THE GROWING LIST

I lifted my legal pad that now bore the names: Della Charles. Angela Pisarro. Elizabeth Flynn. Patricia Boch. Moira Blessing. Each woman was missing a body part.

So was Bunny Alberti. Brenda Fitzer. Tracey Kabrizzi. Janet Atkins.

I felt I was finally looking at the beginnings of a true list of Harvester victims.

My fingers raced as I tapped the familiar names. Then I added Bunny Alberti, nineteen, a waitress, scalped. Dead four years. Case open.

Brenda Fitzer, twenty-five, software engineer, nose missing. Fourteen months ago. Case open.

Tracey Kabrizzi, thirty, folk singer, ears lopped off. Five years ago. Case open.

Janet Atkins, twenty-two, jeweler, missing her tongue. One year. Case open. . . .

BODY PARTS

VICKI STIEFEL

LEISURE BOOKS NEW YORK CITY

To Mom and Dad, for a lifetime of love.

A LEISURE BOOK ®

February 2004

Published by

Dorchester Publishing Co., Inc.
200 Madison Avenue
New York, NY 10016

ISBN 0-8439-5317-9

The name "Leisure Books" and the stylized "L" with design are trademarks of Dorchester Publishing Co., Inc.

Printed in the United States of America.

BODY PARTS

ACKNOWLEDGMENTS

Without the following people, this book would never have been realized; blame me for any errors, not them:

My dear friend Donna Cautilli, whose boundless spirit and homicide counseling experience was my inspiration; Massachusetts State Police Detective Lieutenant Richard D. Lauria, for his invaluable aid and access to the workings of the Medical Examiner's Office and Crime Scene Services; Sgt. Monte M. Gilardi, Trooper Susan Ricci-Howe, and Jo-Anne Nason of Crime Scene Services for their essential aid; Sgt. Steve Byron, also of the Massachusetts State Police, for his willingness to answer numerous questions about procedure; Lt. Walter Keenan and Rolf, Trooper Mark Reid and Mako, and Trooper Reid Rideout and Roxie of the Massachusetts State Police Canine Corps, who introduced me to the world of K-9 dogs; the MEs, Crime Scene Services officers, forensic anthropologist, support staff, and Chief Medical Examiner Dr. Richard Evans of the Office of the Chief Medical Examiner in Boston, whose work continues to astonish me; Dave Badger of the Badger Funeral Home, who offered me advice and information about the funeral-home business; Dr. Tatyana Macauley, for her Czech translations of dog commands; homicide counselors Wanda Henry-Jenkins and Paul T. Clements, who freely shared with me insights into Philadelphia's Grief Assistance Program and the families of homicide victims;

Dr. Barbara Schildkrout, for her advice, role-playing skills, and priceless psychiatric expertise, not to mention her friendship; Andrea Urban, for her support and longstanding friendship, and for her delight in showing me nooks and crannies in Boston I couldn't have found on my own; my writers' group—Barbara Shapiro, Jan Brogan, Floyd Kemske, Judith Harper, Thomas Engels—writers and critiquers extraordinaire; my tireless readers—Bunny Frey, Tamar Hosansky, Pat Sparling, and Patricia Erigero; my cousin, Carolyn Boiarsky, for her technical writing brilliance; Lee Sullivan, for her creativity and heart; The Reel Women Wannabes—Donna, Linda Windels, CJ Williams, Suzanne Hendrich, and Pat Murphy—for ten years of unwavering support; Susan Gray, for teaching me how to never give up; Saundra Pool, who got there first, but was always convinced that I'd get there, too; Barbara Quinlan, who sold us our Eden;

Peter Rubie, my loyal agent, for his perseverance, editorial expertise, and faith in my talents and abilities; my editor, Don D'Auria, for his enthusiasm for Tally and my novel; Peter, Kathleen, and Summer, whose caring and support has endured through the many years; my adored stepkids, Melissa, Mike, and Sarah, who always make me feel welcome and loved; dear Mom, who supported me when the going got really tough; my beloved sons, Blake and Ben, whose tolerance for my writing was boundless, whose support was constant, and whose love is endless; and, finally, my best friend, my other half, my mentor, and my adored husband, William G. Tapply, whose advice and teaching is priceless and whose love is above all price.

I thank each and every one of you for making this book a reality.

AUTHOR'S NOTE

No Massachusetts Grief Assistance Program lives within Boston's Office of the Chief Medical Examiner, whereas Philadelphia's Grief Assistance Program continues to work out of the Philadelphia Medical Examiner's Office. There exist many grief assistance programs throughout the U.S., and they continue to do amazing work with the families of victims of violent death. I applaud them all. Please remember that Tally and her gang at MGAP live in a fictional world.

"If it ain't level . . . LEAN!"
—Bob Wray, bass player

Chapter One

My ancient Grand Wagoneer skidded as I hooked a right into the Office of the Chief Medical Examiner's parking lot. I skated across the lot, the wind snaking beneath my down coat, as I fantasized about hiking flower-filled hills on a steamy summer day. That got me through the side door and into the warmth.

I was late. I'd missed the daily staff meeting at nine, the MGAP meeting I'd called at ten, and the autopsy I'd planned to attend, which was scheduled for eleven.

Starved, I chomped down on a pistachio muffin while I shrugged out of my coat and slipped off my Bean boots.

I tossed Kim Ito's file on the desk. She was the reason I was late. Meeting with her had been worth it—had it ever—but I'd play catch-up for the rest of the day.

I freshened Penny's water. She's my pal, my bud, my confidant, and a three-legged German shepherd who's a former Canine Corps police dog. I gave Pens a pat and a treat, waved at the MGAP counselors in our central office, and flew into my noon group session.

"Hey," I said.

Arlo pulled his harmonica from his pressed overalls and blew a melancholy tune. Like always, Christy waved hello with one of her red braids. Mary and Donna, our two associate counselors, looked relieved, probably because Roland Blessing was being a pain in the ass, per usual. Blessing glowered before he gave me his back.

"How goes it, all?" I said to the group.

"Why do you always start with that?" Blessing asked.

"I'm open to suggestions, Roland."

Blessing sat soldier-straight, face tight with anger, running a hand across his thin pomaded hair. "Ya know, I'm the only one that's forced to be here. It sucks."

In December, he'd joined our group made up of people who'd lost loved ones to homicide. Blessing was required by the courts to participate because he'd threatened the woman he believed killed his daughter. It was either us or jail.

"Moira's dead three years," I said. "Maybe it's time to mourn, instead of being so angry."

He began flipping his ubiquitous Sacagawea golden dollar. Reminded me of those 1930s gangster movies. He knew it annoyed me.

He was filled with fury and full of attitude, yet he was such a sad man. Perhaps that's why I gave him more rein than most.

"Roland?" I repeated, trying to infuse my voice with compassion.

He jabbed a finger at Arlo. "I'm sick of that harmonica shit."

"And you're an idiot," Arlo said.

"Why you fu—"

"Roland! Arlo!" I barked. "You guys know the rules. Attack me, swear at me, whatever. But you don't go after anyone else in the group."

Arlo played a trill on the harmonica.

Blessing snared my eyes. "Fuck you."

"Big whoop," I said. "Anybody can swear, Roland. It's harder being real, digging deep into those feelings."

He shook his head. "You're a pisser, Ms. Tally."

"So I've been told. Can we move on now?"

Blessing leaned close and whispered. "The harmonica really does stink."

"Does it maybe remind you of Moira?"

His eyes grazed the floor. "Maybe."

I put a hand on his back. "Aw, Roland."

MGAP's assistant director poked in her head. "Sorry to interrupt."

"Let's talk about it later," I said to Blessing. "What's up, Gert?"

"I got a newbie here. Ms. Jones, meet Tally Whyte."

In walked a lithe, mahogany-skinned woman who carried herself like a jock. I was jolted by a moment of familiarity. I knew her from somewhere, but couldn't catch the *where*. Damn, I hated that.

We shook hands, and she stared me fiercely in the eye.

"Who did you lose, Ms. Jones?" I asked.

"Sister."

"When?"

"Found out yesterday."

The room rippled with surprise.

"I'm sorry," I said. "Your grief is so fresh. Wouldn't you rather talk one-on-one with Gert?"

"I want *you*." Jones's hazel eyes glinted with anger and hurt. They held secrets, too.

"Sure," I said. "As soon as we're finished here."

Blessing flipped his coin. "Are you done with this chick yet?"

"*Chick?*" Ms. Jones said.

"You heard me."

"Roland," I said, waving Ms. Jones to a seat, "lose the attitude."

"Sorry," he mumbled. "It's the damned police. They haven't done squat about questioning the bitch that killed my kid."

"It's hard," Mary said in her soft Southern lilt. "I know. But our group is all about moving on."

"My Moira, she . . ." replied Blessing. "Forget it."

"You know we'd like to hear," I said. "We care, Roland."

"Forget it!" he shouted.

Christy rolled her eyes. Arlo was trying to keep his laughter in check. Joking, laughs—they were Arlo's medium for dealing with his child's death.

"Talk to us, Arlo," I said.

"They had him." He chuckled, shaking his head. "And there I was, sitting on the edge of my courtroom seat, watching the creep go down. Cheering to myself, mind you. And then they messed up the chain of evidence. We were almost there. Inches, you know? So who knows what'll happen now? He left the courtroom wearing a big grin and giving his lawyer a thumbs-up. Good old Mr. Jolly. I'd like to—"

"I'll talk to Kranak, Arlo," I said. "I'll get his take."

"Thanks. But you can't fix this one, Tally. Not this time."

No, I couldn't. Ideas and suggestions, sympathy and empathy volleyed around the room, then we segued to Christy's obsession, a year after her father's murder, with cleaning up the long-gone blood on her living room floor.

"I can't stop." Christy rolled her eyes and stuck out her tongue—her goofy face. People laughed. So did she.

"I'll spot a speck of something," she continued. "A stain, even a shadow, and then I have to go at it with the Lysol and brushes."

"What about laying new carpet?" Mary asked. "Like we talked about a couple weeks ago?"

"I . . . I did," Christy said. "But yesterday I ripped it up. Maybe I should've picked some color other than red, huh?"

Everybody laughed.

Blessing jumped to his feet. "You people are idiots! How can you flap your mouths about cleaning and fricking carpets when folks you loved were murdered?"

"Because we've all been there," Mary said, her eyes sad and remembering.

Blessing's laugh was sour. "Yeah, right. And you deal by smearin' enough makeup on to cover a pig? No way you been where I been."

"Why attack Mary, Roland?" I said. "Everyone here has that pain."

"My ass." Blessing smiled. It wasn't pretty. "My baby, she was a flautist. Real promising, or so they said. And some bull-dyke bitch killed her and raped her with her own fucking flute after she was dead. Then the bitch took my baby's hands as a goddamn trophy and dumped her in Boston Common, right by the fucking frog pond. Who the hell do you think you people are?" Blessing muttered, *pussy*.

Damn him. I began to stand.

"It's okay, Tally." Mary turned to Blessing. "It took me a long time to live with the fact that my mom's killer got away. The newspapers forgot her. So did the legal system. The police moved on ages ago. And you know, it makes me feel all sick inside."

"So *do* something about it," he said.

Mary worked her hands in her lap, her nerves showing. "What matters is that Mom's gone. She won't ever be back. I *want* her back, Mr. Blessing. So much."

Tears burst from Blessing's eyes. "I didn't even get to say good-bye to my girl. Not once."

"Say it now," I said. "It'll help. Promise."

"Yeah, right," Blessing said. "All you do is sit around and whine."

"Sounds like you're doing all the whining," Ms. Jones said.

"You don't know nothin'," he said.

"Really?" Jones strutted over to Blessing, whom she topped by a good five inches. "I know your type. Your thing is to cause problems. Asshole."

"Who you callin' asshole, bitch?" he hollered.

I flew between them. "Stop! We're trying to do work here."

I looked from face to face.

The air sizzled.

The Jones woman winked at me and sauntered toward her seat. *My God, Jones is my old friend Chesa!*

Blessing lunged after her.

I grabbed his shoulder. "Leave it!"

He balled his hand into a fist. It started to tremble. His face slackened, while his fist shook harder.

"Roland," I said. "Why don't we—"

His arm fell to his side. "I'll leave it. For now." He made for the door.

"Stay," I pleaded. "Let's focus on Moira."

The confused look he gave the group settled on me. "She's all I think about."

"I'm not buying that one," Chesa Jones said.

Blessing gave her the finger. "Fuck you!" He slammed the door.

"*You* were out of line, Ms. Jones." I ran after Roland Blessing.

"Mr. Blessing! Roland!"

He stopped midstride by the side doors, arms waving, eyes wild. "Where are her hands? I want her hands. I just need to hold my baby." He sobbed.

I reached to embrace him.

He searched my face, and I saw hope on his, and a terrible misery. "Roland."

He shoved my arms away. "You can't help. No, you can't."

He banged out the side door, and I was left cradling a grief more familiar than breath.

Chapter Two

When I walked back into the session, I caught Chesa's eye, and gave her a smile. She shrugged. I was dying to talk to her, but we had to finish the session, which we did.

Except she disappeared right as group ended. When I couldn't find her, I dragged my ass back to my office. I figured she'd find me. I sat on the couch, wiped. Penny crawled up beside me and fell instantly asleep.

I believed I'd cut through Blessing's anger last week. Obviously I was wrong.

I tried to reach him on the phone, but had no luck.

Dammit, where was Chesa? And what had happened to her sister?

That morning was just another typical day for me at the Grief Shop, which is my nickname for OCME. Lots of people think working inside the medical examiner's office is spooky. Maybe they're right. Or not. It's all how you see the world.

Located in Boston, the Grief Shop houses the administrative offices and operations for the Massachusetts medical examiner system. True, it's a pretty intense place. Then again, I've been called the same.

We're on Albany Street in a bland, three-story brick building dwarfed by the campuses of Boston City Hospital, Boston University Medical Center, and Boston University Schools of Medicine, Dentistry, and Public Health. We're also smack at the crossroads of Boston's South End and Roxbury neighborhoods.

Medical pathologists, a forensic anthropologist, administrative staff, and an elite State Police Crime Scene Services unit inhabit the Grief Shop, as does the chief medical examiner, Dr. Veda Barrow, who also happens to be my foster mother.

The building contains a state-of-the-art forensic pathology center, three autopsy theaters, two cold-storage facilities, a trace evidence room, and specialized rooms for family counseling and identifying human remains. The latter were part of my bailiwick as the director of the Massachusetts Grief Assistance Program, also known as MGAP.

When MGAP moved into the Grief Shop, we caused the relocation of the Crime Scene Services photo lab and its sergeant's office to other spots in the building, always a bone of contention between me and my pal, CSS Sergeant Rob Kranak.

MGAP is a private, nonprofit organization. Our whole point is to aid the bereaved as death via homicide slams them in the face. We help them thread the emotional maze, as well as deal with legal matters, court stuff, the press, and the cops.

The session with Blessing, Arlo, and Christy was not unusual. Ditto for how Chesa and Blessing mouthed off to each other. When homicide happens, anger, confusion, and fear follow.

There are fewer than thirty professional homicide counselors in the United States. I'm proud to be one of them.

A shadow, then a woman hovered in the doorway, one hand hooked in her belt. The stance—arms crossed, a leg thrust out, aggression vibrating from every pore—Chesa again gave me that fierce stare. I wanted to leap up, but . . .

"I was out getting a smoke," Chesa said.

"I looked," I said, forcing myself to play it cool. "Couldn't find you. Come on in."

She took the chair across from me. "That Blessing's one wired dude."

I nodded. "He's not the only one, if you get my drift."

"Point taken." Head shaking, she scrunched her hands in her jeans pockets. "You didn't recognize me at first. Dammit, I'd have known you anywhere."

"You were, what, thirteen when we last saw each other? It's been twenty years."

"More than."

Screw playing it cool. I leapt up to hug her, felt her bristle, then relax. She hugged me back, fiercely.

"It's so good to see you, but . . . your sister. I'm sorry. What happened?"

She shook her head. "Don't know. Della's the one who told me you were here. Didn't she mention me?"

Who was Della? Then I recalled a striking woman with tiger eyes from last August, named Della Charles. She'd come in, all wild-eyed, ranting about some dead friend of hers. She was obviously high on something. "I'm afraid she didn't talk about you."

Chesa's head jerked, like I'd slapped her. "She couldn't stop talking about *you*. Like you were some big deal or something."

"Believe me, I'm not." I squeezed her arm. "I didn't know you had a sister."

"There's a lot I never told you when we were in school."

"Too much," I said. "How come you stopped coming out to school in Lexington? I tried to find you, but I never did."

"Yeah. Yeah . . . I know. I heard you'd come down to the neighborhood looking for me. METCO was fine, but school in Roxbury wasn't half bad, you know?"

"I missed you. So . . . tell me about Della."

"She got her pretty ass all goddamned dead!"

The boil of Chesa's anger, and her shriek of pain washed over me. "I'm so sorry. A homicide?"

"Damned if I know. She's in some funeral home down in the old neighborhood. I went over this morning. Nobody answered the door when I knocked. Not when I called, either. Gave me the willies." She shrugged. "Thought maybe you'd . . ."

I had case studies to input into the computer, the budget proposal was screaming at me, and so was a fund-raising cocktail party at four.

I gave her hand a squeeze. "Let's go."

The white, one-story funeral home was wedged between two taller brick buildings. Across the street, brightly colored town houses seemed plucked from a Cape Cod village.

We walked beneath a red canopy painted with the name MCARDLE FUNERAL HOME. A stream of water had frozen along the door seal. Chesa tugged and finally the door gave way.

She abruptly stopped. "Getting that call about Della being dead. I'm all messed up. I don't want to see her dead. You going to force me, Ms. Tally Whyte?" Her chuckle sounded scared.

"It's your call, Chesa," I said softly.

"I can barely move." She slumped against the door and tipped her head back. Twin tears crept from the corner of each eye and slid down her cheeks, meeting at the tip of her sharp chin. "Della was *it* for me. I've got no one now."

"Want to get some coffee first?" I said.

"Yeah. Sure. We could grab a bite and talk and . . .

Who am I kidding? We'd better get this done. It's gonna suck."

"Big time."

I wrapped my arm around Chesa's waist and we went inside.

The paneled foyer smelled of age and potpourri and death, just like every other funeral parlor I'd ever been in. I hate funeral homes.

I steered Chesa across the thick ruby carpet toward the viewing room. I'd have liked quiet better than the gloomy classical music that oozed from invisible speakers.

Chesa was shaking, and I tightened my grip on her waist. Where was the funeral director?

"Mrs. Cheadle works here. She's the one who told me. She said Della's in the front room."

We peered through an arch. Upholstered folding chairs formed three lines, like soldiers at parade rest. At the end of the room, Chesa's sister lay cradled in the blue satin that lined a mahogany casket.

A throat was cleared and, startled, we turned.

A small, bearded man in a blue suit nodded solemnly. He wore his hair in dreadlocks—a white guy trying to fit into a black neighborhood, perhaps—and thick glasses magnified blue eyes that I suspected were soft with professional sympathy.

He rubbed his earlobe, then shook first Chesa's hand, then mine.

"I'm Mr. McArdle," he said in a soft Southern voice. "You're here for Ms. Della." He waved us forward.

Chesa rested her hand on Della's face. My throat grew thick with sadness.

I wanted to be alone with McArdle before I asked how Della had died.

After long minutes, Chesa backed away. While I traded her brightly colored soaking-wet scarf for my extra handkerchief, she asked McArdle if there was someplace to pray. He said he had a small altar down the hall and led her out.

I walked over to the coffin. I petted Della's cheek, making her earrings dance. Her patrician nose still arced high above cheeks that, thankfully, McArdle hadn't stuffed with cotton. Even death, and the McArdle Funeral Home's efforts, couldn't steal her great beauty, although her pageboy wig left something to be desired. Her full lips were sealed—with stitches, I knew. Christ. I knew too much.

I held her fine-boned hand in my sturdy one.

Della was young, not yet thirty. Yet she hadn't arrived in a body bag at the Grief Shop. So what had killed her?

I inhaled deeply, faintly nauseated by the mortuary's rose potpourri. I touched her shoulders and again visually surfed her face. Her eyes were too bulbous, too . . .

I drew back a lid.

I wasn't surprised. A wad of cotton stared back at me.

Della's tiger eyes were gone.

I turned, and McArdle was standing in the arch at the room's entrance.

"Did Della Charles donate her eyes, Mr. McArdle?"

He smiled. "You don't miss much, do you? So I was told by her physician. I'm sorry it startled you. Most people don't—"

"Sorry. Habit. Do you know how and where she died?"

He patted my hand. "Ms. Della passed over at Mass General. Exposure. Sadly, all too common with the indigent in winter. They found her half-frozen in the lot across from the Wang. She was malnourished and delirious. I think they treated her for a good twenty-four hours, in hopes of saving her."

"How sad." I handed him my card. "Sorry for prying."

"No need to apologize." He read my card, pulling it close to his nose. "Ah, OCME."

"Would you give me the attending physician's name?"

"Certainly. Would it be convenient if I retrieved it after the return of my assistant? He's running errands and I have to prepare for another service."

"Of course. Chesa talked about paying for Della's services."

He rubbed his forehead, as if he were in great pain. "That will help."

"Pardon?"

"I donate my services from time to time." He shook his head. "My mother rests God-knows-where in some pauper's grave, unacknowledged and unmourned. My aid to the indigent is a tribute to her."

If Veda hadn't stepped in, my dad would rest in a pauper's grave, too. "What a generous and kind thing to do."

"As you are kind. I've watched you with Ms. Chesa."

"Forgive my grilling, but why wasn't Chesa notified about her sister's death?"

"I don't know. I thought that odd, too. Very

strange. Perhaps Ms. Della's physician could help."

Chesa returned, and we confirmed the time for the service and interment, which was to be held the following day.

On our way out, McArdle handed me the attending physician's name over at Mass General: a Dr. Christopher Rutledge.

Back at the Grief Shop, Chesa hung out in the lobby while I tried to reach Dr. Rutledge. I finally left him a message. I left Roland Blessing a phone message, too. The guy worried me more than the typical survivor.

Chesa and I bought some Italian bread and salad on the way to my place, and I cooked up spaghetti carbonara, one of the seven meals in my repertoire and a favorite of Penny's.

"I like your place," Chesa said.

"Me, too." I live in Boston's South End, in a first-floor apartment of a bow-fronted Victorian town house owned by Jake Beal, a successful sculptor who lives upstairs.

My front bedroom, with its bow window, faced the street. The kitchen divided the apartment, and the French-doored living room looked onto a tiny fenced-in yard and Dartmouth Place, one of Boston's prettiest dead-end streets.

After Chesa and I scraped our plates, and I let Penny out back to do her business, we sat in front of the fireplace, legs stretched out, each sipping a glass of cabernet.

We talked about the past and the present, and she studiously avoided any mention of Della.

We'd met when I was thirteen and she was eleven. She was a METCO student from Roxbury. I came from an East Lexington blue-collar neighborhood, something that I doubt exists today in that increasingly affluent suburb.

Even with the age difference, we became buddies. We'd go bowling or roller-skating or to the movies after school. For two years I played big sister, not that *she* saw it that way. She would come to my apartment and was crazy for my dad, but she refused to tell me where in Roxbury she lived or anything about her life there. For a kid, she was very self-possessed.

One summer day, when the heat sizzled off the pavement, I followed her home. She caught me and laughed her head off. The following summer, she vanished from my life as suddenly as she'd entered it.

I hadn't seen her in all those intervening years. Yet she felt as vivid and true as she had years ago.

"Pretty oddball career you picked," she said.

"I'm also a psychologist," I joked. "This just evolved."

She peered around the apartment. "No guy?"

I'd decorated in warm colors and overstuffed furniture, not to mention plenty of dog hair; in shells and rocks and funky paintings of houses; and some of my handcolored photos, too. "Is it that obvious? I'm divorced. I wasn't so hot at marriage."

"I hooked up with this guy when I was in the WNBA. Once I creamed my knee, so I couldn't play anymore, he expected me to turn into Aunt Jemima or something."

"I can't see you playing that."

She stared at her wine. When she looked back at me, tears filled her eyes.

"Della?" I said.

She nodded, biting her lip. "I was thinking of when we were kids, and I used to do the METCO thing to your whitey school. Della tried to talk me into sticking it out."

I slid my hand to hers and held on.

"What happened?" she sobbed. "Why'd my sister have to die?"

"We'll find out. Promise."

A short while later, Chesa reached for her coat.

"Stay here?" I asked. "I'd love you to."

She tugged her cap onto her head. "Thanks, Tal, but I need to be by myself."

I knew all about alone time. "I'll give you a lift to your hotel."

She shook her head. "Just to the T."

"But . . ."

She notched her head and smiled. "I want to ride the rails for a while. Feel the vibration. Hear the thump-thump. Smell other people, hear their chatter. I want to not *be* anyone for a while."

"I understand."

"Knew you would."

"I'll pick you up tomorrow for the funeral."

"Naw." She tugged on her blue cap. "I should be alone with Mrs. Cheadle. We'll meet you there. The three of us can go out after."

"A good plan."

At the T station, she got out of the car and leaned on the windowsill. "Why'd this happen, Tal? Why?"

Before I could answer, she trotted down the T steps. I watched until her blue cap disappeared from sight.

When I got home, I curled on the couch with a

second glass of cabernet. I'd had better days.

Oh, it was great to see Chesa after all those years, but it had put me in a contemplative mood. The past was always with me, especially when I encountered someone who'd known my dad.

I opened one of the French doors. A blast of frigid air down from Canada barreled in, along with the slap of tires on the wet pavement. I walked onto my balcony.

Penny brushed by me to do her business on a patch of lawn.

Chesa was from the old time, the before time. Made me laugh. I was the cobbler who had no shoes himself. Time to let Dad go. I could feel it. Maybe Chesa was the key. Over my shoulder, I surveyed my father's meerschaum pipe collection that sat on my mantle.

When Penny returned, I closed the doors and tried Blessing once more. I left yet another message and included my cell phone number. The guy was hurting. I hoped he wouldn't do something stupid.

Gray filled in the patches of blue sky on the short drive over to McArdle's the following morning. The thick air promised snow.

I was worried about Chesa. Della's funeral would be a closure of sorts, but she'd have a hard go. Everyone did, and Chesa had that tough facade that would make it even more difficult.

The red awning snapped with the breeze as I ducked beneath it. My fingers were tingly with cold. I struggled with the doorknob. It wouldn't turn.

I banged the door a couple of times, trying to free

the ice so it would open. It suddenly yawned and I stumbled inside.

The hall was dark. Too dark. And it was quiet. Unnaturally so. The hairs on my arms prickled.

"Hello?" I hollered.

Nothing. I was a few minutes early, but . . . I tapped the wall until I found the switch. I flicked on a light.

The stand that held the sign-in book lay on the floor and someone had punched a boulder-sized hole in the wall.

Oh, shit.

"Mr. McArdle?" I pulled the pepper spray from my purse and crossed the hall to the viewing room.

Watery sun filtered in from the windows. Folding chairs lay piled in the center of the room. A greasy smell, gasoline maybe, sharpened the air. Fist-sized holes marked the walls here, too, and prayer books and flower stands sprawled across the ruby carpet. Ripped pages fluttered about the floor as I entered the room.

A blanket of lilies remained draped across Della's closed coffin. At least the vandal had *some* respect. Maybe McArdle was at the local police station. All Chesa and Mrs. Cheadle needed was to see this mess.

"Hello!" I called again.

The vibration settled. Then silence smothered me like a cocoon. The place was freezing. So was I. When it warmed, pipes would burst.

I walked down the hall and peeked into the rooms. All trashed.

I called Kranak on my cell phone and told him the funeral home had been vandalized.

"Get out," he said. "The creep could still be there."

"He's not."

"How the fuck do you know?"

"It's daylight. The guy's long gone. Plus, it doesn't feel like it."

"Feelings," he sang in a whisper. "Just get yourself out and—"

I clicked off.

On the basement stairs, I panned my eyes across what was left of McArdle's showroom. Sample coffins and cremation urns lay smashed on the floor. Yards of fabric sat in a wet something.

"Mr. McArdle?" I called.

Nothing.

As I crossed the floor, shards of glass crunched beneath my feet. I stepped in puddles of heaven-knew-what. The smell was worse—antiseptic and fetid.

The vandal had even done a job on the embalming room.

I hustled back upstairs seriously worried about McArdle. Could he be hurt? I hadn't seen any blood. Robbed? Doubtful. Maybe he'd ticked off someone—big time.

I peered out front. What was taking Kranak so long?

I checked my watch. Damn. Chesa and Mrs. Cheadle would arrive any second.

I jogged down the hall and did a more thorough exam of the bathroom. Found nothing. I peered into another room. A VCR was in pieces. Ditto for a TV. Blue and red chairs were sliced open.

Glacial wind knifed through the broken window in McArdle's office. Loose papers flew into the air, then landed on the smashed liquor bottles and puddle of china that littered the floor. What looked like an appointment book lay open beside an overturned couch.

I walked to retrieve it. The wind hushed. I reeled from the smell.

Feces and urine and a whiff of that other indescribable sweetness made me want to run.

Oh, hell. McArdle.

Someone had flipped the couch, the front of which was jammed against the window. Shaking, I crouched down and peeked around an end of the couch.

A body lay jammed beneath a bunch of cushions. I saw a pair of penny loafers and a gloved hand. On Jello legs, I walked around to the couch's other end.

Someone slammed the front door. "Tal?" It was Kranak.

"In here!" I called. "Goddamn it, hurry up!"

My fingers shook as I switched on my flashlight and sprayed light onto the face.

Chesa? No. Oh, God.

Her tongue protruded from her mouth. Her beautiful eyes bulged. One frozen hand gripped her collar, as if she'd been trying to loosen something around her neck.

Blood crusted her eyes and nostrils and painted her mouth with garish lipstick.

I cradled her head and sobbed. I desperately wanted to hold her.

Chapter Three

I sat shivering on a folding chair in the coatroom of McArdle's Funeral Home, the only place that wasn't swarming with cops and forensics and the ME's people. The case officially belonged to Boston Police Department.

A cop walked in and handed me a styrofoam cup of cocoa. "From Kranak."

"Thanks." I took a sip. It warmed me a little.

Where was McArdle? Whoever had killed Chesa must have scared him off. Or maybe McArdle had killed Chesa. Or maybe he was dead. God, I hoped not.

I rested my head in my hands. I wanted Chesa alive.

What had gone on here? Why did Chesa go back to the funeral home?

If I'd insisted she spend the night, things would be different. Or if I'd driven her to her hotel, she'd be alive. If I'd . . . I blew my nose.

She'd been beaten. I tried not to think of her pain. Or her fear. The terrible fear. Chesa was no wimp. The guy must have had a gun. Something. Maybe he'd shot her.

No. Her tongue and eyes indicated she'd been strangled.

Oh, Chesa.

* * *

I'm thirteen, an eighth grader, flat as Kansas, and the tallest girl in my class. In other words, a dork, a beanpole, an Olive Oyl. Dad says I'll like it someday that I'm tall and skinny. He's nuts.

Today, I walk down the street to collect little Jimmy O'Reilly from his junior high. Jimmy's in fifth grade. He lives on the third floor of our apartment house and his mom's got a doctor's appointment or something, so I got guilted into doing it. A major pain.

Jimmy's supposed to be waiting for me by the playground entrance. Of course, he's not.

Near the playground, I spot Brian Donovan and Pat Arnold. They're in eighth grade like me, and maybe a foot shorter than I am. They think they're hot stuff.

They see me and wave like smartasses. You know, salutes, with lots of winks. Brian points to the cigarette he's smoking. It's a joint. What jerks.

I'm about to turn the corner when I realize they're dragging some kid. I move closer. It's a black kid in a blue kilt. Her feet aren't touching the ground.

I don't like this at all.

I walk up to them, and they're laughing and snorting, like scaring the hell out of this little kid's the funniest thing in the world. I can't believe they're not even trying to hide her from me. Her legs are pinwheeling in the air and she's shaking. She's maybe eleven, and even skinnier than me.

Her face is wet and puffy with tears, and her eyes are wide with fear and something else. Hate.

"What are you guys doing?" I say.

"We're getting a piece of nigger ass," Pat says.

"Yeah, right," I say. "Don't be jerks. Let her go."

"No way," Brian says, yanking her arm.

The little girl whimpers, and I want to strangle both boys.

"I'm going to get Sergeant Tommy," I say.

"Oh, yeah," Pat says. "That's gonna matter. Right. Like he'd give a shit if it's Sambo-colored."

"Yes, he would!" I say.

Pat grins, then slaps a hand over the little girl's face.

"Ow!" He pulls his hand away fast.

Ha! She bit him!

Pat starts to backhand her. I grab his wrist. "Don't. Just leave her be."

Brian and Pat exchange slithery looks.

I slap my hands on my waist and widen my stance, so I'm showing them, see, that I'm as tough as they are. "Let her go, or I'll beat the living crap out of both of you." Not that I could. But it sounds decent.

They both laugh, while the little black girl shivers. Poor little kid.

I grab Brian's shirt and ball the front into my fist. I pull him close to my face, so he's on tippy-toes. "You deaf or something? You know I'm dating Kenny O'Toole? You know how pissed he'd be if he knew you'd given me such a hard time?" All of which is a total lie. We went out on one date, and it was a flop because he tried to feel me up and I wouldn't let him.

I slide my eyes to Pat, and I can see he's thinking about it, deciding whether to punch me in the gut while I'm holding Brian or to let the kid go. I squint, trying to look fierce.

Pat shoves the girl at me, and she lands with an "oomph," so I trip backward, releasing Brian.

"We were only bullshitting you anyway," Brian says.

"Yeah," Pat agrees. "It was fun scaring her. So go blow it out your ass. You won't tell Kenny, right?"

"Not if you don't ever touch her again," I say.

The boys give me the finger as they walk away. But they'll leave her alone.

I crouch down by the little girl. Her braids are all mussed and she's got a shiner beneath her left eye. Her dimpled chin wobbles, but she holds it together. I wipe a dribble of blood from her face.

"You were brave, kiddo," I say.

"We sure got 'em, didn't we?" she says.

WE? Ha! Ya gotta love it. "We sure as hell did, kid."

I took a pull on my hot cocoa. They were taking Chesa out now, a white body bag zipped around her long, lean frame. The guys wouldn't look at me. They knew she was a pal of mine.

Dumb place to be sitting, a funeral parlor's coatroom.

"Hey, Tally!" came a voice from across the hall. "You wanna come here?"

I tried shaking off the memories the way Penny shook water from her coat. "On my way." I pushed to my feet, headed toward the viewing room. "What's up?"

Joe, one of Boston PD's forensic techs, waved me into the room. "We got a little weirdness here. Didn't you say the sister was inside?" Joe pointed to the coffin. Someone had raised the lid.

The coffin was empty.

I stood outside on the curb, beside a dirty pile of snow, gulping bitter air that came out in white puffs. Where the hell was Della's body? Freaked me out when Joe showed me that empty coffin. I had to get out of there.

Someone sniggered. A kid in a red bandana stood staring at me. He had a glint in his eye—hard to describe—but he knew something.

I waved. "Hey." I walked toward him, and he slouched against a light pole, waiting for me, or so it appeared. He lit a cigarette as he watched me approach.

He straightened, looking beyond me, eyes narrowed, scared. Over my shoulder, a shadow. Kranak.

When I turned back, the kid was running, his Nikes a white-swooshed blur.

"Wait!" I ran after him. The cold air nicked my throat, and the rasp of my breath hissed in my ears.

The kid widened the distance, and I pumped my arms and legs harder, lengthened my stride. He hooked a right, sprinted up a hill glistening with ice.

He crossed the road and hit a shrub-covered lot at full stride.

I was losing him.

"Fuck!" Kranak hollered, then he dashed past me faster than I could imagine.

The kid looked back, a mistake.

In that moment, Kranak leapt through the air. The kid's hands flew up, a protective gesture, just as Kranak crashed them both to the frozen ground in a tangle of arms and legs and curses.

"He knows something!" I offered Kranak a hand up.

"Yeah. Maybe." His breath came in bellows.

"Don't have a heart attack," I said.

"Gee, thanks, Tal. I'll make sure not to." He pulled

his handkerchief from his pants pocket and wiped the dots of blood sprinkling his scraped cheek.

The kid sat up, slinging his arms across his knees. I offered him a hand up, too.

He spit on it.

Kranak gave me an I-told-you-so look. "Keep it up," he said to the kid. "I'll haul your ass down the station. Your name?"

The kid massaged his shoulder. "Julius Binny."

"So how come you ran from this nice lady here?"

"Fuck you," the kid said.

"Not my taste," Kranak replied. "You know the cliché. We can talk here or someplace warmer, like a cell. Your choice."

The kid pushed to his feet. "Don't you guys ever get tired of the same lines?" His accent was faintly West Indian.

"You know what went down in McArdle's," I said.

Binny straightened the red bandana on his head, hitched up his pants, then tucked his hands into the front pockets. "What's in it for me?"

Kranak rolled his eyes. "You're right. This gets long. Same lines, same responses." He reached for Binny's pocket, then held up a plastic packet with white powder. "Well, lookie here."

The kid's face tightened. "Hey, man. That ain't mine!"

"No? But this little lady just saw me take it from your pocket."

"It ain't. Fuck you."

"I'm freezing my ass off, Tal. C'mon. We'll take Bandana Boy to where it's cozy warm." Kranak reached for the kid.

Binny held up his hands, palms facing us. "All right,

man. Look, I know somethin' cause I helped Mr. McArdle put a stiff into his hearse late last night. That's all, man. I didn't seen nothin'."

I turned to Kranak. "So McArdle took Della."

"Didn't know her name," the kid said. "But, man, was Mr. McArdle ever scared. I mean, shakin' scared. I heard the racket, too."

"What kind of racket?" I said.

"This dude and this chick inside. Fightin'. Hollerin' at each other. Breakin' stuff up. I could hear 'em. They sounded shit-faced."

Kranak grabbed a hunk of the kid's leather jacket and pulled. "I'm freezing. Let's walk. So go on, kid."

"That's it."

"That's not *it*." I was furious that this kid was jerking us around.

"My people see me with you guys . . . It's not cool."

"I don't give a fuck about cool," Kranak said.

We crossed the empty lot. The kid limped.

"Are you all right?" I said.

"My ankle's broke. Yeah, I'm fine."

"Why didn't you and McArdle go inside and help her?" I said.

The kid shook his head. "I said that to Mr. McArdle. He said no way. Said that dude worked for Mr. Wiseguy Harry Pisarro. That he wasn't gonna mess with him. I'm tellin' ya, his teeth were chattering."

Kranak frowned. "And you didn't do squat. Not call the cops. Not see for yourself what was going down?"

The kid shoved his hands into his back pockets. "Okay, so I looked. Peeked in the window. Saw this dude, regular-looking guy. Old."

"Old like me?" Kranak said.

"Little older."

"White, black?" Kranak said. "Hair? Eyes? Come on, come on."

"White. Sorta sandy-colored hair. Thin. Greasy. Hair, I mean. I didn't see his eyes, until . . . See, he's waving his arms at this black chick. Can't see her face. And then he spots me." He wagged his head.

"Julius?" I said.

"Yeah, well. McArdle's long gone, see. And I ain't proud of this, so don't you go repeating it."

"You got scared, right?" Kranak said.

"Damned straight. Guy looked up at me. Saw me. He had the look of death on his face. The look of death."

An hour later, Kranak and I sat across from each other at the Victorian Diner, our usual haunt. It was bright and noisy and normal. Right then, I needed normal.

"Who's the guy, Rob?"

"You think I know?" he replied in his usual charming tone of voice.

"Maybe." I unclenched my fist. I'd found one of Della's dancing-people earrings in the crease of the coffin's blue satin lining. "Still no sign of McArdle?"

"Nope. Got the shit scared out of him real good, as they say."

Kranak could lie with the best of them, and he might be lying now. In his mid-forties, his dancer's lean build had thickened with the years. He had basset hound eyes, a Marine-style flattop, and a mean scar running from his lower right eyelid to the corner of his lips. He scared a lot of people. I adored him.

Kranak knocked gently on my forehead. "Hello? Anybody home?"

I leaned against the booth. "Yeah. Yeah. I'm here. I can't believe you pulled that powdered sugar trick on Binny."

He grinned. "Swear to God, it works every time." He felt behind my ear and produced the same white packet. "Every time."

"You're awful."

"Yeah. Sorry about your friend, Tal." Kranak slurped his tea. "Tell me, how do you like that Roland Blessing for it?"

"Roland Blessing? Where did that come from?"

"You know he's one of Pisarro's goons."

"I can't believe you never told me. The guy's been in my group for four weeks."

"Blessing fits the kid's description, too."

"So do a million guys."

"Not ones with beefs against that Chesa woman." Kranak's charcoal eyes were opaque with secrets. Somehow he *knew* about Roland Blessing's argument with Chesa at group the previous day. "But that was all it was, a heat of the moment thing, Rob."

"Guess you saw that he beat her."

I rubbed my cup. Nerves. "We had dinner last night. Just like old times."

He took my hand. "They're picking up Blessing right now. They got a whole bunch of good prints. We'll see if Blessing's show up."

"You shouldn't have strong-armed me into leaving McArdle's."

"The cops can handle it just fine without your help."

I held Kranak's eyes. "I've got to find Della's body. See that she's properly taken care of. I can't believe McArdle drove off with it." The tears I'd been fighting all morning spilled over. "Damn. It doesn't make sense that Blessing would kill Chesa."

"Does to me. He's a screwed-up shithead."

"If I'd handled him better in group yesterday . . . Yes, they got into it. But it was good for him, you know? Getting his anger out. He's a strange guy, but no way should his anger have spilled over into violence at someone else. Suicide? That I could see."

"This is all about guilt, babe," he said. "You can't save the world."

"Why the hell not?" I chuckled as I felt another prickle of tears.

He pulled something from his pocket and opened his hand. A Sacagawea dollar shined golden in his palm. "This mean anything to you?"

My heart stuttered, then I saw his game. "You didn't find that at the funeral home. You're not wearing gloves and you wouldn't keep any evidence."

"You're too smart for me, Tal. Boston PD found its twin on McArdle's office floor. Face it, Blessing's a fruit loop 'cause his kid got whacked. A pissed-off fruit loop. He did her, Tal." His scowl was ferocious.

I sighed. "I'm going to see that friend of theirs, Mrs. Cheadle. She deserves to know about Chesa."

"You going to tell her about the missing corpse?"

"Probably not."

"At least until we fish the Della woman out of the river."

"What's that supposed to mean?"

"When McArdle realizes his place is trashed, he'll have a corpse on his hands with no place to put her. What's the shrimpy guy gonna do?"

"You can be so crass, dammit." I tugged on my floppy hat and stomped out.

*   *   *

The snow took an intermission as I drove across the Charles and through Cambridge. Once I made it to Somerville, I found the three-story wooden home where Mrs. Cheadle had her apartment.

I'd called ahead and was expected.

I jammed the Wagoneer into a parking spot. The smells from a chowder house mingled with wood smoke and lavender from a funky perfumery across the street. I walked by an Asian grocery, a pet store, and more houses, some with apartments inhabited by Tufts college kids who, even in the cold, lolled on the second- and third-story porches.

Some yellow flower boxes were perched on windows, ready for spring blooms. They made me feel like crying. Chesa would never see the spring.

I rang Mrs. Cheadle's buzzer and an answering buzz let me inside.

The door to my right belonged to a charmer named "Go Away," according to the masking tape stuck to the brass plate.

A red-bereted head appeared behind the door to my left and waved me forward, big smile on her ancient face. I walked down the hall rehearsing how I'd break the news that Chesa Jones was dead.

We sat in Mrs. Cheadle's living room. My wing chair faced the sofa where the old woman held court surrounded by cats of every color and shape. Penny would have loved the menagerie.

I'd learned from Chesa that Mrs. Cheadle had once been a stripper and vaudevillian at the Old Howard in Scollay Square, which was torn down in the 1960s and replaced by the antiseptic Government Center.

Although African American, she was very fair, which explained how she'd passed as white in shows that were proscribed to black entertainers. Memorabilia filled her apartment.

She had to be in her late seventies or early eighties, and her small frame bowed from a humpback. Lines crosshatched her heart-shaped face, and her lips, which smiled easily, were painted red, matching the beret jauntily set on her head. Her black dress was covered with cat hair.

When I told her about Chesa, she rocked as she cried.

I handed her some tissues. "Mrs. Cheadle?"

"I'm okay. Okay. What went on? What happened?"

I gave her a censored version. "Why was Chesa at the funeral home last night?"

She clicked her tongue. "Chesa was a child with deep feelings. A loving girl. She told me she wanted to settle up with Mr. McArdle. She was fighting a terrible grief. Who did you say killed her?"

"The police think it was a man named Roland Blessing."

She shook her head. "I surely hope he didn't hurt Mr. McArdle, too. He gave me a job when I was in a bad way."

My throat felt dry, and I took a sip of tea. "Want to tell me about the girls?"

She pressed a gnarled finger to her cheek and tapped it three times. "Oh, yes. Why, I babysat for the both of them. They were full of vinegar, those two. I can't believe they're both gone." Tears pooled in the wrinkles that circled her eyes.

I told her how I'd known Chesa as a kid. "I wish I'd known Della back then, too."

She patted her lap, and the black cat nestled onto the spot. She stroked him. "Chesa moved around a lot, but she always stayed in touch. Now, Della. She seldom came to visit. The drugs. The alcohol. The child felt displaced, and yet she reached out to her sister and me only infrequently. I think a lot of her coolness had to do with her pride. And her shame."

"The substance abuse?"

"That, and the fact that she earned her living from men. Do you know she modeled years ago? Oh, yes. With her fine looks, I thought she'd go far. But it didn't last. Nothing much ever did with Della."

"When did you last see her?"

"I'd say maybe two weeks ago. She looked good. Healthy. Those beautiful eyes of hers sparkled. I knew she was free of drugs or she wouldn't be visiting me. She promised to come back, too." She shook her head. "Never did, though."

My tongue burned with the words that Della was probably on a bender that resulted in her exposure and death. I couldn't mention Della's missing body, either. The old woman didn't need more grief. "It must have been a shock when you learned Della was dead."

"Upset me plenty. And then I was sick, and that nice Mr. McArdle offered me that time off and . . . I feel it in my heart that I didn't go to the viewing yesterday. Was that a mistake, do you think?"

"Of course not," I said. "I mentioned Roland Blessing. Did you ever meet him?"

She pressed a finger to her lips. "Not that I recall."

I hadn't expected she would have. Blessing must have followed Chesa, maybe even from the Grief Shop. He was clever, not going after her on the subway, but waiting until she'd gone to the funeral home. Too many eyes watched on mass transit.

"Any idea where Mr. McArdle might have gone?" I asked.

"No idea. The man didn't confide in me."

I let talk of Della and Chesa drop, and Mrs. Cheadle began showing me her vaudeville scrapbooks. When her lids drooped, I got up to go.

She grabbed my hand. "Please tell me when Chesa's funeral is. I'd so like to go. And Della's. Yes, I must go to that, too."

On the drive back to the office, I played with Blessing's killing of Chesa like a sore tooth you can't leave alone. If only, if only, if only.

Dammit, I'd get that son of a bitch.

I punched on the radio to get a traffic report. Minutes later, news came on about a Roxbury homicide at a local funeral home. Few details. No suspect in custody. Police were on the hunt.

I felt a terrible emptiness.

I stopped at a music store and bought a CD. Back in traffic, the changer sucked in *Sweet Baby James*. A favorite of my dad's. And Chesa's. From a long-ago time when he'd taken us bowling. I chuckled. First ball Chesa'd thrown was a strike. Dad went nuts with excitement.

I was gridlocked at the light on Tremont. I wished I had more memories like that of my dad.

They were gone from the earth. Forever.

I started to yell, and the light changed, and I yelled while horns blared and people hollered and it didn't matter. It didn't matter at all.

Chapter Four

By the time I got back to the office, I was repeating that familiar mantra about not falling apart. I had to find Della's body and bury her. I had to bury Chesa. And I had to find Blessing. Why had he murdered Chesa? *Why?*

Hell. I'd been through this too many times.

I gave Penny a much-needed walk, then called Mass General. Dr. Rutledge still wasn't on. When I left Della's physician a message to call me, I let the exasperation rise in my voice.

I dreaded facing the group the following week. They'd all feel guilty, which was wrong. Nothing indicated that Roland Blessing would freak out so badly.

But I couldn't help myself. I felt guilty, too.

I stopped by Kranak's office—maybe he had news about Blessing or they'd found Della's remains or he'd heard from McArdle. Unlucky me, Kranak was off on a case.

Frustrated about everything and feeling utterly impotent, I buzzed John Strabo, one of our MEs. He wasn't in his office, so a-hunting I went. I unlocked the double doors to the morgue wing and smacked right into Dr. Tom Fogarty.

"Dammit!" He rubbed his surgically enhanced nose where we'd collided. "Why can't you stay out of our wing?"

"And why can't you not act like a jerk? Have you seen Strabo?"

"He's just begun a post. Excuse me." Fogarty reached for the door.

"Where would I find information on a thirtyish woman who died a few days ago from exposure over at the General?"

He smirked. "Folks don't usually die of exposure at the General."

I mined a bucket of patience. "The woman became ill from exposure out on the streets, Fogarty, then died in the hospital."

He rolled his eyes. "I haven't time for this." He pushed past me, into the lobby.

I trailed after him. "Just give me an answer. Or is it too challenging?"

"You *do* remember how to climb the stairs to the records room, correct?"

"Thank you for that clue. But she wasn't here."

He sighed with exaggerated exasperation. "Of course she was. If she was thirty and died of exposure, in or out of a hospital, they would have brought her here for a post. Period. End of discussion, although it really can't be called that, now can it?"

He walked off mumbling expletives.

And I was left cursing myself. I hadn't been thinking straight. When a person as young as Della dies at a hospital in the state of Massachusetts, it's a given that they'll be brought to the Grief Shop for an autopsy. So why hadn't Rutledge sent her body over?

Then again, maybe he had.

But when I checked with Records on arrivals in the past two weeks, Della's name didn't pop up. Nor did she match any of our recent Jane Does.

What the hell was this Rutledge pulling?

I called Veda, who pledged to get me a direct line

for Rutledge over at the General. As we hung up, she said, "This morning your friend . . . Sergeant Kranak told me all about it. Terrible. If you need me, *bubbeleh*, you know I'm here. Think about taking a break. It might help."

"Help what?"

"Your state of mind."

Her parting comment trailed after her like a rancid perfume.

I slumped onto the couch, my emotions jagged as splinters.

State of mind, my patootie. I reached for a pen, but my hand brushed Daddy's meerschaum pipe.

Daddy buttoning his pea jacket, waving a jaunty good-bye as he walks out the door. And then Daddy broken, his left leg at some crazy angle, fingers missing from his right hand, rivers of blood streaming from his face, his hands, his . . . He's trying to crawl up our front steps. Daddy!

I rocked back in the seat. It didn't *feel* like twenty years ago. More like yesterday.

I went to the bathroom and ran a cool cloth across my face. I looked like shit.

Minutes later I was called to the lobby. A kid—either a jumper or she'd been pushed—had arrived a couple of hours earlier. Now her folks were waiting for me.

I introduced myself and we began our sad journey. After two draining hours, I dragged my sorry ass out of the Grief Shop.

I crossed the parking lot hunched over, with Penny hugging my side. It was rainy and windy, and the chain-link fence clanked like it always did in bad weather. I spotted a man at the back of the lot. He was lighting a smoke as he hugged close to the shadow of a Range Rover. Something glittered . . . maybe a gold coin flipped into the air . . . or the barrel of a gun.

When I shaded my eyes, he nodded to me. His head snaked around, as if looking for someone, then he made a step forward—coming my way. I shrank closer to the Jeep.

"Tally!" Mary trotted out the door, the rain pelting her uncovered head.

"Something up?" I yelled over the rain.

"Sorry," Mary said. "I thought I'd lost my house keys, but I've got them."

When I looked up, the man saluted me, then melted into the puddle of shadow between the parking lot lights.

Spooked, I drove home too fast. The rain had turned icy, the footing slippery on the front steps. Jake flung open our communal front door wearing a scowl. It marred his too-perfect mug, making it almost interesting.

"What's wrong?" I swooped my mail off the hall table.

"You didn't spread the rock salt when you left," he said. "Again."

"Sorry. I meant to. This is all a fake-out because you didn't get my bedroom light switch fixed. Right?"

He raked a hand through his hair, which meant he hadn't, then squatted to let Penny lick his face. A shocking lack of taste on her part.

"You smell like the dead," he said in that Maine way of his, all taciturn and quiet.

"You just smell," I replied.

He chuckled, then crossed his arms. "You have trouble sleeping, I'll be up late."

Jake could be sensitive. When he was in the mood.

"Jake-*ie*," came a breathy voice from upstairs. "Are you coming back? I'm cold."

We had a lousy heating system, too.

Jake showed lots of white teeth. "On my way," he hollered upstairs.

"Can she vote yet?" I asked.

As I walked down the narrow hall to my flat, he thundered back up the stairs. Good thing I didn't have a crush on my landlord.

While I nuked a can of soup, I rifled through my mail: catalogs, electric bill, a VISA come-on, more junk. Nothing from the Winsworth, Maine, police. I'd been waiting forever for a response to the letter I'd sent them regarding my dad.

Earlier, Mary had raised an interesting point: Was there any chance Blessing had killed his own child? I'd thought about it myself and dismissed it. Might bear another look.

I set up my photo oils, cotton balls, and cotton-rolled toothpicks for painting black-and-white photos. I wished I had a picture of Chesa. Instead, I picked one of a magnificent maple, in my mind's eye all yellow-red, with the trunk dark-brown wet from a recent storm. The sky I'd make surreal, using fantastical colors of purple and rose and green.

Except it came out dark and dank and permeated with sorrow. That wasn't Chesa.

I dumped the photo in the trash, then climbed into bed, paint-stained and weary. I wondered what Blessing was doing, what he was thinking and feeling.

Chesa, speak to me.

I wanted to replay our dinner last night . . . and make everything different.

Penny climbed onto the bed and made her nest at the foot. I thought of my ex-husband, and how I'd welcomed his warmth beside me early in our marriage. I pictured his hand seeking my breast, and how he'd cup it and massage it and how my mouth would dry, just like now, while the rest of me grew damp with desire. I could feel his hardness beneath my hand, and then the way he'd curl on top of me, and it felt so good, the warmth, the sharing, the . . .

I rolled on my side and tried to purge the memories.

The drums were bad that night. I fought them off as long as I could, then downed another inch of bourbon.

I didn't dream.

The following morning I barreled into the Grief Shop at Mach speed. I hustled to the central office. Gert was at her desk, Donna was filing, Andy was on the phone.

"Where's Mary?" I tried to keep the panic from my voice.

"Called in sick," Gert said.

"I don't like this. Blessing had an argument two days ago with Chesa. Now she's dead and the police think he did it. Well, Blessing and Mary mixed it up a bit, too."

"Mary?" Andy snorted. "She doesn't mix it up with anyone."

"Shut up," Donna said.

I ran my finger down the chart, then dialed Mary's number. "I don't even know where she lives or—"

"Heddo?" Mary answered in a snuffly voice.

"Mary!" I gave the thumbs up. "Hi, er, I just called to see how you were feeling."

"Better," she said, "but not good enough to infect everybody."

"I hear ya. We talked yesterday about Roland Blessing and Chesa Jones—"

"Yes. I'm doing okay with it. Thanks."

I looked around the room. The faces of my coworkers were grim. Andy glanced away. "Um, just be a little cautious," I said to Mary. "Lock your doors and check who's there before opening one. You know, the regular stuff. Not that you should worry."

"Of course not." Her voice was hushed and heavy. "He's such an angry man."

"He is that. Get healthy. See you tomorrow."

I hung up. Three pair of eyes searched mine. "Yeah. I'm thinking the same thing—did we mess up?"

Gert popped a Bazooka bubble. "Are you kiddin' me? The only person to mess up was Blessing."

"Point taken," I said.

"One more point ya better take." Gert thrust a pink-polished nail in my direction. "Ya know that advice you just gave little Mary? Look in the mirror, Tal."

"I'm fine. And I've got Penny." Before she'd lost one leg, she'd been a first-rate Canine Corps member.

If someone went after me, she'd rip out their throat.

What *had* that guy been doing in the parking lot last night? Penny wouldn't be so hot at stopping a bullet.

Gert blew a purple bubble, a larger one. She scratched Penny's chin. "Good thing she helps in the emotional part, too, since she's the only one you'll let close."

She sashayed from the room.

I was looking for Kranak like crazy. Couldn't find him, and by midday I was cranky and tired and in no mood for his games of hide-and-seek.

He ticked me off even more when he walked into my office and began trolling my minifridge for a Yoo-hoo. He was such a mooch. Then he unwrapped a giant hoagie and started chowing, as if my office were Sardi's.

Okay, so it used to be his office, but it was time for him to get over it.

He pushed a manila folder across the coffee table at me.

Inside were photocopies of several fingerprints. A name was written beside them: Roland Blessing.

"From McArdle's?" I said.

He nodded as he took a swig of Yoo-hoo.

"Did you learn anything about Chesa's movements that night?" I asked. "What about McArdle? Have they found Blessing yet?"

"What do I look like, Info Central?"

"Come on, give."

"Your friend Chesa left the hotel at ten P.M. alone, two nights ago. Last time anyone saw her. Cabbie dropped her at McArdle's. Still no McArdle."

"And . . . ?"

"And they'll find him soon. I'll keep you in the loop. What I know, you'll know."

Which meant he'd tell me as much as he felt like telling me. "And Blessing?"

He tossed his rolled-up napkin into the trash. "Done a vanishing act."

"There's a big surprise."

"It is, matter of fact," Kranak said, clearly annoyed with me. "See, they've got him, solid. Down at that bowling alley. Probably doin' an Irish jig, if I know—"

"Don't be a bigot."

"You think that well of me, huh, Tal?"

Kranak's words stung. "I'm sorry. I . . . I know you were making a joke." A feeling of enervation washed over me. "Go on."

"They pile into the place, the Golden Shamrock Bowling Lanes, and he's nowhere around. Poof. He had help. Boston PD's not sure which kind. Pisarro? Some other hood? Family? Naw. Doesn't have any family left. Hard to guess."

"Have them check the cemetery. Blessing went there a lot to talk to his daughter. What about Della's body?"

"It hasn't turned up," he said.

"I love that phrase, Rob, 'turned up.' Not exactly proactive."

"So what?"

"Look, I need to put Della to rest."

"Oh, she's at rest, all right."

"Christ. I know McArdle took her, but—"

He held up his hands, as if in surrender. "God save

me from your buts. I'll call if I hear a peep. And watch your ass, eh? I've grown fond of it."

"Not so fast. You're on my class list at Northeastern for the spring semester. This is the fifth year you've signed up for my class. Are you going to show this time?"

"Maybe." On his way out, he did that *Beavis and Butthead* laugh he knew I hated.

Just before I left the Grief Shop for the day, I pulled open a file cabinet in our central office and flipped through folders. I was hunting for Blessing's MGAP record. I finally buzzed Gert. "Blessing's folder is missing."

"The cops came by yesterday," she said. "After lunch, lookin' for his stuff. I told 'em they couldn't have it, but I think while I was talking to one, the other one scarfed the folder. Hang on."

Minutes later, Gert returned carrying a plain manila envelope and wearing a grin. "Of course, I'd made a copy."

"Gert," I said, taking the envelope from her hand. "You are a gem."

"Don't I know it."

When I left the building that evening, I found myself checking nooks and crannies in the parking lot, and white-knuckling Penny's leash, and groping for the pepper spray, which was damned awkward, since I carried keys in my hand, too.

The lot was empty, except for me, which pleased me enormously. Later that evening I brewed myself some thick Turkish coffee, crawled beneath the coverlet on the couch, and tried not to think of Chesa. I'd watch her autopsy.

I wanted to be there for her.

I reached for the folder. The courts had *forced* Blessing into counseling. Why hadn't I seen his murderous rage?

It wasn't fun reading. He claimed employment at the Golden Shamrock Bowling Lanes in Southie. When the court had insisted we take him on, it had included his rap sheet. Blessing had committed a variety of misdemeanors, but no mention was made of Harry Pisarro. I didn't doubt that Kranak was right about that. And the Binny kid had mentioned Pisarro by name.

The recorded crimes were old—from long before Moira had been killed three years earlier—and most were stupid scams that ended up hurting only Blessing. I reread his evaluation form, an instrument we give to each potential counselee. Mary had recorded the data, while Gert had done the evaluating. Blessing was deeply depressed and probably used drugs to medicate his emotional pain. The only legit job he'd worked since his daughter's death had been at the bowling lanes. He'd verbally assaulted a woman he termed "the bull dyke." She was his daughter's landlady and he'd accused her of lusting after Moira, who at nineteen was a promising flautist attending Emerson College.

Like so many loved ones of homicide victims, Blessing's grief was on hold, the process aborted. He'd been plagued by the media, and like most victims' family members, he felt huge levels of anger and frustration and fear. Although he'd tried to hide it, he was terrified he would fall victim to the same killer.

His paperwork noted his refusal to have any sort of one-on-one counseling. His continuing interference with his daughter's landlady had gotten him arrested and attending our group was a condition of his not being jailed.

He was angry. I'd seen firsthand how verbally abusive he could be. So why hadn't he harmed Moira's landlady, the woman he believed had killed his daughter, and instead picked on Chesa?

I put Blessing's folder aside for a minute and switched from coffee to Cline's great mourvedre. I busted Jake for his snooty wine tastes, but nothing took the edge off better than a crisp red.

I opened the written sketch on Moira Blessing's homicide. She'd apparently been a cautious and quiet girl totally into her music. Her death had been as grim as Blessing had described in group. The killer had strangled her, then mutilated her. She hadn't put up a fight and they'd found the underground drug Ecstasy in her blood. Her father said that was ridiculous, that she'd never take a drug like that.

The well-prepared killer had then taken her hands as trophies—it appeared he'd removed them with some type of sharp axe. Moira's sexual assault with her flute took place after she was dead. It was strange, yet comprehensible, in that it isn't uncommon for human predators to have erectile dysfunction.

The night of her death, she and her father were to meet for dinner at a restaurant near the Public Garden. On his way to the restaurant, which was on a well-lit street, Blessing crossed through the park.

Geesh. *He'd* been the one to find her body. I read the transcription of Blessing's tape.

*As I walked across the park to meet my girl, I heard
Moira's flute . . . playing . . . she was playing . . . so beautiful, ya know . . . and I followed the tune, had to, she was
calling to me . . . and I went off the path hollering her
name . . . "Moira!" I called and called and . . . and then I
crossed the grass . . . following that sound . . . and the grass,
it was wet . . . I remember that, it seeping through my
sneakers . . . seeping . . . just like . . . I tripped . . . didn't
fall, not me . . . see, there was something on the ground.
. . . something I couldn't see . . . a thing . . . beneath a
greenish canvas covering . . . all lumpy and funny and . . .
and I wasn't hearing Moira's flute anymore . . . and I . . .
I . . .*

He hadn't been able to continue, but Gert's note
said that Blessing had looked beneath the canvas and
found his daughter. It said she was clothed—thank
God he didn't see his dead child naked, with a flute
sticking from her vagina. But he'd seen the stumps of
her arms, where her hands belonged. He'd screamed,
and been unable to stop screaming until sedated. He'd
ended up in the VA hospital in Jamaica Plain.

Terrible, terrible world. The killer must have been
a monster to lure Blessing to his daughter's body.
What could Blessing have done to deserve such a horrible revelation? Or maybe it wasn't that at all.

I wiped away the tears I hadn't known I cried.

So how come, after three long, miserable years, he
turned homicidal? What triggered it?

And the more pressing question: Would he kill
again?

Chapter Five

I checked my watch. It felt like midnight, but was just after eight. I didn't like the anxious feeling that was building inside me. Blessing's anger came out of his pain. Apparently his fury had reached pressure-cooker proportions. Why now?

I threw on some jeans, then dialed the precinct that handled SoWa, where Moira had lived out her final days.

SoWa was one of Boston's artistic areas and where my landlord Jake had his studio. Moira's landlady still lived there, and it was there he'd been arrested for stalking her.

"I'm concerned," I told the officer on duty. "It's probably nothing. Just check on the woman."

"We know Blessing. He's a couple fries short of a Happy Meal. We sent a patrolman over earlier, and the lady's fine. We're keepin' an eye out 'cause of that Roxbury thing."

"Great. You think there's a chance Blessing's got it right about the landlady?"

He chuckled. "No way. When the kid died, we got the landlady at some gallery opening. Five, six sworn statements. Plus she's got arthritis in her hands. No way could she have chopped off the kid's hands."

"Then why would Blessing focus on her?"

"She's all he's got. The case is cold as a Maine morning."

"A shame. Thanks for the help."

"We live to serve."

Having counseled the families of homicide victims in and around Boston for twelve years, I knew a lot of people. A *lot* of people. Some of my counselees were simply acquaintances who'd moved on once they emerged from hell. Many others became friends, since we all belonged to an exclusive club. One, admittedly, no one wanted to join.

That's why I whistled Dixie. She's a lawyer friend who grew up and still lived in Southie, and who specialized in domestic disputes, annulments, and green card cases. I met her when they'd brought her brother into the Grief Shop in a body bag.

"Hey Dix," I said.

"So, you're in a mess," she said in a brogue that could butter toast. She pulled it on and off like a spring sweater.

"I need some help."

"I'm not surprised, once I read about Rollie. Him hurting your friend and all."

"You know Blessing?"

"Sure. Not well. Bad temper Rollie has, doesn't he?"

"Yup. But I never saw any violence in the man."

"I couldn't tell ya. So what can I do?"

"I need an escort to the Golden Shamrock—a bowling alley in your neighborhood."

Dixie bellowed a laugh. "You're crazy, you know."

"Well, of course I am."

"I'll send ya with my new honey, Mick. I wouldn't step foot in that hole meself. Too ugly by half."

* * *

Dixie always had a new honey, and her Mick was waiting for me outside the door to the bowling lanes. The place defined hole-in-the-wall, with a scuffed door that might once have been blue and windows greased with smoke and God knew what else. I didn't want to know what else, actually.

Mick was a skinny-bean who pumped my hand with glee. He reminded me a little of Dixie. Same gray eyes, same toothy grin. He raised an eyebrow. "Are you sure you want to go in there? It's a pit."

Not a trace of a brogue. Leave it to Dixie. "Got to do it, Mick."

"Then let's go."

Inside, we drew a lot of looks from men sipping beers at the bar, which was on our right. The joint rumbled with noise from the bowling lanes, the bar, and the jukebox, which was playing Elvis's "Love Me Tender." The smell wrinkled my nose—a tad too much testosterone for my taste.

Straight in front of us lay the candlepin lanes that gave the place its name. In New England, candlepin bowling rules.

They say the Irish in Boston are more Irish than the Irish. Maybe it's true. Or maybe not. But the Golden Shamrock was different, and not just because it was a bowling alley. Not just any Southie resident hung out there, but guys who considered themselves badasses. First off, understand that it was a guy place. Some patrons had done time, while others took out their anger on their wives and kids. Some dealt drugs and others collected guns for the IRA. Some did both. And a few were nice. A very few. Even they generally had a past.

I felt confident because Mick was with me, not to mention Penny, who drew more looks than I did. Without her in my life, even with Mick I wouldn't have gone there. A shower of beer soared across a table as Mick and I wove our way to the bar.

I spotted a state cop I knew. He winked, and I wondered if he was socializing or hunting Blessing like me. I squeezed my way through. I got pinched once. Penny bared teeth, and that was that. I slid onto a bar stool with green leather smooth as a baby's bottom. Golden shamrocks glittered on the pine-paneled walls. I rested my elbows on the scarred bar and faced the fogged mirror.

The bartender, with striking black-Irish looks, walked over.

Above the music of the Chieftains and the swoosh, ker-thunk, and smash of the lanes, Mick ordered a beer. Then he faded into the background as we'd discussed earlier. If things got weird, he'd jump back in.

"Diet Coke," I said to the bartender.

"Don't have any," the bartender said.

Right. "Coke, then."

"None of that, either."

"*Really?* What *do* you have that's nonalcoholic?"

"Water." He smirked.

"No mixes?" I said.

"All out."

The word "jerk" came to mind. "Water it is, then." I laid down a twenty.

He poured me a glass of plain old tap water, sans ice.

He peeked over the edge of the bar before sliding the water in front of me. "That Mick's new dog?"

"Nope. She's mine. Or maybe I'm hers."

"Huh. Had a pal whose Canine Corps pooch got mustered out 'cause she got her leg blown up."

I scratched Penny's head. "That sounds like my Penny. Jimmy Devlin?"

"Yup," he said. "Be right back." Minutes later, he was pouring a can of Diet Coke into a frosted glass. "The name's Skip."

I nodded, having obviously passed some arcane test. "I'm looking for Roland Blessing."

Skip laughed. "You . . . and a million other pissed-off people. I wouldn't want to be in Blessing's moccasins right now."

"How long did Blessing work here?" I asked.

"C'mon, he never worked here. He's a regular, though. Fancied himself a member of the Golden Shamrock club."

"Which is?"

"Just a bunch of bozos that come here every night."

"So what's your take on him?"

He shrugged.

"I'll play you for the info in darts."

"You'd cream me. I stink."

So did I, but why share that information?

Skip poured a shot for himself. "Blessing wasn't such a pain until little Moira got killed. Then he started acting pretty strange. Odd. It got worse. Couple nights ago, he came in all paranoid like, and—"

Skip's eyes tracked to the door. He gave me his back.

"Skip?" I said.

The rumble of chatter and clink of glasses and snick

of pool cues hushed. A ball crashed into pins, then silence there, too.

In the mirror I saw a tall man with white hair and black brows cross the room. He wore a long camel's hair coat and trendy black pants and a black t-shirt—Armani, maybe—which made him look like an aged Hollywood producer on the make for a young chick.

He was headed my way. Penny growled when he got close. I caught his grin in the mirror.

Boy, did I know that grin. Most at the alley wouldn't, simply because Italians didn't frequent bars in Southie, just like the Irish stayed away from the North End.

But there were other, more compelling reasons.

His name was Harry Pisarro. It would be easy to romanticize him. I'd put him in his early sixties and at about five feet ten inches. His silvered hair crowned a tanned face blessed by a Roman nose and expressive lips that smiled easily. When I'd met him three years ago, I'd have had to be made of cardboard not to be impressed by his courtly manners and elegant speech and his power to make whomever he spoke with feel important.

Kranak said he was a mob bigwig. But even mobsters need counseling when their daughters get garroted by loose-cannon lovers.

He gave plenty to the homeless. He walked in AIDS marches and supported the Boston Ballet. He donated big bucks during MGAP's fund-raising month, and for the past three years, on the anniversary of his daughter's death, he sent me two dozen roses. His grief for his daughter had been real.

But Pisarro was no benign wiseguy. I'd also counseled two families of petty crooks who'd tried to fish

Pisarro's waters and ended up floating in the Charles. Pisarro's wife, with her fearful eyes and too-loud demeanor, often wore bruises that I suspected came from Pisarro. I'd also heard rumors that he was the source of the serpentine scar that ran down Kranak's face.

That, more than anything, made me dislike him.

I swiveled in my seat. "Hello Mr. Pisarro."

"Harry. I've told you the name's Harry."

I nodded. "How are you doing?"

He held up a leather-gloved hand. "Fair."

"It takes time."

"Yes. And what, might I ask, are you doing in the Golden Shamrock, Madame Tally?"

"Just sharing a drink with my friend, Mick."

"Is that so?" Pisarro's eyes slid to Mick.

Mick's Adam's apple bobbled.

Skip made his way back down to us. He was wiping a shot glass.

"Ah, Skip," Pisarro said. "The on-the-take cop."

Skip flushed.

"So what brings you down to Southie, Mr. Pisarro?" I asked.

His smile was warm as the Sicilian sun. "I hear that someone who works for me has committed a heinous crime, one that involved you, Madame Tally."

Now it was my turn to flush. He'd somehow made Chesa's death seem dirty. "I'm surprised you admit Blessing worked for you."

He nodded. "On and off. As one of the computer technicians at my club. He wasn't half bad at it. Unfortunately, he was more off than on. I hired him because of his daughter. But it's not acceptable, what he did to your friend . . . and you."

The door banged open. Pisarro's two flunkies pivoted, hands sliding beneath their jackets.

Kranak?

Pisarro bowed, notched his head at his men, then strode toward the back.

I turned to Skip. He was gone, too.

"You just happened along, right, Rob?" I asked, unable to keep the exasperation from my voice.

"Keeping an eye on you, babe."

"Don't call me babe, dammit. I'm pretty ticked that you barged in on me like that. I was trying to learn something about Blessing."

Kranak hoisted a beer to his lips. "What's to learn? With Pisarro on his trail, the guy's toast."

Thursday morning, four pairs of eyes were glued to me as I assigned that day's work load.

On the white board, I wrote Gert's name beside the victim of a drive-by shooting. I gave Andy the family of an indigent woman who'd apparently been mugged. Most likely no one would show. It was Donna's day for filing, while Mary took the phones.

I scratched my name beside the third victim, even though no one would arrive to mourn Chesa Jones.

I'd been the one to ID Chesa. By now, she'd been assigned a number, and a tag dangled from her toe. She'd been photographed and examined, clothed and nude, weighed and measured and X-rayed.

Did Chesa have scars? Tattoos? A mole? That would be in the report, too, which would also contain her fingerprints and old broken bones and needle marks, if any. They'd have checked her hair and fingernails and skin and taken fluids from her body for testing at the lab. Was she on drugs? Did she have cancer? Was she anemic?

I knew so little about Chesa.

She was all set for Strabo's knife that morning. Why did I feel this compulsion to watch? It would be agony.

"So what's everybody looking at, huh?" I asked.

"Nothin', Tal." Gert rested her hip on the desk. "You notice your skirt's on backward?"

Shit. I reached down to twist it around. "No, it's not, Gert."

"Just wanted to see if you were paying attention."

I knew enough about grief to know I was acting pretty desperate. I wanted Blessing found. I wanted Chesa's murderer behind bars. I wanted it done. *Now.*

I knew it didn't work that way. It didn't mean I didn't feel it.

If I could locate McArdle, find Della's body, that would help.

I dialed city records and connected with Betsy Croll.

"Hey, Betsy." I told her about McArdle. "First name Joseph. I've searched the Web for his number and come up with nada."

A pause while she searched, then, "I've got nothing on a Joseph McArdle," Betsy said. "But the mortuary building's owned by a Gateway Properties, Inc."

I jotted down Gateway's address and phone number.

"Who owns Gateway?"

"Doesn't say," she replied.

*   *   *

Minutes later, a tentative knock before Strabo's bald
head peeked around the door. "You still want to see
the Chesa Jones cut?"

"Thanks," I said. "Be right down."

I walked through the morgue wing's doors and
donned sterile scrubs for Chesa's autopsy.

Three autopsies were in progress in room two.
When I entered room one, I expected to see Strabo
talking into a microphone, with Chesa's body on the
steel table.

The room was empty. It was freezing, the blowers
that kept the air fresh were working at furious speeds.
I'd forgotten my sweater.

A door flew open and Tom Fogarty breezed in.

Hell.

He glanced at me, his blue eyes impassive, then
frowned at the empty table, then the door. Fogarty
tapped one foot.

His eyes locked on mine and a smile crept along
his full lips. "That nut case Schliemann was in yesterday when you were off somewhere."

"Did he find a new mummy?" I asked.

"Who knows?" He shrugged. "I kicked him out."

"He's a harmless old man."

"I banned him from the premises."

"You are such a bum."

"Thank you." He checked his watch. "Where is that
damned corpse?"

With a grunt of disgust, he stormed from the room.

*   *   *

Minutes later, a metallic rumbling came from the corridor, then a masked Fogarty blew back in followed by a Boston PD detective I'd seen at Chesa's crime scene and a technician pushing the steel gurney that held Chesa. I tied on my mask as Fogarty and the tech hefted Chesa's body onto the table. The rigor had receded. Only her neck remained stiff.

The technician handed Fogarty the X rays. Fogarty spoke into the microphone while he studied them. Nothing broken except several metacarpus bones, not atypical of a basketball player. Several of her teeth were false, also not atypical.

He spoke of the swelling and bruising around her mouth and nose and eyes, and how she had apparently been beaten by a blunt object, possibly a bottle.

He remarked on the lack of defensive wounds to her arms and hands. Ditto for any marks marring her wrists or ankles. She hadn't been tied. Had she been drugged? Was she too drunk to put up a fight?

I listened to Fogarty drone on about Chesa's head, the petechiae—small bleeding sites in the moist mucosa of Chesa's lips and inside her mouth. He examined Chesa's eyelids and found petechiae there, too.

I stuttered an inhale.

The detective gave me a sharp look. I wouldn't meet his eyes.

Chesa's face and neck were a dark red, her eyes bulging. There was a bruise, an inverted *V*, on her neck.

Fogarty's voice hissed into the microphone, his dispassion irrationally bugging me.

He concluded Chesa had died slowly and painfully from strangulation.

"... consistent with homicide," Fogarty mouthed for the recorder.

Tears tickled my eyes. I swiped my forearm across my face.

Fogarty lifted the knife to make the *Y*-shaped incision across Chesa's chest, then vertically down to the pubis.

Rather than seeing Chesa now, I saw her as an eleven-year-old getting her insides opened up. Then I saw myself. I wore tattered jeans and a sweater set, a blue one with pink flowers—the one I'd worn when I'd found my dad. Then I pictured Fogarty slicing through *my* flesh, slowly, methodically, while he examined me, talked about me, verbally dissected the crime against me as my husk lay open and unprotesting on a cold steel gurney.

I turned and left the room.

Chapter Six

I gently closed the office door behind me. Penny whined. I steadied myself on the desk. I was shivering. I'd never done that before—mentally exchanged bodies on an autopsy table. I ran a chilled soda can across my forehead.

A soft knock. "Come in," I said. I cleared my throat and in a stronger voice said, "Come on in."

"Hi, Tally." Mary's soft brown eyes met mine, then slid to the window. "I, um, I got a funny phone call last night. I thought you should know. Is it a bad time for you?"

"Not at all." Mary's mother was a homicide. It had bent her. Forever. Just like it had bent me.

She'd been with us for three years, and was becoming an excellent counselor. She was sweet and quiet and insecure, and plastered on more makeup than a chorine. The mask was her arsenal against pain. I "got" it only too well.

"Tell me about the phone call," I said.

"He said . . . He said he was watching me. Donna and you, too. That he missed us. That we were special to him." She shrugged. "Gert agreed that I should tell you. It might be nothing, but . . . It could have been Roland Blessing."

"Did he threaten you?"

"Not really." She chewed her lip. "Not in so many words. But his tone made me nervous. You know what I mean?"

"Sure do. Did you tell the police?"

"Yes. Right away."

I nodded. "Please be extra careful, Mary."

"Oh, I am. Donna and I called the police in our towns and they're going to keep a watch out for us. You should have a watch, too."

"Will do, Mary. Thanks."

After she left, I fixed a hot chocolate. Blessing's call was an odd thing to do for someone with his profile. The incompleteness of that profile bothered me. I phoned Dixie, who confirmed that Blessing had no one. That fit. He could be watching us to connect.

According to Dixie, he lived in a ratty little tenement. She said he'd spent all of his money on Moira's music lessons and her apartment. Made him sound noble. Except she also told me about his phony scams, where he'd claim to be collecting for the police benevolent association and take money from old people not savvy enough to know he was a con artist.

I was sure he gave a piece of that pie to Pisarro.

"He's a minor leaguer," she said. "But he loves hanging around the big boys. He loves the tough stuff."

"Does he? I can't see that. Oh, I know he does bad things, but I see him as scared, as a man who uses other thugs as camouflage."

"No way," Dixie said. "He's a big-mouthed—"

"That's my point. He's mouthy, not an action guy. And yet he killed. Can you get us inside his apartment?"

"I don't know, Tal. If he found us, he'd be one angry boyo."

"Come on, Dix."

"Lemme see."

An hour later, she called back with a yes. We made a date for the following morning, then I leashed up Penny and headed for Newton and the Haywood Funeral Home.

Time to make arrangements for Chesa's service. I was also betting Dave Haywood could find McArdle for me. I just hoped he wouldn't ask me for a date.

Thirty minutes later, I parked in front of a mortuary graced with stately pillars and a porte cochere.

I tugged slowly on the car door handle. Chesa's death was dragging at me.

Come on, kiddo, crank it up. I flicked my hands through my Medusa curls, dabbed on some lipstick, and went inside.

Dave Haywood was walking toward me down the

hall. Haywood was one of the best in the business. A jovial man with a runner's build and a Cornhusker face. His family had been planting corpses for generations.

"Yo, Tal! Long time no see." Haywood smothered me in a hug and held it a wee bit too long.

"Can we talk in the annex?" I asked.

"Sure. You look like you could use a drink." He led me through the viewing rooms to the cheery, yellow-painted apartment at the back of the mortuary.

"I can almost taste the Old Grandad, but since it's only noon, how about some coffee."

He got out the coffee fixings. "You're off your feed, Tal. I can see that. Though, of course, you always look stunning."

Yeah, right.

"I've got center-ice seats for the Bruins next Sunday. Feel like going?"

"I always go to Veda's on Sundays." Lame.

"Raincheck?"

"Dave, I . . ."

"I'll come up with something even better."

Swell. I smiled.

"So, Tal, if it's not the Bruins, what *can* I do for you today?"

I made arrangements for Chesa's service and cremation. I then explained about Della's missing corpse and McArdle.

He sat our mugs on the coffee table and slid into the chair facing me. "Strange, strange world. We get pretty protective of our dead. Could be why he took her."

"Do you know McArdle?"

"Doesn't ring any bells." His hand wandered to mine and he rubbed it.

After a beat, I moved it away, allegedly to stir milk into my coffee. It was one of those awkward guy/girl things I hated. I covered by sipping coffee.

"I can understand McArdle being terrified of Blessing," I said. "But it's frustrating that he hasn't resurfaced."

"He's a probable witness to your friend's homicide, right?"

"I hadn't thought of it that way, but sure. He could stay hidden until Blessing is caught."

"He sounds like a wimp."

"Maybe a little nervous. But he seemed a decent guy. You know, the kind who'd do the right thing. He even does some pro bono work for the homeless."

His eyebrows shot up. "Freebies for the homeless? New one on me."

"I'm pretty desperate to find him so I can bury Chesa's sister. And I'd like to talk to him. He was one of the last people to see Chesa alive."

Dave leaned back in his chair. "Ever think this McArdle wasn't on the up and up?"

"No. Why wouldn't he be?"

He shrugged. "You know how much a funeral and interment costs. Was he buying these freebies burial plots or cremating them?"

"He implied burial."

"It sounds odd to me. I'll check out the pro bono thing. We're a small community. One of my colleagues'll know if somebody's doing freebie funerals for the homeless."

"Just get me McArdle's home phone or address." I pushed to my feet.

"No problem. Hey, how about tickets to that new show at the Colonial?"

"Dave, I . . . sure."

The following morning, I presented a box of Krispy Kremes to Dixie O'Toole, while she was in the middle of taking curlers out of her rich, brown hair.

I was bubbling to check out Blessing's digs, but no one ever rushed Dixie.

She snagged the donut box. "Be ready in a sec." When she emerged from the bathroom, each hair was in its perfect place, with the sides and back rolled up into a retro 1940s hairstyle. Although it was winter, she wore a polka-dotted silk suit and terrific stacked heels.

"You're such a glamour puss," I said.

"Gotta be," she replied, tucking her purse beneath her arm. "For the prices I charge, this colleen's got to look the part. Ready?"

"Am I ever."

Dixie walked nowhere, so we drove two blocks over to Roland Blessing's digs. The front door was un-locked and we climbed the rickety staircase with one eye over our shoulders. Dixie produced a key—God knew how she'd gotten it—and after we tugged on gloves, she pushed open the door to Blessing's apart-ment.

"Didn't I tell ya it was a slum?" she said.

"Slum? You're being too kind." The room consisted of a saggy bed, crates as tables, a dresser, a TV, an orange beanbag chair that drooled those little white pellets, and hooks on the walls that equated a closet. Talk about depressing.

"What are you hoping to find?"Dixie asked.

"The key to Roland Blessing."

We started prowling the apartment.

I lifted the grungy bedcovers. "Yuck." On a crate beside the bed sat a plastic photo cube, yellow from age and nicotine. Its pictures showed a freckled toddler, a carrot-topped eight- or nine-year-old, a teen in overalls, a striking young woman with flowing strawberry-blond hair. All Moira. Her eyes, from toddler to adult, had stared clearly at the camera. A serious girl.

Why hadn't Blessing taken the cube?

"Look what I found, Tal."

Dixie held up a rusted tin wastebasket with an empty box of Clairol blond inside.

"Shit. Now we have a blond Blessing."

"Maybe," she said. "Let's hurry up. I'm afraid the cockroaches are gonna sneak into my clothes. How're you doing?"

"Nothing much so far."

"I meant your dad, and you know it."

"Better. Dad's dead twenty years. I still miss him."

"Richard's gone five years now. Wasn't he laughing beside me just yesterday?" She held up a sheaf of papers. "Looks like old bills. Interested?"

"Telephone?"

She paged through them. "Gas. Electric. No phone."

"Leave them."

"This thing with your dad. It wrecked your marriage."

"And not Mark's wandering eye? Let's hustle in here."

"What came first with Mark, Tal, the chicken or the egg?"

"Mark claimed I was 'emotionally inaccessible.' Bullshit. He never said squat until I walked in on him and that chippy flopping around our bed."

"He was a shit. But maybe, Tally-O, it's time to move on in all ways."

"I'll take it under advisement, counselor." I peered under the bed and pulled out a long, narrow case with clasps and a handle. Moira's flute case. I snapped the clasps and gently lifted the lid. Inside, the indentation for a flute carved the bed of bright blue velvet. Of course the flute was missing. Her killer had used it to—

A noise? I bent my head close to the case. Ticking. Had it started when I'd opened the case?

Holy shit! "Dix, we gotta get out of here!"

I pushed her out the door, and straight into one of the thugs I'd seen with Harry Pisarro yesterday.

"Ticking!" I said. "Could be a bomb."

The three of us scrambled for the stairs, my legs working overtime, and we thundered down and landed, stumbling over each other, racing to the door when—

An alarm. Loud. *Ding, ding, ding, ding, dinggggggggg.*

We stopped, panting, waiting, bent in half from our sprint.

The dinging finally ceased, then silence.

We looked at each other, chagrined that we'd all made fools of ourselves over an alarm clock. Stupid.

"Looking for something?" I said to the thug.

The guy blinked fast. Pisarro's boys weren't known

as free thinkers. He pointed a finger at me. "I remember you."

"Just tell Harry we say hi."

I was glad when we were back on the street. "Okay, so it wasn't a bomb."

Dixie repinned her hair. "Why would he put an alarm clock in a flute case?"

"God knows. It was good for us. Keeps us on our toes."

"Oh, sure, Tal. I needed that. My life's too boring."

I laughed. Couldn't help it. "Pisarro's doing the same thing we are? I keep thinking I'll read about Blessing's corpse in the paper. If I were Blessing, I'd skedaddle."

"Naw. He's a Southie kid, just like me. Not as cute, maybe, but he's got the same innards. He won't leave."

"And Harry Pisarro knows it."

After Dixie and I parted, I called Mrs. Cheadle to see if she knew how to locate McArdle. She didn't. With Penny riding shotgun, I drove around Roxbury and asked about Chesa and her sister, Della. Nobody recognized either of their names, or my description of a tall woman with yellow cat's eyes and close-cropped hair. I tried to find Binny, the kid with the bandana, which earned me some slithery looks, but no takers.

I hoped to hell McArdle hadn't just dumped Della's body in the river, like Kranak had joked early on.

Maybe his landlord knew where he was. I headed for Government Center, the part of Boston most like

New York's urban canyons and a planet away from Roxbury. I found Gateway Properties, but its door was locked. When questioned, a custodian said that mail also arrived at Gateway for a Daniel Brown.

As I left the building, my cell phone bleeped. Gert.

A bomb had blown apart a North Shore post office. The remains of seven victims, plus the alleged perpetrator, were on their way in. So were their shocked families.

I zoomed back to the Grief Shop.

Chapter Seven

The next three days were intense. The post office bomb had not only blown apart seven lives, it simultaneously shattered the lives of the victims' loved ones.

That meant dozens of individuals we calmed and consoled as they asked *why?* again and again. I called in two friends, homicide counselors from Philadelphia's GAP, to help out our crew, and we muddled through. But it was rough.

By Sunday we'd begun group grief sessions.

That same day, I carved out some personal time, and Mrs. Cheadle and I held a small, postcremation memorial service for Chesa at Haywood's. Some of her Ithaca chums attended, and they spoke of Chesa in glowing terms.

Ashes in hand, Mrs. Cheadle and I furtively deposited a pinch of Chesa at the Fleet Center, where the Celtics and Bruins play. We scattered the rest in the harbor, the cold stiffening our fingers, then I took Mrs. Cheadle to lunch at Locke-Ober's.

We talked about Chesa, and Mrs. Cheadle regaled me with tales of her vaudeville days, of the Old Howard and the Foys and Ann Corio and Sally Keith-Queen of the Tassels, and other once-famous names now lost in the mists of time. Della's death and her missing remains were strangely absent from the proceedings.

On Monday morning I again checked the papers to see if Pisarro had done in Blessing. So far, nothing, so I assumed Blessing continued to breathe.

As I drove to work, I counted the days since Roland Blessing had beaten and strangled Chesa. Six days. The cliché was true—it felt like a lifetime.

I did the thing in my head, where I ran the tape from a week earlier, and Chesa had been alive, and we'd laughed and made dinner and reminisced. I saw us high-fiving and clinking glasses. I pictured her taking in life's breath and exhaling.

I saw Chesa's childhood face segue to her mature one. In Eastern mythology, when you save a life, aren't you responsible for it forever?

I poked my head into Kranak's office.

"Anything on Blessing?" I asked.

Kranak shook his head.

"Lab results on Chesa?"

He swiveled away from me.

"Where's the report, Rob?" I peered over his shoulder. Chesa Jones was neatly typed on a blue folder.

Kranak intended for me to see it. He wanted me to take it, didn't want to hand it to me.

I swiped it. "Stop trying to protect me, Rob."

"Who, me?"

I carried the folder to my office and closed the door.

According to the lab's tox reports, Chesa had pumped a ton of alcohol into her system. So, in other words, she and Blessing had belted down a few. No, more than a few. She'd had recent sex, but no trace of semen. Rough sex, from the looks of it.

I stroked Penny's fur.

Was it rape? Damn him.

Blessing had beaten her, using a bottle to pummel her again and again and again. Wham, her face. Wham, her eyes. Wham, her nose, blood spurting. Wham, the side of her head and her jaw and her temple and . . . Then he'd strangled her.

I tried to picture it and stumbled over the image.

Christ. I hoped Pisarro would cut off his balls.

Gert buzzed me. "Fogarty sent his usual dippy memo about the budget."

"And?"

"And we're $100,000 short."

"Get your wizard's wand out and let's go to work."

"Oy."

At noon, I walked into group knowing we'd talk mostly about Blessing. Guilt and surprise and sorrow volleyed around the room. Arlo played his harmonica, then told anecdotes about Blessing that lacked bite or new information.

"He asked me out," Christy said.

"You're joshin' me," Arlo said. "He's got thirty years on you."

She ran her hands across her knees. "I know. It was sorta yucky. I said no and he didn't hassle me or anything. I think it was all about my hair."

Of course. Christy's red hair matched Moira Blessing's.

"I saw him," came a whispered voice from the corner. Mary.

"When?"

She nodded. "Two days ago. Across the street, at B.U."

"What makes you—"

"I don't know." She sat up straighter. "His hair was almost pure white and so was the beard he'd grown. It must've been bleach or something. And I accidentally bumped into him, in the crowd. We made eye contact." She blew her nose.

I sat beside her and slung an arm around her shoulder. "You okay?"

"Sure I am,"she answered gamely. "But it scared me a lot."

Arlo played *Twilight Zone* notes on his harmonica. "Let's all watch our backs."

Arlo's words clung like a static-filled skirt. Were we all in danger? I jogged across the lobby and out the door. Burrr.

Arlo and Christy were talking while they walked to their cars.

"A minute, Arlo?" I hollered.

"Not now, Tal." He flicked his cigarette butt over the fence.

I trotted up to him, shivering. "Come on, Arlo. Just a sec."

His eyes slid to Christy, whose head was tilted with unasked questions.

"It's about that report you filed with the courts," I said, lying.

"Oh, yeah. Sure. Let's go."

Back in my office, I offered Arlo a seat. "Let's be straight with each other, Arlo. You're holding something back about Blessing. I'd like to know what."

He laughed and flapped his leathery construction-worker's paw. "You've got the stuff, don't you? Okay. I got this idea where to find Blessing." He pulled over a chair. "See, he goes over to the VA hospital once a week."

"Which one? Jamaica Plain? West Roxbury?"

"Neither. I think it's the downtown clinic. He claims he was a Navy SEAL. Vietnam. See, I've got this plan to go get Blessing for the cops."

"Pardon?"

"He killed that friend of yours, right?"

"Yes, but—"

"So I go get him. I can take him."

"Take him? Oh, come on, Arlo. Be serious."

"I am." He snugged on his cap. "I think it's a damned fine plan."

"It stinks. Blessing beat my friend, then *strangled* her. He's not someone you want to mess with."

He played a couple of *Star Wars* notes on his harmonica. "Remember that fight we almost had, him and me? He's a chump. I can take him. Easy."

Arlo as vigilante. Idiocy. Here was the bluster of a man desperately trying to be in control of something, *anything* in his life. "Forget it, Arlo."

"I can take him."

I doubted Arlo would find Blessing. But what a disaster if he did.

I dialed the cops to tell them about Blessing's visits to the VA hospital, except I disconnected just as someone picked up.

My gut was singing off-key notes. A lot of them. I wanted Blessing bad, but . . .

I thumbed through my Rolodex. Tish Snyder and I had taken a bunch of classes together, what was it? Ten years ago.

She'd worked at the VA hospital in Jamaica Plain.

I called the hospital. Tish didn't work there any longer. I clicked off.

This was ridiculous. I was neglecting my clients, my staff, my friends. Chesa's killer would be caught just fine without my help. In fact, Harry Pisarro would probably do to Blessing what he'd done to Chesa.

Leave it, I told myself.

One more call.

I phoned the VA clinic downtown and on a hunch that he had one, asked to speak to Roland Blessing's case worker. Bingo, except the guy wasn't on. I left my number and a message saying I was a homicide counselor who'd been counseling Blessing about his daughter, Moira, and dropped Tish's name.

Now I was done, done, done.

I got back to work at my real job, but had difficulty concentrating. MGAP was humming, so I began to transcribe more files into the computer, an ongoing process.

An hour into it, Veda buzzed me.

"What's up?" I said.

"Come up, Tal," Veda said. "Bring the information you have about Rutledge."

Rutledge? Ah, Della Charles's attending physician. Right.

Penny and I wended our way upstairs, past the conference room, the Grief Shop's administrative offices, and doctors' offices. The Chief Medical Examiner's office sat near the lunchroom entrance. Hard to imagine a more unpretentious spot. Veda liked her out-of-the-way location, just as her direct predecessor had.

When Veda opened her door, Penny leapt onto her, paw on shoulder.

"*Sah-Nay!*" Veda commanded in impeccable Czech. Penny instantly sat and Veda grinned. "Ach, my little Czech puppy, how are we today?"

Penny's nose butted Veda's hand.

I got the English version of "sit" in Veda's best Jewish-mother voice. At sixty-something, she resembled Dr. Ruth, except for her bright-red hair. She handed Penny a treat, then sat behind her desk.

"Obviously there's a problem," I said.

She nodded. "Dr. Christopher Rutledge. He's the problem."

"How come?"

She opened a manila folder and passed it to me.

A Dr. Christopher Rutledge *was* on staff at Mass General. Except, according to Veda's scribbled note,

Rutledge had been out of the country for the past
month.

No way could he have been Della's attending physician.

Chapter Eight

No Rutledge. No Della, either. And no McArdle. My
head was spinning.

I had a few minutes of downtime before I convened
one of my more fractious postal bomb bereavement
groups, so I made a much-needed call to one of
MGAP's primary donors. A knock, then Mary walked
in. She was bright and intuitive. And she had such
pretty eyes. I just wished she'd lose some of her in-
security, along with the heavy eyeliner and mascara.
We were working on it.

I finished my call. "What's up, Mary?"

"It's sort of about Mr. Blessing."

She was extremely deferential with me. I suspected
she'd been the same way with her mother. I smiled.
"Whatever it is, I'm all ears."

She cracked a smile. "You know I like working
here."

"As much as your editorial job at the magazine?"

"I can't believe you even remember that." She
grinned. "I like it more. By a lot."

"So what's the scoop?"

She rotated her charm bracelet. "Gert mentioned
that Della Charles, the one whose body disappeared,
was the sister of your friend, right."

"Yes."

"I think I met her."

"Where? When?"

"I mean, I'm pretty sure it was her. A few weeks ago. In a jazz club."

"Did you talk to her?"

She nodded. "This is the really stupid part. It was when I went to the bathroom. There was a woman in the stall and there was no toilet paper, so I passed her some from my stall. When she came out, she thanked me. She introduced herself as Della." Mary shrugged. "I think it might be the same lady from the description Gert gave me."

"Was she with anyone?"

"Two guys. One had a cello case, but he wasn't playing there. The other one, well, I think it might have been Mr. Blessing."

Whoa. "Blessing? Did you talk to him?"

She shook her head. "He always made me nervous. I know it's not much, but I thought you'd like to know. She seemed nice. She was so pretty."

"Thanks. Some food for thought. What made you wait so long to tell me, Mary?"

She twisted her charm bracelet. "I felt dumb. I didn't think it mattered."

"Well, I'm glad you told me now."

"Can I do anything for you?" she asked.

I'd been that desperate to please once. Before Veda. "Sure you can."

I flipped my Rolodex and wrote down a name and number. "Give Mrs. Cheadle a call for me and see if she's free tomorrow morning? I'd like to visit her."

"Will do! Um, do you think I look like Gert? She said we were sort of alike, but there's no way."

The hope in her eyes was painful. Gert had an infectious smile, bubbly personality, and curves that didn't quit. "You look like you, Mary. But I can see a similarity to Gert in your smile."

Mary's laugh was melodic.

It would be good to hear it more often.

What was Blessing doing with Della? And who was the cellist? Was he Della's friend? A lover? Could he have had a part in her death? Blessing hadn't reacted to Chesa like he'd known who she was. Then again, the women had different last names and only faintly resembled one another. And from Mary's description, Della sure didn't sound malnourished and homeless. Why would Blessing know Della?

When I arrived home, I fed Penny, and then myself. I phoned Jake, who breezed in minutes later. I forced myself not to drool over his great ass and wide shoulders and crooked smile.

"Wazzup?" he said, helping himself to a beer.

"Feel like doing a sketch for me?"

"Of?"

"This woman who, well, she died, and . . . of her sister, too."

"How'd they die?" He swigged the beer, all casual, but his eyes were intense.

"The one, Della, I don't know. The other, my friend Chesa, was murdered."

He thunked down the bottle. "Nope. I don't do dead people. Not that kind of dead, anyway."

"Jake, it matters to me."

His jaw bunched. After long moments, he stomped out. "I'll be back with my charcoals."

Thirty minutes later, when he hadn't returned, I lifted the phone to call. I held off. Who was I to demand he do this thing?

Sixty minutes into it, he opened my door, sketchbook and charcoals in hand. While I described, Jake sketched. We did several revisions, but in the end, he'd captured Della and Chesa.

"They're beautiful," he said. "Especially the one named Della."

Before I could thank him, he tore the sketch off the pad in one fierce motion and left without a word.

Hours later, I propped the sketch of Della and Chesa on the dresser in my bedroom. I'd scanned the sketch and made a Web page for them. I'd linked it to the MGAP pages, since we got so many hits. You never knew—somebody might recognize one of them or have seen them somewhere. Couldn't hurt.

I climbed into bed feeling an itch part of me wished Jake would scratch.

An incessant *brinnnnggg* made me grope for the phone. The clock said seven. I'd overslept. Pale light filtered through the window. I snuggled the phone beneath my chin and my shoulder. "Yeah?"

"I saw her. I saw *them*."

Blessing? I wasn't sure. "Who did you see?"

He stuttered a sob. "I still hear it, Moira's flute. Oh, Christ, help me, please. Help me." It was a wail.

"I can. I can help you, Roland." Phone cradled to my neck, I threw back the covers and shrugged on some clothes. "I can come meet you. We can talk."

"I've been watching. But I can't get close. Can't."

"Roland. I want to help. Just tell me wh—"

"Here!" he shrieked. "Here!"

The phone went dead.

I held my head in my hands, shook it, tried to get rid of the cottony feel. Blessing's call was deeply disturbing.

I phoned Boston PD, then Kranak, knowing if I didn't tell him, the Boston cops would.

"You sure it was him?" Kranak said.

"Not at first. But, yes. I am. He sounded frantic. Disorganized. Not good."

"Not good is right. Christ, Tal. Did he admit to killing your friend?"

"No. He asked for my help."

"Right. You could help him, by being dead."

"I don't think so, but I'm pretty sure I saw him in the OCME parking lot. It felt like he was watching me."

"Cute. Did you share that with anyone?"

"You. Just now."

"I'm putting a bug on your line."

"Fat chance."

"Yeah, fat chance."

"Sorry. I said the same thing to Boston PD. A lot of people call me, Rob. People who trust me, who tell me intimate things. I won't allow those conversations to be overheard."

"Jesus. You're a fucking bleeding heart."

"Thank you."

I got out my notebook and added a couple lines to my profile of Blessing. What had he really wanted? He seemed terrified. Of Pisarro, maybe.

He'd said, "I saw her. I saw them." Chesa? Chesa and McArdle? Who else?

He'd wanted to meet. To tell me what? He could see me as an authority figure and was seeking absolution for killing Chesa. Or maybe he wanted to kill me, too. Needed it. Because I'd challenged him. He sounded desperate, like he had to talk to me. Back to the absolution thing, or it was something I couldn't see yet.

I grabbed a mug of coffee and drove over to the VA clinic.

The outpatient clinic was dark and quiet and filled with a silent anguish. I approached a tweed-jacketed man whose rimless glasses skied the tip of his nose.

I introduced myself, and pale eyes peered over those glasses. He lifted a clipboard, studied it, while I stood there getting more and more annoyed.

"Dr. Jaeger," I said, using his name tag as a guide.

"In a minute," he answered, in a tone that would normally have had me walking out of there in annoyance.

He finally laid the clipboard down. "You called. You're looking for information on Roland. You won't get anything from us."

"I'm trying to understand what—"

"I know exactly what you're doing. And it won't work. So why not just trot on about your business and leave us to ours."

I folded my hands in front of me. "I counsel the families of homicide victims, Dr. Jaeger. I counseled Roland Blessing."

"I don't give a—"

"I'm desperately trying to understand why this man brutally murdered a friend of mine. And I need to know if he'll kill again."

He barked a laugh, then his smile faded. "You don't understand. When you do, come see me. We'll talk."

Jaeger was summoned by a woman holding a phone. He gave me a quick salute and walked off.

I spoke with a nurse, a patient, and a clerk. Each smirked, shook his head, and gave me nothing.

The folks at the VA clinic didn't believe Blessing had killed Chesa. It was obvious in their demeanor. Jaeger especially did not see him as a killer. But they didn't like him, either. Not one bit.

All that did was serve up more questions

Gert and I shared a bagel and coffee around eleven. Circles rimmed both of our eyes—from Blessing, from the budget, from work.

"When Blessing called me," I said "he referred to 'her.' Who's he got in his sights? You? Mary? Donna? Moira's landlady?"

"You?" She blew an immense bubble and popped it with a long nail. "Let 'em tap your line, Tal."

"Can't do it. Chesa's dead days. They haven't caught him. Christ, I can still see her, lying there all—"

"Sometimes they never catch them."

"I know."

I submerged myself in work and surfaced around two to check on Dave Heywood's progress in finding McArdle. He hadn't made any, but promised he'd have something for me tomorrow or the next day. After we hung up, I surfed the MGAP database for any hint of McArdle. Bingo. He had another funeral home out in bucolic Harvard, Massachusetts, not the university, but the town an hour or so west of Boston at the opposite end of the spectrum from Roxbury.

I dialed the number. Maybe that's where McArdle was hiding out with Della's body until Blessing got caught.

A recording answered. I'd called some number at the Harvard elementary school. Someone could have transposed the numbers on the report. I called information, but they had no listing for a McArdle Funeral Home in Harvard or any surrounding town.

Huh.

What was McArdle pulling? Where was the guy? All I wanted was Della's remains. It shouldn't be that much work to get a corpse.

I checked my watch. Ouch. I barely made it out of the building in time for my appointment with Mrs. Cheadle.

I took Storrow Drive, a mistake, since the picturesque route that ran along the Charles River was immobilized.

The winter wind frothed whitecaps and a hardy kayaker, read: crazy person, paddled his craft down the river that in spring would be filled with colored sailboats and sculls rowing in rhythm. Even today, joggers bundled in sweats ran the path alongside the river, sidestepping patches of ice. College kids toting backpacks ducked their chins from the wind as they walked, and a few hardy mothers pushed babies in strollers. Would I ever push my child along the Charles? Would I ever have a child?

The traffic inched along, and I finally was able to take the exit ramp and cross the Charles. By the time I popped out onto the opposite side of Cambridge, I figured Mrs. Cheadle might have passed on to a better life, it had taken so long.

I punched the buzzer on Mrs. Cheadle's outer front door, hopping from foot to foot from the cold. No returning buzz, so I tried the outer door. The knob turned, and I headed for Mrs. Cheadle's blue-painted door.

I knocked twice, and when she didn't answer, I searched my purse for my pad so I could leave her a note.

Something crashed inside the apartment.

"Mrs. Cheadle?" I hollered.

Silence.

"Mrs. Cheadle?" Her door opened beneath my fingers. Bad sign. A clank. The chain and a wallplate had been ripped from their casing. Hell.

I peered into blackness—the lights were off and the shades lowered. Pepper spray at the ready, I stepped into the room.

Someone elbowed me in the back. Hard. "Shit!"

My arms flailed, but I still fell, my cheek connecting with a sharp-edged surface. "Ugh!" I thudded to the floor.

I rolled and glimpsed a dark sweatshirt, baggy pants, and gloved hands before he slammed the door shut, plunging the room back into darkness. I lurched to my feet, cheek throbbing, and yanked open the door.

I raced down the hall, through the alcove, and onto the front steps.

Empty. The street was empty.

"Mrs. Cheadle?" I called, stepping back into the apartment.

Again, silence, except for the mewling of a cat.

God, I hoped she was okay. I flicked on the wall switch. Nothing happened. I sprayed the room with my mini-Maglite. Kitchen table on its side. Two over-turned chairs.

What if there was a second guy?

I tightened my grip on the pepper spray, then followed my light into the living room. An overturned table, lamps broken, two chairs on their sides. Smashed knickknacks from Mrs. Cheadle's vaudeville career. The son of a bitch had kicked in her TV, too.

My stomach clenched. Someone else was in the apartment. Maybe it was just the cats. Or Mrs. Cheadle. I hoped Mrs. Cheadle.

A movement. I jumped. Her gray cat reclined on the sofa, licking his belly.

"Mrs. Cheadle?" I repeated, hating the shaky thread to my voice.

I shined my light into the bedroom. It looked less disturbed. It also looked empty. I peered under the bed. Four reflected cat eyes stared back at me.

Goddamn, I hated this.

A noise, behind me. I turned, still on my knees. The glint of a butcher knife coming at me.

Crap! I tackled the knife-wielder's legs and pushed them upward with all of my strength.

He was so light he flipped onto the bed, landing flat across it with an "oomph," and I caught the shine of the knife as it flew from his hand.

Juiced on adrenaline, my fingers shook as I pushed the pepper spray toward his face with one hand and shined the light in his eyes with the other.

Except the "he" was a tiny "she"—white hair askew beneath a beret, a wrinkled face, a housecoat bunched around her hips.

"Mrs. Cheadle, it's Tally." I said. "Oh, shoot. I'm sorry."

She folded her hands and squeezed her eyes closed. "Praise Gypsy Rose, who was watching out for me." She held out a hand. "Come on, young lady, help this old woman up. I've been scared out of my wits."

Chapter Nine

I helped Mrs. Cheadle stand—she barely came to my shoulders—and we tottered into the living room. I righted a chair and eased her into it.

She repinned her hair, straightened her beret, sighed. She told me where the circuit breakers were, and I flipped them on. When I reappeared in the living room, Mrs. Cheadle was surrounded by half a dozen cats draped over the back of the chair, on its arms, and in her lap.

"You give that thing here," she said, motioning me over.

I handed her the knife and she tucked it beside her. "Makes me feel secure, even if I know it's a lie."

"It scared the heck out of me."

She chuckled, and her skin folded into a million wrinkles. "Did I?"

I pulled up another chair, so we were knee to knee, and took her hand in mine. It was cold and fluttered like a trapped bird. "Are you *really* okay?"

"Seems to me I'm in better shape than you, Tally. That's quite a mess you've got on your cheek."

It felt tender and swollen beneath my fingers and would earn me another of Jake's biting comments. "I'll call the police." I reached for my cell phone.

"No point. They're not going to do anything except make me fill out a mess of forms."

She was right, of course. Not much time would be spent on a B&E. "Can one of your friends stay with you?"

She shook her head. "My pals—this would scare them something terrible. I'm all right."

"What exactly happened?"

"I was about to do my laundry, when I heard a knocking at the door. I shuffled into the kitchen as fast as these old legs would take me. 'Mrs. Cheadle?' he said through the door, and I didn't care for his voice. Not one bit."

"You didn't recognize it?"

"I did not. And it sounded too sweet. Like he wanted to wheedle me out of something. Or scare me. My kitties were growling, too. I tried 911. The line was dead. So I grabbed that big butcher knife, and headed for the laundry room."

A calico cat leapt onto her lap and she began to stroke it. Her eyes drifted to the smashed knickknacks, the framed posters crumpled on the floor, and television with its gaping hole. She tucked her chin, so I couldn't see her face.

I could replace her TV. But who could fix the broken memories? "Can I get you anything?"

She raised her head, and her eyes shimmered with fury. "Just that man's head on a platter. To go on with my tale. He started hitting the door hard, and I'm thinking, Now what's there to steal from poor old me? as I went around closing the drapes. By that time, I'd made it back into the laundry closet. I slipped inside and switched off the circuit breakers. About then he broke down the door."

"You sound very prepared."

"Oh, I am. Happened before, twice. When I was dancing, and when I was a child, there was . . . Oh, yes. I've learned that darkness can be a friend. He was angry, that man, breaking things up. I know all about angry men. I was shaking scared. Then there came a crash and a yelp."

"The yelp was me."

"It appears you've saved this old hide." She chuckled, then her eyes, gray from age, filled with tears. "What's it all about, I'm wondering? There's little here but me and my kitties."

I was thinking Roland Blessing. "Did you ever see a strange man at the funeral home with Chesa, perhaps?"

"Didn't see Chesa there. Not once."

"Could you have heard something unusual at McArdle's?"

"No. Ah, you mean about Della. Well, I hesitate telling you this, Tally, but Della's remains are missing."

So much for keeping secrets from Mrs. Cheadle. "Yes. A young man helped Mr. McArdle place her in his hearse the night Chesa died. And, well, we can't find him. Perhaps your break-in has to do with Della and Roland Blessing."

"That man who killed Chesa? He didn't know Della."

"I think maybe he did." I told her what Mary had seen.

"I regret the day I introduced her to Mr. McArdle. If I hadn't, Chesa would—"

"*You* introduced them?"

"Della came to pick me up here for a lunch. That same day, Mr. McArdle kindly gave me a lift home from work."

"Would Mr. McArdle's assistant know something?"

"Not likely, since he didn't have any assistant. None that I ever saw."

Nothing was connecting. "Think. Was there anything unusual at the funeral home that was odd or . . . I don't know . . . strange?"

"Strange? Only thing strange was finding Della that time."

"You found Della?"

"Well . . . yes. Please, let me clean up my things. Then we can talk better."

"I'll clean," I said. "You supervise."

She cried as I swept up the broken tokens of her vaudeville career. I could still feel the intruder's anger. It reminded me of Blessing's fury, and of the destruction I'd seen at McArdle's. This was no random break-in.

We finally sat down over a pot of tea.

"Della was the first and, praise be, the last corpse I saw there," Mrs. Cheadle began. "Scared me half to death. Those rooms off the basement were locked up tight. Mr. McArdle said that he'd clean them himself. But last week, when I was mopping the basement floor, I tripped over my bucket. Dirty water went everywhere, and it drove me crazy when it seeped beneath the embalming room door."

I poured each of us more tea.

"I needed to wipe up that mess," she continued. "So I went upstairs, telling myself that I should leave it be. It would dry. But I'm a neat and tidy person. I went into his office for the key, and since he was out, I felt no reason not to borrow it for a few minutes." She smiled a conspirator's smile.

"Wasn't *anyone* else around?" I asked.

"Not a soul, which was typical. Mr. McArdle didn't do what I'd call a brisk business. And so I unlocked the door, but I didn't look on the table. On purpose. I thought I'd be in and out lickety split. But as I'd finished mopping, I noticed a dress draped over a chair. It had bright purple and green embroidered flowers. Just like one Della wore. She'd done the embroidery herself. I thought, Oh, no, and I stole a peek. And of course it was our beautiful Della. Lying naked on that old enamel table." She pulled a scarlet kerchief from the pocket of her housecoat and dabbed her eyes.

"What a terrible shock."

"Yes. I had this urge to cover her. Which was a foolish thought."

"It's very natural, in fact."

She shook her head. "I wasn't myself. Horrible, but I'm embarrassed."

"Don't be. Someone you loved was dead. Unexpectedly so. And there she was, not even covered by the dignity of clothes. Especially given Della's eyes." I'd seen much worse, but what a horror for that poor old woman.

She stirred her spoon around and around in her tea. "Her beautiful eyes. But that's not what I meant. You see, I got all caught up in those awful stitches. Big, ugly things."

"Della's body had stitches?"

"Oh, my, yes. A whole lot of them. You know, the ones funeral people do after they've cut the body open to prepare it."

"Mrs. Cheadle, morticians don't cut open bodies. Their incisions are maybe two, three inches long."

She raised a hand to her cheek. "Really? Well, someone had cut poor Della wide open." She ran her hands from her shoulders to her breasts to her solar plexus and navel and abdomen. She abruptly stopped. "The stitches went all the way to her privates."

She'd drawn a *Y*—the classic autopsy incision.

Since she never came through the Grief Shop, who had autopsied Della Charles? And why?

I lingered at the door, saying good-bye to Mrs. Chea-dle. We made another date for tea, and she stroked my cheek, as if I were one of her cats. I hated leaving her.

"Oh, Tally!" Mrs. Cheadle said. "I forgot something. Terrible, this age thing. The goon in my apartment. He said, and please excuse the expression, 'Fuck Pisarro.' I don't know who that is, but it might mean something."

"Yes, it sure might."

At the truck, I called a kid I knew, Nicky Pelletier. Nicky agreed to watch Mrs. Cheadle for a day or so,

since she'd refused to go anywhere safe. Then I phoned
Kranak and filled him in.

I started the truck and cranked up the heat. I did a
U-turn and made for the heart of Cambridge and the
lair of Harry Pisarro.

Chapter Ten

Although it was barely two, the diluted afternoon light
gave the bustling streets of Cambridge a soft, impres-
sionistic air. I called information, then punched out
the number for Byte Me, the cyber café owned by
Harry Pisarro. One of his flunkies said Pisarro would
call me back. He did, instantly, and I asked if now was
a good time.

"Any time's a good time for you, Madame Tally."

"I'm on my way."

Pisarro greeted me with a toothy smile and a kiss on
each cheek. He handed me a glass of merlot, and insisted on giving me the tour. The floating ebony bar
snaked around stations where young adults sat pounding computer keys or jerking joysticks. More stations
hugged the walls, as did booths shaped like horseshoes.
The place was dark, the voices muffled, except for an
occasional gamer's shout.

Neon flickered, and synthetic music, low and
strange and hot, pulsed just beneath the purr of conversation. The mingling of incense and cigarettes and
dope tainted the air.

It was like I'd entered some subterranean world and my skin crawled, mostly because I was drawn by its allure.

We threaded through rooms that hummed with sitar music and glowed with black lights, past a computerized alcove dubbed "eBay," and took a seat at the back of a small room where neon stars constantly burst on the walls and ceiling.

Pisarro waggled a finger and an antipasto platter appeared.

We ate as we exchanged pleasantries. Timing was everything in this game.

I finally sketched Mrs. Cheadle's break-in. "Blessing's *your* man. I believe you're pushing him too hard. I think he's so frightened, so angry, he's lashing out at anyone and everyone. You've got to back off."

He twirled his wineglass. "Is that so? Why would Roland Blessing, one of my computer techs, assault some old black woman in Somerville?"

"You already know about the homicide. It's a long story."

"I have all the time in the world, Madame Tally," he said in a soft voice that invited confidences.

I explained about our bereavement group and Chesa's confrontation. About Della and the McArdle Funeral Home and Chesa's death. As I wound up with Mrs. Cheadle's break-in, his lips pulled into a sad smile. "Let me understand. You believe Blessing terrorized some poor old woman because I'm putting the pressure on him?"

"Perhaps. Yes. He's terrified."

Pisarro growled. "He should be fucking terrified."

Oh, hell. "I think he's focused on Mrs. Cheadle because Blessing thinks she knows something that puts him in jeopardy. If that's the case, he'll try again."

He closed his eyes, inhaled. "Madame Tally, I owe you a debt for my darling Angela. In fact, it was because of Angela's terrible death that I hired Roland Blessing. I pitied him because of his Moira. I related to him on that level.

"I'm also fond of you. But no one tells me what to do."

The mobster who killed people and buried them beneath train tracks was revealed. "I understand that."

His indigo eyes laughed. "You're a piece of work, Madame Tally."

"I've got to go."

He held up a hand and a roly-poly man with a cadaverous face materialized.

"This is Johnny Bones," Pisarro said.

"Nice to meet you, Mr. Bones," I said, trying to sound truthful.

"Bones will watch your Mrs. Cheadle."

"*Pardon*? I don't think so. No siree."

"Oh, yes siree, Madame Tally. Someone used my name while committing a crime against your friend. Someone who might come back and try to hurt her further. Someone who might be in my employ, like Roland Blessing. And if he got to her, *I* might be blamed. We can't have that, now can we, Madame Tally?"

I didn't give a rat's ass if he was blamed. "I think that's a poor idea."

"But I think it's a fine one." He whispered in Bones's ear, then stood. "It's all settled. Bones will watch your Mrs. Cheadle. He'll also escort you to your truck."

There were pluses for Mrs. Cheadle. But I hated it. "Thanks," was all I said.

"For you, Madame Tally, anything."

"So you'll let up on Blessing?"

"I'm afraid *that* is not possible."

He kissed my hand—the palm. Then his eyes traveled upward, pointedly surfing over my breasts, and locking on mine. There was heat, but it was more like a clone of sexual ardor than the real thing.

He sickened me.

"No one is what they seem, Tally Whyte. Remember that. No one."

I drove to Charlestown Harbor's Constitution Marina and the dock where Kranak kept his boat. The dock lights glowed dully as I neared Kranak's home, a forty-two-foot repro Friendship sloop. He'd painted her maroon, with black trim, and named her *Far Away*. Stars winked from their blanket of black that paled to a muted amber just above the incredible view of Boston Harbor and downtown's lights—picture-postcard pretty. The Pru and the Hancock glowed majestically, surrounded by lesser buildings that glittered like party favors. A man lugging a plastic sack of groceries trotted by. A bell clanged, followed by the thrum of a revving motor. I filled my lungs with the cold night air, loving the briny smell of the sea. A sharp pain reminded me of sailing and my childhood in Maine and . . .

Kranak's boat was dark and silent. The breeze toyed with a frizzed tendril of my hair and I tucked it behind my ear. I stood there for a long while, oddly comforted as I watched Kranak's boat bob in the gentle swells. I considered climbing aboard and waiting for his return.

The bleat of a ship horn startled me out of my reverie.

I leaned against a piling and wrote Kranak a note.

Having problems seeing Blessing as Chesa's killer. My gut and all. Let's talk. T

I retraced my steps up the dock, tightening Chesa's scarf around my neck for warmth.

I retrieved Penny from the Grief Shop, and we drove home. When I unlocked my front door, the hair on my arms prickled. So did the fur on the back of Penny's coat. I felt an "otherness" that didn't belong. Penny trotted through the rooms emitting a low, throaty growl. I licked my lips, telling myself I was being stupid. But in the kitchen, I found a dirty plate I'd left beside my bed sitting in the dish drainer, washed.

I picked up the pace, trying to ignore the creepy tune playing down my spine. A stiff paintbrush I'd left on the easel now sat in the brush box, cleaned. In my bedroom, the morning's rejected tights that I *knew* I'd left on the bed were missing. I found them in the *wrong* dresser drawer, folded.

I ran upstairs and pounded on Jake's door.

"Yeah?" he said, when he opened it.

"Were you in my apartment today?"

"No."

"Someone was."

"I've been here all day. If anybody'd tossed the place, I would've heard."

"It wasn't tossed. It—"

"What?"

"I don't know. I'm upset, dammit!" I gripped the door. "You and Veda are the only people who have spare keys. *Someone* was down there today."

"You're paranoid."

"And you're rude." The son of a bitch laughed.

"You accuse me of going downstairs and smelling your panties and *I'm* rude?"

"I never said that. But it's just the kind of thing you'd do. Neaten the place up, I mean. Well if it wasn't you, then who?"

He brushed past me down the stairs and thundered into my apartment.

I traipsed after Jake as he cruised my place. When he finished, he leaned against the fireplace mantle. "There's only one question. Is this all a ruse to get me to talk to you again?"

"Spoken like a true egoist," I said.

"Hold up the mirror, Tal."

I waved a hand. "You're not making things any better."

"No?"

I stood. We were in for one of our sessions. "Red or white?" I asked.

"Perhaps a woodsy—"

"Be thrilled it's not Ripple." I reappeared with a Cline mourvedre and two glasses. "I didn't bring the cork, so you can't sniff it, Mr. Sommelier."

"You're no fun." A smile from Jake, the first I'd seen since last evening. Spectacular, per usual.

"Bottom line—someone was in here. A little ghostie didn't move and clean all of those things."

"You're always buzzing around in the morning," he said. "Maybe you were thinking deep thoughts and forgot you did all of that straightening?"

My first sip of wine took my anxiety down a peg. "It wasn't just straightening, Jake. Things I left dirty—don't say it—were cleaned. It's creepy."

He shook his head.

I didn't dare tell Jake how the apartment's atmosphere had been thick with "presence" when I'd arrived home. I looked up. Jake was wearing a small smile, as if he thought I was a little coocoo, a little overworked. Just a little tired.

If it was Blessing, he'd really gone 'round the bend. Of course it wasn't Blessing. Not his style. Pisarro, maybe. Checking up? Or Veda. Sure. She was always coming over. Forgetting stuff. Then retrieving it.

"Thinking deep thoughts again?" he said.

"Always." I gulped some wine and laughed. Maybe I'd imagined the whole shebang.

"Don't ask me to sketch dead people again." He frowned. "Please."

"I'm sorry. I shouldn't have. I just needed to see them, you know?"

"I know." He knocked back more wine. "You don't like me much, do you?"

"Where did that come from?" I said. "I like you." My foot was wagging and I stopped it.

"I've got tickets for the new show over at the MFA."

"Saw it."

"It opens next Monday."

"Oh. Take one of your girls." I wasn't about to compete with twentysomething models.

He stomped across the room. "What is it, Tally? What bugs you about me?"

How do you tell a guy you're not pretty enough to date him? "Nothing, Jake."

"Or don't I have enough edge, like your buddy Kranak? Or some other boy in blue. Huh?"

"Kranak wears a suit."

His eyes narrowed, as if to laser my secret thoughts. "Your wine was halfway decent for a change." Then he left.

I was exhausted, but couldn't sleep. I got out the glue, my magnifying glass, some paper towels, and Mrs. Cheadle's broken ceramic hula dancers I'd stuffed in my purse. I laid the pieces on a tray on my painting table and went to work.

When I moved the tray to let them dry, I saw it. It must have somehow gotten stuck to the bottom of the tray and when I lifted it, it clanked onto the painting table.

A golden Sacagawea dollar.

Chapter Eleven

First thing Wednesday, I left the baggie with the golden dollar on Kranak's desk, with a note asking him to check the dollar for prints.

Strike one, Kranak wasn't around. Strike two, neither was Dave Heywood. I was itching to find out more about McArdle. Strike three was calling the Harvard, Massachusetts police about McArdle's funeral home out there. I was told that yes, there had been a McArdle Funeral Home. And that it had burned two years earlier. No arson, no, no, the officer assured me, and, no, he had no idea where McArdle was now. He'd left town and had given the land to a teen center, which the cop would happily show me if I cared to stop by.

Cross-eyed with frustration, I hopped onto the Web and ordered Mrs. Cheadle a new television. At least I could make something happen.

I phoned Billy Christenson over at the State Crime Lab in Sudbury. Billy had taken the cop sensitivity class I taught at Northeastern.

"I need help with some print sets taken by Boston PD."

"I'll try," Billy said.

I gave him the particulars of Chesa's death at McArdle's. He said he'd call me back ASAP. An hour later, he did.

"They got seven clean sets, after ruling out you, a lady named Mrs. Cheadle, and the dead woman, Chesa Jones. Massachusetts APHIS came up with only one on the seven, a Roland Blessing. No other hits. Ditto for the FBI database. They mailed print copies to New York, Jersey, and the other New England states."

Most people think there's this giant national database of all fingerprints. The FBI has a pretty good one, and there are other national ones, too. But no single database contains all of the state prints. Each state has its own APHIS system. And in Massachusetts, out-of-state print confirmations are still done through the U.S. mail, since digital files can be tampered with.

"I'm looking for anything on this McArdle guy, Billy. Call me if you get a hit?"

"Will do."

I poked my head into our central office. Empty. I was about to page Gert, when my phone rang.

"Tally Whyte," I said.

"In my office. Now."

Veda. And she sounded pissed.

I trotted upstairs, Penny hugging my thigh. As I neared Veda's office, the door opened. She walked out, followed by Fogarty.

I forced a smile. "Hi Tom, Veda."

"Looking for handouts, Tally?" Fogarty tightly clutched a manila folder.

My smile widened. "Aren't I always?"

Veda crossed her arms.

"I'd better be off to my meeting with the Warner's PR woman." Fogarty grinned. "*Street Fighter*'s going great. Oh, FYI. Your bud Kranak got a reprimand from his lieutenant. Something about a little funeral parlor thing." Fogarty bustled out, his lab coat flapping behind him.

The word *dickhead* came to mind.

Veda sat behind her massive desk, hands folded. "*Must* you get into it with Tom? Every . . . single . . . time. I can't afford to lose him, Tally."

"Why the summons?"

She poured us each a mug of coffee from the carafe on the file cabinet. We both sipped, our eyes meeting as they'd done a thousand times. I saw kindness there, and worry. Veda had a patent on that emotion.

Finally, she ran a hand across her grizzled hair. "Gertrude inadvertently mentioned the sketch you had Jake do of Chesa and her sister. I saw it on your desk."

I took a sip of coffee. "You know what Chesa meant to me. It's a reminder."

Veda sighed, then stared out at the gunmetal sky. "This hunt for Roland Blessing. It's hurting your work. You're preoccupied."

"He was a client. Chesa, a friend. And you're overstating."

"People are talking. People are worried."

"If that's true, I'm sorry. But I haven't shortchanged MGAP."

"Perhaps this is not about Chesa Jones at all."

Veda knew me better than anyone on this earth. "Perhaps."

Veda refilled our mugs. "Say it, please."

"So maybe it is about Dad. And Chesa, too. Maybe I blame myself that I wasn't there for her."

"As you did for your father. But that I understand."

"The odd thing, Vede, is that the stuff I'm learning about Blessing isn't adding up. I usually have a pretty good read on my clients. Not this guy."

"Your clients are victims. This man is a killer."

"And a victim, too."

The pencil in Veda's hand snapped. "Listen to you. A victim. You frustrate me endlessly. That's the point here. It's dangerous for you to get so involved, to dredge up your father's death, to leave yourself open to Fogarty's machinations."

I rested my hands on her desk. "You know I won't back down."

Veda tossed her broken pencil into the trash. "You'd think with the death of Arlo Noyce, you would."

"Pa . . . Pardon?" I tried to stop my hands from shaking, failed.

"I thought you knew. I'm sorry, Tally." She shook her head. "He was the John Doe we talked about at this morning's meeting."

"The decapitation?"

"Yes. He was ID'd a short time ago." She sighed. "Someone had a notion about a harmonica they found with him."

Oh, Arlo, what happened to you?

I hobbled to the bathroom, stomach cramped so bad I was bent in half. Although Veda tried to help me, I shooed her off, just like when I was a kid.

Downstairs, Gert was on the phone and Mary was perched on a stool, updating the flow chart, while Donna read a list from her clipboard.

Everyone looked lousy, their faces tear stained and puffy.

"Veda just told me about Arlo," I said. The flow chart named Gert as on deck for Arlo's sister. "Just the sister?"

"A brother's flying in from Michigan," Gert said. "The kid . . ." Her lips wobbled.

"I'll do the sister, Gert," I said.

"Why would Mr. Blessing cut off his head?" Mary said.

Donna started to cry.

A soft knock, then Strabo peeked in. He looked

around at the crying women, now a chorus, and crooked a finger at me.

Outside in the hall, he laid a hand on my shoulder. "They found the guy's head."

"I guess that's good." I hugged myself. "Yes. That's good."

"The head—the killer had shoved a harmonica down the dead guy's throat."

It was late by the time I waved good-bye to Arlo's grieving sister and brother-in-law. Everyone had gone for the day but Gert, who was blowing giant Bazooka bubbles, sniffling, and furiously pounding computer keys.

"Remind me to kill Fogarty," she said.

"Will do."

"Some guy from the state lab called. Quote: 'I've got something for her.'"

I got Billy's voice mail at the crime lab. Damn. I left a message saying I'd wait for his call.

Marking time, I checked on Mrs. Cheadle, who was fine according to her watcher, Bones. *Call, Billy. Call.* Waiting stunk. Maybe I'd take harmonica lessons. I laughed. I'd be lousy at it.

Oh, Arlo.

I was angry. Furious. I started ripping up budget sheets. Screw Fogarty. Screw the budget. Screw—

I tossed the shredded budgets, so they flew across the room like so much confetti.

"Nice," Gert said from the doorway.

"Come on in, Gertie," I said. "Feel like a shot of bourbon?"

"We've got Trip's tonight, remember?"

"I'm not going."

"You gotta. To let off some steam over Arlo. C'mon, Tal."

I got two paper cups from the bathroom, then poured us each a finger of Rebel Yell. It went down smooth. "How are Mary and Donna doing?"

"Not bad. I've talked to both of them."

I tipped the cup at her in a salute. "Thanks." I told her about Arlo's big plan to catch Blessing.

"You tell the police."

"Days ago. Obviously they didn't dissuade him."

"I'm gonna head over. You coming with me?"

"In a while."

I worked late, until I was alone with the night shift, and the dead.

I tried Billy once more, around eight, then left for Trip's. I searched the parking lot for Blessing. It was empty of rats, at least the two-legged kind.

But I'd swear, from somewhere in the darkness, the mournful notes of a harmonica drifted on the breeze. The tune being played was "Amazing Grace."

Chapter Twelve

That night, our group sat around the scarred, circular table at Trip's, a bar on East Berkeley named for that venerable stallion, Secretariat. Get it? Triple Crown?

Owner Toots Schwartz's idea of decor was Budweiser signs, an awful white-faced jockey statue, and framed prints of local Suffolk Downs winners.

Off-duty cops and attorneys from the DA's office

mixed with Grief Shop staff and a smattering of Bruins players. For some reason, they found Trip's irresistible.

So did we: a bunch of gal pals who shared drinks, problems, and laughs most Wednesday nights. Tonight, Shaye, Gert, Belle, Dixie, Reen, and I sat elbow to elbow at the round table.

Shaye ran a woman's shelter and Reen was an FBI agent in the Boston office. Belle was also an agent, of the literary kind, who specialized in mysteries and thrillers. Along with Gert, Dixie, and myself, we were quite a crew.

I was lucky. I had some great friends.

Crumpled napkins and abandoned swizzle sticks lay scattered beside drinks ranging from piña coladas to bourbon.

We talked about Blessing and Chesa and Arlo most of the night. Normally, Gert and I didn't bring our work to the table. But this was different. This was personal.

"Where's Penny?" Dixie said.

"I dropped her at home," I said.

"So why is Kranak avoiding you?" Belle asked.

"Maybe it's my imagination," I said.

"Imagination?" Shaye said, using that sarcastic tone I hated. "You?"

"Oh, come on, Shaye," Dixie said.

My cell phone bleeped. "Hello?"

"Hey, it's Billy."

"Hold on a sec." I walked to a corner of the bar and covered my ear. "You have McArdle?"

"Nope. A woman," he said. "A Della Jones."

I rested my fanny on a table. "That can't be, Billy."

"My specialty."

"No, seriously. Della was dead when she arrived at the funeral home. Days dead. In the coffin dead."

"Sounds like creature-feature material, Tal. Lemme get my notes." A pause, then, "Okay, the prints say Della Jones, aka Della Charles. We got a hit from New York state. Couple years ago, this Jones woman was arrested for taking a swipe at a cop, and they printed her. They found her prints all over that McArdle Funeral Home."

"What the hell does 'all over' mean?" I felt like I was suffocating.

"Um. Downstairs. The embalming room to be exact. Also the upstairs bathroom. Coat closet. And what's labeled here as McArdle's office. On a shelf."

I thanked Billy, then slowly walked back to the table. I wondered if Kranak knew.

"You look like shit." Shaye said.

"They found Della Charles's fingerprints in a bunch of places at McArdle's."

"Wasn't she the missing corpse?" Belle said.

"Yup. According to the funeral director, she died at the hospital. But that's bullshit. She was *alive* at some point at that funeral home."

"Do not adjust the dial of your television set," Gert said in sonorous tones.

Shaye bashed Gert's arm. "Quit it." Her laugh was nervous. "So maybe it was a crack house. Maybe she OD'd. She could've been trading screws for lines of coke, which is why he was going to give her that freebie funeral. What do you think, Reen?"

"I think I'm not involved." The diminutive FBI agent caught a Bruin's eye and they began a game of sliding miniballs up the mini-alley. The hockey player obviously didn't know Reen Maekawa. Poor, clueless Bruin.

"Can we please table this weirdness, huh?" Gert took a swig of Miller. "You think I should go out with that newspaper guy, or what?"

"How can we not talk about Della?" I asked.

"Because it's creeping us all out," Dixie said. "The guy keeps harping on your body, Gertie. Not a good thing."

"Speaking of . . . ," Belle said. "How's Herb, Shaye?"

"It's the weight thing." Shaye said. "I'm sick of it. Either he likes what he sees or he moves on."

"Why do guys do that?" Belle glanced at her dainty breasts.

Gert rolled her eyes.

"It's not just guys," I said. "We buy into the beauty thing, too."

"Like it matters to you," Shaye said. "You're pretty and thin."

"Pretty's relative." I pictured Jake's parade of models. "And you mean skinny. Yeah, I know. When it comes to me and men, I admit I'm affected by their looks. We pretty much all are."

"Count me out," Belle said. "I just like money."

"Looks don't affect me, either." Shaye adjusted the muumuu that covered her ample form. She looked from Belle to Dixie to Gert to me. "All right. Half the time I loathe myself and the other half I loathe the people who are judging me because I'm fat. I'm working on it. Okay?"

"Some men like Rubenesque women," Belle said.

"My ass," Shaye said. "They want perfection. Like you."

"Perfection?" Belle said. "Are you kidding? Guys think I'm cute, but they like bigger boobs than I sure as hell have."

"Ah, Belle girl!" Dixie said. "I've got big ones, and all they do is get in the way."

Gert belched, we all laughed, and things were okay again.

Reen strode over, lips atwitch.

"You creamed him, didn't you?" I said.

"Fifty bucks. Dumb hockey goon." She pulled out a chair and straddled it, just as most of our group said good-bye.

"Stay," Reen said. "It's early."

"Gotta go" was mumbled and money was laid on the table.

I should have gone, too. But I needed Reen's ear, and maybe her help.

She retrieved another Old Grandad for me and a piña colada for herself.

"Della's fingerprints at the funeral home point to homicide," I said.

"Maybe." Reen's eyes slithered across the crowded room.

I told her about the case. While I talked, Reen stroked the mole beneath her left eye that was actually a tiny tattooed Japanese character. "Maybe I'll find McArdle in some esoteric database."

She tilted her chair back on two legs. "Perhaps."

"I'm just using you as a sounding board."

"Are you?" She allowed her lips to twitch into a semismile.

"Of course," I said, hoping to stoke her competitive juices. "Kranak would get his nose out of joint if you, say, maybe checked around about McArdle and Blessing in some of the more exotic FBI databases."

She nodded sagely. "I wouldn't want to offend Sergeant Kranak."

Not exactly what I'd hoped for. "You know how Kranak can be."

"Yes," she said, eyes hooked on a black-garbed, gaunt-faced man at the bar arguing with a lump of a guy in a down vest.

"You think Kranak could access some of those databases?"

She slammed her chair back on all four legs. "No."

"No, he couldn't?"

"No, I will not enter into this, Tally."

"Fine. I understand. You're busy. But you love a mystery, right? Mary, one of our associate counselors, saw Della Charles and Roland Blessing together."

"Finis," she said.

I'd done well, considering.

I crossed Appleton, keys in hand, eager for the warmth of the town house, a greeting by Penny, and my cozy bed. The porch light was still out, which meant Mr. Fixit Jake had again forgotten to change the bulb. Typical.

A cover of clouds hid the stars and the air was thick with snow. A cat mewed, and someone's metal garbage can clanked to the ground. Raccoons.

I placed my foot on the first step. At least I'd intrigued Reen. Maybe if—

A scraping sound on my right. I spun around.

A faceless man in an overcoat materialized out of the inky blackness.

Blessing? I swallowed, or tried to. "Yes?"

"Excuse me if I've frightened you." He raised his gloved hand to the brim of his old-fashioned fedora. "I'm lost."

He was clean shaven. I could see that much. His citrusy aftershave tickled my nose. His voice was rich and sexy—like a radio performer's—and had a dash of twang.

He was nervous—I felt it in the darkness. Or maybe it was excitement. Whichever it was, I didn't like it.

Could he be a disguised Blessing? "What are you looking for?"

"132 Chandler," he said. "A friend's house."

He didn't sound like Blessing. Not at all. "Chandler's a couple of streets over." I pointed with my free hand.

"I must've gotten turned around, ma'am." A flash of perfect teeth reflected in dim glow of the light down the street. I wished I could see his face.

I grabbed the railing, as if to climb the steps.

"Wait," he said.

"I've got to go. My husband will be getting anxious."

He chuckled, softly. "Of course he will. Have you ever been lost in a strange city?"

"Sure." I climbed a step, sideways, so I stood above him. My gloves felt squishy from my sweaty hands. If all was innocent, why didn't he just leave?

He moved up a step. We were again on a level, and he leaned close, so near his face almost grazed my cheek. His moist breath brushed my ear. I prepared to jerk my knee into his balls.

"That's it!" he said, straightening. "Sung. The perfume you're wearing. A favorite of mine."

"Who *are* you?" I hated the ragged thread in my voice.

He smiled again; then he reached into his pocket. "My name's—"

"Don't move, asshole!" Reen shouted as she ran across the street, gun drawn.

"Wha—?" The stranger spun around.

"Hands on your head. Don't budge." Reen patted him down left-handed. Her right hand pointed the rock-steady gun at the man's belly.

"Reen!" I said. "He just needed directions."

"Perhaps." She stepped backward and lowered the weapon. But she didn't holster it. "No weapons."

"Can I put my hands down?" His velvet voice shook with fear.

"No," Reen said.

"I didn't mean anything. Really. Let me go now? Please?"

"How about it, Reen?" When I turned back, the stranger was running down the street.

"Okay. I was scared shitless." I handed Reen a bourbon and sipped my own. We sat on the couch, feet on my burlwood table, decompressing. "But, geesh, you tore into him like a frigging SWAT team."

"You should have told him to get lost." Her eyes cruised my living room, a place she'd visited dozens of times.

"I know. But once I realized he wasn't Blessing, he seemed harmless."

She pressed her hands to my face. "And if I hadn't arrived?" She reached into her pocket and produced a business card. Her eyes narrowed as she read: "Bernard Trepel. Aliant Systems—Sales. Lubbock, Texas."

"I can't believe you snatched his card." I pulled it from her fingers.

"The card was in one of his pockets. I felt it. I took it. Perhaps a client's and not his."

"Lubbock, Texas?" I said. "He had a twang. What possessed you to follow me?"

Reen's gaze ricocheted off my face. "I did not like the guy at the bar. He kept sneaking peeks at you."

"The skinny guy?"

She shrugged, her eyes surfing the room, always busy, always moving. "The baldie in the down vest."

"I only saw his back."

"He left right after you did. He reminded me of that Blessing person."

"And you followed him." Penny laid her head on my lap, and I stroked her soft fur. "Thanks. I've gotten paranoid about everything. I hate it."

She shrugged. "You'd hate dead more."

I grinned. "My guardian angel."

Reen's nostrils flared. "You could use one. No light. Your landlord's a shit."

"He's really not. Just forgetful. You can get so sour on people."

"I have to go." Her eyes pulled down their shades.

"I'm sorry. I . . . Thanks for watching my back. You really think the guy in the down vest was Blessing?"

She shrugged, and her hair rippled like a black waterfall.

"Can I keep Trepel's card?"

She smiled. "You are as transparent as watercolor on rice paper."

"You'll help with this McArdle thing, yes?"

She touched the tattoo beneath her eye. "Perhaps I should focus on Blessing."

"Don't. Everyone's pushing him, Reen. He's going to do something bad."

She raised an eyebrow. "You friend's and this Arlo's murder aren't bad?"

"I don't mean that. It's just . . . I can't explain it. But Blessing shouldn't be hammered."

"All right. McArdle's it is, then."

I hugged her, which she tolerated like a mama dog putting up with an exuberant pup. I walked her to the door. "Lock up," she said.

"I always do."

"Sometimes, Tally, you need a keeper."

Sometimes I wished I had one.

The drums kept me awake. I'd heard them for years, a remnant of my father's death. Tonight they echoed around my head, softly, sinuously.

I sat in my bed at 2 A.M., Penny sprawled beside me, an unread book on my lap. Some nights, the drums pounded tha-thump, tha-thump. Tonight, they played their tune low and slow.

Chesa. Where was she—her soul, her essence? And where was Della? Maybe dancing with her sister, although I doubted it. Just as I doubted my dad was waltzing the mother I never knew around some heavenly ballroom. But I wished it were so.

My mouth watered. More bourbon would silence the drums. Penny started licking my chin.

If a lion did that, would his sandpaper tongue flay the skin off my body?

I downed a shot of bourbon, then instead of fighting

the drums, I lay back, my hands cradling my head, and tried to decipher the message they were sending me.

The following morning I had another session with Arlo's sister, along with his brother who'd flown in from Michigan.

"The police said it could be Roland Blessing who killed our Arlo," Teresa said.

"Perhaps," I said.

"He was in your victims group, too, wasn't he?"

"Mr. Blessing? Yes."

Her mouth pulled into an angry snarl. "Why didn't you see it coming? You're a shrink. How come you didn't know he'd kill Arlo?"

"I never thought Arlo would find him, Teresa."

"You mean, he was looking for him?" she said. "And you let him?"

"It wasn't a matter of me letting—"

"These shrinks," spat Arlo's brother. "They're all full of shit."

Kranak continued to avoid me. After lunch, I drove out to Newton for my appointment with Dave Haywood.

I was pretty strung out by the time I flopped onto Dave's apartment annex couch.

He handed me a Diet Coke. "That McArdle guy." Head shaking, he straddled one of the kitchen chairs. "I'm just thinking how a guy sets up a phony funeral home."

"Phony?"

"Oh, yeah. All smoke and mirrors. No license. No paperwork. There are no records on him or his place."

"Places. He had one in Harvard, too. So it was all a sham?" I said. "Why? How?"

Haywood nodded. "A fake funeral home operation is damned hard to do. He'd been in Roxbury how long?"

"I was told three years. So how did he do it? And why?"

"He must have faked the necessary paperwork," Haywood said. "Or maybe he didn't bother with paperwork. So he hangs out a shingle. Who would question it? The embalming is more complicated."

A door closed somewhere in the mortuary. "I was told he did at least a few funerals. He must have done one in the Harvard place or he wouldn't be in the MGAP database. But who says he embalmed the corpses? See what I mean?"

"Unfortunately, I do."

"Maybe he just tossed the corpses. Or the funeral home in Roxbury could have been a front for a bookie joint or a drug house."

"You said your friend's sister was alive there," he said. "Maybe she died there, say from an overdose, and so McArdle puts on this phony funeral."

"Except for the autopsy stitches. I guess they could have been from an operation. Sure. Della could have been sick. That's why she was operated on. And she dies at McArdle's. And because his cleaning lady, Mrs. Cheadle, tells Chesa about her death, he has to put on the funeral. Yes. And Mrs. Cheadle, by telling Chesa, who told me, put a big kink in the works. See it?"

Haywood nodded. "I see it. Almost too well."

"That's why Della's coffin had to be real."

"Real?" Haywood said.

"In the basement, I found all these bogus coffins that Blessing had smashed."

His laugh boomed and he slapped his thighs. "There's your 'why.' You should have mentioned the fake coffins earlier."

"Considering Chesa's murder and McArdle taking Della's corpse, it struck me as secondary."

"My compadres would kill me if they knew I was laughing about it. I think we're wrong about this drug business."

"Huh?"

"What you've got here in McArdle is a flimflam artist. It's the old bait and switcheroo. Shows the expensive coffin, sells it to the family, lays them out in that, then substitutes a flimsy pine or cardboard box. Like we've talked about, he doesn't even have to bury some of them. He can recycle. Some of these guys even bury people, then at night go dig 'em up and sell corpses for research. Nasty stuff, but even a few legit morticians have been known to pull the coffin switch. Don't repeat that, either. This guy could make thousands a year, and I'd say he took off not just because he was afraid, but that someone would discover the scam. People get mighty pissed when they learn their loved one is rotting in some cheapie pine box."

"You think that's what he did with Della's remains?"

Haywood reached for my hand. "Guys like this, Tal. Well, he might have even dumped her in a river, a landfill, somewhere secret. You told me she was homeless, right? With the sister dead, who's going to miss her?"

"Not a soul."

"Yup. You give it a little time, he'll resurface. Guys like him always do."

"All I really want is Della's body. McArdle can go scratch."

Haywood's eyes got puppy-dog warm. "Same old Tally. Trying to watch out for the wounded."

I extricated my hand from his. "I told Chesa I'd take care of matters. That's all. A promise is a promise."

He pushed the forelock off his brow. "We could be good together again, Tally."

I patted his lapel. I liked Haywood. "But not good enough, Dave. Not good enough."

I fumed all the way back to the office about McArdle. A flimflam artist. A phony. A sham. Christ. No wonder he was hiding out.

Chapter Thirteen

The remainder of Thursday felt all wrong. It proved to be a sleepy sort of day—no new homicides, nor suicides. Yet I was irritable and jumpy. I shared lunch with Gert, going over budget matters while we ate tuna sandwiches. Because Andy was out sick, I covered his four o'clock group. It felt as if I had a ton to do that wasn't getting accomplished, yet when five rolled around, I was grateful to leave work on time for once.

Instead of heading home, which is what I'd planned, I drove to the VA clinic.

*   *   *

"I told you no," Jaeger said as he breezed by me on his way to his office.

"He's killed again. Arlo Noyce, another man in my homicide counseling group. A good man."

Jaeger slapped his palm on his office door and entered.

I hollered after him. "Arlo didn't deserve to be beaten and decapitated!"

I took a seat in a waiting room chair. A pony-tailed vet studiously ignored me. So did the other doctor, who notched her head at the vet. Both left the room.

Now it was just me and the chairs.

I sat there for forty-five minutes. Dammit, I would not leave until Jaeger spoke with me.

Jaeger, his chapped lips pursed in a frown, poked his head out of his office for the nth time. "*Why?*"

"Because an old friend was murdered. Blessing was in my group for a month, yet I never saw it in him."

"So? You made a mistake. We all do."

"I won't leave it. At least, not until we've talked. I'll sit here until you relent or I grow roots. There's no reason not to show me his file."

"So you can open him up like a can of beans?"

"Oh, come on." I got so in-his-face, I could see the pores on his nose. "You're just being pissy. He's already being hunted by the cops and a mobster. Get real."

"And fuck you." He vanished in a swirl of white lab coats.

So I'd pressed a tad too hard.

I sat back down and began picking at the table's chipped formica.

A cleared throat. Jaeger. Crooking a finger.

"I made some calls," he said. "You're lucky. A friend

of mine, Tish Snyder, vouches for you. Come on back."

Hallelujah.

Jaeger sat on the corner of his desk while I read Roland Blessing's VA file.

We had shore leave. The boat . . . the ship . . . Christ, would I ever get that right? It lay in the harbor like a fat, old woman. It wasn't fat or old, just big. Biggest thing I'd ever been on.

So five of us, we rode most of the way to town, but then . . . We were all wobbly, see, no shore legs. So we got off and . . . Well, we walked for a while. We were warned. Yeah. Yeah. But, you know, five guys. Like we were worried?

So our legs, at least mine, were all rubbery at first. After maybe half a mile, they started feeling better. The bugs were bad—it was twilight. We weren't used to these big suckers, not on water like we were. Then Jimmy, he hears a noise, and we stop and we get all quiet. But none of us hears nothing. So we go on, all eager to get to town and the booze and babes and . . .

The first one, he hacked Jimmy's head almost from his neck. The shriek, and then, and then. . . . I can hear the snap, snap, snap of his black pajamas, as the Cong moves so fast. I see this knife, arcing up high in the geek's hand and I go for my gun, but . . . I don't know . . . I don't know why I just watched him slice off Reaper's nose, then he . . .

I don't want to do this no more. Can we . . . ?

No, huh. All right.

So I'm there, watching, swallowing all this saliva and licking' my lips and . . . I finally got the gun out,

*ya know, and it's real heavy in my hand, but . . .
Marty. He's such a great guy. My best buddy from
growing up. We went to school together and . . .*

*I don't see why I couldn't move, but I couldn't and
all I can smell is Marty's fucking Brut cologne and
I'm watching, like a movie, and Marty, he's calling
to me to help, help, help.*

*And there's blood, man, and I'm covered in it. And
it's warm and sticky and tastes sweetish, like a penny
maybe, on my tongue.*

*And I sat down in the road—they were going to
get us, I knew they were going to get us all no matter
what we did—and I'm all ready for the feel of that
knife, you know, and I'm wondering where it'll go in,
and how it'll feel, and I'm hearing noise and screams
and singing. Trippy stuff. "Inna Gadda da Vida."
Yeah. That was it. And I gotta sit there and wait for
my time.*

So I woke up in the VA. That's all I remember.

"Not pretty reading." I softly closed the folder. Not
pretty at all. "So he wasn't a Navy SEAL."

Jaeger shook his head. "Took quite a bit of the
training, but he couldn't cut it."

"You never think about the Navy having clerks, especially in Vietnam. But everyone has pencil pushers,
don't they?"

"By all accounts," Jaeger said. "Blessing's story was
true. Needless to say Blessing was out of the Navy in
a flash. He landed in a VA hospital for six months.
Diagnosed with post-traumatic stress disorder. His
symptoms were a complete inability to take action in
any sort of crisis. He'd freeze up, and it progressed to
where he could barely cross the street."

"Some people aren't meant to be warriors," I said.

"No. A variety of sounds and smells and sights triggered his frozen states. Something as simple as an amber light turning red or getting honked at by a car could provoke his symptoms.

"If someone jostled him in a department store, if he smelled nutmeg or Brut cologne, if he was yelled at by friend or foe—all precipitors that flashed him back to the confrontation with the Viet Cong. He once stressed out so badly at a stoplight that his car had to be towed, with him in it."

"I see he tried to kill himself with carbon monoxide."

Jaeger nodded. "Twice. Two half-hearted suicide attempts. Neither serious. Over time, he mentally recovered to where he seemed able to function in the real world."

I read between the lines—how Blessing had latched onto Pisarro and how he gravitated to men of action, so that he was coupled with them in words, if not in deeds. Someone had made a note that he became all bluster because he had so little substance.

"Then his daughter was killed," Jaeger said.

"Moira." I leaned forward. "Sure. When Moira was murdered, his symptoms slammed back. So now, whenever he's angry, which is often, and he goes to take action connected to that anger, he freezes. Period. He doesn't even need the stimuli anymore. Just a memory of them." I cut my eyes to Jaeger. "You believe he's incapable of physical violence. Is that correct, Doctor?"

"Yes."

"Every day I deal with patients who experience post-traumatic stress disorder. If what I'm reading about Blessing is accurate, then I'd have to agree."

"Simply put, Blessing's illness would prevent him from murdering anyone."

I wasn't sure I agreed. I thanked Dr. Jaeger, whose head was shaking.

"What are you going to do?" he asked.

"Review our casework on Blessing. Then talk to the police."

"Good luck."

The bitterness in his voice spoke volumes.

At home, I reread Blessing's MGAP file. Right there in black and white: A month ago—Blessing's first session—he'd gotten totally pissed at Arlo. Started shouting about Arlo's cologne. I'd bet Arlo wore Brut.

Blessing had griped about how Arlo stank, then had tightened his hands into fists. He'd pulled back an arm, ready to pound Arlo, who was more than ready to pound back. But Blessing had frozen. His eyes had become unfocused, all far away, and he'd just stopped. The remembering. Technically it was a recollection of an event that precipitated his post-traumatic stress disorder. I saw it in my clients again and again.

Blessing wasn't just seeing, but actually experiencing the massacre over and over. And over and over again, he'd be powerless to protect his friends. How sad that the same held true for his daughter.

I wondered if Moira's killer knew of Blessing's handicap.

It was all there, and I fell asleep contemplating Roland Blessing's pain, my grandmother's quilt pulled up to my throat.

Chapter Fourteen

The alarm bleeped. Dammit. Too early. Way too early. Coffee. Oh, yeah.

I groped for Baby Ben's alarm stalk. Except where was the clock? I pushed myself up. Right. I was on the living room couch. My watch read 4 A.M.

"The phone. Shit!"

I found the portable just before the machine clicked on.

"I'm here. I'm here?"

"You Tally Whyte?"

"Who is it? What's wrong?"

"Kranak said you asked a lotta questions. Lieutenant Capistran. Mass State PD. We gotta situation here."

I cradled the phone as I pulled on my sweats. "What kind of *situation*?"

"It appears one Roland Blessing has taken one Dottie Brylske hostage. And he's askin' for *you*."

Penny bounded after me into the Crime Scene Services police van. Kranak was behind the wheel, chewing a bagel.

"Where's Blessing?" I asked.

"He's taken her to Newburyport, for Christ-knows-why." He handed me a plastic travel mug filled with coffee.

"Thanks. Brylske was his daughter's landlady, yes?"

"Yeah. When Blessing started hollering for you, Capistran called me to get the scoop. I said I'd pick you up, since you drive lousy."

"Gee, thanks, Rob."

It was dark out, and bitter cold as we drove north toward Newburyport. "Rob, I have serious reservations about Blessing as a killer."

"Oh, right. That's why he kidnapped this woman—because he's a puddytat. FYI, that dollar you left in my office. I got a good print off it. Blessing's."

So Blessing *had* been in my home. Creepy city. "Hear me out, huh?" I launched into Blessing's VA file and his behavior at our group that now made terrible sense. "He freezes, Rob. Call the original incident what you will—cowardice, fear, whatever—but remember he was a clerk. Hadn't seen any combat. Hell, he's a techie geek for Pisarro. He just hangs with the tough guys."

"That freezing shit was thirty years ago. Times change. So do people."

"Once his child was killed, his post-traumatic stress disorder became as fresh as today. It's all in the file."

"File my ass. He's good for your friend. We got a dozen prints, the gold dollar, also with prints, and the kid who saw a guy who looks just like Blessing and works for Pisarro arguing with the Chesa girl. You yourself told me the motive."

"Sure it seems to add up, but it's all wrong, given his psychological profile."

He rolled his eyes. "If it looks like a killer and feels like a killer—"

"It's not necessarily a killer, Rob. It feels wrong."

"Let me offer this: Blessing's prints were all over the scene of Arlo's homicide, too. Ditto for a witness

seeing them together. You gotta face it, babe. He did
'em both."

We pulled into Marshview Way in Newburyport at
5:10 A.M. I hoped we'd made it before Blessing did
something weird.

Talk about a zoo. Lights and noise and TV stations
and cops in all sorts of uniforms. Beyond the down-
slope of a pretty Gambrel house, the marshy river me-
andered toward the sea. A dozen boats with huge
spotlights bobbed in the water, all focused on a boathouse maybe big enough for a speedboat. Kranak hustled Penny and me through a gauntlet of cops until
we finally made it to Lieutenant Capistran's side.
Kranak peeled off, and I was left with the stocky lieutenant.

"What's happening?" I said.

"Blessing's in the boathouse with the Brylske
woman," Capistran said. "The negotiator says Blessing's in your grief group or something. The guy's already killed two people. You knew them both, right?"

"One was a friend. The other was in our group. But
I'm not sure Blessing—"

"We don't want the landlady to be a third."

"Now what?" I tilted my head back to inhale a big
lungful of air.

He pointed to a frail-looking man in jeans and a
huge sweater. "Go talk to Stan, our negotiator."

I introduced myself. "How does Blessing sound?"

"Fucked up," the negotiator said. "And weepy. He
hasn't stopped crying. What can you tell me about
him?"

I told as much as I knew, and he frowned when I said Pisarro.

"The woman he's using as a hostage," I continued. "He thinks she killed his daughter. She couldn't have done it. But she makes a good focus. She's gay. I've been told she has a wise mouth and a tough manner."

His eyes narrowed. "Christ. Let's see if we can't get them both out in one piece."

He held up a finger while he pressed his earphone tight to his ear. He nodded repeatedly. "You want Tally Whyte?" Pause. "I'll put her on."

He motioned with his hand, and a black-garbed cop handed me a headset. I slipped it over my head. "Are you there, Roland?"

"I'm glad you're here." Blessing's voice shook with fear or nerves. I hoped he wasn't on drugs.

"I'm glad to be here, too," I said.

"Your father was killed, wasn't he?" Blessing sobbed. "Knifed. It's what I heard. Blood everywhere. You remember the blood, how it pumped from his body?"

I shuddered. "I do. How's Ms. Brylske feeling, Roland?"

"Pain." He chuckled. "It's terrible, that pain. Moira felt it, you know. This bitch cut her hands off. I want them. All I want is Moira's hands. And she won't give them to me."

"Ms. Brylske didn't cut off anything, Roland. She doesn't have Moira's hands. I heard she's a nice lady. Her name's Dottie, by the way."

"She's a bitch. And she did cut them. She did! She must have!"

"No, Roland, she didn't. You're trying to turn

Moira's landlady into her killer. But you can't, can you? Because she didn't do it."

I heard shouting, then whimpering in the background. Then a slap.

"Roland, please talk to me. Ms. Brylske's a good person. Like Moira was. C'mon, Roland. Let her go. We can go somewhere. Talk. Just you and me."

"Your friend, she had a big mouth, too." Pause. "I don't know how I ended up here. I don't understand."

"We can talk about it, Roland."

"It . . . I don't know. I . . . I'm confused. I miss my baby."

"Like I miss my dad. From what you've said, Moira was a lovely, gentle soul."

Capistran signaled he was sending in the troops.

"No!" I hissed to the negotiator. "Not yet. I can get him to come out peacefully."

He nodded, then made eye contact with Capistran, who shook his head back and forth. He then spoke into his headset. Like a wave, the black- and Kevlar-garbed officers crouched toward the house, moving like a black blur in the night.

"Are you there?" Blessing said to me.

"Of course. Come on out. Please, Roland."

"Maybe. I'm going to let this dyke go now. Will you talk to me alone? I'm scared. I don't understand."

"I will, Roland. You know I will." *Wait* I mouthed to the negotiator.

He held up a finger, then Capistran spoke into his headphone. The troops halted.

Almost there. "Are you going to come out that side door, Roland? I need to know, so everything will be cool when you come out."

"Side," he said. "Oh, yeah, I need to talk about

Moira and Arlo and . . . What's that? What? Holy shit." Click.

"He hung up!" I said to the negotiator. "Roland! Roland!"

A boat motor thrummed.

The troops moved—black shadows.

A keening howl shred the night.

Capistran bellowed "Blessing!" on the bullhorn and the negotiator was talking madly into his headphones. So was I.

Silence from Blessing.

Shots booming and wood splintering and windows shattering, then the black shapes poured into the boathouse.

The negotiator pressed his fingers to his headset. "Yeah. Yeah. Christ."

I ran toward the boathouse.

Someone grabbed my arm, so I was flung back around. Penny growled. "*What*?" I said.

"She's dead," Kranak said.

"No!" I whooshed out a breath. "Dammit, dammit, dammit. Where's Blessing?"

He shook his head. "Gone."

"Gone? Gone where?"

Kranak shrugged. "They'll find him."

I wandered away, hands pressed to my face, trying not to feel that poor woman's fear as Blessing took her life. How could I have been so wrong about Blessing? How?

I waited and waited. But they found no sign of Roland Blessing.

* * *

The cops and I talked for maybe an hour, trying to figure out where Blessing might go. He wasn't that bright a guy, yet no one seemed able to catch up with him. Now, the search would intensify.

I filled in the state cops on what Dixie and I had found in Blessing's room.

They knew all about it. Kranak hadn't, and I could feel how pissed he was.

The hearse arrived to take Dottie Brylske to the Grief Shop. Damn.

"Can't believe you didn't tell me about going into that bozo's place," Kranak said on the way home.

"I knew you'd get mad at me."

"Gee, Tal. I wonder why?"

"Your sarcasm is unbecoming."

"You see how easy it is to go wrong with that shrink stuff, Tal."

"I don't see anything, Rob. Nothing's adding up for me. Not a damn thing. At least maybe I can help find Blessing."

"You stay out of it."

I stayed silent, is what I did.

God, what a waste. Poor Dottie Brylske.

I slept for an hour or so, then dragged myself to the office.

No headline blared Roland Blessing's capture. *Somebody* had to know where Blessing was.

"Hi, guys," I said.

"We heard you had a bad night," Gert said.

"Real bad."

"I took the Brylske woman's family. They're on the way in."

I filled my mug with coffee. "I'm glad you're doing them. I should stay out of it. Fogarty in?"

"He did the Brylske post."

I trotted up the stairs, fast, so I wouldn't chicken out.

Fogarty's door was open, and he was hunched over what looked like budget sheets. God, I'd hate his job.

"Hey, Tom."

He swiveled, blinking fast as his eyes refocused. "Oh, this is rich. You must want something big to come up here."

I shrugged, going for nonchalant, and took the chair beside the desk. I pulled a pair of Celtics tickets from my pocket. "Luxury suite. Center court. Old-timers' night. They're saying Bird's going to show. I'm sure you know we're playing the Knicks that night. Any interest?"

He laughed, but couldn't quite hide the hunger in his eyes. "Who did you kill to get these?"

"No one you'd know."

"Sure I'd be interested. Who wouldn't?"

"They're yours. All I need is the key to the database for a month."

He pushed out his lower lip. "Why do you care about how many traffic vics arrived here last week? Or the average age of people who died at home alone? Huh?"

"The why doesn't matter, Tom. The point is, do you want these tickets?"

He removed his half-glasses and twirled them by a stem. "To get the key, you'll have to do a walk-on for *Street Fighter*. As you. Tally Whyte. Homicide counselor."

"Not a chance."

"Oh, there's a chance. They want you, much to my disgust, and they'll kiss my butt if I get you on board."

Months earlier, I'd turned down the new Spenser-wannabe TV show. Especially as myself. "Forget it."

I scooped up the tickets and headed for the door.

"Only way you'll get the key, Tally."

I walked out the door.

With the database, I could see if Blessing had any other connections at the Grief Shop. Maybe he was tied to some other crime that ended in a homicide, or even a seemingly accidental death.

The more I learned about Moira's death, the more tools I'd have to find Blessing.

And maybe an arrow would point to Blessing's hideout. A neon one.

All the possibilities felt like fleas on my skin. I kept wanting to scratch them.

I buzzed Fogarty, who ten minutes later traded the tickets and my appearance on *Street Fighter* for a month's worth of daily encryption keys.

I began tapping keys, digging into what I hoped was a secret gold mine about Blessing.

"Tal, can you come here for a sec?" Gert said. "Dottie Brylske's partner wants to meet you."

"Sure." I raked my fingers through my hair. "Let's get it done."

I hugged Lin Brylske-Harry. She was short and sinewy and had a pretty face marred by a terrible grief.

We sat in the grieving room. Lin kept rolling and unrolling the hem of her shirt.

"How can I help?" I asked.

"I heard you were there." She frowned. "Was she very scared?"

"I think she might have been. But only for a short while."

"Why did he think she killed his daughter?" she asked.

"Dottie was someone concrete to light upon. When the real killer isn't available, people do that. They need someone to hate, to get angry at, to point a finger at. I'd guess you're feeling many of those things right now."

She rocked, arms wrapped around her waist. "Someone put him on to Dottie. He didn't think that at first. Point of fact, Dottie and Roland were friends. Then he changed, maybe four months ago. That's when he settled on Dottie as little Moira's killer."

"Have you told this to the police?"

"Sure. Dottie told them. A couple of times." Rocking. Rocking.

"I see. Is there—"

"If she wasn't scared, she wouldn't have died."

"Oh, Lin, I wish that were so. But I'm afraid that's not true."

"Of course it's true. My big girl's heart wouldn't have burst if she wasn't so scared. Wouldn't've. My big girl." Lin Brylske-Harry held on tight and sobbed.

I mouthed to Gert. *Heart?*

Gert nodded. "Cause of death. Heart attack. You didn't know?"

"I sure didn't."

*   *   *

I was up half of Friday night working on the Grief Shop database. Saturday morning I was back at the keyboard, trying to make better friends with columns of figures and names and statistics. I wasn't succeeding.

I'd left Penny home, and except for the sparse weekend shift, nobody was around, including MGAP and CSS. Most of the Grief Shop's staff worked weekends only on an "as needed" basis. It was quiet. Too quiet. Dead quiet.

I was glad Burt the security guard was on and that a key was needed to enter the building.

Another hour passed. I was going nuts that I couldn't find Moira Blessing in the database. Although her death had taken place more than three years earlier, her file still should have been on record.

But it wasn't.

So who had erased Moira from the Grief Shop's records?

Just as I was leaving, Gert and Mary arrived. Gert was the on-call counselor.

"You being noble, or what, Mare?"

She smiled, shook her head. "Nope. Lin Brylske-Harry's going to stop by, so I said I'd spell Gert for a while."

"Sounds noble to me," Gert said.

"Get this." I explained about Moira missing from the database. Both looked at me as if I'd had one too many.

"Fine," I said. "Sure it's all in my head. Feel free to hunt for it yourselves."

Chapter Fifteen

I met up with Dixie on Newbury Street. Blessing or no, I wasn't going to miss our longstanding outing.

By dinnertime, shopping bags fanned from our hips.

"We're bad," I said.

"That we are," Dixie said.

We giggled like schoolkids.

"Come on," I said. "I'm starved."

We left our packages in my car, then arm in arm walked toward Copley Plaza.

I sobered when I saw the same blond man I'd seen at Domain duck into a shop as we approached.

"Wait a minute, Dix." I popped into the store. The man was trying on a hat. I slinked toward him, feigning fascination with a similar hat.

He pulled off the hat. "Problem?"

I gave him a fake smile. "Not a one."

Of course it hadn't been Blessing. What was I thinking?

Sometimes I loathed winter. When I pulled up in front of my town house that evening, darkness filled every crevice and crack of the street. I cautiously opened the truck door.

Bare branches clacked from the large oak that bowed halfway across the street. The sidewalks were empty. Something clattered above my head. I pivoted.

Someone had left an aluminum folding chair on their rooftop deck.

Down the street, lamps spilled warm light onto the pavement. Jake still hadn't replaced the bulb above our place. I'd do it myself that weekend.

I crossed the narrow street, one hand awkwardly clutching my shopping bags, the other holding my flashlight and keys. As I climbed the steps, I caught a movement behind me. I snapped around. Nothing.

I felt like shouting, "Come out, come out, whoever you are."

I scooped up the FedEx box resting against the door, unlocked the door, and scooted inside. I slammed the door behind me. I sighed.

Except where were the thundering paws and the howl of greeting? "Penny?"

No answering woof.

Right. Jake had taken her for a romp. I drooped. A girl needs a little greeting, a little fuss, especially after the day I'd had.

I headed for the kitchen, turning on lights as I went.

I glanced at my answering machine. Holding steady.

I dropped the FedEx box on the coffee table, noting the Byte Me return address. Huh. I fired up my Mac. While it loaded, I nuked some frozen beef burritos, changed into cozy sweats, and returned to the living room carrying Trepel's business card.

I dialed Aliant Industries in Lubbock, Texas, and eventually got Bernard Trepel's recorded voice, complete with twang. His recording said he was still on his "New England loop." He was real. He was normal. At least he sounded normal.

I left a voice mail with my name and number and

an apology for Reen's heavy-handedness the previous night.

I was disgusted with myself. My paranoia today with the blond guy. My fear tonight parking the truck. My terror and anxiety about Trepel. I'd joined the paranoid hall of fame.

Roland Blessing was taking over my life. No way would I let him do that.

I checked my e-mail, then plopped onto the couch, pulled the tab on my Diet Coke, then the one on the FedEx box. Out came a bubblewrapped something, that became a burgundy leather photo album as I unwrapped it. No note.

Crap. I had a bad feeling about it. I bit into a burrito and opened the book.

A laughing waif, maybe six years old, stared back at me. Hands on knees, head tilted back, wearing a swimsuit. A chime of memory. Immense periwinkle eyes and midnight hair and a hint of a pointy chin reminded me of . . .

Of course. Angela Pisarro, Harry's murdered daughter. No mistaking those eyes or chin.

Why had Pisarro sent me an album of his dead child?

I leafed through the book. Angela grew from little imp into a lovely teen with a shy smile. Sometimes she'd stick her tongue in the corner of her mouth and her eyes pranced with mischief. The imp revealed.

More pictures. Angela in English riding clothes, as Dorothy in a school play, in a cap and gown at high school graduation. She'd grown into a young women of uncommon beauty. These latter photos were the ones that Pisarro had shown me after her death. The same ones that had appeared in the newspapers.

Her face had matured into an elfin shape, and she'd

cut her hair into a short pixie. Her eyes took center stage in her gamin's face.

I flipped the page. My burrito slipped from my fingers.

Angela's corpse.

Mounted just like the earlier ones were crime scene photos of Angela's homicide. Someone's palm had been greased to get them.

Angela lay on her back, naked, a red scarf draping her face, arms tied above her on the brass headboard. Padding beneath the wrist bands. Whomever had tied her didn't want her bruised. *Whew*. More pages of the same. Horrible, dehumanizing stuff.

Three years ago, I'd known little of the case. I'd been fly-fishing in Montana that July and had returned just prior to Angela's funeral. Pisarro had personally requested my assistance, and I'd attended the wake, services, and interment. I'd also had several private counseling sessions with Pisarro, which his wife declined to attend.

I'd never seen the crime scene photos or Angela's body at the Grief Shop.

I flipped to the next page in the album.

Angela on the table beneath Strabo's knife.

Good God.

I scanned the autopsy photos. One item was particularly noteworthy.

Angela's periwinkle eyes were missing.

I found a note from Pisarro at the back of the book.

> *Dear Ms. Tally:*
> *Odd how my Angela's eyes were missing, just as you described the woman Della's missing eyes.*

The police never found Angela's eyes. No one knows about their absence, including my wife, except the police and the people at your house of death. And the killer, naturally.

I've been looking into things. Could someone be trafficking in stolen eyes? Word has it, they go for large sums.

Please return the album at your earliest convenience.

Your friend,
Harry Pisarro

Selling eyes? *Selling eyes?* Absurd. Or was it?

I dumped the rest of my dinner down the kitchen pig.

Had Chesa been surprised that Della had donated her eyes? It felt like so long ago. Had we even discussed it?

Angela's killer, her musician boyfriend, had met a grim death while in prison. No one dared mention Pisarro's name.

What if the boyfriend *hadn't* been Angela's killer?

Boy, if I were going to sell eyes, I wouldn't choose a mobster's daughter as donor.

I carefully rewrapped Angela's photo album. Sending me the album was his cry for help. Much as the thought lacked appeal, I'd call him tomorrow.

I flicked on the TV, then reached for Penny, looking for a cuddle. No Penny, of course. I phoned Jake.

"Yeah?" He sounded Down East dry, as if I'd disturbed him.

"Thanks for taking Pens, but would you bring her home now?"

"I don't have Penny," he said, his voice sharp.

"Oh, come on, Jake. She's not here."

"I dropped her off after our park romp. Goddamnit, you're starting to sound—"

"Later."

I flew off the couch. "Penny!"

I looked in closets and out back and even under the bed.

I opened the cellar door and flicked on the light. "Penny girl?"

Silence. But then a sound. A *snore*?

I started down the steps, peered around the railing, and spotted her curled in a corner of the dirt-floored cellar, asleep.

"Penny, come."

Still no response. I trotted down the steps.

A vibration, like a small tremble of an earthquake. I gripped the rail and gingerly put my foot on the next step. The staircase teetered like a drunk.

Up? Down? Which? Where?

The tread swayed wildly beneath my feet and I jumped.

I landed with a thud and a whoosh, just as the steps collapsed in a groan of noise and a billow of dust.

I tried to catch my breath, couldn't at first, so I lay there feeling the grit inside my mouth and the dust scraping my eyes.

A wet tongue began bathing my cheeks.

"Great," I choked out. "Now you wake up."

Penny didn't say much.

"Tally!" Jake hollered from the top of the stairs. "What the hell are you doing?"

"Nothing," I choked out. "Just resting down here on the cellar floor."

"What happened to the staircase?"

"Justifiable homicide," I said, finally understanding the meaning of those words.

"What?" he hollered.

"Just get me out of here."

An hour later, I was clean, my scrapes covered with Betadine, my entire body one big ache.

Penny, on the other hand, appeared just jim-dandy.

"Why didn't you bark, you dumb dog?" I said as I mixed her dog food and kibbles. "You should've barked. Having a nice nap down there, were you?"

Her eyes bobbled from me to her food dish.

Jake returned to the kitchen wiping his hands on his pants. "Timbers rotted."

"You're sure?"

"Yup. I'll get someone on it right away."

Right. I placed Penny's dish on the floor. After she inhaled her food, I walked her out back on the leash, not wanting to lose sight of her. Not that night.

"Well?" Jake said, as I locked the French doors to the back.

I felt a chill. "An intruder put Penny in the cellar. Sometime this afternoon, since you had her with you this morning. I think he drugged her."

"She could have snuck down there herself."

"Oh, right. The cellar door, which I *always* keep closed, happened to be ajar? Where were you today?"

He tossed me a black look. "The studio. What are you implying?"

"Nothing. I'm *saying* that someone put Penny down in the cellar."

Jake turned me by the shoulders. "I know you think Blessing got in here once, but . . ."

I shook off his hands and cruised rooms again, looking for missing money or jewelry or art. I released a pent-up breath when I saw Dad's meerschaum pipes were just as I'd left them and was relieved that Della's single dancing earring still sat in my jewel box. I searched for shuffled papers or bankbooks or magazines, for mussed clothing, drawers, shoes. All seemed in order. Too much in order. Again.

Earlier, I'd been too preoccupied. The coffee mug I'd left in the sink that morning had been put in the dishwasher. The phone book I'd left open to Plumbers had been closed. Creepiest of all was the full toilet paper roll in its cradle in my bathroom.

I know I'm a bad girl, but I'd used the last piece that morning and had failed to replace the empty tube with a full roll.

My visitor had. Cripes.

My earlier paranoia whammed back.

I wished the son of a bitch had stolen money or the TV or the Nantucket baskets I collected. That I could understand.

But an apparition who'd flitted about tidying up and who'd locked up my dog, who was trained to attack intruders, but hadn't? That gave me the shivers.

Jake stared at the embers of the fire I'd built earlier. His right eyelid twitched, a sure sign of worry.

"Nothing's missing, Jake."

He nodded.

I phoned Kranak.

Chapter Sixteen

While I talked on the phone to Kranak, Jake vanished like a wraith. I rechecked all the locks and went to bed with Penny snuggled beside me. Hours passed before the knot of tension in my belly relaxed.

Sunday morning my entire body ached. I poured some coffee and headed for the couch. "Wowsa!"

Jake was asleep on my sofa. Endearing, but creepy, too. I'd slept through his arrival.

"Howdy, Tal." He left with a smile and a wave. At least until he passed Kranak. Both sneered, their eyes shooting poison darts at each other.

"Cut it out, guys," I said to thin air. Far too chipper behavior, if you ask me.

Jake had vanished, while Kranak was unpacking his crime scene kit. Penny barked, and in walked two guys wearing security firm uniforms.

The installer's pink sheet said they'd been hired by Jake Beal. And Jake wasn't even installing it himself.

Minutes later, two carpenters breezed in and began taking measurements for the new cellar staircase.

I was starting to feel like Bilbo in *The Hobbit*.

Kranak shooed everyone away until he'd given the place a thorough going-over. CSS kit in hand, he moved from room to room print dusting and eyeballing and measuring. He looked through closets and beneath my bed and inside desk drawers.

I followed him around and went "gack!" when he dumped my hamper stuff on the bathroom floor. Did

I want Kranak to see the red teddy I sometimes wore to bed?

"You're drivin' me nuts," he finally said. "Get lost."

Instead of losing it, I phoned Mrs. Cheadle.

"Doin' okay, Tally," Mrs. Cheadle said.

"How about lunch this Thursday?"

"Oh, that would be fun. Just so you know, I've started a journal of recent events. Might kick-start this ol' brain."

"No one needs a kick-start less than you. But the journal's a good idea. I'll pick you up at noon."

"I'll be wearing my finest."

After we signed off, I tossed Penny her Kong out back. When my arm became a rubberoid, we went back inside. Kranak was seated on the sofa, tapping his foot.

"Tea's on the way." I brought him a steaming mug. "Find anything?"

"Nothing on the surface. I got some prints, probably some pal of yours. I checked out the mess downstairs. Like Mr. Sculptor said—rotted timbers. Were they helped? Hard to tell. It's gotta be Blessing, and he's acting like a fruity kazootie."

"He seems to be obsessing on me," I said.

He took a pull on his mug and frowned. "This tea sucks. Is it from the last century or what? So what are you hiding from me, kiddo?"

Just Pisarro's album and allegations. "Not a thing."

"You're full of it."

"Thanks. So tell me your thoughts on Della Charles being alive at McArdle's."

He frowned. "Alive? Who says?"

"Boston PD found her prints all over the funeral home."

"Huh? Fuckers didn't call me. Pisser." His face reddened. "I wonder why not."

"Me too."

Later that Sunday, Penny and I drove out to Veda and Bertha's house in Lincoln.

Bertha is Veda's much more retiring sister. She's soothing and mellow and hilariously funny when she's had a few, which is unfortunately a wee bit too often.

That night, Veda and Bertha plied me with sauerbraten and spaetzle. My favorites. Oh, hell. Somebody had blabbed about my stair collapse and both were in full-blown worry mode. Veda hugged me in her furious way. I hugged her back. It felt good to be loved.

Bertha belted down one too many margaritas. No one does the Flamenco quite like my Jewish foster mother Bertha.

I waited until she crashed before telling Veda about Blessing's presumed visit.

"Have you seen a doctor?" Veda asked.

"I'm fine." She knew not to push.

She shoved the brownie plate my way. "Have another."

"I'm stuffed."

"You've fed half your meal to Penny."

"She's stuffed, too."

She slapped her thighs. "So. Blessing invaded your apartment. Again."

"Maybe. Probably. Whoever it was, it was . . . upsetting."

"Yes." She nodded.

"I suspect Rob's half-convinced my intruder was

Jake. Rob loathes him." I refilled our coffee mugs. "Jake would never lock up Penny."

"Jake would never lock up anyone." We began clearing the plates. "Maybe Jake has seen Blessing around the town house."

"Most days he's at his studio. I'll ask the neighbors. I can't figure how he got in."

"Who has a key?" Veda said.

"You. Jake. Me. That's it."

She sat back in the chair—a tiny woman with intense eyes that were now closed. One finger tapped her red lips. She sighed as she raised her lids. "You've got to back off of Blessing. Take it easy. Leave it alone."

How to leave Chesa? Except it was more complicated than that. I didn't believe Blessing had killed her.

I forced myself to relax. "It's so creepy, the way he fixes things up, as if he's trying to put my life in order. And he stuck Penny in the cellar. That was the worst." I explained my conflicted feelings about Blessing.

Veda flapped a hand. "What about that Bobby Plantegenet?"

A blast from the past. "I counseled him—what?—a year ago. His thing with me was all about transference."

"I also know he was stalking you."

I gnawed my lip. "He moved away."

Her eyes flashed. "So perhaps he's back. If it's not Blessing, perhaps it's someone like Bobby. You come into contact with many people on the edge."

"Excuse me?"

"I carry a gun."

"No way will I."

"That pepper—"

"No gun."

She stood and ran her hands down her red dress, straightening it.

"Veda, I . . ."

She started scrubbing dishes, splashing water, and cursing. She also ignored me. When I left, she bussed me with an annoying air kiss, just to emphasize her anger. She always lost the Gun Discussion.

I knew she was scared for me. I was scared for me, too. I fought tears of frustration. Why did everything lately feel like a fight?

Over breakfast and *The Globe* Monday morning, I hungered for an article about Blessing's capture. No such luck.

He had to be smarter than we'd thought, a modern Houdini, or maybe someone was helping him.

Given my druthers, I'd go for the latter.

Like, who? The guy had no one. By the time I arrived at the Grief Shop I recalled Moira Blessing's missing file. I headed for the records room, and her hard-copy folder, and ran into John Strabo. He'd done Moira's post. "Hey, John. Got a sec?"

When Strabo and I returned, Gert and Mary were all smiles. Then Mary's eyes lingered on Strabo, and vice versa. Hummm. Veddy interesting.

After he left, Mary pushed a button on her computer.

"Voila!" Gert said "Moira's report!"

"Someone misspelled her first name," Mary said. "And left off the *B* in her last."

"You're both brilliant."

"We know," Gert said.

Over lunch at my desk, I reviewed Moira's record. Nothing much new, until—

"Holy shit."

The McArdle Funeral Home had performed Moira Blessing's memorial service.

Chapter Seventeen

McArdle had retrieved Moira's body from the Grief Shop and performed her memorial service.

There it was—plain and clear. What my gut had been hollering, but I hadn't been hearing for all of the noise about Blessing.

What the hell was going on?

Roxbury funeral homes did *not* perform services for Irish girls from Southie.

I tapped McArdle's name in the Grief Shop database and held my breath.

Chesa's name appeared, of course. So did Moira's. Plus an Elizabeth Flynn, a name that chimed some dissonance. The database notation was from two years earlier.

Only three names? Three funerals wouldn't pay the water bill.

Then again, as Haywood said, McArdle's was a phony operation. A scam.

Even so . . .

What were my antennae picking up on Elizabeth Flynn? I asked Gert.

"Remains found in a field, ripped to shreds." Gert's voice crackled with anger.

Of course. Flynn's homicide had sparked a media feeding frenzy. Her killer had never been caught.

"I worked with her dad," Gert said. "Chief Petty Officer Henry Flynn. What a crusty old bird. All depressed 'cause he wasn't around when his daughter got killed."

"Then who handed Elizabeth's remains over to McArdle?"

"Check with Andy. He caught the case."

Andy walked in tightening the knot of his tie. As if it would matter to me. There was a lot of stuff that Andy didn't get. He brushed the chair for dog hairs and sat.

"How about you look this over?" I handed him the counseling report I'd reviewed on Elizabeth Flynn's survivors. He started to read.

I poured us some coffee and handed him a mug. In his early thirties, Andy still looked like a kid, and he tried to cloak his youthful appearance with wing tips, blue suits, and a perpetually solemn expression. Of all of my counselors, Andy had the least empathy for the survivors. I never quite lost the feeling that his efforts at MGAP were fodder for the doctoral dissertation he'd yet to produce.

When he closed the folder, I said, "Your notes say Sven Gunderson was Elizabeth's uncle. He identified the remains. But where's the follow-up? You're terrific at helping survivors navigate those shark-infested waters."

"Gunderson didn't feel like swimming. He ducked

out. Her father . . . We couldn't get in touch with him. We couldn't find him."

"Flynn had no other relatives?" I said. "No best friend? Lover? Employer?" According to Dr. Lulu Redmond's studies, each victim has seven to ten close surviving family members.

"Correct. Just Gunderson. He handled everything."

Both Chesa and Della were unusual in that respect, too. So was Moira, with just her dad. And now Elizabeth Flynn, with only her uncle appearing at the time of death.

"So here we have her uncle," I said. "He's the one carrying all the terrible emotions of her death by homicide. He doesn't seem very broken up about it."

"It was a little odd. He seemed frozen. You know. But he was organized. He'd lined everything up. The funeral home, the service, the interment. It was like he'd—"

"—been through it before?"

"Yeah."

"And had he?"

"I don't know. He went poof, see? Didn't return my follow-up calls. Didn't answer our letters. I can only do so much, Tal."

I took a pull of coffee. "Your report doesn't mention the mortuary's name."

His eyes shifted to the wall. "Never got it."

"Why?"

He shrugged. "Gunderson didn't ask for my help. I forgot."

I nodded. "Thanks for reviewing this with me."

After he left, I flopped my feet onto the ottoman. Andy was hiding something.

The question was what and why?

* * *

The following day was filled with a flurry of activity, as well as a budget crisis. Funny how that greased my mental processes.

To quote E. M. Forester, "Only connect." Chesa's death had sparked a chain of events. Or had it? Perhaps the chain had begun with Della's death. Or maybe Elizabeth Flynn's. Or preceding that, Moira Blessing's.

Were all four women's deaths connected by more than just McArdle's funeral home? Was there a daisy chain of deaths? If so, when did the chain really begin?

Kranak would say I was stretching connections. But the vibe was screaming "yes!" Once before I'd visited Roxbury, with little success. A return trip was in order.

As Penny and I drove to the McArdle Funeral Home, I occasionally looked over my shoulder. I loathed being watched.

I patted Penny's head. "Good girl."

"Ohuuuuu."

"You're right, girl. Something's up."

I wondered what Blessing was doing at that moment. Hiding. Running. Maybe.

I parked several doors down from the funeral home. Some kids were building a snowman in front of a sea-blue town house. Across the street, two men huddled in an alcove, sipping from paper bags.

I leashed Penny and stepped from the truck.

A woman appeared. She wore a thin pink coat that brushed her ankles, and over it a hooded sweatshirt, the hood pulled on her head. A frayed glove covered her shaking, outstretched hand. She was grinning. "You gonna get a ticket, parking like that. I'll watch your car for you."

I pulled out a five and held up the sketch of Della and Chesa. "Have you ever seen these women?"

The money disappeared beneath the woman's coat. "Nope."

I got out a ten, but hung on to it. I pointed to McArdle's. "You know anything about McArdle or that place?"

She swayed, then steadied herself on the truck.

"I know a good women's shelter," I said.

"Don't need no shelter."

"When did McArdle's open?"

"I'm not so good with dates. Maybe three years ago."

Some teens strutted toward us down the sidewalk. Her eyes slid to them, then back to me.

"You try Jazz." She pointed to a brick building, tore the ten from my hand, and took off, running with a clumsy, loping gate.

All because of the teens. They were dressed like clones: leather jackets, black pants hanging low, black Nikes, reversed black baseball caps, and smart-ass grins.

The apparent leader also wore a red scarf tied around his head. He was the kid Kranak and I had run down the day I'd found Chesa. Julius Binny.

Penny and I approached the boys, who whistled and made kissing sounds. One tugged his groin.

"*K noze*," I commanded Penny in Czech. Telling her to heel put her instantly on alert. I pulled one of my cards from my pocket. "Remember me, Julius?"

"That's one funny lookin', three-legged dog." Binny slouched against a lamppost, his eyes challenging mine.

"Play it that way, if you like." I held up the sketch for all the boys. "Did any of you ever see these women?"

"They're fine lookin'," Binny said, his eyes laughing at me.

"Real fine," echoed two others. "But we ain't seen 'em."

"You recognize them," I said to Binny.

"Yeah. The one chick I saw arguin' with that dude." Binny thrust out a goateed chin. "The other one I put in the hearse. Before she got dead, she was hotter than you."

Binny knew a hell of a lot more than he was telling. I was getting ticked. A bad thing. "The one you saw arguing? She's the one I found inside McArdle's. Murdered."

"That fag wouldn't kill nobody," said the shortest of the quartet.

Binny grabbed the kid's throat. "Mr. McArdle wasn't no fag. He was cool."

"I hear," squeaked the kid. Binny cut him a mean look, then released him.

"Where's McArdle?" I said to Binny.

His lip curled. "How should I know?"

"You know," I said, losing patience.

His hostile brown eyes telegraphed his signal. The other three slid around behind me, just as the leader made a grab for me.

He got a chestful of dog and bared fangs an inch from his throat.

"If your friends touch me," I said. "She'll rip your throat out."

"Okay, okay, okay," the leader said. "Get her off."

"Tell your buddies to get lost."

"Go!" he said to them. "Now!"

The sounds of feet running and, from behind me, hands clapping. But I didn't move my eyes from the leader.

Someone laughed. "Not bad for a white missy."

"Now, where is McArdle?" I repeated.

"I don't know, man," he choked out. "I just ran errands for him. Once I loaded that stiff in his hearse, I never saw him again. Swear to Jesus."

"Why don't I believe you?"

"Talk to the asshole behind me. He knew McArdle real good."

"*Lehni*," I said to Penny.

When her paws touched the pavement, the kid raced for his cronies, one hand flying behind him in a third-fingered salute.

I slipped Penny a treat, then turned. A middle-aged African-American man stood on a stoop—the same brick building indicated by the old woman. The man was pointing a handgun at the boys. As they sidled off, he slipped the gun into the pocket of his maroon velvet smoking jacket. He was grinning. "Thanks for the show. That's some dog. What are you doing down here, missy?"

"I'm trying to find McArdle. Are you Jazz?"

"What? I smell of music?"

"The calluses on your hand."

"I play cello." His grin widened.

Mary had seen Della with a cellist.

An icy rain began to pelt the streets, making dull, thudding sounds on the cars.

Penny and I ran up the steps and scooched beneath the alcove's overhang. I showed the man the sketch of Della and Chesa.

He tucked a wad of chewing tobacco into his cheek. "Striking. Never saw them, though."

"The one on the left was named Della. You never took her out to a club? Maybe Roland Blessing went, too?"

His eyes narrowed. "I'd go now, missy. Weather's turnin' to snow."

"The kid said you know McArdle."

"Persistent puss. Lotsa people know McArdle, just not ones'll talk to you. Strange fella. We'd talk music. He didn't know much, but he liked *learning*. Same as you, loved that dog of his. Restoree. Got hit. Died." His eyes drifted beyond me. "Well, look who's here. See ya."

"Wait a min—"

"Hey!" Tommy Taylor, an annoying *Boston Herald* reporter, trotted toward me.

"Well, if it isn't Tally Whyte," Taylor said as he ran up to me.

"I'm late, Tommy." I reached for the truck door.

He snatched the sketch from my hand. "You looking for that Blessing dude? Did he kill these two women? Was one of them your friend? That's what I heard."

I opened the truck door. Tommy held on to it. Penny growled.

"So?" he said. "What's the story? You know I'll find out one way or another."

"Get lost." I got the scraper out of the truck and started clearing the windshield.

He popped an Altoid into his mouth. "So sad. And I came all the way down here just to tell you something."

"You're so full of it."

"Am I? Your office told me where you were. So here I am."

"My office wouldn't tell you squat."

"Sure they would." He scratched his scruffy beard. "If I had something important to tell you."

"My a—"

The stench of oily smoke wrinkled my nose. I panned the street and spotted Binny. He was racing around the corner of McArdle's.

Vroom! Flames shot from the funeral home windows.

"Shit!" Taylor ran toward McArdle's.

"Hold it!" I grabbed his jacket. "What did you have to tell me?"

Another boom! Glass and wood rained down on us. The funeral home screeched, as if in pain. Smoke boiled into the air.

Penny leapt onto Taylor's chest, immobilizing him.

"*What*?" I said to him.

"A nurse pal at Mount Auburn Hospital called me," Taylor screamed back. "Some old black lady at the hospital kept calling, 'Help Tally.' The nurse recognized your name. That old lady mean something to you?"

"*Lehni*." Penny jumped down from Taylor and we ran for the truck.

On the way to Mount Auburn, I called the fire in to 911.

I pressed my hands to the glass outside of the intensive care room where Mrs. Cheadle fought for her life. Machines hummed and gum-soled shoes squeaked and hushed voices broke like small waves against the ward's pervasive sea of quiet. I walked into the room.

Mrs. Cheadle was taped and injected, and a ventilator tube erupted from her mouth. She'd arrived two hours earlier, according to her attending nurse, and in the past hour had slipped into a coma.

She'd been stung by bees. *Bees!* She was allergic and had gone into anaphylactic shock.

"I'll take care of your kitties," I told her. "But they'll miss you. You've got to get well. Come on, Mrs. Cheadle."

A nurse tapped lightly on the glass.

I leaned down and kissed her. No response.

Pisarro's watchdog, Bones, was pacing the ICU's waiting area. His gray suit was rumpled, its knees stained.

"I don't understand," I said. "Bees in January."

He blotted his face with a balled up handkerchief. "I know. I let down Harry."

"*Someone* had to get in there and leave live bees. Someone who knew Mrs. Cheadle was severely allergic to bee stings."

He sucked his thumb. "One of 'em got me. They was swarmin' all over the place. Who ever heard of bees in winter? I thought they hibernated or something."

I had assumed that, too. "Who went inside her apartment?"

"Nobody. For real. I even took the flowers from the delivery kid, just to be sure."

I knew. Somehow, that was how the bees got to Mrs. Cheadle.

What did she know that might cost her her life?

I walked out of the waiting room dialing Kranak's number.

Chapter Eighteen

I finally connected with Kranak. "You've been wrong. Wrong all along about Blessing. He didn't kill Chesa. Maybe not even Arlo." I told him about Elizabeth Flynn and Moira Blessing.

"Stay out of what you don't know," he said.

"And what about Mrs. Cheadle?"

"What do you want me to do, arrest a bunch of bees?"

"Blessing was set up, Rob. Just look into this McArdle guy."

"Should I start calling you lieutenant, or what, Tal?"

"Why are you copping this attitude with me?"

"Because you're a pain in the ass, sticking your nose in where it doesn't belong."

"Thanks for making me feel swell, Rob."

"My specialty. Now get lost."

Get lost? I didn't get it. Not at all.

* * *

When I opened the door at work just after three, Fogarty was leaning against a lobby chair, tapping his thigh. Along with his lab coat, he wore a smile. A big one.

I beamed back. "Hi, Tom. Having a fun day?"

He chuckled. "I received a call from Tommy Taylor. Something about a murdered woman in Roxbury. Drumming up publicity, Tally?"

I ignored him as I crossed the lobby. I really wasn't up for any more confrontations that day.

He eyeballed me tip to toe. "So you're poking around again. Yet another publicity ploy for MGAP. It's a bad misstep, Tally."

"Publicity ploy, Tom?" I longed to shake him by his lapels. "Why are you so desperate to get rid of MGAP and me? It can't just be the money that OCME gives us."

"Irrelevant." He turned to leave. "By the way, Taylor said that funeral home burned to the ground. There are no bodies. No records. No nothing to report on. He sounded angry. Arson in Roxbury isn't much of a headline grabber."

"Look, Tom—"

"Boston's own little Street Fighter," he mimicked in a nasal voice. "Taylor called you that. Your little trip to Roxbury should send Veda's blood pressure skyward."

"You wouldn't dare."

The bastard actually *winked* as he walked away.

* * *

I shook off my fury at Fogarty and my worry that he'd yap to Veda. I had bigger worries. Mrs. Cheadle, for one.

Even so, both he and Kranak sounded like they had bees up their butts. Speaking of bees, I found a bee man and we agreed to meet at Mrs. Cheadle's place. I also dug up a bunch of people to rotate with me taking care of Mrs. Cheadle's cats.

That accomplished, I bought some cat food, then headed over to Mrs. Cheadle's to meet the bee man.

Mr. Puzas, the bee man, met me on the sidewalk. He wore blue coveralls, and his black hair was pomaded to perfection. He didn't smile. Once inside the building, I explained about the cats as he donned head gear and gloves.

"Don't bees hibernate in winter?" I said.

He shook his head. "Nope. They're around. You just don't see 'em. And they don't die when they sting ya, either. That's another myth. Most people don't know bees. Don't understand 'em."

"Please remember it's a crime scene," I said, although Boston PD was nowhere to be found.

"Gotcha, ma'am. I won't touch a thing. I'll wear gloves, and the kitties'll be fine."

Sprayer in hand, he entered the apartment. Minutes later, he poked his head out. "All set. She's got screens, so I opened the windows, too."

Inside it was freezing, but thankfully bereft of live, stinging bees. Dead ones were scattered over the kitchen and living room floors, and several of Mrs. Cheadle's cats were playing kitty Ping-Pong with bee corpses. It looked like a lot of bees to me.

Why attack Mrs. Cheadle? I still wasn't getting it.

"If the bees arrived with the flowers," I said to

Puzas. "How would someone pull that off?"

He hooked his gloves on his belt, then walked over to the floral bouquet resting on a side table in the living room. He eyeballed it. Then he parted the flowers and peered downward. Next he got out his flashlight, which he beamed into the vase.

He finally leaned down and smelled a rose. "This guy was smart." He pointed to the green glass vase. "I'd bet that inside this vase is a second glass container."

"Let's see, shall we?" I snapped on a pair of latex gloves, laid the flowers on the table, and slid two fingers into the vase. "Oh, ho. Look." I held up a vial that reminded me of those glass rose stem holders, only fatter.

Puzas grinned. "I'm *good*. Yes I am. The bees were in there. Notice how you couldn't see the vial through the dark green glass of the vase?"

I put the vial and the flowers back. "But how does it work? How are the bees kept inside the vial, then released at the right time?"

His eyes swept across the dead bees lying on the carpet. "I read about somethin' like this once. You put candy in, that's what you do. Some kinda sweet, like a Jolly Rancher, as a stopper. Then the bees, who eat sugar, eat though the candy and escape. The flowers coulda been here for hours before the bees ate through and escaped to sting your pal. The timing would take some practice. Pretty damned cool, if you ask me."

If Mrs. Cheadle wasn't fighting for her life, I'd think it was cool, too. It *was* clever. Horribly so.

I thanked Mr. Puzas and paid him.

"I'm a student of bee lore," he said on his way out.

"Bet you guessed that. Your friend's lucky, by the by. Half the people who are allergic and get stung don't make it."

When I reentered her apartment after walking Mr. Puzas out, the cats flocked around me, rubbing my legs and purring. I dished out the food I'd brought. I refreshed their water bowls, took care of the litter box, and washed up. Then I snapped on the latex gloves again and searched the kitchen. I found nothing.

In the living room, an overturned bowl of soup and a juice can lay on the floor bedside her overturned TV tray. My eyes burned with tears. Damn him.

Since Boston PD wasn't interested, I emptied the water from the vase into a baggie, then dropped it, the vase, the flowers, the bee vial, and some bees into a shopping bag, intending to deliver it to Billy at the crime lab. Normally, I'd give it to Kranak. But he wasn't acting normal. Not even a little.

I hated feeling like we were playing on different teams.

I searched the living room. Nada.

Where was the journal she'd mentioned starting?

I opened the trunk that served as her coffee table and thumbed through her scrapbooks. The pages of her life. I squeezed the bridge of my nose, trying to release the awful pressure. Let her be okay, I prayed.

I came up empty in the bathroom and the bedroom, except for a throng of cats that accompanied my explorations. I checked the closets. No luck.

Hell.

I *knew* Mrs. Cheadle hid things. Where? The apartment wasn't that big. Maybe her attacker had found what he'd wanted.

I pictured him slithering around, rifling her stuff, being neat and oh-so-tidy. Like Blessing in my apartment? Or like McArdle? Or someone else entirely?

He'd worn gloves, I was sure. I was also sure he knew that if an errant hair or fiber attached itself to something in the apartment, it would matter little. Forensics wouldn't scour the place. Look what Kranak's reaction had been.

My adversary—I'd come to think of him in those terms—was clever and intelligent. I sat back on my heels. But Mrs. Cheadle was no dumb bunny, either.

I trotted back through the apartment.

The scrapbooks. This time, I took them all out. I carefully fanned each book's pages. Maybe . . .

Midway through the third book, I discovered a letter from Chesa. I slapped on a Post-it, paged through the rest of the book, then went on to the other scrapbooks.

I found more Chesa letters and the diary pages Mrs. Cheadle had begun.

Yes! Thank you, Mrs. Cheadle.

Penny and I were halfway up the town house steps when I jerked my head around.

Jake had replaced the light, but it was a weak, pallid thing against the ink-black of the empty street. Clouds hid the sliver of moon. The cars parked curbside would make a perfect hiding place. So would any of the alcoves or doorways.

Creepy night sounds amplified. I was sweating. I gripped the heavy shopping bag in one hand and clamped the remaining albums awkwardly beneath each arm. Someone had been inside my home two nights ago. Just two nights.

I chewed my lip. I didn't want to put the scrapbooks or the bag down. I'd already gotten out my keys. But even with Penny beside me, I felt vulnerable. Timid, even.

"Tally!"

I whirled, teetered, then fell on my bum. Hard.

"Tally, it's Reen."

The bubble of euphoria made me dizzy. "Well, Goddamnit, help me up."

I changed into sweats, then Reen and I drove to McDonald's. On the way, I filled her in about events, including Elizabeth Flynn.

"Your case, yes?" I said.

One eyebrow shot up. "An old case. A terrible one."

"Tell me what you remember."

She closed her eyes. "Too much." A pause, then, "A Monday—hot, humid—in August. A kid taking a shortcut to his friend's house stumbled over Flynn's remains. I remember the smell, being out in that field with her. Even in the open, the air was close, thick. It stuck to us all.

"Flynn lived in Harvard. Each morning, Flynn worked out at a health club named Orchard Hills in Lancaster, then headed off to her job at the Apple Valley Nursing Home in Ayer. Both towns are within five miles of Harvard."

"McArdle had a second funeral home there," I said.

"Flynn was last seen at the health club on a Saturday morning. The kid stumbled on her three weeks later. She'd been kept somewhere else all that time.

"Flynn was twenty-seven, a health nut, a vegetarian. She'd been in extraordinary shape. People called her beautiful. Two witnesses saw Flynn leave the club that morning with an unidentified person in navy sweats. One witness claimed Elizabeth's arm was slung over the guy's shoulder. She heard them laughing, she said."

"Was the man ever identified?" I asked.

Reen stroked the tattoo beneath her eye. "No. Flynn was found nude and dismembered, torso slashed open, breasts removed, body parts scattered in a small area. We never found her purse or clothes or gym things. She was full of Valium.

"All evidence pointed to asphyxiation by ligature as the mechanism of death, and then she'd been cut apart and dumped. Hunks of her flesh were missing, especially from her torso and face. All animal bites. I can still see her face.

"Maggots had eaten out her eyes."

A whimper.

I looked up. The McDonald's guy handing us our meals had turned pasty white. His outstretched hand shook.

I took the meals from him. "It's just a movie."

His Adam's apple bobbed. "Oh," he mouthed, giving me a tremulous smile. "Really? You guys going to do tryouts or something?"

"Not yet," I said. "But when we do, we'll be sure to get in touch."

*   *   *

"Why hack Elizabeth up?" I said on the drive back to the apartment. "Think about it, Reen. Why not bury her or toss her in some deep lake or quarry pool? The killer wanted her remains found."

"To crow about his handiwork," Reen said.

"Sure. Or maybe he thought animals would eat all the remains."

"For the past two years in Massachusetts, no one has repeated the style of Flynn's homicide. Some of my colleagues believe her killer has left the state."

"Was her killing assessed as impersonal or personal?"

"Impersonal," Reen said as we parked. "Killers who intimately know their victims don't tend to chainsaw their bodies and spread them around fields."

"True, unless they're wacko. A serial killer? Except there's no serial. Which brings us back to the McArdle Funeral Home."

We climbed the steps to the apartment. "You remember all of this very vividly."

"It was unforgettable."

"What about the missing father?"

"He was off on some sailing trip. He could not be reached."

"Did you meet the uncle?"

"No. When the state police tried to interview him, he'd already left for parts east. Saudi Arabia, I think."

"Maybe Mrs. Cheadle's scrapbooks will enlighten us."

Thirty minutes later, we'd culled all the letters and diary entries from Mrs. Cheadle's dozen scrapbooks, and they lay stacked on the breakfast bar where we'd been working. I handed Penny a fry, the last from our McDonald's dinner.

"Feeding Miss Penny fries is not a good thing," Reen said.

"I only do it occasionally," I lied. "How are the birdies?"

Reen fixed us drinks. She handed me a tumbler of bourbon. "Fine. My new one, Bubba, might be pregnant."

"You'll be a grandma."

She punched my shoulder. "I was surprised to find letters from Della Charles."

"I know. Mrs. Cheadle led me to believe she didn't keep in touch. We've got dozens here."

"An old woman's poor memory or something else?"

"You're too suspicious. Let's read."

It was hard, the reading. Della and Chesa were dead, Mrs. Cheadle in a coma. Hearing their thoughts, their worries, their dreams brought them pulsing to life.

It was as if they sat beside us, peering over our shoulders. Chesa was beside me the whole time, giving me plenty of sass.

"Did you note Della's enthusiasm about meeting this Shelley?" Reen said.

"Yes. She calls him Shel."

She stroked her tattoo. "So, she met a man approximately one week before her death. A 'special' man. Perhaps Blessing using a false name?"

"Blessing would be the last person to carefully draw a woman in. He's more the sledgehammer type. This Shel is obviously charming. It doesn't mean he killed her."

"Correct."

"Whoever this Shelley was, he appears to have offered Della something no one else did—safety, security, respect."

I handed her Mrs. Cheadle's diary pages. "I'm going to call the hospital."

Mrs. Cheadle's condition remained critical. They feared pneumonia.

I sagged in the chair. Penny rested her head on my lap and I stroked her nose. Frustration felt like my Siamese twin.

Reen held up a finger. "Come look at this, Tally, from Mrs. Cheadle's diary."

I followed her delicate finger across the lines of fountain-pen script.

He'd know I'd been there, Mr. McArdle, but I expected I'd tell him anyways. My Della was still lovely in death. At peace, somehow. I'd swear her eyes followed me when I turned to leave. I fetched a blanket from upstairs and covered her.

"Her eyes." I reread it. "Della still had her eyes when Mrs. Cheadle found her in the embalming room."

"Yes," she said. "Perhaps McArdle took her eyes, which would be why he didn't want Mrs. Cheadle talking. Disturbing that the same McArdle handled Elizabeth Flynn and Moira Blessing's services, but no others."

I told her what Harry Pisarro speculated about his daughter's eyes.

"Selling eyes is a stretch." Reen slapped me on the back. "You know, I see this McArdle person with Roland Blessing in some fashion."

"You think the two of them killed Chesa?"

She nodded. "They had means. Opportunity. Motive? Maybe she learned something significant about her sister's death. Didn't you tell me that McArdle lied about Della Charles's attending physician?"

"Yes," I said. "There is cutting and missing eyes and Moira's missing hands, Reen. But I'll never believe Blessing had a part in killing his daughter."

"You could be wrong about that."

"This is crazy. We're talking about funeral directors killing people and taking their eyes and cutting them up."

"Crazy are we? Let me bring all of these loose threads to my people. Perhaps we can weave something whole out of them. Step back, Tally. It's time."

That night, I surfed the Web for body organs. I was amazed by what I found.

Many sites were spawned by urban myths and paranoid people. But I found a legit piece about a guy in L.A. who'd been arrested for running an illegal organ harvesting route outside the United States. I found several articles on the L.A. Coroner's Office, which got into hot water for illegally selling corpses' corneas.

And several years earlier, someone at the Philadelphia ME's office had earned headlines for plucking brains from bodies and giving them to the University of Pennsylvania med school. The worst were the dozens of articles detailing the poor in nations like Egypt and Pakistan who sold their own vital organs—kidneys, lungs, and corneas. A perfectly legal practice.

I found no substantiated article about the harvesting or sale of body organs in the United States.

That didn't mean it didn't exist.

I called Jake, hoping for some company. When his machine came on, I left a message for him to call.

He didn't.

Chapter Nineteen

The rest of the week I raced around—fund-raisers, work, errands, more work. The budget frenzy, with Fogarty at the heart, was heating up. By Saturday, I was wiped.

That morning, as I washed my face, my hands slowed, then stopped. Plum semicircles smudged beneath my bloodshot eyes. I'd swear I'd lost ten pounds and the skin sagged from my bony face. My curly hair was limp, my lips chapped.

"Wuff!"

I peered down at Penny, who held her leash in her mouth.

"You don't care how I look, do you, girl?"

Her paws did a little dance.

"Okay. We'll go in a sec."

I smeared on moisturizer, a brush of blush, and peach lipstick. Before Penny and I headed out, I took a final peek in the mirror. I still looked like shit.

Although the maples and oaks were skeletons and the browned grass crunched beneath my sneakered feet, the air that morning promised spring. After Penny frolicked, searching out her dumpsite with care, I drove to the Grief Shop.

I needed to talk to someone with more wisdom than I possessed.

Veda was on the phone when I entered her office. I pecked her cheek, poured myself some coffee, and took the seat across from her.

When she hung up, she held up the morning's *Herald*. "You would think they'd get a fresh picture of you."

Taylor had printed the story about the fire after all. "What can I say? Believe me, I didn't intend to become the *Herald*'s poster girl again."

"Tom's feathers are ruffled."

I grinned. "Thank heavens for small favors."

"Have you been eating right? You look—"

"Like hell? I've scheduled the face lift for next week. Can we talk about stuff?"

I told her what Reen and I had discussed. "How does it feel to you?"

Veda shrugged. "I remember a case out in Idaho back in the early sixties. A man who got his jollies cutting up people. Each and every one had had polio. He had been denied admission to med school because *he* had polio. Needless to say, this was long before the Americans with Disabilities Act. When the police caught up with him, he said he was killing and autopsying folks to find a cure for the disease."

I took a pull of coffee. "Horrible and sad, especially since polio was pretty much eradicated in the United States by the late fifties. When I came in this morning, I checked—Moira's eyes were gone, too. Strabo attributed it to maggots. Like with Elizabeth Flynn. He's seldom wrong, but . . . maybe the same guy took them."

Her black eyebrows crashed together. "Imagine the equipment needed. And the skill and manpower necessary to harvest eyes. To keep them germ-free and viable. Not to mention the transportation issues."

"I know."

She walked around her desk and took both of my hands. "Special Agent Maekawa spoke with me this morning. I'm disturbed. I had no idea your involvement was so deep in searching for your friend's killer. And that's why you either must give up this hunt of yours or take a leave of absence from MGAP."

"Pardon?"

She squeezed my hands. "You heard me correctly. Your safety. I'm so worried."

"Well, of course I'm not taking a leave."

Pain filled Veda's eyes. "If you want OCME's funds for MGAP, you will."

I choked on my anger. "This isn't like you, Vede. Threatening me. My program. Just so I'll stop searching for answers about a friend's death. You haven't the right."

"I love you. That's my right. But this is professional. You're disabling your program by this obsession." She looked away. "Don't fight me on this."

I jumped to my feet. "Of course I'll fight you."

"Then you must weigh your options, Tally. Either you leave off your investigation or you leave MGAP until this is over. Make the correct choice."

*   *   *

I threw up in the bathroom, my head pulsing, then beelined it for my office. I downed some migraine pills, then pored over budget sheets. Even with grants, we *had* to have the OCME's money, access, and space. I sighed. Gert could run MGAP.

Tough to get the words out. My throat felt thick, constricted. Hard to swallow. Impossible to *see*. I blinked fast. I felt trapped, confused. And angry. Really, angry.

I closed my office door, leaned against it, and cried. Silently. Always silently.

Maybe Veda was right. I should leave off. How could I leave MGAP?

How could I not?

I got Veda on the line. "My leave request will be in your hands within the hour."

Chapter Twenty

I sat in bed, book open on my lap. Penny was still asleep, her snout resting on my feet. She wuffled out a sigh. She liked these languorous days we were living.

During the past week and a half, I hadn't dug up more on McArdle. Or Blessing. Or learned more about Chesa or Moira or Elizabeth or Della or even Angela Pisarro. I hadn't contacted Angela's father, either. Or Dave Haywood. Or the Crime Lab.

I hadn't called Reen. And she hadn't called me.

Kranak was MIA, too.

Dottie Brylske was laid to rest and the search for Blessing intensified. At least, that's what the papers said in their two-line mention of the case.

I'd barely managed to drag myself to the hospital to see Mrs. Cheadle. I'd called each day, too, but the fact that her body had gone into some catatonic holding pattern enervated me further. The pneumonia ran rampant, and she remained in the ICU.

What did it all matter?

I knew I was in a depressed state. And I didn't give a damn.

Watery sun splashed onto the yellow comforter. Early February. Punxatawney Phil hadn't seen his shadow. Maybe this year he was right and spring was on its way.

I'd brought my "courage" stone home from work, the one my dad had carved, but I couldn't bear to touch it.

Courage my ass. I was a wreck.

I reached for my mug of coffee and took a pull.

I heard the front door opening, then a pause. Jake deactivating the alarm, then footsteps down my hall.

I turned the page of *The Fellowship of the Ring*. Comfort food for the soul.

"Yo, Tal." Jake leaned against the door frame. His jeans hung low on his hips and an oily stain formed a *U* on the hem of his white T-shirt. He ruffled Penny's fur. "She's not getting enough exercise."

"I take her for romps every day," I said.

His eyes cut to mine. "She doesn't look well."

He meant I didn't look well. "She's doing fine, Jake."

"What about class tonight?" he said, crossing his arms.

"I'm canceling it."

His right eyelid twitched. Mr. Worry Wart.

"The opening last night was fun," I said.

"Superficial chitchat used to bore you."

"So I've changed. I liked the guy's work, too."

His gray eyes darkened. "I found it forced. Mentioned it last night."

"Did you? Oops, must've missed that. Sorry."

"Dammit, Tally, all you've done is lie in this bed for a week and a—"

"I've got to finish this book, Jake. See you."

He kicked the heel of his boot against the door frame, then left.

That evening, I dragged on some clothes, then took the T over to Northeastern. I stood outside my classroom and taped the cancellation notice to the door.

"Ya kidding me."

I didn't turn. "Long time no see, Rob. What's up?"

"I'm taking your class. Remember?"

"There is no class." I stepped back so he could see the cancellation notice.

He ripped it down. "Sure there's class."

I started writing a new notice on the extra paper I'd brought. "You know that Veda pressured me into taking a leave."

His hands dived into his rumpled pants. "Nobody here's gonna know about it. I'll lay a fifty nobody brings up your leave."

I taped the new cancellation notice to the door.

The hall rang with voices. I spotted Gert and Mary and Donna and . . . Wow. John Strabo. Of all people, *they* didn't need bereavement training. "What's the deal, Rob?"

"I, uh, happened to mention your class tonight. Nobody can stand that you're not harassing them at work."

My eyes burned. "I didn't bring my class notes."

"Hundred bucks says you'll do swell. Christ, I can't believe I'm saying this."

"A hundred bucks, Rob?" I ripped down the notice. "You're on."

All nerves, I slid onto the scarred desktop, crossed my legs Indian fashion, and panned my eyes across a room of cop faces: interested ones, blank ones, bored ones, angry ones. Typical of the first night of my cop class at Northeastern University on counseling the families of homicide victims.

But not a single face said, "You screwed up, lady."

I held the eyes of each of my friends: Strabo, Donna, Mary, and Gert. Each wore a faint smile. I almost laughed when Gertie winked.

I'd sat in front of similar classes for five years. It never grew old.

I smiled, relaxed my clenched abs with a few deep breaths, and went for it.

". . . And by the end of this course, you'll have acquired some counseling techniques. More important, you'll have gained greater empathy and understanding for the victim's loved ones. You're all trained specialists with incredibly difficult jobs. But here, you'll be the bereaved. *You'll* be the ones who've lost sisters and parents and children to homicide. And you'll feel just a little bit of what the real families are feeling. It's going to be a bitch, but . . ."

Ninety minutes later, I brought what had been an utterly normal class to a close. As everyone filed out,

I hugged my friends. Kranak gave me a grin, silently mouthed, "one hundred bucks," and walked out. The man was a pisser.

Ten after nine. I sat at the desk swiftly putting the officers' completed questionnaires into alphabetical order.

I'd been an idiot to even think of canceling. I loved teaching and working with cops and—

A crunch by the doorway. Ah. Kranak couldn't wait to collect his winnings. As I turned, something cold and hard pressed against my cheek. A gun.

Oh, shit. My eyes climbed upward. "Who the—"

"Hi, Tally." Roland Blessing. Big Tom Cruise grin. And eyes filled with terror. They darted around the room, pinball fashion, then settled on me. He was panting.

I moistened my lips. "Roland. Put the gun down. C'mon."

"Can't, can't, can't."

"Sure you can." Shit. He was on something. PCP, maybe. An upper of some sort.

"They're all following me," he said. "They'll get me."

"Not if you—"

"Asian chicks were the same way. Sweet, sweet, then . . . WHAMO!"

Bile soured my mouth. "Roland. Sit down. Talk to me. Please."

"No time! Notimenotimenotime! Being followed. That little Asian hottie. Just like the other one, I escaped her." He giggled.

"You escaped, Roland?"

He shook his head. The gun trembled against my cheek. "I didn't. Not really."

"What were you looking for in my apartment?"

"Not me." He sniffled. "Don't you see? The monster, the monster. It's more games, don't you see? I'm so tired."

"I understand tired. How can I help?" Most nights I brought Penny to class. But not tonight. Tonight there wasn't going to be any class. I swallowed hard.

"Anyone ever say you look just like Laura Dern? She's one a my favorites. Blond. Long and lovely. Great smile. Better ass."

Twilight Zone time. "You're hurting me with the gun, Roland."

"Sorry." The pressure eased. Then he slid his butt onto the desk, slung an arm over my shoulder. He rubbed his stubbled face against my ear.

I shivered. Oh, Christ. I squeezed my eyes tight to stop my feverish blinking.

"I'm scared, Tally."

"Of what?"

"I killed someone."

"You're not a killer, Roland."

"I am. That landlady. Stupid. All of a sudden, she went into this *thing*. I never meant for her to die."

Was it my turn? "Dottie Brylske was an accident."

"But she's dead!"

"But not by your hand. And you didn't kill Chesa or Arlo either, did you?"

His arm snuck around my waist. "But I can now. Oh, ho. You'll see. I've finally found it. In a bottle. Remember 'Time in a Bottle?' What about 'Guts in a Bottle?' "

"What are you on, Roland?"

"The best," he said. "I feel great. And Moira. I can almost not think about Moira."

"Is that what you want? Not to think about your daughter?"

"No. But it's hard to remember now." He rested his chin on my head. "You understand. And I'm glad."

I started to push to my feet.

He slammed me down and screamed. "Stay put." Snick.

He'd cocked the hammer. "I'm right here." My fingers trembled as I groped for the purse flap, crawled beneath it, started inching inside toward the pepper spray. When I looked up, his eyes were on my hand. Tears ran down his face. "Don't you get it? Now I can be strong and powerful and all those things. Finally. Shel gave that to me. Shel knows the same pain, up close and personal. Oh, yes. It's Shel's best friend, too."

"Shel?"

"Shut up!" He pinched my nipple, twisted it, hard. I bit my cheek so I wouldn't cry out.

"I left my notebook," came a voice from the doorway.

My head snapped around, banged into the gun barrel.

Kranak stood there looking large and relaxed, as if it were an everyday thing to walk in on a crazed killer holding a gun to his friend's face.

Crowding behind him stood Gert and Donna and Mary and Strabo, their faces tight with terror.

"What the fu—" Blessing's eyes widened.

"How goes it?" Kranak said as he entered the room.

Blessing lifted the gun from my cheek to his mouth.

"No!" I cried.

The boom froze me, and then bits of warm blood and brains rained onto my head and shoulders and face.

Kranak wiped my face with one of those scratchy paper towels. He'd already made sure I was in one piece, then used his cell phone to call for backup and body-baggers.

No one else was around, which I saw as a plus.

I wasn't doing so hot. I sat shivering at the desk, staring at the red blood and gray glop dotting my hands and jeans and white turtleneck. A deflated eyeball with a blue iris lay on my ring finger. It stared up at me.

"Look, Rob, Blessing's eye."

Kranak frowned, then he retrieved a fresh paper towel from the dispenser and ran it across my hands. The glutinous smear made my stomach heave.

"You gotta go?" He started lifting me from my seat.

"No. No, I'm okay. Sort of." I pulled a handi-wipe from my purse.

Kranak took the towelette from my shaking hand and continued his ministrations. "What was the deal?"

"Blessing was a wreck. He referred to someone named Shel. In a letter to Mrs. Cheadle, Della Charles also referred to a Shel."

"Yeah, so?" Kranak said.

"I don't believe Blessing killed anyone. You shouldn't have pressed him so."

"Pressed him? What are you talking about, 'pressed him'? I walked in and the guy whacked himself."

"You terrified him."

"Christ, Tal. I'll chalk this up to you being upset." Kranak crouched down, touched my cheek with his fingertips. "Come on. You're all wiggy about this guy."

"I was so scared. What made you come back?"

"I forgot my notebook."

A Snoopy notebook lay on one of the desks.

I laid my head on his shoulder and laughed.

Chapter Twenty-one

I pulled myself up the town house steps, one slow step at a time.

It was midnight, though it felt like 4 A.M. after too many bourbons. Kranak and I had just spent two hours giving the police at Boston's D-4 station all the details of Roland Blessing's visit to my classroom.

Blessing's terrible death left so many questions unanswered.

I shucked my clothes and stuffed them into a garbage bag, then grabbed a bottle of cabernet and a glass. Penny slipped inside the bathroom as I closed the door. I turned on the tap, tossed in some bath salts, and surrendered to my rampant paranoia by locking the door.

Penny wuffled a sigh, and I gave her a massive hug. "Why am I still scared?"

She lapped my face.

I felt loved.

Wine in hand, I sank into the claw-footed tub. Christ. Blessing could have killed me tonight, and instead, I'd watched his brains Jackson Pollock all over me. Oh, boy.

I feared closing my eyes, but the steam and heat and soothing water made my lids droop. I fought it, knowing I'd see Blessing, but my lids closed and . . .

Daddy. In our living room filled with junk-find furniture, his precious model ship and meerschaum pipe. We walk to the porch. We're supposed to go to the movies, but we're arguing about Winsworth and visiting, and he refuses. He won't go.

Why can't we go back to Winsworth, Daddy? Why not? What are you hiding?

And I'm so mad, I won't go to the movies. No, I won't.

I stomp back inside the house, but Daddy opens the door. He says he's going to work instead, and he grins and waves a jaunty good-bye.

"Have a day, daughter!"

And I know he's only faking, that we really are going to the movies, but . . .

A shout! I run outside. Daddy's sprawled on the steps, blood frothing from his mouth and running out of his nose, his hand reaching upward. For me. Reaching.

Daddy! Daddy! Daddy!

A knock at the door.

I shrieked, sloshing cabernet over the rim. Droplets, Blessing's blood, splatter onto to the bath bubbles. Should've gone for the Chablis.

"Are you okay, Tally?"

I inhaled a sob. "I'm just fine, Jake. Thanks. Now go away."

"I'll wait."

"Don't bother." I brushed a curl from my face and felt something soft and squishy—a glob of Roland Blessing's brain.

My stomach spasmed.

"Tally?"

"Just go away, Goddamnit! Just go away!"

I dragged the curtain around the tub and turned on the shower. I rested my cheek against my knees, while the shower pounded the hell out of me.

Thursday morning I called Jake to apologize. All I got was his machine. My phone rang off the hook, given the *Globe* and *Herald* articles cheering the death of Roland Blessing and noting my unfortunate part in it. I turned off the ringers.

The horror lingered. I kept hearing Blessing's voice. I'd turn quickly, feeling a "something" behind me, see his face in the mirror instead of mine. I took four showers. Scrubbed myself raw. Obsessed on Blessing's words, and how desperate he'd seemed.

I thought about Shel, and felt even more spooked. Who was he?

The reporters out front didn't help, and I checked the door locks a dozen times.

My feelings were typical victim fallout. Knowing that didn't erase them. I could taste the fear. Just like twenty years ago, after my dad. And the paranoia. And pain.

Even so, I felt more alive than I had since leaving MGAP. I was awakening, all tingles and prickles, like the way your arm feels when you've slept on it.

Right after I hung up from trying to reach Jake for the fourth time, a bunch of CSS officers swarmed into my apartment. Half were out of their jurisdiction. Kranak's doing. They printed the place, lifted fibers, spritzed chemicals, and waved Luma lights. Billy was among them and whispered how he'd found nothing on the bees or the vial so far.

As they were leaving, Kranak said we should have a drink that evening. I said, no way was I going into a public place. We agreed to meet at his boat.

Afterward, I cleaned up the mess they'd made, then started in on the loads of laundry and dishes left undone while I'd wallowed in depression. Around three, someone buzzed the front door. I peered through the peephole. Expecting the media, I was surprised to see a delivery guy holding an immense rectangular box. Flowers.

Bees anyone?

I pressed a couple dollars into the guy's hand as I took the box.

"You all right, ma'am?" he said.

"Just peachy."

I laid the box on the redwood table, then pressed my ear to its surface. Silent as a tomb. A laugh riot, eh? I had options. I could chuck the box out back or call the bomb squad or wait for Jake, who probably wasn't speaking to me. I could even call Mr. Puzas, except I wasn't allergic to bees.

A lunch of paranoia wasn't so tasty.

I slid the white lid upward.

The scent of roses billowed into the room. My God. Dozens of blush and yellow long-stemmed roses.

A card rested on the green tissue paper. "Be safe, my dear. I think of you always. Harry Pisarro."

I nearly fainted with relief.

So how come it gave me the creeps?

That evening, I walked beside Kranak down the dock, Penny heeling by my side. The rumble of passing boats, the lap of water against the pilings, the crisp sea smells, even the sight of Old Ironsides failed to lighten my contemplative mood.

Kranak hopped onto the boat and offered me a hand down. I felt shaky, my legs rubbery as I stepped onto the teak deck. Kranak pressed numbers into a keypad, then opened the cabin door. I held the rope rail as I descended into the narrow cabin.

I was enveloped in warmth and the smell of chocolate. The place was cozy, the ceiling low, with mahogany framing brass portholes curtained in blue-ticked cotton.

He seated me at the dining booth while he brewed us cocoa. Penny sniffed around, then lay on my feet. A comforting weight.

"So how come you wanted to see me, Rob?"

"Later. Just talk, kiddo."

I stretched my legs across the booth. "Do you believe in evil, Rob?"

Silence, then, "I don't see stuff that way."

"I try not to, but I sometimes feel things."

He peered over his shoulder. "I *think* 'em."

"Dammit, Rob, you know I do, too. Last night was so weird. Blessing started talking about Laura Dern and Asian chicks and asses and hotties and—"

"You gonna do your men-as-shits riff again?"

"It was disturbing how he deconstructed women, like a lot of men do. His behavior was troubling. Strange."

"Wow, that's a news flash, Tal." Kranak placed mugs of hot chocolate on the table. He slid into the seat across from me.

"Stop being a brat." I replayed Blessing's words for the umteenth time. I felt the gun's pressure, and the cold metal that gradually warmed. Kept seeing Blessing's eyes. Desperate. Frantic. Haunted. So scared, he'd killed himself. I felt the blood . . .

"Don't go there, huh?" Kranak said quietly.

"Right. Look at this. Last night, Blessing flipped from frantic to tearful to paranoid to sexual and back again. I'll bet the lab shows he was on PCP, or something similar. A high dose. FYI, suicide is common during acute PCP intoxication."

"So who gives a fuck?"

"I do, you dirt brain!"

"Tut, tut, tut, Ms. Touchy-Feely."

"Blessing said he'd finally found some courage," I said. "That mattered. He was a guy who could not *act*." I told Kranak what I'd learned at the VA clinic.

"Who cares why he did it? With or without the PCP, he killed those women. Now he's dead. End of story."

"You haven't been listening. Roland Blessing didn't kill them. Or if he did, something evil was following him around, acting as an enabler."

"Something evil? C'mon, Tal. Evil walks on two legs."

"True. But haven't you ever felt that . . . absence of light? There's something dark and purposeful connected to the women's deaths. It's close. Like the fog that cradles your boat at night."

"Sad. Too many episodes of *Buffy the Vampire Slayer*."

I laughed. "This is a lot scarier than some TV show. What if Pisarro got to Blessing? Maybe I've been misreading this all along. Maybe Pisarro killed Chesa. Maybe he's been harvesting eyes for profit. Maybe McArdle and Blessing were his puppets."

"And maybe the tooth fairy's got a hard-on for me. Pisarro did his own kid?"

"Pisarro's grief for Angela was real. It's a stretch. But look how he connected Della and Angela's missing eyes. Next, he's pointing to some organ-selling trade."

Kranak shook his head. "Now *that's* a stretch."

I sipped the hot chocolate. "I'm trying to untangle Blessing's words. I think he caught onto Reen following him. I also think whoever killed Chesa—let's say Pisarro or McArdle—met up with Blessing. And Blessing became his patsy. And where's McArdle? A scam artist. Maybe more? He's involved with these killings."

He stroked his scar. "Blessing say that?"

"No."

"Did he even mention the guy?"

"No. Not once."

When he dropped me off, he didn't pull away until Penny and I were safe inside the apartment.

Funny thing was, I never learned why he'd wanted to meet with me.

The following morning, refreshed after a solid night's sleep, I ate a huge breakfast of bacon, eggs over easy, toast, and more bacon.

I pushed back the curtains to the French doors. A leaden sky cast gray across the wide pine boards and Oriental rug. Dammit, movie moments like that always showed gorgeous sunshine splashing in. I laughed.

I would figure a way to make Veda rip up my leave

request. I also needed to talk to the Roxbury cellist
again. But first I'd mend a fence or two with Jake.

Jake and I went to the Gardner Museum cafe for
lunch. His choice. He picked at his tuna. Starved, I'd
already devoured mine and was eyeing his. He swiped
a napkin across his bushy mustache. "You can't have
it."

"Shucks."

He batted an errant rubber plant leaf for the tenth
time. "Stupid place for plants."

"You knew this place was small. Your choice, remember?"

He tossed his napkin onto the table and walked out.

I'm a hell of a fence-mender. I signed the charge
and ran after him.

The Gardner's a trip. Completed in 1902, it's shaped
like a square, its inner courtyard lit by an immense
skylight and filled with lush greenery. Mrs. Gardner
designed her museum after a fifteenth-century Ve-
netian palace. She filled it with dramatic sarcophagi,
paintings by Rembrandt and Titian, and fabulous furniture of earlier ages. Tiny by modern museum stan-
dards, I found it magical and mysterious. If I'd
encountered a pantalooned troubadour or an armored
knight, I wouldn't feel surprised.

Now all I wanted to encounter was Jake.

Not on the second floor. On the third, I passed
through the Veronese room, and entered the Titian
room. Jake stood alone, gazing at Titian's *The Rape of
Europa.*

I walked up behind him and rested a hand on his arm. He shook it off. I pressed my forehead to the back of his neck and whispered, "I'm sorry about two nights ago. For being so rude. For yelling at you. Try and understand?"

He shook his head. "Can't."

"Yes, you can."

"Nope, I can't. You went to his boat last night, Tal."

Whoa. What conversation was *he* having? "Jake, dammit. Look at me."

He turned, his jaw rigid with anger. "You're half in love with him, Tally."

"*Kranak*?" My feelings for Kranak were complicated, for sure. But love? "What does he have to do with any of this?"

"What's wrong with *me*?" He poked at his chest.

I tried not to laugh at the primal man thing. "Nothing. You're a great guy."

"Then why won't you even look at me?" His eyes were hot now. Unnervingly so.

I punched his arm. Smiled. "Face it, Jake. You're too cool for me."

His mouth twitched into that smile that always hovered near the surface. "You're a pain in the ass, Tally Whyte, which is part of the reason I'm crazy about you." He kissed me hard and hot, his tongue probing my mouth, his hands cupping my butt.

I pulled my face away. "Forget it, Mr. Macho. Look. I like you a lot, but I damned well don't want to line up behind the last model you screwed."

"How can you be so dumb?" he said.

"*Me*? You're the one who's clueless if—"

"You listen." He abruptly released me. "I admit I've

made love to some of those women. Mostly, I haven't. It's you I care about."

And how long would that last? "Let's go home. We'll screw, get it out of our systems, and forget about it."

He laughed softly. "Damn, but you're romantic. And you've got it all wrong."

He dragged me around the museum and into a closet I didn't even know existed. He flipped the turn lock, pulled down my leggings as he kneeled and . . .

By the time I unzipped his jeans, the word *ready* inadequately described my state.

Chapter Twenty-two

The zip of Jake's fly boomed inside the darkened closet.

"I can't believe we just did it in a closet at the Gardner." I groped for my bra.

He kissed my fingers. "Nice."

Nice? So what had I expected, love talk? "Go peek. See if anybody's out there."

"Here." He handed me my bra, then cracked the door. "Not a soul."

We held hands as we ambled across the Long Gallery toward the Gothic Room, both affecting an interest-in-art look that I was anything but feeling. What had I done?

A movement to my left made me jerk. Two women sat on a bench, their heads buried in a book.

"You said 'not a soul'," I hissed.

"I didn't see them. Who cares?"

I tightened my hand in his and we continued our studied progress to the arch.

"Tally! Ms. Whyte!"

Oh, crap. I turned. "Why, Mary," I said. "Gee. Hi."

I wasn't happy. I was also unlucky. Mary and her friend did a different museum each week, and wasn't it cool that this week was the Gardner's turn?

Jake, the rat, concocted some lame excuse and vamoosed.

Mary, her friend, and I ended up back in the Gardner's eatery, sharing a cup of coffee, all because Mary was freaked by having a ringside seat at my brush with death two nights earlier. She and I made a lunch and museum date for the following Monday.

After we parted, I visited Mrs. Cheadle. The dear old gal remained in a coma. I drove over to Roxbury pissed at the world, and as I climbed the cellist's steps, I got madder and madder. Penny stood beside me while I stabbed the cellist's buzzer over and over. I wouldn't leave until I got some answers about McArdle.

Even at three, the sun was still bright in the sky. The days were lengthening. Icicles from the recent snowfall jutted like monster's-teeth on the lintel above our heads.

Footfalls, a pause, then the door opened.

"Hello, Mr. Cellist."

He scratched his goatee. "I wondered when you'd pay me a return visit."

Brown led us through rooms filled with tapestries and paintings hung from mahogany-paneled walls and massive furniture crouched on hand-loomed Persian rugs. He offered me a leather chair in a den lined floor to ceiling with books. A cozy fire crackled behind a glass-doored fireplace and delicious smells steamed from the silver coffee and tea service.

"Call me Jazz or Danny or Mr. Brown. Your pick."

Daniel Brown. Gateway Properties. McArdle's landlord. Why wasn't I surprised?

No music played, which surprised me. *Gulliver's Travels* lay open on the table.

Brown pointed to the food and drink. "Help yourself."

The coffee smelled like hazelnut, the tea, of oranges. He'd piled éclairs and fruit tarts on a porcelain platter.

I felt like the stranger come in the from the storm who was treated like an honored guest. Hadn't he been murdered at the climax?

"Thanks for the food," I said. "But—"

"Inez's pleasure." He gestured to a corner of the room. A pretty black-haired girl of maybe twenty sat tucked in the room's corner.

"It looks delicious, Inez."

Her smile swept to her brown eyes.

"I do pastries sometimes," I said.

Her eyes moved to Brown.

"Inez doesn't speak," Brown said.

The girl's face crumpled. She awkwardly rose using crutches I hadn't seen to support her. A long, Indian-patterned skirt draped her legs.

"Inez's nap time," Brown said after he'd closed the door behind her.

"She's lovely," I said. "Your daughter?"

He grinned. "Wife."

"The crutches?"

"Inez lost her feet and her voice in a car accident."

"I'm so sorry."

He laughed. "You *are* sorry, aren't you, missy? Your face tells a thousand tales. After reading about your brush with death in the paper, nice to see you in one piece."

"Thank you." The air changed. I couldn't say how, but it thickened. "When I first asked you about McArdle, why not tell me you were his landlord?"

He rubbed the book's cover with what I'd call affection. "McArdle was a friend of a sort. And I pitied him. I've never met a human being, man or woman, who despised himself more. I'll say nothing against the man." He lit a cigar, then smiled around it.

"Go on, please."

"Understand that I never knew him well. Like everyone, I saw a part of him, never the whole. Our church fathers saw him as a religious soul who seldom attended, but tithed substantially. One of those teen thugs saw him as a saint for rescuing his cat. Yet that old crone who panhandles hated him for refusing to give her a cent, or so she said. And the drug users loved him for letting them flop at the mortuary."

"Roland Blessing, the man who . . . died the other night. Did you ever see him with McArdle?"

"No."

"What about Della or Chesa? Are you sure you never saw them alive?"

He grinned, his teeth tight on the cigar. "Now there I lied to you. And I've regretted it since. That beautiful Della. Whole bunch of people were hanging out over there, spaced out. She was one of them." He shrugged. "McArdle was cowering in that office of his. I took him home with me."

I lowered my voice. "Someone saw you out on the town with Della one night."

His eyes traveled to Inez's portrait. His yearning was palpable. "I slept with her."

"Was McArdle angry?"

"He didn't care."

The way he tucked his hands—he was lying. "Where could McArdle be hiding?"

Something crashed upstairs.

Brown made for the door. "I have no idea where Mr. McArdle is at."

Penny whined. I was tempted to follow. Had Inez fallen? Had a panic attack? A fit of some sort?

What I didn't expect was Brown to breeze back into the room wearing a smile and carrying a bottle. "Port," he said. "Excellent vintage."

"Inez is . . . ?"

"Resting, of course." He handed me a dainty glass filled with the dark liquid.

I sipped. Outstanding. "What did Inez think of McArdle?"

He looked away.

"She didn't like him, did she?"

"He helped Inez when others shunned her. You see?"

What I'd seen was a woman who'd been profoundly damaged far beyond the loss of her feet and her speech. "Has she gotten some professional help?"

"We've tried. Nothing." He sagged, and I caught a snapshot of a man defeated.

"The mortuary fire. You must have lost a great deal."

"I was insured. I lost very little." He tipped the glass of port to his lips. "McArdle was the loser there."

"How do you think Della died?" I asked.

"No idea. None. But drugs would be a good guess. She loved that H." He poked the fire to a blaze. "Time to go, Missy. Best not come back."

At the front door, I laid a hand on his arm. "What's bothering you about what he did with Della's body, Jazz?"

"Nothing I can say for sure."

"Then guess. Speculate."

"Why tell you?"

"Because I'm asking. It matters."

His face tightened with anger. "There was talk. That was all."

"Dammit, Jazz. Stop playing me like one of you instruments."

"All right!" he barked. "Some people around here. . . . They're into Vodoun. They'd talk about eyes. Empty eyes, like McArdle's. Missing eyes, like Della's. Oh, yes, I knew about that. A lot of people got scared. Wanted me to turn McArdle out."

"But you didn't. Because he threatened to tell Inez you'd slept with Della?"

"Wrong! I wouldn't because . . . because he scared me, too." He snapped the door closed.

Chapter Twenty-three

I made for the truck. McArdle was far more complex than I'd imagined. That a man like Jazz Brown could be scared of him was shocking.

Penny walked beside me, and I half hoped I'd spot

Julius Binny or the old woman in the pink coat. My nose got sniffly from the chill.

I'd been at Brown's a long time. The fading light matched my gloomy thoughts about Inez and her husband. I heard Veda's voice, nagging me for lugging around other people's sorrows. I missed her. We hadn't spoken since she'd forced me to take a leave.

Maybe Jake would be waiting when I got home.

I was drawn to the collapsed wreck that had once been the McArdle Funeral Home. Penny and I stood before the burnt-out shell. Crime scene tape ran across the yawning maw that had been McArdle's. Only the rear wall of funeral home stood.

I pressed against the police tape, peering into the rank, rubble-filled hole. I could make out the embalming table and a sink, but little else.

Where are you, McArdle? What have you done? *Who* are you? The breeze stung my face, and I turned to go.

Penny whined. Suddenly, she scooted beneath the crime scene tape.

"Penny, come!"

She jogged toward the back of the building.

"Dammit!" I followed, walking the narrow perimeter that skirted the hole. Even minus a leg, Penny was swifter than I. She loped ahead of me, and vanished behind the rear wall.

"Penny, dammit! Get back here."

I heard her yip, then she suddenly reappeared, did a little dance, then bounded behind the wall again. "What the hell?"

I hugged the house to my left. To my right yawned the maw of black, with its deadly spikes of timber and glass.

I rounded the corner and there she was, circling a patch-sized dead vegetable garden. Around and around she went in a dizzying spiral, whining the whole time.

"Penny, come!"

She bounded to me. Whined. Pranced. Then shot back to the same patch of earth. She urinated, then begin to dig, except the ground was frozen and . . .

Oh, *hell*. Penny—the Canine Corps star—trained to detect human scent. *Dead* human scent.

Della Charles.

I called Kranak on my cell, then waited as night oozed into each corner and crevice, cloaking me in darkness. I stamped my gradually numbing feet and tried not to think of eyeless corpses and bogeymen and Vodoun.

It was useless talking to Penny. She acted like she'd been planted there.

The breeze became a wind that barreled between buildings. The chain-link fence behind me rattled. Stuff inside the McArdle sarcophagi flapped and groaned.

What was that? A shadow? A man standing, watching, stepping toward me and . . . gone. Nothing. Nothing. Just a cat. Sure.

Just an alley cat.

Wailing sirens and screeching tires shattered the night, and lights, like frantic apparitions, strobed hunks of buildings, cars, people huddled before a bus stop. I saw it all through the skeletal window in the wall that offered my view to the world.

My brain burst from its coma.

Of course the "something" beneath that garden wasn't Della Charles. Not unless someone had planted dead vegetables in the frozen ground atop her grave.

Then again, a "something" was there. A something that made Kranak apparently call in several branches of law enforcement and maybe the Army Reserve.

Vehicle noises amped up and heavy-duty lights beamed onto the site. People barked words, and someone hollered, "You okay, Ms. Whyte?"

"Just peachy," I shouted back. "Careful coming around."

Pounding footsteps, then uniformed cops and black-garbed ones and plainclothes detectives poured into the rectangular area behind the funeral home. They stopped short of where I stood, and Kranak pushed his way through the crowd.

"What's with all these troops?" I asked through shivering teeth.

"You're freezing," Kranak said. "Come on. Let's go."

"What's the deal, Rob?"

A photographer kneeled and shot Penny from different angles, then said, "That should do it." He was followed by a tall woman dressed in a black Canine Corps uniform. The state trooper was attached to a golden retriever who started whining and digging, just as Penny had.

"Sar?" I said, recognizing Lieutenant Sarah Benjamin of the Massachusetts State Police.

"Hi, Tal," Benjamin said. "Leave it to Penny to find a buried corpse in winter."

On that note, Kranak hauled Penny and me out of there.

*   *   *

We wove through people setting up lights, unrolling more crime scene tape, and barking incomprehensible words into walkie-talkies.

It felt like I'd stumbled onto a weird movie lot.

Dozens of people and reporters clustered on the street, trying to get closer. We passed Strabo, who patted my shoulder, and several CSS forensics people waved.

Although I peered around, I saw neither Danny Brown nor Julius Binny. Then my eye snagged on a petite form wearing a jacket lettered with "FBI." Reen.

What was she doing there?

Back at the office, I gave Kranak my detailed report of how I'd ended up in McArdle's veggie garden. All the while, I kept chewing on why so much manpower had hauled ass to the site.

"How come you're taking my statement and not Boston PD? Huh?"

He ignored me, and took yet another in the parade of phone calls that had interrupted us.

I got some kibbles from my office and fed Penny. Someone arrived with sandwiches, and Kranak and I ate in silence. Then I finished my recitation.

"That'll do it." Kranak flipped off the tape machine. "You okay to drive home?"

"Of course." I raked a hand through my curls. "Why are you telling me nothing?"

He didn't answer.

"*Excuse me*, but how come McArdle's looked like the D-Day assault?"

"How about you let it go, Tal."

I smiled. "Happy to. Even though I've been investigating Chesa's and Arlo's deaths for weeks and had Blessing's gun to my face and watched Mrs. Cheadle in intensive care, I'd be happy to leave it in your competent hands."

"Finally you're talking sense."

"Are you *nuts*? Leave it? I left MGAP for it!"

"Christ. I'll get some coffee. With bourbon."

He returned minutes later with a bottle of Old Grandad. "I bagged the coffee."

It would be worse than I'd imagined.

Kranak took a pull of bourbon, then another. "They found a body. No ID yet. Nude. A mummy, for Christ's sake. A woman."

A body. Some once-living person, hidden for how long? A family, unable to mourn their dead for what, months, years? Renewed grief when the body was identified. I belted back more of good ol' Grandad.

"Cut it out," Kranak said. "You can't take on all that woe."

"I . . . You know I get the blues. Continue."

"Fogarty did the post. His take is that she's been dead about a year, maybe more. Somewhere in age between twenty-five and thirty. Brown hair. No legs. Chain-sawed off, probably to fit into the box."

"Christ. I told you about Elizabeth Flynn. She was—"

"I know. The way I see it, McArdle starts chopping up Mummy Lady. But something happens. He's disturbed at his work, gets bored, whatever, and he's got to get rid of her quick. So he sticks her in the box."

"What kind of box?"

"An old wooden crate. Penny's got one hell of a nose. Canine Corps brought three dogs. Only that golden with Benjamin caught the scent. We might be able to do a match of the saw marks between Mummy Lady and the Flynn woman."

"That's something. The woman's eyes?"

"Gone. Fogarty thinks maybe surgically. Tough to be a hundred-percent sure at this late date."

"You've no idea who she is."

"Nope. We're looking for the usual open cases, disappearances, stuff like that."

"Anything else?"

"Fogarty's still dicking around, but it'll be the lab that gives us most of the info on this one."

"Cause of death?"

"Not readily apparent." He scratched his temple. "My first mummy. I didn't like it much. Makes my skin crawl, even after all I've seen. But it's like she'd been preserved in that crate as a . . . you know, like how the Egyptians buried their dead. Like, maybe, he was saving her for something. There was a Bible in there with her, a Gideon's, and her head was resting on a foam pillow, if you can believe it."

"I'm sure you can do something with the pillow or bible. You're a wizard at that stuff." I sat on the end of his desk, arms crossed. "Okay, Rob. What's really going on? Ever since Chesa's homicide, everyone's been doing a dance about Roland Blessing. Except now there's another homicide tied to McArdle's place."

"No homicide yet. Just a body. She could have died from natural causes."

"Oh, come on. How come I don't hear you saying, gee, maybe Blessing didn't kill Chesa and Arlo? Maybe he was set up. But, why? Two and two aren't making four."

"Not for us, either."

"Who's *us*, dammit?"

He pushed away from his desk. "You're not going to like this."

"It's a little late for that, isn't it?"

"We've been on this McArdle guy for a couple weeks—Maekawa, me, some other people. Maekawa's been keeping an eye on you and searching about a million databases for any info on him, funeral home scams, stuff like that. I've been poking my nose all over the place. Others have been checking out the Flynn and Pisarro homicides."

"How is Angela Pisarro connected to McArdle?"

"He assisted the Williams Funeral Home in the collection of her remains."

"I didn't know. But her eyes were—"

"Taken before he got a hold of her. It's complicated, Tally. Like this ball of twine we're trying to untangle."

I was steaming. "And what have you found?"

His thumb and index finger made a zero. "Nothing. The harvested organ thing is looking good. Pisarro's no dummy."

"And?" My eyes narrowed as Kranak squirmed in his seat. "Or maybe you don't want share with me, eh Rob?"

"Blessing was involved with McArdle. We're not sure how. We think Blessing met McArdle when the latter handled Moira Blessing's funeral. The bottom line here is we got people selling eyes, maybe other organs, too. 'McArdle' is a fake, naturally. Whoever he is, he's involved with a bunch of other people, including Harry Pisarro. But given mummy woman downstairs, I'm expecting a whole lot more firepower will be added to this thing."

"So who is Shel? Both Della and Blessing referred to someone named Shel."

"Never heard of him except from you."

"Interesting" was all I said. Kranak wouldn't want to listen to any of my crazy notions. But he sure wasn't hearing the same song as me.

"What's with the funny face? You connecting with your inner detective?"

"Har har," I said. "My leave was awfully *convenient*, wasn't it?

"What tipped you off about how Veda faked sacking you?"

I averted my eyes. My hands shook I was so livid. If Kranak hadn't blurted it out, I never would have guessed my leave was a setup.

"Tal?" Rob lurched out of his chair. "I'm . . . Shit. You hadn't guessed, had you?"

"Who gave Veda the order?"

He swiped his hand across his face. "People."

"Someone pretty high up to squeeze Veda. Or was it her idea from the get-go?"

Kranak shrugged.

"I want to hear the whole pathetic tale. Now."

Chapter Twenty-four

I clocked it to Veda's house in Lincoln in twenty-seven minutes. Maybe a state record. If I'd run some lights, I would've made it in twenty, but I hadn't the guts.

I pounded on the door, hollered, not giving a damn whom I woke up. Then I remembered my key. I unlatched the lock just as Veda was swinging open the door.

"I can't believe what you did to me!" I hollered.

Veda pulled me inside and gave me a ferocious hug.

"I'm gonna barf," I said.

"Later." She tightened the sash on her bathrobe. "After you've had some food."

"I don't *want* any food," I protested as she dragged me into the living room. "My dear friend Kranak's feeding me bullshit. Reen's involved, too. And so are you. Goddamnit, Vede. You're the one that hurts the most."

"Of course you want food."

My mouth flapped again, but by then she'd vanished into the kitchen. Penny disappeared, too, in search of her beloved Burt—Veda's highly masculine cat. Go figure.

I slumped on the ancient chintz couch and lifted the lid on Veda's not-so-secret cigarette stash.

"Don't you dare," echoed Veda's voice from afar.

I lit it with her crystal lighter, a petty revenge that felt great. I put my feet up on the cocktail table, right by the cluster of frigging Hummels that I loathed. Another teensy piece of revenge. I was getting into this.

I inhaled smoke, coughed, inhaled again. Just like riding a bicycle.

Veda bustled in, her tiny body dwarfed by an immense tray that held huevos rancheros, blue corn chips, salsa, and guacamole, a special favorite. Plus a Diet Coke and a steaming carafe of coffee. Like I would forgive her because of some great food.

She set plates, napkins, and cutlery on the table. "Feet off the table, young lady!"

I jumped. Childhood dies hard. "With all that food, Kranak must have alerted you." It came out as a growl.

She nodded.

"He sneaked out on me, the bastard, before I got a full explanation."

"He said you knew about the charade in my office."

I mounded guacamole on my plate. "It didn't feel much like a charade to me."

"As intended."

I stomped off and chucked kindling and newspaper atop the logs resting in the cavernous fireplace. I lit the thing. Ah, the satisfaction of a ferocious blaze.

I slid back onto the sofa and downed a huge forkful of huevos rancheros.

"Ah, so we're eating again," Veda said. "These past weeks, you could have starved to death."

"You've been talking to Jake behind my back."

"Of course."

"Traitor."

"Who?" she asked. "Jake or me?"

"Both of you. So I wasn't hungry for a while. Big whoop."

Veda's eyes clouded with pain. "I know about the depression. The days and days you spent in bed. I haven't seen you like that for twenty years. Not since your father's homicide."

I wiped my mouth with the soft linen. "I've been dying, Vede. How could you separate me from MGAP. You know what it means to me."

"How could I not?"

Her hand, blue veined and liver spotted, knuckles like knobs, covered mine. She cried, silently. Veda never cried, except at movies and birthdays.

"Oh, Vede, don't." I ran around the table and kneeled, hugging her tight. "I'm okay now. Promise. I bet I've gained two pounds in the past two days."

"You wouldn't even talk to me. Never before had you done that."

"I was so hurt. And angry. I was a mess." I chuckled. "I'm still a mess. Just not as big a one as I was a couple days ago."

She dabbed her eyes with a corner of her robe. "I see. All it takes is a near-death experience with a killer. I must remember that."

I kissed her papery cheek, then returned to the couch and mounded my plate with food. "I haven't forgiven you. I'm still angry."

Her eyes searched mine.

It was a moment, as our eyes, our bodies, our hearts shot love back and forth. It held all of the memories of my father's death, my salvation through Veda, and the years she nurtured and supported me. It was the time my boyfriend left me for a cheerleader, and when I'd nursed her, after she'd broken her hip.

There were many more moments: shopping and movies and the death of my dog, Pal; cooking and fights and her beaming face at my graduations; her discovery that her eldest brother had died in the Holocaust; my discovery that my beloved father was a con artist.

Big, small, they all flowed between us in that second of time. I smiled. "I love you, you know."

"And I, you. Always." She slapped her lap. "Now we can talk. Ah, the police. They've been interested since Pisarro sent you the album."

I folded my legs Indian fashion and dived for more

guacamole. "So why make me take the leave?"

"The danger with Roland Blessing. Little did I know. . . ."

"Poor Blessing. He wouldn't have harmed me."

"Or so you believe."

"Who's involved?"

"Our Boston police, the state police, the DA's office, and the FBI. Reen's a large part of it."

"So they're after McArdle."

"They have been for weeks and may have found his hideaway.

"Where?"

"I don't know." She produced a wan smile. "Are you really all right?"

"Some stinky residue, but nothing I can't handle."

"Reen and Robert worried you were in danger."

"I'm not stupid. I take precautions. It's not like I go around ready to draw my frigging forty-five."

She smiled. "You finally bought a gun?"

"*No.* It was an expression. Come on. I'm pooped. You're pooped. Bed."

I gave Penny a run while Veda tamped the fire. We climbed the stairs arm in arm.

"I'll be back on the job on Monday."

"They won't permit it, Tally."

"Sure they will. Or I'll give the *Globe* a call. The *Herald*, too."

"My dear, that's—"

"Blackmail." I grinned. "Isn't it grand?"

First thing Saturday, Gert called to say our night at Trip's had been switched to Monday. When I told her I was coming back to work, she screamed, "Yes!" I was absurdly pleased.

After we hung up, I cleaned the house. In the middle of pouring yet another can of Drano down the bathroom sink in a vain attempt to unclog it, Jake breezed in.

"How about you knock, huh?" I said.

"How about you not being such a priss?" He grinned.

I anticipated the Big Kiss. Didn't happen. I tugged my sweater lower, so it covered more of my sweats. I felt like a frump. "You here to fix the bathroom sink?"

"I'll do it next week. You're upset."

"Who says?" I put my cereal bowl in the sink. I waited for his arms to snake around my waist. Finally, I snuck a peek. Jake was crouched down petting Penny.

I flopped onto the couch, wishing for one of Veda's cigarettes. When a girl got dumped, she always looked less needy when smoking a butt.

Time to take the offensive. "Jake, screwing in the closet was cool. A first for me, although I assume you've done it before, since you knew all about that closet."

He pushed to his feet, his hands resting on his hips. "Well, I think we accomplished our mission."

His jaw bulged from his tightly clenched teeth.

"That's a straight road to TMJ," I said.

He laughed, loud and hard. "You are one ball-buster of a woman."

I flounced into the bedroom, waited a few beats for him to leave, then reemerged.

He was sprawled on the sofa, Penny beside him, the traitor.

"I assumed you'd left." I felt like an ass.

"I got us a reservation at a B&B in Bar Harbor. Up for it?"

"No thanks." That would make Jake and me a "something."

"Don't have to make love, ya know," he said.

"I thought that was the point."

"If you change your mind, call me." He gave Penny a final chin scratch and left.

I sulked, got over it as I soaked in the tub. How to sort out my feelings for Jake?

That I didn't know. But by the time I pulled the plug, I realized I'd better talk to my former professor, Dr. Barbara Beliskowitz, a forensic psychiatrist. I might be decent at analyzing people with aberrant behaviors, but Barbara was the best of the best.

"Come in. Come in," Barbara said in her deep, honeyed voice. She offered me one of her big, toothy smiles that rose all the way to her intelligent gray eyes.

As I sank into one of the huge couches in her art-filled living room, I breathed in the room's calm. It felt swell.

"It's been too long," I said. After we filled each other in on our lives, she drew out my feelings about Blessing and his suicide.

"Anger," I said. "Remorse that he's dead. Fear, of course. I haven't probed these feelings very deeply."

"That's fine. So put them in your pocket for another day."

"Will do." I sketched her the tale of Della and Chesa, Arlo and Mrs. Cheadle, and Elizabeth and Angela and Moira. "The police believe this is all about an organ-harvesting ring. That these organs are being sold for profit."

Barbara poured us more coffee. "And you?"

"I agree that organs are missing, especially eyes. The police, the FBI, they're not stupid. But they hear 'wiseguy,' and sometimes they lose perspective. They think Harry Pisarro is tied to these crimes."

"And you don't?"

"I did for a while. But now? No. Although most of the kills were organized, the killer's anger, his passion was intense. I don't get why they're missing that."

She clasped her hands. "You're linking all of the women's deaths?"

"I think they must be tied together. Both Elizabeth and Moira were hacked up in some way. It appears the mummy lady was chainsawed. The disturbing thing is the ardor, the passion. People selling eyes for profit aren't motivated by their emotions."

"I couldn't agree more. Perhaps a serial killer, you're saying to yourself."

"Yes. Might these organs have been taken as trophies?"

"Possibly, which would indicate some personal, psychotic motivation. This killer would have lost complete touch with the usual meanings people have in their lives. Think of the proportions. His degree of rage and paranoia. The idea of causality."

"Yes," I said. "Those feelings of fury and paranoia would have reached psychotic proportions. At the same time, he's disconnected from their cause."

"Of course," Barbara said. "Remember that eyes watch you."

"They do," I said. "They see into your soul."

"If he's harvesting their eyes and keeping them, he's

keeping a specific part of them, in order to have them, to hold them to him."

"Harvesting. Yes." I sat back on the sofa. I could see Blessing so clearly. The sweat, beading his forehead, dripping down his face, him tossing the coin. I felt his hand shaking as he pressed the gun to my face. I tasted bile.

"Tally?"

"Sorry, I . . . Blessing said a lot of stuff to me that night. But one thing keeps humming around my brain. He words were 'Shel knows the same pain, up close and personal.' The overriding pain in Blessing's life was his daughter's homicide."

"Ah. Perhaps this Shel, then, has also been infected by the pain of homicide."

"Yes! That's how I interpreted Blessing's words. That a loved one of this Shel's was a victim of homicide, too. This Shel could be the killer or Blessing's puppeteer."

"This is scary stuff," Barbara said.

"Tell me about it. With the power this guy seems to have over women, he could be extremely handsome?"

"Like Bundy. Sure. He was a charmer. Or, it could be some unattractive man, one who gave off very safe vibes. Be careful, Tally. I'm worried."

Barbara wasn't the only one.

Back home, I pulled out my stack of notes on the killings, along with the profile I'd begun on Blessing.

Poor Roland—all talk and the only action he was capable of was killing himself.

As I reread, I came to believe I should concentrate

on Elizabeth Flynn. Unlike Moira or Della or Chesa or the mystery mummy, Elizabeth had a living father and a former boyfriend. Unlike Angela, they weren't criminals.

Dear God, six women dead. All by the same hand?

And Arlo? Was he a victim of his own braggadocio? I was afraid so.

I found Richard Blanchette's number. Elizabeth's former boyfriend agreed to see me as long as I didn't mind a bunch of pals making plans for an upcoming ski trip.

I drove over to Blanchette's. When Elizabeth was abducted and killed, he'd been hiking in Alaska for two months. All provable. He still felt guilty about her death.

Early that June, Elizabeth had taken up with a new friend. "Her buddy," she called him. Blanchette said she was oddly secretive about her new pal. He worried it was a guy, and that Elizabeth was sweet on him.

I wondered if Elizabeth's new friend was named Shel. Blanchette didn't know.

That evening, Veda and I took in a DeNiro flick, after which I watched *Now, Voyager* on the boob tube, cried, went to bed, and dreamed of sailing with my dad on Penobscot Bay.

Back from food shopping on Sunday, I checked my messages for the umteenth time. Jake hadn't called. Reen hadn't returned my calls or my pages. But, oh, hell, Mary had phoned.

I'd forgotten about our Monday lunch. I'd have to reschedule. A knock, then Jake breezed in. "My TV's on the fritz. Thought I'd watch the Celtics down here."

"Did you now?" was all I could think of saying.

He tossed his sketch pad and pencils on the sofa, then beelined it for the kitchen.

"Look, Jake, I'm sorry about Bar Harbor."

"No biggie. It's halftime. You eat?" He began rummaging through my cabinets.

"No, but—"

"I'll make us sandwiches."

"Your can opener's on the fritz, too?"

Pans clanked and the fridge door opened. I sat, arms crossed, fuming. I'd spent too much time making love with Jake in my mind to want him in my face. I paged through his sketchbook. God, the man had talent. "Why the sketchbook?"

"Always draw during the game." He handed me a sandwich.

"You can stay if you sketch someone for me."

"Anyone dead?"

"Not that I know of." Between bites, I described McArdle.

Jake finished the sketch as the buzzer sounded on the Celtics game. It drowned out his wail, caused by a guard missing an easy layup in the final nanosecond.

Jake groused while I cleared our dirty plates. I returned with a brandy-filled glass for each of us.

"Where are your snifters?" He nuzzled my ear.

"Be happy I'm plying you with booze."

"Bad, Tal." He explored my breasts.

I was having too much fun to stop him.

"Who's the guy in the sketch?" he asked.

My mouth dried, while other parts of me moistened. "Jealous?"

He laughed.

"McArdle."

His hands ceased prowling my body. "The funeral home creep? Fuck my nose. Next time you want me to sketch a pervert, tell me *first*."

"I never used the word *pervert*."

He stormed out, and I stomped into the bedroom furious with Jake *and* myself.

Which is why I didn't notice Gladdy, at least not for a minute. I was in the middle of shucking my clothes, when I froze.

Gladdy was gone.

I blinked several times, hard. Tried to push down the well of panic.

An antique highchair stood in a corner of my bedroom. The chair was ancient, far older than I was, and held together with square-head nails and wire. In the chair sat Gladdy, the baby doll my dad had given me on my sixth birthday.

"*Gladdy*." The cliches were true—tattered, battered, and scarred—I loved Gladdy with a passion that sprang from pages and pages of childhood memories.

I walked slowly to the highchair. I reached out to touch it, but pulled my hand back. I would have Kranak print it.

But what was the point?

I knew *he'd* taken my Gladdy. He wouldn't leave prints or hairs or fibers. I inhaled a stuttered sob.

She was only a doll.

I found the golden dollar hours later. It lay in a crevice of the high chair.

Had Gladdy been taken before I'd gone to Blanchette's? I didn't think so.

Tears burned my cheeks.

She was only a doll, Goddamnit!

I shook with fear and fury. He'd gotten in through the alarm and locked doors and . . . Screw him.

I donned a pair of gloves, then lifted the Sacagawea dollar into a baggie.

The night he died, Blessing had said he was sick of games.

So was I.

Chapter Twenty-five

Monday morning, I dropped the baggied dollar on Kranak's desk. I'd noted the time and date on the bag, but knew it would still come back with Blessing's prints.

The killer's message? He'd controlled Blessing. Now he was going to control me.

My ass, he would.

When I walked through MGAP's doors, Gert, Donna, Mary—all wore big smiles. Even Andy showed animation. It felt swell. I spent the morning relishing tasks I'd done a thousand times. With two questionable deaths over the weekend, we were all busy.

"There's no way I can do lunch and a museum today," I said to Mary.

She nodded. "Sure. Maybe, um, I could come with you tonight to Trip's?"

Gert's look said she was worried Mary's delicate ego would get bruised by our raucous crowd. I worried, too. "Mary, I—"

Mary's leaf-green eyes said "please."

"We'd love you to join us." I'd make sure Shaye bagged the heavy makeup barbs.

"I'm so excited," she said. "Oops. I've got a session in five minutes." She laughed—a rare and pleasant sound. "I'm glad you're back. It's like you've never been away."

Alone for the first time that morning, I sat behind my desk and took a welcome breather from the chaos. My gaze rested on my dad's meerschaum shaped like a horse.

Dad hated fear, but he'd taught me to respect it. I'd been scared last night. Too scared. By some creep I thought of as . . . the Harvester. Yes. The name suited.

One man. One will. Killing how many women?

The name, the malevolent sense of purpose gave me the willies. I wrapped my hand around my courage stone, felt its familiar weight and perfect fit.

Like Dad, I hated fear too.

I rubbed the stone with my thumb.

I was about to go in search of Kranak, when he walked into my office juggling a torpedo-sized sub, two cans of Diet Orange Crush, and a stack of napkins. He sat on the couch and unfolded the wax paper, revealing an Italian sub oozing hot peppers. He slid half and a Diet Crush my way, then took a humongous bite.

I bit down on my half of the sandwich. Heaven. "Blessing's prints were on the dollar, right?"

He nodded. "We printed the house. We got zip."

"Did you notice the date?"

He gulped some soda. "Sure did. You should keep a cleaner house, Tal."

"It wasn't Blessing. He took my doll, Rob. Oh, forget it. Just hang onto the coin."

"Eat some more. Got it in Little Italy. You don't get better than that."

And you didn't get friends better than Kranak. I took another bite. "I forgive you, though you didn't ask. So where's your investigation at?"

His scar whitened. "Forget it."

"Won't the media glom onto it any minute?"

"The media can go fuck itself." He tossed the balled-up wrapper into the trash.

I opened a binder and showed him Jake's sketch.

He craned his neck. "He looks like a geek with a beard."

"McArdle. Jake drew it. It's dead on."

A snort. "How come, Ms. Samantha Spade, you never had da Vinci sketch the guy before?"

"It didn't occur to me. My imperfections are showing." The signs were there—the flicker in the eyes, the studied nonchalance, the cough into the napkin. Kranak was dying to get the sketch. He reached for it.

I snapped the binder shut. "Keep me in the loop."

"Fine." He grabbed for the binder.

"Too glib." I pulled it onto my lap. "Veda says you know where these organ sellers hang out. Call me when you're going in."

He laughed. "This is a *major* operation. With international shit, as well as national happening. I'll do my best. That's all I can promise."

Somehow I'd find out. "I guess that'll have to do." I gave him the sketch.

"I know you think some maniac is doing this." He rested a hand on my shoulder. "Wrong. We've got this thing locked up. We've got homeless people going into the joint, but not coming out. We've traced international couriers back to Cambridge. Now we're waiting for the payoff. Money's changed hands. The whole magilla's sewed up."

"You've got tunnel vision," I said. "He's taking trophies, Rob."

He rubbed his belly. "You give me *agita*. Blessing did those people. He's dead."

"No, he did not. He was a *mask*, Rob, for the real killer. And a victim, too."

"All psychobabble. Our little band of merry men aren't cuckoo. They're smart. Big bucks smart."

"Grrrr. Will you listen?"

"Nothing to listen to. The Pisarro kid? Her lover knocked her off, then removed her eyes 'cause he didn't want her 'seeing' anyone else. The Flynn girl? Strabo says maggots ate her eyes."

"What if the Harvester took something else?"

"Who the fuck is the Harvester?"

"The killer of six women."

He laid a hand on my shoulder. "You're connecting crimes that aren't related. Give it up, Tal. Now."

Kranak was wrong. He was all facts and figures and fingerprints. But he made me think about Strabo's take on Elizabeth's eyes. Strabo was seldom wrong, but . . .

What if John Strabo had lied or made a mistake? I reviewed Flynn's autopsy report, then waited outside the autopsy theater where Strabo was doing a post.

"Five minutes, John?" I said, after he'd exited the room.

He nodded, and I followed as he trotted upstairs to his office. He held the door for me, per usual, then flipped his lab coat back, glanced at the clock, and sat. "Go."

"What led you to believe Elizabeth Flynn's missing eyes were eaten by maggots?" I took the chair beside the desk.

"The usual signs."

"Really? You told Kranak that, yet when I reviewed your report, you skirted the issue. You're so meticulous. Why not specifically mention the maggots?"

"So I forgot to write it down. So what?"

"It's not like you."

He flapped the pockets of his lab coat. "This is ancient history, Tally."

I sighed. "Not really. It affects how Kranak relates to Elizabeth Flynn's homicide. He's not connecting it to any others."

He massaged his forehead. I was right. Strabo wasn't sure about how Elizabeth Flynn's eyes were removed. "John?"

"A couple years ago, when Sophie and I were going down the shitter. The kids thought I was this big villain, and I did, too, and . . . things got out of hand emotionally."

"I remember."

His chuckle sounded more like a gasp than a laugh. "Of course you do. You were the one I dumped it all on, weren't you?"

"It was a tough time for you, John."

He tossed his paperweight into the air, caught it. "But now Sophie and I are at least communicating. The divorce is proceeding. The kids are more accepting. I'm seeing someone new."

Maybe Mary, according to the grapevine. "So your life's more settled. Then why fudge it with Kranak?"

He smoothed a hand across his hair. "But I'm not, am I? I mean, if I'd failed to note in my report that Flynn's missing eyes *might have been* surgically removed, my ass would be on the line with Veda. Comprende?"

"Veda understands pressure."

"She'd crucify me."

"You're wrong. C'mon, John. You've got to tell it like it is."

"I stand by what I told Kranak."

I was furious as I walked back to my office. Okay, I could accuse Strabo of covering his ass, but where would that get me? Nowhere.

I should face it. The combined forces of the FBI, state police, and DA's office had lit on something concrete about the illicit sales of human organs. They were trained, bright people dealing with this. They knew things that I didn't and had resources I couldn't possibly possess.

Except they didn't see the angles that I saw. They hadn't counseled Pisarro or Blessing or Chesa. They hadn't met McArdle.

Somewhere, somehow, they'd hopped onto a different track from mine. And it was the wrong track, dammit.

More women would die. I could feel it, and it terrified me.

*   *   *

I called Elizabeth Flynn's dad, and he gave me the phone numbers in New Hampshire and Saudi Arabia for his brother-in-law, Sven Gunderson.

"When did you last speak with Mr. Gunderson?" I asked Chief Flynn.

He snorted. "That old coot? Not since before Elizabeth died. He spends most of his time in Saudi Arabia now. Last time he was back in the states, I was at sea. It's been . . . difficult for me. Since he took care of Elizabeth when I was away, well . . . I've avoided hearing about it. It's hard talking about my only child's death, you see?"

I did see, sometimes too clearly.

I called Gunderson and got his machine in both places. I left messages referencing the chief and my phone numbers.

After I hung up, I realized how many other threads I'd let drop in the previous weeks. The bees. The Binny kid. Pisarro. I grabbed my pad and made a list. A long one.

I was wrung out after my three o'clock bereavement group. I tried Reen again, and slammed the phone down when yet again I'd landed in voice mail hell.

Damn her for avoiding me. I'd get her tonight at Trip's.

I checked with Kranak, who had no ID on the mummy woman yet.

I was about to retrieve the mummy woman's autopsy report, when in walked, unannounced, the husband of a stabbing victim. I was on deck, so off I went, definitely *not* down the yellow brick road.

I got out of there at six-thirty, my list still acres long.

Mary added to our numbers that night at Trip's, and my fears were unfounded. She did fine and became big buddies with Toot's dog, Farful, by feeding him fries.

"So where's Reen?" I said.

"Don't know," Dixie said, exhaling a cloud of smoke.

Shaye lowered her voice so we all had to crowd in. "I heard that she was involved in some big whoop-de-do task force."

"Wow," Mary said.

"And?" Belle stroked her gorgeous swan neck.

"And that's it." Shaye said. "You're conspicuously quiet, Madame Tally."

"You ever miss your period?" I said.

"Every month!" Belle smiled. "It stopped early, at thirty-six. No more mood swings."

"Thus sayeth the queen of moodiness," Shaye said.

"Cute, Shaye." Belle pursed her Clara Bow lips, then burst into giggles. "True."

"Are you pregnant?" Mary asked.

I frowned. "Just curious." Hadn't Jake worn a condom in the closet? Sure he had. Except who can see in the dark?

Chapter Twenty-six

Jake was invisible when I arrived home. Ditto when Penny and I left for work the following morning. Our lovemaking in the closet felt like a dream.

I was PMS grouchy, still no period, and imagining myself pregnant, a too, too ridiculous thought.

I was still in the glooms when Billy called from the crime lab about the bees that had put Mrs. Cheadle in a coma.

"The vial and vase are generic,"he said. "Found in a million places. The lab discovered the remains of what appears to be a hard Jolly Rancher–type candy. They found the residue at the neck of the vial."

I told Billy how the bee man said a candy stopper trapped the bees in the vial until they ate through.

"Heck of a murder weapon," Billy said.

A knock on my door. "Come on in," I hollered. I glanced up. Fogarty, who took a seat across from me. Peachy.

"Go on, Billy."

"The vase was covered with fibers and dirt and detritus."

Bones had handled it. A florist, too? Perhaps. "Prints?"

"None that match anything through our APHIS database. I'm still working on the bees. Not my specialty, and I've been real busy here, Tal."

"I understand. And thanks a bunch."

The confirmation of the candy was pretty cool, but

what did I really have—a Jolly Rancher–type candy, a generic green vase, and some bees. Frustrating.

"Sorry, Tom," I said to Fogarty. "I've been trying to reach that guy all morning."

"Back at it, eh, Tally?"

"At what?" I snapped.

He pushed his glasses up on his nose. "I came for the budget."

I handed him the blue folder. "Anything else?"

"I didn't . . ." Fogarty's mouth flapped. "No. Welcome back."

He tucked the folder beneath his arm and left. No sniping. No snide remarks. No threats. What the hell was going on?

The phone rang. "Tally Whyte here."

"Her name was Patricia Boch," Kranak said. "Cute kid. A veterinarian. She—"

"Whoa. Who are you talking about, Rob?"

"The mummy."

I pulled over my pad. "Go on. Sorry to interrupt."

"Boch disappeared a year ago. Running in the woods out in Amherst last March. She did it every day. Prepping for the Marathon."

Amherst. Nowhere near Harvard or Boston or . . .

"Gotta go," Kranak said.

"Wait a minute. A veterinarian? She doesn't fit your homeless profile."

"She fell on hard times after that big splash she made. Mental problems. Lost her practice. Theory is that she was going for the comeback trail. Happens all the time. When I know more, I'll pass it to you. See ya."

"Wait!" I screeched.

"Check out that autopsy report. Ta ta."

Like I needed Kranak to be cute? I paged through the report. Nothing. Nothing. Whoa. Her torso and head were cut open in a manner consistent with an autopsy. Just as Della's had been.

Patricia Boch's liver was missing.

So now they were on to selling organs, not just eyes.

That afternoon, Veda left around two for a conference in Bangor. Around three, Fogarty peeled out of the parking lot in his red Miata.

Now was the time to search the Grief Shop's database for missing body organs.

The system was cranky and slow. Her liver. Maybe the Harvester collected more than eyes. I alerted Gert that I would be busy, possibly for several hours.

She nodded, "Sure ya will. Uh, huh."

An odd response from Gert. Then again, lots lately struck me as odd. I opened the database.

My pager vibrated.

Mount Auburn, Mrs. Cheadle's hospital.

I padded down Mount Auburn's hushed halls, then passed the ICU waiting room. Bones sat with his elbows on his knees, head in his hands, sobbing.

In joy, no doubt, that he'd saved face with his boss. Mrs. Cheadle had awakened.

I opened one of the heavy ICU doors, entered the suite, and walked to the desk. The nurse who'd called and who was present many of the times I'd visited, grinned.

She cocked her head. "Not long. She's doing great, but we've got to play it cool."

"I plan to."

I took Mrs. Cheadle's fragile hand in mine, and for

the first time in weeks received an answering squeeze. I pulled up the chair and smiled into the half-opened eyes that peered back at me—weary, but alert.

"Tally." Mrs. Cheadle's voice quivered. "Where've I been?"

"On a bit of trip." I rubbed her hand against my cheek. "I've missed you."

The tiniest of smiles. "Me, too."

Joy bubbled through me.

"Don't cry," she said.

"Who, me? Cry? I'm so happy."

"So am I."

Her eyelids drifted downward, and I waited contentedly until I was sure she slept. When I left the room, the nurse assured me that while a long recovery was in store, Mrs. Cheadle was on the mend.

Bones was a wreck, and I tried to convince him to relax a little bit. He wouldn't have any part of it. This bulldog was not leaving its bone until the bone left the hospital.

Funny about how little stuff trips people up. When I left Mount Auburn, I spotted an adorable black VW Bug parked near my truck. I love Bugs, and so I took notice when it pulled into traffic moments after I did.

I turned onto Storrow Drive. The Bug turned too, and I got chilly all over. A few minutes later, I slowed my truck to see if the Bug was still with me. Sure was. Damn.

Now I was pissed. I mean, here I was high from visiting Mrs. Cheadle. And some creep was pulling me into a puddle of paranoia.

I peeled off Storrow and drove across town, from

Clarendon to Commonwealth to where I crawled between Tremont and Washington, traffic clogged, per usual, and I looked in my mirror. The Bug was three cars behind me!

I'd had it.

I jammed on the brakes and tear-assed down the street toward the Bug.

I rapped on the Bug's window. "Hey, I'm talking ta you!" I said in my best *Taxi Driver* voice.

His window wheezed down and he smiled.

Were we kidding here? "Why the hell are you following me?"

"What'ja talking about?"

Horns honked, and cars crept around us, and drivers hollered curses.

"You've been trailing me since the hospital in Cambridge!" I said.

"Huh? I was visiting my sis over at Mount Auburn. I'm going to Chinatown. So?"

"That's a bunch of bull."

More horns, and someone hollered "Hey, Lady!"

And I looked around and . . .

What was I doing?

I hopped back into the Jeep.

What planet had I just been visiting?

By the time I hit Albany Street, I'd given myself a good lecture for acting like a totally paranoid asshole. That's when the reality of Mrs. Cheadle's recovery sank in.

She'd live. She'd be okay. A million tiny muscles in my body relaxed. I inhaled a sob, then bawled my heart out.

I sat in the parking lot at work, scraping tissues beneath my eyes. Good God, I looked like a raccoon. As I scraped harder, I exhaled a long, weary breath.

The monster had failed with Mrs. Cheadle. "Yes!"

I dabbed on some blush and left the truck, ready for battle with the Grief Shop database.

Chapter Twenty-seven

Moments later, I leaned out my office door and whispered "Gert."

She rounded the corner, her lips blowing an immense purple bubble.

I pointed to my computer. "So what's up, Gert?"

She popped the bubble, slurped up the mess. Chew, chew. "What?"

I squinted at her. "You've got something cooking, my dear Ms. Gomez."

"So?"

"So why are you pissed at me?" I fetched us two sodas from the fridge.

She flipped the top of her Dr. Pepper. "You know, I was in charge for a while around here. I was the go-to girl."

"Woman. You were. And you did a hell of a job. I apologize for acting like a jerk. You know how weird I get when somebody touches my computer."

She flopped into the chair facing my desk. "Only-child syndrome."

"I know it's stupid." I began scrolling through a list of names, summaries, and case file numbers. "This is the sort on body organs that I'd planned to do."

"Thought I'd help out."

"Er, Gert. How did you know about that?"

"I heard you talking to Sergeant Kranak."

I shook my head. "You're good at this computer stuff, aren't you?"

She chewed. "I'm good at a lot of stuff. The sort doesn't look so hot to me." She saluted, a smirk on her face, and left.

I scrolled down the list of names. Angela's flew by. So did a bunch of Jane and John Does, but no victims leaped out as unusual. I brushed aside my disappointment and pressed the print button.

The printer's familiar whine put me into the zone.

I was back at McArdle's. The Lysol smell, Della's elaborate casket, the slow and sonorous music.

I petted Della's cheek, making her earrings dance.

Della's gold earrings. They were shaped like jointed people. I'd found one.

"Holy shit!"

I raced home, then hustled to my jewelry box. Della's earring lay in a jumble of jewelry. I held it up. The gold glinted in the lamplight and the jointed legs danced.

My memory was correct. The VW Bug guy had worn its exact duplicate.

I called Kranak and told him some guy had tailed me that afternoon, and would he check out the license plate?

I also told him I'd bet the car was stolen.

After we signed off, I plopped onto the couch with a box of Triscuits and a Diet Coke. I hadn't recognized the kid. But what had I really seen that afternoon?

A guy with a dangly earring poking through ragged blond hair that sat beneath a Patriots cap. He'd worn a leather jacket and had smiled at me with a set of crappy teeth only a mother could love. He hadn't taken off his sunglasses.

Long blond hair. Lousy teeth. Patriots cap. Sunglasses. Bottom line—I hadn't seen much of the actual person.

So who was he? The Harvester? Someone working with him?

Penny whined and I gave her a Triscuit.

He'd *wanted* me to see him. Did he want me to see the earring, too? Sure he did. He was waving a red flag at me. Creepy, creepy, creepy.

I scurried around the house checking windows and doors. I rechecked the alarm system. It didn't mean squat.

I flopped back on the couch. He'd been playing games with me from the get-go. What was he telling me that I wasn't understanding?

That night, as I tried to decipher the organ printout, I felt a host of dead crowding me: Chesa, Della, Angela, Elizabeth, Moira, Arlo, and now Patricia Boch. What names didn't I know yet? What faces was I still to learn?

The Harvester was always a move ahead of me.

"Why hasn't he hurt me, girl?" Penny perked up her ears. I started punching out Jake's number, but disconnected on the second ring.

He wouldn't want to hear this. I wished Reen

wasn't treating me like I had smallpox. I could call Veda. And get her sick with worry. Dixie? What could she do?

I pushed my glasses back onto my face and lifted the printout. I was all alone in this. A faint echo of the drums, those awful drums, thrummed in my head.

Hours later, the phone bleeped just as I was reading about a poor soul who'd been eviscerated. Nothing was jelling. *Something* had to be there. It had to.

"Hello?" Crackle, crackle, hiss, spit. "Hello?" I repeated.

"Sven Gunderson calling. Hank's brother-in-law. You left a message for me?"

"Mr. Gunderson! Good to hear your voice. I've been trying to connect with you. I'm with MGAP."

"What's that?"

Background laugher. Music. I was having trouble hearing him. "Sorry about the acronym. The Massachusetts Grief Assistance Program."

"Yeah? So?"

"It's about Elizabeth's death. Remember Andy Nogler? He's part of MGAP. We're the ones who assisted you when you were at the morgue identifying Elizabeth."

Click.

"Hello? Mr. Gunderson?"

Silence, then a dial tone.

I considered dialing him back, then decided to call the chief. Except it was after eleven. Morning would have to do.

My eyes blurred when I lifted the printout. I bagged it. "Time for bed, Pens."

I showered, then tucked myself in, reassured by the

bottle of bourbon and the pepper spray on the bedside table.

It would be nice to have Jake beside me.

Was I nuts? I patted Penny. She was safe. Her love was true.

The phone rang. The clock read midnight. "Hello?"

"Ms. Whyte? Sven Gunderson again. I just had a little palaver with Hank Flynn, who says you're the real thing. I didn't want to upset him, so I didn't say a word about Elizabeth, but . . . mind telling me what's going on here, ma'am?"

I propped myself up on an elbow. "I'm looking further into Elizabeth's murder."

Silence.

"You there, Mr. Gunderson?"

"I'm . . . Yes, I'm . . . here. I didn't know. Didn't . . . Lord almighty. You mean it's true? Little Lizzie's really dead? Murdered? Oh, Lord."

Oh, Lord was right. "Forgive me, but . . . something pretty strange is going on."

A sniffle, then nose blowing. "Now that's some understatement, ma'am."

I told him about Elizabeth's homicide, about "Mr. Gunderson's" visit to the Grief Shop and MGAP, how he'd identified Elizabeth's body and arranged for her funeral service and cremation. "I wanted to ask you about the funeral home and its director."

"Ms. Whyte, I swear to the almighty God, I know nothing about any funeral home. I was never to your MGAP. I never saw Elizabeth's body. And I sure as bejesus never identified her. I don't know what's happening here, but I haven't been in the states for over three years."

We talked for another fifteen minutes. After we said good-bye, I mulled Gunderson's words.

That someone had played a charade identifying Elizabeth was obvious. Was it the Harvester, reaping what he'd already sown?

Andy Nogler. Had he suspected "Gunderson" was a fraud? His notes had stunk. In fact, they'd been downright strange. Why hadn't he raised any doubts about "Gunderson?"

If he'd spoken, would Chesa and the others be alive?

I was going to fry Andy Nogler's ass.

Chapter Twenty-eight

I awakened terrified. I wasn't alone. I felt it. Someone was watching me. *My god.* The tang of smoke. I feigned sleep, snuck a peek. Black, except for my neon alarm pulsing 5 A.M. Penny's weight. Gone. Where was she?

I pretended to move in my sleep, flopped an arm over the side, wrapped my hand around the pepper spray.

I wished I had a knife, a gun. No. No gun.

What to do? Stay there? Let him get me? Get up? What?

I lurched up, finger pressed to the nozzle. "Just don't move, you creep."

"Promise I won't."

"Goddamnit, Jake! What the frig are you doing?"

"Watching you sleep." Jake's voice was lackadaisical, annoying.

"How?" I said, flipping on the light.

He held up a Yankee Candle. "Didn't wake you. Not at first, anyway."

I corralled my hair in a scrunchie. "You've got balls."

"I needed to see you asleep."

"Why?"

He lit a cigarette and inhaled, one of those deep, satisfying inhales. A ribbon of smoke plumed toward the ceiling, adding a strangeness to his face, as if he wasn't Jake at all. I liked it. I liked the way he drew in the smoke. It compelled me. "I didn't know you smoked."

"Gotta go."

I scrambled after him. "Dammit, Jake Beal. You hold on. This is the creepiest thing you've ever done, watching me in the middle of the night."

He flicked his cigarette into my sink, where it hissed as it landed. "You're right. Didn't think of that. I've got to get to the studio."

I stomped. "It's five A.M."

"My show's in a week."

"I forgot. But spying on me . . ."

He leaned in for a kiss.

"No way," I said. "I've got yucky morning breath."

He grinned, then kneeled and lifted my T-shirt.

Oh, my.

On my way to work, I was still fuming at Jake. I mean, he was driving me nutso. Why couldn't he be normal and say, "gross, morning breath" and leave? Instead he'd . . .

Dammit all. Jake Beal was definitely doing a number on me. And I was loving every minute of it. Well, almost every minute. Which was bad, bad, bad.

At a red light, I made a quick call to the hospital. The friendly nurse said Mrs. Cheadle was still battling the pneumonia, but they hoped she'd be out of ICU in a few days.

When I drove into the parking lot, I hit a wall of people. My God, had there been some horrific accident or mass homicide? I parked, and Penny and I plowed through the crowd of snow-dusted humans wailing and weeping and wringing their hands.

"How many died?" I asked, as Gert pulled me inside and slammed the doors.

"The zoo out there's for some religious guy," Gert said. "Strabo thinks one of his followers fed him rat poison. His flock's going nuts."

I stomped the remaining snow off my boots. "So who's dealing with them?"

"We've got two people out there in the thick of it." We walked toward my office.

"Sorry. I didn't see them. I'm in a crabby mood. Any other decedents?"

"Homeless guy. Looks like he drank himself to death." She handed me the list. "There's no meeting this morning. I updated the board, too."

"Great." I ran my finger down the list's page. "I don't see Andy's name."

"He called in sick. Again." She sat with her hands pressed between her knees, madly chewing gum, eyes pasted to the inch-thick stack of printouts on my desk.

"What's this, Gertie?" I asked, lifting the printout.

Her eyes glittered. She combed her bangs with her nails—Ms. Casual.

I scanned the first page. Brenda Fitzer, missing nose. Jose Alvarez, missing fingers. I flipped pages. Mario Basch, missing teeth. Janet Atkins, missing tongue.

She was nodding, a smile splitting her lips.

"Missing body *parts*?" I said.

"Last night, well, I got to thinking. Ya know? Body organs. Body parts. Stuff missing. That Patricia Boch you're so interested in. She was missing her legs, right?"

"Yes. But Kranak thinks McArdle was interrupted as he was hacking her up."

"What if it was more than that?" she said. "Well, see. I got to wondering. What happened to her legs? Where'd they go, I mean? And I thought, hey, what if . . . I like to do 'what if.' So I did a new sort this morning, looking for missing body parts. It came back pretty good, don't you think?"

"I think you're brilliant, is what I think." She'd grown so much in the past four years. And I hadn't noticed, not enough. I grinned "I think you're way cool."

"Thanks," she chirped.

"Let me look at this—"

Splat! against my window.

"Those weirdoes are throwing vegetables!" Gert said.

Off we went to calm the Followers of the Eternal Light.

*   *   *

I think the snow, more than our efforts, calmed the Followers. It got so bad that Northeastern cancelled that evening's cop class. I put aside my lesson plan and picked up Gert's body parts printout.

An hour later, my pulse was racing. I buzzed Gert.

"She took Penny for a walk," Donna said.

I lifted my legal pad that now bore the names: Della Charles, Angela Pisarro, Elizabeth Flynn, Patricia Boch, and Moira Blessing. Each woman was missing a body part.

So were Bunny Alberti, Brenda Fitzer, Tracey Kabrizzi, and Janet Atkins.

I felt I was finally looking at the beginnings of a true list of Harvester victims.

My fingers raced as I tapped the familiar names. Then I added Bunny Alberti, nineteen, a waitress, scalped. Dead four years. Case open.

Brenda Fitzer, twenty-five, software engineer, nose missing. Fourteen months ago. Case open.

Tracey Kabrizzi, thirty, folk singer, ears lopped off. Five years ago. Case open.

Janet Atkins, twenty-two, jeweler, missing her tongue. One year. Case open.

I hadn't made it beyond *O*, but I already had cross-offs. In fact, all the men, as well as several of the women, had lost a body part during a fight or in an accident or because of spousal abuse.

I did an age sort. The victims fell between nineteen and thirty, with Elizabeth, at thirty, being the eldest. Moira was the youngest.

I'd found nine "possibles," plus Arlo and Chesa. My God.

The victims lived all over the state: Amherst, Boston, the North Shore, the Cape.

I didn't see one consistent connection between them.

Mary buzzed. "There's an old gentleman here, Tally. I'm not . . . would you?"

"On my way."

I slumped at my desk and wiped my eyes with a hunk of tissues. He was the sweetest old man. Eighty-three. He'd been brave as I'd walked him through identifying his wife of fifty-seven years. His beloved was dead because some shitty creep had assaulted her for a lousy ten bucks on her way back from her weekly bridge game.

I sighed, and laid my head on the desk. To catch my breath.

Just for a sec.

"So this is how our illustrious MGAP leader spends her time."

Who? "Reen!" I sputtered as I lifted my head. "You're here."

She glided to the coffee maker and began brewing a pot.

She wore a navy blazer, tan slacks, and a starched white shirt. She'd leashed her fall of hair into a braid. Her gum-soled Bean boots lay abandoned on the floor, while their snow melted onto the carpet. As the coffee brewed, Reen's eyes surfed the room.

"You've been avoiding me," I said.

She shrugged.

Same ol' Reen. No apologies. No guilt. Sometimes, I wished I was like that.

"I've seen *you*." Her lips tilted into one of her rare smiles.

"It sounds like a throng's been watching me—you, Blessing, maybe others."

"Blessing was unfortunate. I'd been watching, but . . . my duties. That night, I presumed a roomful of cops would keep you safe. It goes to show about assumptions."

"There's someone else after me, Reen."

Her elegant eyes widened. She set a mug of coffee in front of me. "Have some high test."

"I've missed you."

Her eyes cut away from mine. "Tell me about this follower."

I told, and she sat back in the chair, her eyes unusually still. Her only movement was her index finger stroking the tattoo beneath her eye.

After long minutes, she inhaled deeply. "Yes. I'm not surprised. Kranak. I expect he's told you some of what we've been doing lately."

"He has."

"I think we are wrong, at least in part. We appear to have found a nest of organ harvesters. Or something. But I think these are two very different cases. Perhaps your speculations about body parts as trophies has validity."

I was giddy. If Reen believed, I'd found a real ally. Others in law enforcement would search databases, do interviews, track leads.

"I have all of this data, Reen. Gert did this incredible sort and it's all here." I collected the pad, the sketch of Chesa and Della, the printout. What was I forgetting?

She held up a hand. "I may believe you, but convincing my superiors won't be easy."

"But . . ."

She shook her head. "Patience, Tally."

"Patience? I have none left. More people could die!"

"From everything you've said, this person is not cycling more frequent kills."

"The Harvester could have killed someone last week!"

She shook her head. "But it's unlikely."

"Can't you just . . ." I hugged my waist. "I don't know. Give them all the stuff and then, after your big hoo-ha, you'll be all set."

She walked around the desk. "Try to understand. After we've smoked out the nest, the special agent heading up our operation will realize that the cases are not completely intertwined. She'll be receptive at that time. It's politically wise. You see?"

"What if I go to the DA?"

"But what do you really have? Many theories, but little evidence that's concrete."

"I have nine names, Reen."

"And that's all they are—names. You know little about their individual cases. I expect the DA, who's fully involved in our operation, will see you as a pest."

I tried to see it from Reen's point of view. "I'll wait for you, then. And I pray that no one else dies in the interim."

"A wise choice."

The fist snapped back on my heart. All I saw was more waiting. Endless waiting.

Chapter Twenty-nine

I enlisted Gert's help.

Her eyes widened as I told her about the Harvester. "Oh, yeah. I get it. Nobody's paying attention, so now you want little Gertie's assistance." She pouted.

"I've underestimated you, Gert. I'm sorry."

She toyed with the end of her braid. "I'm thinking. Considering, ya know?"

"It's scary stuff, G. I understand if you don't want to get involved."

She grinned around an immense bubble. "If there's action, I want in."

Good God. "Action? Um, I'm not sure." I handed her the body parts printout. "We need to learn about these women as people. Make some calls. Review autopsy reports. Check Web page hits. Stuff like that."

She nodded. "I could set up a Web guest book."

"You could do that?"

She beamed. "Piece of cake. We'll get this monster."

"Not a monster. Picture a guy maybe thirty, thirty-five. Someone unprepossessing, even invisible. Yet a person who appears kind. Self-deprecating. Serious. Lonely. I doubt he uses force to lure them in. It matters that they like him."

"Like a hurt puppy."

I smiled. "Yes. We can't resist that, can we? My profile sees sex as a part of it, but I question that he's capable of intercourse. Think of how some of our clients lost their sex drive after losing a loved one to homicide. I think he experienced the same. We know this guy, Gert. Better than most people. Better than the cops."

"I bet he didn't get a lot of hugs growing up, either," Gert said.

I hugged her. "Thanks for helping."

"Donna and Mary will want to help, too."

I shook my head. "I'm not sure—"

"We're not talking about strapping on Magnums here."

"No, right." I shrugged into my coat. Penny instantly came to attention. "I'm off to see Chief Flynn and Harry Pisarro. I'm hoping that Elizabeth's and Angela's environments provide hints about how they're all connected."

My truck trudged along despite the snow as I drove west down Route 2. I met Chief Flynn, and immediately liked the bearded and gruff merchant marine. Funny how much he reminded me of my dad.

While the chief gave me a tour of his Asian-style home, his golden retriever, Zipper, romped with Penny. Over sandwiches and tea, I learned that Sven Gunderson had called the chief after he'd hung up with me. He'd shaken Chief Flynn with the news of the masquerade. The chief had taken it well, considering.

The chief left me alone to search Elizabeth's room. It was minimalist and serene, and featured a rock garden, a bonsai, and a small area with candles for prayer.

I found no signposts connecting her to the other

victims. In the chief's den, we flipped pages on years of scrapbooks featuring Elizabeth as infant, toddler, high school science and track star, young-adult competition-winning bodybuilder, and mature nutritionist who lectured on women's health issues.

Here was a life, gone. She'd worn this great smile when she'd graduated college, like she could take on the world. She was really into her body, but she was also plain, like the room where she slept. A no-fuss kind of woman.

In so many pictures, she looked up at her dad with such pride.

God, I ached for him.

I skimmed several articles that she'd written, a spread on her in *Shape* magazine, and the manuscript she was working on about nutrition. I searched for a journal and found none, and delved into the chest at the foot of her bed hoping to find some hint of the killer or a connection with any of the other women. Nothing looked promising.

I found no clue of the new friend her old boyfriend had mentioned. Hoping for nuggets, I brought her manuscript with me. But I was definitely not feeling lucky.

As I was leaving, the chief pointed to an urn on the mantle. "Elizabeth's ashes."

"Oh," was all I could reply. I suspected the ashes on the mantle were not his daughter's, but from some fireplace. I hadn't the heart to tell him.

After several wrong turns, I drove down a freshly plowed, birch-lined drive toward Harry Pisarro's home in Carlisle. At the end of the drive sat Pisarro's home—a swooping modern structure shaped like the prow of a ship.

A large, two-storied wing floated above snow-covered lawn. Mile-high windows reflected the dull afternoon light. Acres and acres of fence surrounded the property.

I left Penny in the car and walked up the flagstone path to the paneled double doors. Before I hit the buzzer, one of the doors swung wide. Expecting a flunky, I was surprised by Pisarro himself.

"Come in, Madame Tally." He kissed each cheek.

Yuck. I stomped my feet free of snow before entering a two-storied foyer the size of a small home. Paintings hung on the free-floating walls and sculptures stood on pedestals. A couch faced a glass-enclosed lap pool. I wondered who swam and who watched. To my right, a staircase wound behind a curved wall.

"Lovely," I said.

"Isn't it?" Pisarro led me into the open-style kitchen. "Coffee? Wine? Soda?"

"Nothing," I said. "But thanks."

Pisarro nodded, then clasped his hands behind his back. "I'm afraid my lovely bride won't be joining us. Come."

He led me to an open staircase facing a cathedral-ceilinged living room. We passed more artwork as we climbed, then walked down a narrow hall.

Pisarro was unusually quiet, much as he'd been in the days when I'd counseled him following Angela's funeral. He swung open the door at the end of the hall, but turned his back to the room and faced me.

"I can't go in there. I'm sure you understand."

As I entered Angela Pisarro's room, her father shut the door behind me.

The room was pink and quintessential "girl." Lace frothed from the skirt of the roses comforter, decorated the pillows, and fluffed the dresses of the dolls resting against them. Framed pictures of horses and competition ribbons lined the walls. Angela had left home for college at BC. Where were her dorm things? The posters? The mementos of the mature Angela?

The room—all candy pink—brought to mind a prepubescent teen.

I opened drawers and peeked under the bed and explored the closet. All filled with stuff from Angela's childhood and teen years.

When I closed the door behind me, I'd learned about the child, but nothing of the young woman who'd been killed.

I found Pisarro sipping a drink as he stood beside the kitchen counter. His eyes, red and moist, tracked me, but he remained silent.

"Angela's college things?" I asked.

He pointed out the window, to the a room above the garage.

"Mind if I look?"

He shrugged.

"This is hard for you, isn't it?" I said.

He grimaced, his lips pulling back from his capped teeth. "You know what I am, Madame Tally. A hood. A thug. A wiseguy. When she learned what I did, she hated me. And I never loved anyone more in my life."

"I'm sorry."

He cupped my cheeks and kissed me.

I drew his hands away. "Don't."

His gray eyes smiled. He wrapped his arms around me, pulled me tight, so I felt his erection. He ground his hips against mine.

If I freaked, I'd end up raped. "Stop, Harry. Stop it now."

His lips smashed down on mine, his tongue hot and wet and probing. I freed my hands and shoved hard against his chest.

I sprang backward—he'd released me—and I stood panting, back bowed, fists clenched, shaking. And he saw my fear. His eyes laughed.

"Are you sure I should stop?" he asked in a horribly normal voice. One hand reached out and began massaging my breast. "Nice."

I slapped his arm away. "Stop now." I inhaled a deep breath, a calming one, when all I really wanted to do was run.

But if I did, that would give him more pleasure.

I laced my shaking hands together in front of me. "Angela's things aren't above the garage, are they?"

His wolf grin said how much he loved the encounter. "I burned them. But the room's quite lovely. A tropical garden, a large bed, champagne chilling."

"I'll be leaving, then." I walked around the lap pool and crossed the foyer, my back prickling the whole time.

A hand drifted onto my shoulder, light as a butterfly. I didn't turn, but felt his breath on the side of my face. "You really missed something special, Madame Tally."

"This isn't about sex, Harry. It's about you feeling

some deep pit of loss. It stinks, you doing this to me, and you know it."

The hand slid off me and I walked out the door without looking back.

I sat curled on my office sofa, shoes off, Penny's head resting on my feet. I called Jake's studio, something I rarely did.

"Yeah?" he said in that distracted voice he wore while working.

I wanted to hear warm words. Comfort words. Love words. Words that he'd go punch out Harry Pisarro's lights. "Did you get my sink fixed yet?"

"Thinking about it. Yup."

Why couldn't I make my mouth ask for help?

We hung up, and I wrapped my arms around Penny. "Oh, Pens. I feel like shit."

In the bathroom, I brushed my teeth again to wipe away the taste of Pisarro. I pulled up my sweater, and began scrubbing my breasts. My hand slowed. That was *it*!

In my office, I dived for Elizabeth's autopsy report. I was an idiot. The killer hadn't taken her eyes as a trophy.

He'd sliced off her breasts. *They* were his souvenir.

Once my fury with Pisarro segued from boil to simmer, I called Bones on his cell.

We chatted for a few minutes. Mrs. Cheadle was not saying much, but seemed alert. A good sign. "Bones, um, is Mr. Pisarro at the club tonight?"

"Every night but Sunday. You gonna talk to the boss?"

"I saw him this afternoon, but I might stop by the club tonight. Thanks."

Hoping Bones wouldn't alert his master that I'd called, I phoned Pisarro's home for the second time that day. The maid answered, and I requested Mrs. Pisarro. Seconds later, a woman who slid over her *R*s in typical Boston fashion came on the line.

"Mrs. Pisarro? It's Tally Whyte."

A laugh. "Did you fuck him this afternoon?"

I cleared my throat. "Mrs. Pisarro, I'm calling about Angela."

"Yes?" Her voice was harsh and slurred.

"Do you have any of Angela's more recent things? I saw her room and—"

"He likes to keep her a child. No. I tossed everything. Didn't Harry tell ya that? Made a big fire. Just like he told me to do." A sniffle. "How come?"

I explained.

Quiet on the other end, then "Oh, come on out."

I drove out to Carlisle again, the snow deeper, the going harder. Blessing's assault felt like years ago, instead of a week. Then again, it seemed like yesterday.

Penny perked her ears as we pulled down the Pisarro driveway. Byte Me was open late. It was only six. But I kept expecting headlights in my rearview mirror.

My back itched, too, as I walked up the path wishing Penny was beside me.

The front door cracked, then a tall woman with

pageboy brown hair and bangs, a slash of red lips, and periwinkle eyes waved me inside.

"It's in there," she pointed to a box sitting on a club chair. Her manicured hand held a lit joint. "If you tell him about Angie's stuff, he'll . . . Don't tell him."

"I won't." I lifted the box, which was surprisingly light.

"Take care of it?" She started to cry. "He burned everything else. Made me throw all my treasures on, too. Her clothes and books and pictures and . . . all my baby's precious stuff. This is all I could hide."

"I thought we could talk. I'm trying to learn about Angela."

She took a drag on the joint, exhaled as if it was a cigarette. "What about?"

"What her life was like. How she spent her time in college. I still don't have a clear picture of those years."

Mrs. Pisarro walked to a soaring window, pushed aside the curtain, and peered out. "You got to go."

"I . . . Is there anything you can remember? Anything at all?"

She leaned her head against the wall. "Last couple years, Angie didn't talk to me so much. Listen, you *got* to go."

"Of course. Thank you. I'll take care of Angela's things. Are you sure I can't help you in any way?"

A smirk. "What do they say? I'm beyond help." She closed the door behind me.

I stowed the box in the trunk, then slid behind the wheel.

Headlights bobbed down the drive.

I couldn't back out, so I gave Penny the "ready"

command. She sat beside me, ears forward, body tense.

A black Suburban pulled in front of the garage. The automatic door yawned and the car eased inside.

Pisarro.

I wanted to zoom backward down the driveway. Which would make me both chicken *and* stupid. It could also lead to physical and mental pain for Mrs. Pisarro.

Just before the garage door closed on the Suburban, Pisarro ducked beneath it. He walked over, his one hand holding a lit cigar. Tonight he wore black pants, a black T-shirt, and a silver-gray jacket. He also wore the smile I'd come to hate.

I powered down my window.

"Madame Tally," he said, reaching for my hand that rested on the sill.

I moved it to the steering wheel. Penny growled.

His hand slid into his pants pocket, and I imagined him pulling a gun and shooting Penny. Or me.

He produced a toothpick and began probing his teeth. "When you didn't visit my club tonight, as you mentioned to Bones, I thought perhaps you might venture out here. Our maid confirmed it. So what brings you to my fair domicile this evening?"

"I left my notepad in Angela's room."

A raised eyebrow that crinkled his tanned forehead. "Really?"

"Really. I called Bones because I wanted to avoid you. Now I'm off."

He walked behind the truck, to the cargo area. Penny's eyes tracked him.

"What's in the box?" He pointed to Angela's things.

"Some stuff of mine. Why do you care?"

He stepped away from the truck and I slowly backed up. Pretty dumb to run over Pisarro, but putting the pedal to the metal never sounded so good.

Just as my car door was level with where he stood, he motioned with his hand. Again I lowered the window.

"I'll be seeing you," he said.

"Will you? I doubt it, Mr. Pisarro."

"Harry." He held up a finger. "Marilyn will regret she gave you Angela's things."

I stomped the brake. "Your wife gave me *nothing* but my notebook. But if you hurt her Pisarro, I swear to God, I'll tell Kranak what you pulled on me this afternoon." I ran a finger down the side of my face, just where Kranak's scar rested.

He laughed, softly. "You're learning to play the game, Madame. I like it."

"And I mean it."

I varoomed backward down the driveway, hoping I didn't smash into one of the damned trees.

Chapter Thirty

On my way back to town from Pisarro's place, I called Barb Beliskowitz, my psychiatrist friend. "He's taking parts, Barb." I described what he'd taken, including Elizabeth's breasts.

"As you're speaking, I keep thinking . . ."

I waited. Barbara liked to pause, think, then speak. More people should try it.

"I keep thinking that these parts . . . dead," she said. "It would ruin their beauty."

"Yes. They'd wrinkle and prune, even preserved in formaldehyde."

"They'd be horrible." Her voice was distant, as if she, too, were picturing it.

"Corrupted," I said. "His trophies."

"But a collection, Tally. A very personal collection." Penny's head dropped to my lap, and she wuffled a sigh. "And they're all hideous. Now that they're removed from their owner. But he doesn't see that. Because they become transitional objects. Like what a child does with a blanket or a teddy bear." Or a doll named Gladdy.

"Yes," Barb said. "The object is still the bear or blanket, but also it's more than that. It can take on the qualities of the child's mother, a beloved dog, some caregiver."

"Correct me if I'm wrong, but wouldn't these removed body parts retain their beauty in his eyes?"

"Oh, yes. Very much so."

As I pulled onto my street, I thought about collections. Barb's living room was filled with exquisite Native American art and her collection of old miniature stoves. Nantucket baskets lined my wide windowsills and sat on tables. I also collected Zuni fetishes. Dad collected meerschaum pipes and Veda accumulated first editions. Most of us collected things.

But the Harvester's collection of putrefying body parts was not merely beautiful to him. Each item possessed the spirit of a beloved caregiver.

A caregiver who was a victim of homicide.

*   *   *

After I arrived home and alarmed the apartment, I cranked up the heat. The Harvester was playing havoc with my oil bills.

I carried the box of Angela's things into the bedroom and began reading the contents. Jake appeared and began "fixing" the bathroom sink. I tried not to think of our last meeting. Not easy.

I put aside Angela's folded poster of Queen Amidala. Poor Marilyn Pisarro. She hadn't many tokens left of her daughter. A few photos, a couple of magazines, some theater programs, a bunch of ski pins, and a few receipts that bore Angela's signature. The kid had dotted her "i"s with a heart. I lifted an *Oklahoma* theater program and scanned for Angela's name. She'd been in the chorus.

"Goddammit, Tally Whyte!"

I lay down the program. "What's up?"

Jake stomped into the bedroom holding a roll of toilet paper. "This!"

"Wow! A toilet paper roll. So is the sink working?"

"Not exactly. But you need toilet paper when using the facilities. I was using them when I discovered there wasn't any."

"There was some on the roll."

"*One sheet*. Threaded out the bottom, which is the wrong way to begin with."

"Gee, Jake, if someone consistently *fixed* stuff in the bathroom, before the fixtures became antiques suitable for the Smithsonian, then I might pay more attention to the niceties."

He nodded fast—the chicken-pecking look. "Oh. Oh, yeah, sure. I don't do enough around here? I don't do the garden? Shovel the snow? Care for the bird feeders?"

"That's because you imagine you're Mr. Outdoors or something. How long's the sink been screwed up? A month? And what about the porch light that took days to get a replacement bulb? Or the thermostat from hell? Or the leak that goes plop onto my head each time you shower? Shall I continue?"

"And what about when the oil burner goes? Who calls the repair guy? Huh? Huh?"

I stood. "Do the words 'empty the trash' have meaning for you?"

More chicken nodding. "Cute. I empty it."

"When? On national holidays? If I didn't drag the cans from the hall to the sidewalk, it would ferment."

Sputtering and chicken nodding and toilet paper waving.

I burst out laughing.

"What?" He slammed his hands on his hips. "*What*?"

I couldn't stop laughing. "We sound like we're married, for God's sake. Besides, when you get really pissed, you look like a chicken."

He bared his teeth. "A chicken?"

I lowered my voice and purred. "What can I say?"

He held the stern face a moment longer, then grabbed my ass and pressed me to him. His tongue teased my mouth, and I wrapped one leg around his butt.

The phone rang.

"The machine'll pick up." He slithered his hands beneath my T-shirt and cupped my breasts.

The phone bleeped again.

"I can't, dammit." I hung on to Jake as I reached for the receiver.

"Hello?" I said, getting hotter as Jake pulled down my sweats.

"Kranak and Reen have something big happening tonight," Gert said.

"Hold on," I told her. "Jake, I've *got* to take this."

He snapped my sweats back around my waist, mouthed *your loss*, then disappeared. I heard water sounds from the bathroom. Sigh.

"Explain, Gert," I said.

"Mary just saw them both run out of here. She said Kranak was in his Kevlar vest. She heard Reen say something about Cambridge."

"Can you follow them?"

"I already am."

"I'll call you on your cell," I said as I leashed Penny. "I'm on my way."

I raced down Appleton as fast as the snow allowed. "Gert? Can you see them in the streetlamps?"

"Sorta," she replied. "They're two cars ahead."

I crossed Clarendon, hooked a left onto Berkeley. The light hung me up at Columbus. I cursed Kranak for not calling me. I'd bet they were going after their alleged organ salesmen. "You on Storrow yet?" I said to Gert.

"Just hopped on."

"Gotcha."

I zoomed through the light at Stuart, but the one at St. James nabbed me. Through the light at Boylston, I passed by Louis, which was the original building for MIT, then I was clear until I hit Storrow. I hoped my cell battery held out for this little escapade. I also hoped this wasn't the proverbial wild-goose chase.

I crossed over Storrow, then curled back onto the four-lane highway headed west. It was snowing again, swirling tiny flakes that made the visibility lousy.

The phone crackled. "Well?" I said.

"We're passing where they keep the Harvard skulls."

"Any flashing lights? Sirens?"

"Nope. Oh, shit."

"What?"

"Somebody cut me off. This isn't as easy as it looks in the movies. For sure not in the dark. They're going awful fast for this snow."

The MIT dome glowed across the river, then on my left, the BU campus, and again on my right, the Hyatt Regency. A pickup honked as it passed me on the right. Hell. I punched the gas pedal, then switched to the right lane.

"You still have them?" I asked Gert.

"Yup. We're crossing the river, and they're headed . . . Shit!"

"What? What?"

"I'm caught at the light," Gert said. "They made it through. They're not going so fast now, so maybe . . . Here goes."

I zoomed.

"Well?" I said.

"Shit! The second light caught me, too, but . . . Oh, screw it. They're bearing right. Going into Cambridge. I'll try and keep up."

My mind could see where she was. I just wasn't

there yet. My wipers *kathunk kathunked*. Penny barked. She was pumped, too.

I crossed the Charles, bore right, blazed through the first light, which was green.

"Where are you?" I said.

"Look around the corner. Second light."

I stopped at the second light, which was red, and peered to my right. A cop leaned on the driver's-side door, talking to Gert through the window. I couldn't see her face, but the bubble she blew nearly touched the cop's nose.

Hell.

I pulled up behind the cop car. When he drove off, Gert climbed into my truck and Penny rearranged herself, flopping across Gert's lap. I took the ticket from her, whistled, then tucked it into my bag. "Expenses."

"Dammit," she said. "I get points for that."

"Sorry. This was a stupid idea of mine, anyway. Like we could chase down Kranak and Reen."

She pulled a string of bubble gum from her mouth, then sucked it back inside. "Maybe we could find 'em. Ya know, cruise Cambridge looking for their car."

I squeezed her shoulder. "We can try."

A boom. The truck shuddered.

"Holy shit," Gert said.

A fireball shot into the air, arcing high above the buildings of Cambridge.

"I think we just found them," I said.

I followed the flames that licked the night somewhere around Fresh Pond. I sped down the road, rounded

the Fresh Pond circle, and tracked the semicircular
glow, which appeared to be behind the Fresh Pond
strip mall.

I climbed the hill, turned right into the mall, and
got stopped by a cop.

I flashed my credentials, fed him some bull, and was
waved through.

Cop cars and fire engines littered the lot, but the
mall itself wasn't burning. I wove around back, saw
the movie theater, also not in flames, and again was
stopped. The fire was down a small road out back,
behind the mall.

I parked in the movie lot, jammed my curls beneath
a baseball cap, and Gert, Penny, and I threaded
around cars and trucks parked at crazy angles as we
ran across the lot and down the road.

To our left, a hilly state park paralleled the road.
On the right, maybe a quarter-mile down, a six-story
building was in flames. Fire licked through its burst
windows and spiked from a huge hole in the roof. The
left-hand side of the wooden building had collapsed
like a closed accordion, but I saw movement on the
building's right side. Someone ran across one of the
gaping windows.

Shouts and screams and sirens and the whoosh of
thousands of pounds of water pressure shooting
streams onto the building were deafening. As we drew
closer, more cops stopped us. Each time I finagled our
way through with my MGAP credentials and mention
of Kranak.

The fire lit the night sky to a surreal orange. Sparks
shot into the air, and smoke boiled like a dirty halo
around the building, playing peek-a-boo with the
flames. My nose and eyes ran. The acrid smell was

terrible, a combination of burning wood and chemicals and . . . flesh?

I shivered beneath my down jacket.

I heard the chatter of media people arguing with the cops. I fished around in my bag and handed Gert my wool cap. "A disguise."

She tugged it on, then leaned close, hollering over the noise. "Ya got one for Penny, too? Hello?"

The cop world knew my three-legged Penny.

We wove among firefighters and law enforcement and EMTs. I finally spotted Kranak, who was talking to Reen near the chain-link fence that surrounded the building. I pulled Gert back into the shadow of a tall truck. Nearby, a cluster of SWAT-style cops holding serious weaponry, FBI on the backs of their jackets, watched as the building burned. Media trucks rolled closer, and several privileged reporters moved in and spouted commentary into their handheld mikes while the cameras whirred.

Someone in law enforcement had alerted the press prior to the raid and had given them special access privileges. Cute, eh?

The crowd "oohed." I followed the tilted heads. Someone stood at one of the sixth-floor windows. The person appeared to sway, holding on to the sill. A fire truck backed toward the building, then began uncranking its long ladder.

My God. The person catapulted out of the window and fell to the ground. He lay there, unmoving. Firefighters rushed toward him, then lifted him and ran from the building amid a rain of sparks.

Another fireball varoomed from the building, shooting like a rocket toward the moon. More explosions, more screams and shouts and groans and crackles and then, a thunderous rumble.

The building collapsed.

When I got home, exhausted, sooty, ears ringing, I dragged my butt to the shower. Gray-black water swirled down the drain, along with gritty crud from the fire. It went 'round and 'round, and I swear when I closed my eyes, I saw that poor trapped human dive to oblivion. I squeezed shampoo into my hand, then lathered my hair. But it hadn't been a dive. More like something fake, like a doll, arms and legs limp, not as I imagined in a plunge like that. I didn't even hear the person scream.

Hard to tell from far away, but his build reminded me of McArdle.

Thursday morning, early, I slammed the newspaper onto Kranak's desk.

"Yeah?" he said around a mouthful of Egg McMuffin. The flesh framing his bloodhound eyes was puffy, the eyes themselves spidered with red. Brown stubble bristled his chin and upper lip. But not his scar. Never his scar.

I felt bad for him. But not that bad. "You said you'd do your best to tell me when this organ-selling raid was happening."

He slurped a dose of coffee. "So I did my best. I couldn't call."

I flopped into the chair facing his. "Did you find your organ sellers?"

"Right now it's a big, friggin' mess. But from the

looks of it, we found something." He shook his head. "Maybe what we need."

"The man who died, was it McArdle?"

"You mean the guy you saw swan-dive from the building?"

So Kranak had spotted us the previous night. "Yes."

Kranak rubbed his eyes with his thumb and forefinger. "You haven't heard."

I excavated for patience. "No, Rob. I haven't heard, whatever that's supposed to mean. I just got here and came straight to you. Stop being cutesy."

"I'm not, Tal. I swear." His hand slid across the desk and grasped mine. "The guy who fell. We . . ." He squeezed my hand. "It was Doc Strabo."

"John?" My brain, sluggish, wasn't computing. "What was John doing there?"

"He was the man, Tal. The point man, we think."

"You mean the body organ thing? But, Rob, I just talked to Strabo yesterday. He wasn't a . . . a point man. You've known him almost as long as I have. How could you think that?"

Kranak gave me this funny look. "Why else would he have been there, Tally?"

"In the warehouse?" I thought of John's kids— Summer and Gabrielle. I'd been to their baptisms and christenings. I'd partied at Strabo's house half-a-dozen times. I'd yakked with him over coffee and bagels about cases and politics and movies and . . .

"He had motive, Tal," Kranak said. "The separation and child support cost him big bucks. Opportunity? What better place than the Grief Shop? Means? Ditto. See how much sense it makes?"

I snapped my hand from Kranak's and hugged my

waist. "It doesn't make any sense. Not any. How can you be sure it's John Strabo?"

"Half his face wasn't burned, Tal. And fingerprints don't lie."

"But Strabo's not the Harvester. He hasn't been killing women for body parts."

"We got our harvesters: Strabo, our head honcho, and two more dead. A black kid, a thug, named Binny. Same kid we think set the fire at McArdle's. He's the one who told us about Blessing the day you found your friend. Now we're thinking he might have been the shooter."

My neck hair prickled. "It wasn't Binny, Rob."

"We'll see. We got a white guy, too. Thirtyish. He looked pretty well set up."

Somehow I knew it wouldn't be McArdle. "Reen didn't tell you about all of the stuff I've found, did she?"

He shook his head.

I rose, unable to shake a dreamy sense of unreality. "I'll see you later."

"Whaddya mean, later? Come back here."

"Later."

The atmosphere in MGAP's central office was hushed as I passed out the day's assignments and updated the board. I'd occasionally blow my nose, runny from tears. Strabo. Dead.

An organ thief? I did not believe it. But . . .

Questions flitted around my head, like who would care for Strabo's dog? Would Mary be devastated by the death of her (maybe) sweetie? Had Strabo jumped, or had he lost his footing and fallen?

I assigned Gert the family of the Binny boy found at the warehouse. Andy looked puce, so I gave him the Jane Doe—cause of death still unknown—who'd been found that morning under a snowbank. I doubted he'd be called on to comfort a family member. I wrote my name on the board beside Strabo's. I would counsel Sophie Strabo, as well as her girls.

The police had yet to inform me that Sophie was on her way in. I had an hour before my first group session. I fielded calls for awhile, one from a counselee who was getting remarried, others from legal aid and a funeral home in Brockton.

I took a breather, walked Penny, then reached for Patricia Boch's autopsy report. Couldn't do it. Not yet.

I entered the large refrigeration room, and walked between the steel gurneys that held the dead cocooned inside body bags. I found Strabo, and shuddered as I unzipped. The left side of his face was blackened, so I walked to where I could talk to him while looking at the man I remembered. I stroked his hair.

"Hey, John. What's the deal? What happened? Why did you lie about Elizabeth Flynn's eyes? I mean, really. Did you know the Harvester? Did you know he took her breasts? What were you doing in that warehouse? Your actions don't make sense.

"Remember when we got stuck on our way to a crime scene and almost drowned in a flood? Boy, that was crazy, wasn't it? I hear you, John. God, I wish you'd smile. Who's going to open doors for me now? You were always so courtly.

"I'm going to miss you. So much. I'm so sorry this happened. So sorry. I'll try and help Sophie and the girls. Oh, John."

I stumbled back to the office, washed my face, then pulled Patricia Boch's report in front of me. She'd

been buried in a pine box at McArdle's for maybe a
month, maybe two. Prior to that, it was estimated
she'd been dead from seven to seventeen months,
housed in an atmosphere dry enough to mummify her.

I turned the page. Fogarty had done the post. He
might be a pain, but he was tops when it came to
performing autopsies. Patricia's eyes were gone, but
so were her liver, heart, pancreas, brain, and other
organs. Her killer was having a high time playing doctor. Or maybe he was into an Egyptian thing. Christ.

Cause of death? Inconclusive.

I flipped to the photographs. There she was—a
brown-haired woman with a wide nose, an overbite,
and a high forehead. Attractive, but not model-
beautiful.

I'm so sorry, Patricia.

Patricia's pictures were strange, disturbing. Mum-
mified. No legs.

Something else was bugging me.

I rested my chin on my fingertips, and studied the
photos.

Talk about an odd picture. Patricia's torso, arms
and head included, lay on Fogarty's table. Standing
beside her head were her feet. Her feet?

I paged back through the text. The killer had removed her legs from her upper thighs to just above
her ankle bones.

Why leave Patricia Boch's feet?

Weirder and weirder.

Feet. No feet. Feet. What was it about Patricia's
feet that so disturbed me?

The phone rang. Sophie Strabo was on her way in
to officially identify John.

Chapter Thirty-one

After walking Sophie Strabo through the misery of paperwork, talking to the ME who'd autopsied John, and IDing her estranged husband's body, I'd lost my appetite. I sat hunched over my desk. I felt like a gnome who hadn't seen daylight in decades.

Feet. No feet. Feet. No feet.

While I doodled, I concocted this elaborate chart with a star enclosed by a circle, all of which signified nothing.

Nothing.

There was some deal going on, I just wasn't getting it.

The phone rang. "Ms. Whyte?" said the jovial voice. "Bernie Trepel here. Returning your call."

"Gee, um, hi, Mr. Trepel." I flopped my feet onto my turtle footstool. "Again, let me apologize for our rude behavior in Boston."

"That's why I'm calling. Your name didn't ring a bell."

"The night on the steps. When you asked for directions. And my friend pulled a gun on you. *That night.*" I kept my voice light, going for gee, *wasn't that a riot?*

"You know, ma'am," he said, his Texas twang thickening. "That's mighty strange. 'Cause I can't recall anything like that happening to me."

"But you must—"

"Believe me, ma'am. I'd remember somebody holding a gun on me."

After we signed off, all pleasantries, the meaning behind Trepel's words sunk in.

Like the guy in the VW bug, "Trepel" must have been following me. I mean, why else impersonate some out-of-town businessman?

Wrong. Here I was assuming the man on the steps was Bernard Trepel. He could have been any Joe with Trepel's card in his pocket.

Did I really believe that? What if Reen hadn't shown up?

I called Trepel back at Alient Systems. "Sorry to bother you, Mr. Trepel. Quick question. What do you sell for Alient Systems?"

"Taxidermy supplies. Best in the West."

Taxidermy supplies? Talk about creepy.

I started doodling again. Feet. No feet. Feet.

No feet!

I scratched a message telling Gert where I was headed, then flew out the door.

Penny and I sat in the den of Jazz Brown's luxurious home.

"Please, Jazz," I whispered. "Would you ask Inez to leave the room?" I glanced at the pretty woman. She smiled back at me.

He shook his head. "It won't make a difference, don't you see? Are you still digging up things for the cops about Mr. McArdle?" Jazz flicked a spot off the lapel of his smoking jacket. "I'm done talking about him."

Inez frowned, then reached for Jazz's cello and bow.

She closed her eyes, then began to play Pachelbel's Canon in D. The resonant music swelled, filling the room.

I leaned toward Jazz. "What exactly happened to Inez's feet?"

His eyes widened. He stubbed out his cheroot. "She'd gone to run some errands. Taken the car. She should've been gone ten, fifteen minutes. Going on to an hour, I started to worry. I was frantic by twenty-four."

I could imagine. "What did the police say?"

"We seldom call the police down here. Not if we can avoid it. I was looking for her. Friends were, too. Neighbors, Mr. McArdle included."

I was jolted by the music. Strident and strong, it grew progressively more frenzied. Inez whipped her head around, as she strummed the bow, her neatly pinned hair tumbling around her shoulders.

Jazz crossed the room and gently tried to remove the bow from her hands. Wild-eyed, Inez fought him. Penny whined while Inez and Jazz played tug-of-war with the bow. Inez shook her head fiercely. Jazz finally took her in his arms and rocked her. She raked her nails down the side of his face.

He lifted her from the chair, and her mouth yawned wide with a silent scream far more unsettling then the real thing. He carried her upstairs while she beat his head and shoulders with fists smeared with the blood that ran down his face.

Twenty minutes passed. Penny lay on my feet, visibly upset by Inez's violent outburst. Should I leave? Stay?

I peered out the curtain behind the sofa. Twilight. In winter, a gloomy, foreboding time.

Soft footfalls on the stairs. Jazz reentered the room, but left the door open. "She won't wake up, but I like to listen." Blood seeped through the gauze on his cheek.

"I'm so sorry," I said.

"Happens. Too often to count."

"Please finish your story about Inez's accident?"

"Not much more to tell. Mr. McArdle found her. Showed up carrying her three days later. She'd been in a car accident. Ran into some pole or other. The car was totaled." He smiled a sad smile. "The little man even had the damned thing towed home. He could be like that—kind, thoughtful."

I kept my trap shut.

"The accident was somewhere out in the sticks. Can't even remember the town's name. They had to amputate her feet. They'd been crushed. She had no ID on her. Nobody knew who she was. McArdle stumbled on her when he was picking up some body or other. If not for that, who knows when we'd've found her? Mr. McArdle even paid the hospital bill." He sighed, slowly, as if it was an effort expelling the air from his lungs. "Ever since, she wasn't right. Couldn't speak. Can barely think. You saw how she gets, frantic and furious. Oh, my darling girl. My darling girl."

He bowed his head into his hands and sobbed.

I hugged him, and murmured soothing words that I knew helped not one bit.

"We were to have kids," he said through his tears. "Lots of 'em. And her career. A tragedy."

"She still plays beautifully," I said. "Even if it's only for you."

His laugh was ironic, bitter. "What's that? Nothing.

Nothing compared to her magnificent dance. My Inez was a rising star with the Boston Ballet."

Night had fallen when I returned to my truck. I believed the Harvester had taken Inez's feet. To my knowledge, she was the only living victim. I tried Reen, failed to get her—damn her for playing cat-and-mouse with me again—called Kranak as I sped across town, desperately needing to tell him what I'd figured out.

I drove to his boat, thundered down the pier, Penny flying past me with excitement. I leapt onto the deck and beat on the cabin door. "Kranak, open up!"

The deck vibrated. Someone else had jumped on board. Someone I couldn't see.

I hadn't watched for a follower, hadn't thought about it as I'd raced across town. "Guard," I signaled Penny, who instantly tensed.

I pounded the door again. "Kranak! Kranak!"

The boat swayed, almost imperceptibly, as the "someone" lurched toward me, his body obscured by the tarp covering the furled mainsail.

I backed up a couple of steps and flexed my legs to leap off the boat.

"Memmmooorrrieess. All 'lone in th' moonligh'."

No. Couldn't be.

"I'llllll remember, somtin', somthin."

Kranak? Singing *Cats*? I peered down the starboard side of the boat.

"Memmoorrieess. All I've got are the mem-o-ries. La la, laaaa, la."

My God. It *was* Kranak. Drunk, his feet perched on the rail, his right arm wrapped around one of the stays, his left arm and most of his body hanging out over the icy sea. What did he think he was, a flying Wallenda?

I grabbed his belt, hauled his ass onto the boat, and dragged him downstairs to the cabin. I settled him in his bunk and doused him with coffee. Yet another mangled chorus of *Cats* that would have given T.S. Elliot hives, then, "Reenie stood me up."

Reenie?

He snorted, gave me a goofy grin, and passed out. In the ten years I'd known him, I'd never seen Kranak drunk. Could it be love? Now that was some picture. Kranak and Reen sure had a lot of explaining to do.

The drums were soft that night. So muffled that I strained to hear them. They whispered *fool, fool, fool.*

The Harvester wasn't simply collecting random body parts. No. He was keeping his victims' most notable feature as a souvenir.

I heard Chesa's laughter, as if to say *finally*. Della's golden eyes mocked me.

I rested my head on the pillow, my brain whirling with thoughts.

Patricia's runner legs. Elizabeth's shapely breasts. Angela's periwinkle eyes. Inez's ballerina feet. Inez— she'd never been to a hospital, never had a car crash. She knew that McArdle had mutilated her, then returned her to his "dear friend" Jazz.

Who wouldn't be mute, living through that nightmare?

And Moira Blessing, of course. He'd taken her flautist hands.

Had Blessing known? Is that why he'd gotten involved with the Harvester, for revenge? And had his revenge turned against him, and he'd become the killer's pawn?

Sickened, I groped for the bourbon. I pressed my hand around the bottle, pleased at the thought of a dreamless night.

Sleep snuck up like a thief, and I embraced it.

I got to work by 7:30, but Kranak was already out on a case. Mary and Donna were in early, too, as was Gert. I told them my sickening conclusion about Inez Brown.

"I finished the printout," Gert said. "We've got five new possible victims. I've started checking out their backgrounds. The body parts thing fits, Tal. This weirdo keeps the best, the most talented, or most beautiful parts of them."

"Or what he perceives as the best," I said.

She nodded. "We've got the Web guest book up, and Donna and Mary are on top of the Web e-mails and reviewing the older phone calls we received right after you posted Della and Chesa's Web page."

I battled a headache. "Dammit, what connects these women?"

Gert shook her head. "Shouldn't the real guys be doing this?"

"Absolutely," I said. "I'm going to talk to Veda."

She blew a bubble, popped it. "Andy had some gossip on the warehouse thing. He heard it didn't work out or something. You know anything?"

"Not a thing."

I corralled Veda after the Grief Shop's morning meeting. Her face tightened when I told her my conclusion, her lips thinning to a blade of red.

"Ach," she said, disgusted. "It makes a horrible, sick sense. But *how* is he choosing them? *Where* is he finding them? What? They all simply go with him like Red Riding Hood and the Big, Bad Wolf?"

"I'm worried about Inez," I said. "Her safety, Vede. What if the Harvester saw me going into Jazz Brown's place?"

"I will talk to Joe Finelley at the FBI. Today. Now. It's warranted."

"God, that would be great." I shoved the fat manila folder bound with a rubber band across her desk.

She held up a hand. "Make copies. Give me those, eh?"

"Sure. I'm not thinking."

"Didn't sleep well, *bubbeleh*?"

"No."

"Jake?"

"He's enveloped in his upcoming show. You going to go?"

The worry lines on her face momentarily smoothed. "Of course."

"Have you heard any more on the warehouse thing?"

"No solid confirmation. Not yet. The grapevine says they were selling corpses' corneas. Kenya. Egypt. Russia. Syria. Japan. Several people in L.A., too." She bit her lower lip. "How could John do such a thing?"

I didn't believe he had.

I opened my office door. "Oh, Jake." The vase of black-eyed Susans brought tears to my eyes. So sweet. And I'd thought all he was focused on was his opening. The card showed a Smiley face and read: MY WORK IS A SYMPHONY WHEN I THINK OF YOU.

I could just see him at his studio, chisel in hand. Made me positively romantic. I sniffled again. Lately my emotions were centimeters from the surface.

"Hey, Pens. Look what old Jake sent us." Buoyed, I pulled over the day's list, which bore a Post-it from Fogarty. He wanted to see me ASAP. Talk about a downer.

I read the list. Five decedents in. Four in car crashes. One unattended.

A calm day for homicide counselors. The unattended appeared to be a coronary and the vehicular deaths seemed to be exactly what they appeared to be.

I entered our central office and saw Andy. I simmered. "How're you feeling?"

"Fine," he answered, his nose poked into a statistics book.

"The Jane Doe yesterday? Anything happening with her?"

His head popped up. "Nope."

"About Sven Gunderson—"

"I've got group in two minutes." He beat a swift exit.

I was headed for Fogarty when Gert handed me an inch stack of papers. "Here are transcriptions of the e-mails, phone calls, and Web responses."

"I'm dying to look but you hang onto them."

"Shouldn't they go to the FBI?"

"They will. But this stuff is all linked to our Families of Homicide Victims pages. We'll have to screen each response. I won't have the FBI poking inside our people's heads. Fogarty's hollering for me. The budget. Could Mary or Donna do this photocopying for me?"

"They're up to their eyeballs, Tal. Me, too. Like Andy, I got group. In an hour—"

"Naw. I'll take care of it."

Off I went to the copy machine. The faster Veda got the FBI onto the Harvester, the better I'd like it.

Chapter Thirty-two

Ten minutes later, Fogarty found me in the photocopy room.

"You didn't see my note?" he said.

"I saw it, Tom. Sorry. I have to get this done for Veda."

He glanced at the sheets I was copying, then tucked his hands into his pockets and flapped his lab coat. Just like Strabo used to. I turned away and collated pages.

"Something wrong?" Fogarty said.

I cleared my throat. "Nothing. What's up?"

"I'd like you to see the Jane I'm working on."

I stapled several pages. "Since when have you needed my—"

"Don't, Tally." He rested his hand on my arm.

I searched his eyes and saw not a hint of Fogarty-the-adversary.

"If it's bad, I don't want to know." And I didn't, dammit.

Fogarty bent his head close. "Please," he said quietly.

*   *   *

We stood in autopsy theater number one, the least-used of the two main theaters. That in itself was odd. The second oddity was that no other corpses or breathing humans working on them were in the room. Just Fogarty, myself, and a single body, which lay beneath a white plastic sheet, the third oddity.

"This is the Jane?" I said.

"Yeah. Pretty grim stuff. Her face."

"What's with the sheet, Tom?" I said, reaching for it.

He held up a hand. "Don't, Tally. Not yet. I—"

I lifted the sheet, staggered, and caught myself on the autopsy table.

Someone had peeled the skin off her face, so only the flesh and structure beneath remained. Like a hunk of refrigerated meat.

All forty facial muscles, down to the striations, were delineated on the skinless face. The face's hills and valleys were pink and red. Found beneath a snowdrift, she'd frozen. Due to the freezing, only small areas oozed blood.

He'd left her hair. Her distinctive and beautiful black waterfall of hair.

A sob escaped. I turned away, hugged myself. No, of course it couldn't be. It was some stupid Fogarty joke. Except . . .

I started pounding Fogarty. "You shit! You absolute shit!" I hit him harder and harder, but I couldn't see, the tears blinding me, making me crazy.

He grabbed my wrists, and the fight leeched out of me. All I could do was stare at the naked, mutilated corpse.

"Reen."

I finally turned back to Fogarty. "I apologize. She's my friend."

"I swear I didn't know," Fogarty said. "I've heard the gossip about what you're investigating. I thought it might be a body parts issue."

Oh, Reen.

I dug my nails into my palms. The pain felt good.

Bruising around her neck consistent with strangulation. Her eyes. No burst blood vessels. Maybe she wasn't strangled. I got dizzy. Breathed in and out. I scanned the rest of her body. It looked good. Fine, really. A few old bruises. I couldn't touch her yet. Could not.

I narrowed my lids, tried to see Reen beyond the mutilation. It *could* be another woman of Asian extraction.

I was a great kidder. And now I was kidding myself.

I lifted her hand. Reen's hand. He'd stolen the skin off her fingertips, too. He'd wanted time to pass before we ID'd her. He hadn't counted on my seeing her.

He'd left her teeth. He knew dental records took much longer to ID.

I squeezed her hand tight. Her beautiful, beautiful face. And the Harvester had stolen it. Damn him! He had no right.

Something hard and mean and acidic formed inside me. A jagged thing from when my dad died. For years, I'd sanded its edges until it was smooth and small.

Now it was back, full-blown, and I relished the rough canker of hate.

"It's Reen Maekawa." I faced Fogarty. "An FBI

agent. Her dental records will prove me right. Call the FBI."

Word of Reen sped through the Grief Shop. Gert and I were talking when I learned that Kranak was back. I raced down the hall, hoping to soften the blow about Reen. I spotted him as he stormed out the building.

I blew through the doors after him. "Rob wait!"

He gunned his car out of the lot.

Minutes later, I handed Veda the Harvester paperwork.

"Strabo and Reen," I said. "Two friends gone in as many days. And Rob. It's bad, Vede."

"Very."

"I want to shake Inez Brown, make her talk, suck out the secrets I know live inside of her." I sighed. "But that's not going to happen."

Back in my office, I called Jake. I just wanted to hear his voice. "I love the black-eyed Susans, Jake. They cheered me up."

"Huh?" he said. "Oh, yeah. That was the point. Bye."

As I hung up, I heard a shouted, "Wait. Wait."

"What?" I said.

"How did you know they were from me?"

Jake was definitely in drifty artist mode. "One, you *always* send me black-eyed Susans. Two, the card was a clue. Duh."

"I sent the flowers, but I don't think I enclosed a card, Tal."

"Sure you did. I . . . Never mind. Talk to you later." I gently placed the phone in its cradle. I stared at the enclosure card I'd tucked into the corner of my blotter.

MY WORK IS A SYMPHONY WHEN I THINK OF YOU, it said.

And a smiley face. What was I thinking? Jake would *never* draw a smiley face.

I began to shake. I growled. That son of a bitch had touched Jake's flowers.

I flung the vase across the room. It smashed against the wall, becoming a jumble of flowers and glass and water as it smeared its way down toward the floor.

Saturday morning, early, I sat in the Grief Shop conference room, one floor above MGAP. Large windows, majestic oval table, comfortable chairs. The temperature was set at sixty-eight, but it felt like ninety from the FBI agents' boiling fury. Even the air smelled of anger. It wasn't pleasant.

Kranak was there, too, as were additional state police Crime Scene Services and Investigative people, and three detectives from Boston PD. At my insistence, Gert was also present. Veda had poked her head in a few times, but hadn't entered the room.

The previous night, at the behest of the FBI, I'd typed copious notes on Della and Chesa, as well as filled in gaps on Angela Pisarro, Patricia Boch, Elizabeth Flynn, Moira Blessing, and Inez Brown.

CSS had also taken charge of what was left of the flowers, vase, and card. They weren't happy with me for smashing it.

Along with my typing, I'd spent hours recounting the details of the Harvester's attentions to me, as well as connecting the whole Roland Blessing thread. The

FBI insisted on giving me a guard, since they concluded I was some kind of object of affection to the killer.

Funny, I'd figured that revolting ditty out all on my own.

Profound silence filled the room as people sifted through what I'd gathered on the Harvester.

I'd sat in on sessions like this before, and if this had been a typical one, jokes and chatter would have ping-ponged from person to person—pressure-valve stuff in preparation for the task ahead.

Today was different. Today one of our own lay downstairs on a chilly steel table.

And so it was quiet. Preternaturally so.

Cold, midmorning light bladed in. I got up and twisted the vertical blinds to shield us from the sun. Nobody else seemed to have noticed.

It's one thing for a monster to lure and kill innocent women. It's another when he somehow hooks a savvy and armed law enforcement agent.

How had the Harvester gotten to Reen? Everyone asked that question, since everyone was convinced it was the Harvester. What about the guy had made Reen drop her guard? Earlier, some of the agents had postulated that the killer was physically large. Everybody knew he wouldn't disarm her with his charms. Not Reen.

To me, a mousy guy like McArdle getting to Reen seemed far more plausible than some hulking male overpowering her.

Everyone agreed he was clever. Had to be.

When I'd told them about McArdle and the pseudo-Gunderson, some liked the team idea. Except the lead agent noted how serial killers most often worked alone.

That was the thing with the Harvester case—each lead complicated a prior supposition. Frustration was shortening tempers big-time.

Some magical photocopier had overnight produced two dozen sets of my notes and files and charts. I'd also carted in Angela's box and Elizabeth's scrapbooks and albums. Autopsy files and crime scene reports littered the table, too, along with a huge carafe of Starbucks coffee, three boxes of donuts and muffins, a dozen phones, and two FBI laptops connected to Washington. Two additional desktop computers had been wheeled in on carts, as had two sets of compact portable file drawers.

Someone had hauled in an erasable whiteboard, and others had scrawled names, causes of death, missing body parts, locales, and added a whole bunch of arrows in red and green.

It looked like a mishmash to me.

On the large wall opposite me, someone had hung a huge map of Massachusetts. Thirteen red pins dotting the map denoted where each woman had been found and blue ones marked where each had lived.

The dead women were here, too, staring at us from a gallery thumbtacked on the end wall's bulletin board.

Reen's elderly mother had flown in from Hawaii. Although I'd offered my place, she was camped at the Copley Plaza until Reen's body was released. Mrs. Maekawa intended to fly her daughter back to the islands, where Reen would be interred.

Kranak was a mess. I'd swear he'd lost weight overnight and new lines etched his beefy face making him look almost feral. He'd refused to talk with me.

Made me feel like crap.

The FBI had sent a shrink over to Jazz and Inez Brown's place. Poor kid. The psychiatrist reported that if, and it was a big if, Inez ever could be brought back to herself, it would take many months of work. Jazz Brown, understandably, was furious at the invasion. He'd booted the shrink out of the house.

The FBI had gone after Mrs. Cheadle, too, but she wasn't in much better shape than Inez, and they'd learned nothing new.

They'd sent teams to rescrutinize everything—the rubble at McArdle's and the warehouse in Cambridge, my town house, Mrs. Cheadle's apartment, and all of the leads I'd followed on my own. They even sent an agent to Mount Auburn to interview Bones, who was dating an ICU nurse, I later learned.

The chief, Pisarro, and the relatives of the other possible Harvester victims were reinterviewed. FBI forensics reviewed the autopsy reports for all the women on my list, as well as Strabo, Chesa, Arlo, and the two men from the warehouse fire.

"You think he set the whole warehouse thing in motion?" I asked.

No one answered, which was pretty typical.

Special Agent Kathleen Lauria was the agent in charge of the multiagency task force. A head shorter than me, Lauria parted her wheat-colored hair in the middle. It brushed her shoulders as she moved. Her manner was softer than Reen's, and her caramel eyes gave the impression that she thought deeply about things. Maybe she did. When she listened intently, her tongue played with her crooked front tooth.

She was doing that now as she read Julius Binny's

file. Her head bobbed up, and she pushed the file across the table toward me.

It said Binny led a small, two-bit gang of toughs. Family deceased, except for a married sister in Chicago. The file listed his age and height and gang colors.

My eyes shot to Lauria. "You know the Harvester tied things up pretty neatly when he roasted Binny in that fire." I told her about my encounters with Binny. "I'm convinced the kid has been doing the Harvester's bidding all along. He spun Kranak and me a great yarn when we first found Chesa Jones's body. He implicated Blessing, and we bought it. He's the one who torched McArdle's in Roxbury, at McArdle's bidding, I'd bet. He liked McArdle a lot. Poor kid. Like Roland Blessing, the killer is a master at getting people to do his bidding, then getting rid of them."

"Thanks," she said. Lauria's head snapped to the time line on the whiteboard. She and another agent bent their heads together to talk.

The Harvester's list was lengthening. How long could the media be kept in the dark? I could imagine the brouhaha they'd make. Something told me the killer wouldn't like that.

A blue-blazered agent stuck a cigarette between his lips, but didn't light it. I sympathized. Like him, I longed for the real thing. In the past couple hours, we'd processed heaps of data and made plenty of lists, but only a few findings emerged. The Harvester had used surgical instruments found in an operating theater and a chainsaw on both Patricia and Elizabeth. His MO was inconsistent, although he liked the use of Valium and somehow got his victims to swallow the pills, presumably to quiet them. It was probable that he dumped the capsules' powder into some strong-tasting drink.

A knock at the door, then Andy Nogler walked in, rumpled, eyes red, lips bowed in a frown, followed by yet another FBI agent. The agent shook his head, then sat beside the lead agent and began whispering in her ear.

"What's up, Andy?" I said.

Andy pulled a chair beside mine and leaned close. "These Nazis got me out of bed at five. They've been putting me though the wringer about this Gunderson guy."

I peeked across the table at the two agents deep in hushed conversation. "Mind if Andy and I step out for a minute?" I asked.

The lead agent shook her head. "Just don't walk off."

"Not a chance." I led Andy to the hall outside the room.

Chapter Thirty-three

"What's going on, Tally?" Andy asked when I'd closed the door behind us.

"That man you counseled, Gunderson. He might be involved in the homicides of several women, including Elizabeth Flynn and Agent Maekawa. Aside from Strabo, who's conveniently dead, you're the only one who talked to him."

"That was two years ago." He slumped against the wall. "He wore a baseball cap and had a handlebar mustache. That's about all I remember. They showed me a sketch of some little shrimp I didn't recognize." He chewed a cuticle.

The sketch—McArdle, I'd bet. "How can you be sure that the sketch wasn't of Gunderson?"

Andy jiggled his hand. Nerves. "Gunderson had black hair, for one."

"The sketch wasn't in color."

"It was just different. All right?"

"No, Andy. Not all right. What are you holding back?"

He slapped his thighs. "Not a thing."

"It's me, Andy. Tally. I know you. You've been hiding stuff about Gunderson from the get-go."

Two red spots blossomed on his cheeks. "I thought he was gay."

"Yeah? And?"

He paced in a circle, hands clasped behind his back. "Did you know I am?"

"No. Did you date him or something?"

He notched his chin. "It's not anybody's damned business. This Gunderson . . . I really thought he was Flynn's uncle. But, yeah. One date."

"And this is what you've been hiding all this time?"

He nodded.

I rested a hand on his arm. "I don't care that you're gay. All right?"

He shrugged off my hand. "That's what everybody says. But there's this weasely suspicion that I might do something queer because I am one, right?"

"Oh, come on. What's the real deal, Andy?"

He fiddled with his watchband, avoiding my eyes. "Because we drank. We met at my apartment. And I got blotto. We . . . we did some grass, too."

"Did you have sex?"

He shook his head. "We kissed. That was it. And it wasn't very good. He was really awkward and . . . he was plain strange. That's all I remember. I think I might've passed out. In fact, I know I did. How the hell can I tell this to those suits in there?"

"I expect they've heard more vivid stuff."

Another gnaw on the cuticle. "Will you sit with me while I do?"

Forty minutes later, Special Agent Lauria and I walked down the hall toward the conference room. I'd just learned how good she was at inspiring confidences. Lauria had been warm and disarming with Andy, and he'd readily told her what he knew, which was a repeat of what he'd told me. She'd just released him, with a warning not to stray.

"Any help?" I asked.

"The gay thing might be." Her tongue tickled her crooked tooth. "What's your take, Ms. Whyte?"

"No team is doing this. McArdle and the fake Gunderson are one in the same. Ditto for the VW guy and 'Trepel.' "

"According to your fellow, Andy, Gunderson was the same height as him—five-ten. Yet you described McArdle at about five-six."

"So McArdle as Gunderson wore lifts."

"A handy man with disguises," she said.

"I think he's more than handy. I think he's outright great at it."

She nodded. "Unfortunately, I think he's great at a lot of things."

A half hour later, Lauria received a phone call. An FBI profiler from Quantico had landed at Logan and was on his way in.

The room's tension ratcheted up a notch.

*   *   *

Professor Arnold Jarvis was immensely fat. His gait was slow, his languid affect accentuated by a pair of granite-faced clones who accompanied him into the conference room. After Jarvis was provided with juice and a sandwich, he stood by the window that overlooked the Boston University medical complex while he ate.

Gert leaned close. "This is something."

"Just what, I'm not sure."

"I think he's cute."

"Jarvis? He's about fifty, Gert. And he looks like a beach ball."

"So?"

Everybody shut up when Jarvis took a seat at the table head, carefully opened his looseleaf notebook, and folded his hands in front of him like the church and the steeple.

"What we have here is a man who feels deeply inadequate."

His voice was soft and Midwestern flat, so that I had to strain to hear each word.

A Boston PD detective raised his hand. Jarvis removed his glasses. "Yes?"

"Why inadequate?"

"I will get to that." Jarvis smiled, and it wasn't pretty. "As I was saying, inadequate. But only a part of him feels that way. Another part feels highly superior and accomplished. He's clever and knows it. Our killer is between the ages of twenty-five and thirty-five and a Caucasian. Will there be any other questions?"

No one opened their mouth.

"Good. He may have been abused as a child—verbally, sexually, and, perhaps, physically—by his parents. Or the abuse could have come from classmates or a favorite teacher or a beloved relative. In any case, he finds himself ugly, inside and out. Hence his kindness to the people of the Roxbury neighborhood, as well as this Mrs. Cheadle, albeit he ultimately tried to take her life. I'm sure there are others he's been kind to. He needs to be liked. He perceives the women he kills as likable and admirable, thus he takes a souvenir, if you will, from each. The very best part of them, as he sees it.

"We would find few mirrors, if any, in his home. His purchase and maintenance of the funeral homes indicate that he has above-average financial resources with which to carry out his projects. He's no Dahmer, who lived in a squalid, small apartment.

"He lives in a house, perhaps on acreage, since his use of a chainsaw to dismember some victims would disturb close neighbors. I see him in the suburbs. Not the country—too many people stand a chance of knowing his business. Yet not the city, given his postmortem practices. The funeral homes were holding tanks, as well as theater sets. Nothing more. He's intelligent, and he gathers followers easily.

"He most likely operates, to date, in Massachusetts. We've found no MOs quite like these killings in our database. He is of the organized killer variety. If we use this Della Charles, aka Jones, as our first *discovered* case, albeit not the first case, his elaborate staging of the funeral parlor scene indicates a patient, well-funded person willing to put time and elaborate efforts into acquiring his prey. Once he was discovered, he coolly constructed a method to mask his kill. He also likes to tidy up. Hence, his theft of Della Charles's body and his retrieval of Elizabeth Flynn's, as well as his use of a cleaning woman at the funeral parlor. Something interrupted his disposal of Patricia Boch's remains, thus her burial behind the funeral parlor."

Someone sneezed, and Jarvis stared down his stubby nose at the perpetrator.

"To continue. The discovery of Flynn was a smoke screen. The same holds true for Angela Pisarro, Moira Blessing, and other victims. He *allowed* them to be found and I hate to think of what other souls he's dumped or buried at his home."

He'd like to keep them close. Of that I was sure.

"He is modestly successful at his day job." Jarvis smiled. "Get it? Day job?"

We all smiled on cue back at Jarvis.

"If, in fact," Jarvis continued, "he needs or chooses to be employed. He may be reserved, at times painfully so. Or he could be loud and boisterous to mask his social anxieties. He concocts idols. In other words, he develops crushes on those he admires."

"Sexual ones?" blurted out an FBI agent.

Jarvis removed his glasses and twirled them by the stem. "I don't know yet. He appears not to have sexually molested any of his victims before their death. Only Moira Blessing was raped after she died. No semen was found and he used her flute as a sexual device. Was this obfuscation? I suspect so, but can't be sure. I, for one, do not believe that we have a sexual predator on our hands, but something far more unusual. A person enchanted with the perfections of others."

"Reen's face," Kranak growled. "Her pretty face."

Jarvis's smile was condescending. "All in the eye of the beholder, eh?"

"So how come he left Officer Maekawa's body by one of the fishmarket stalls?" an agent asked.

Jarvis chewed an arm of his glasses. "Simple. He's evolving. Where he once wanted to deceive us, hide his doings, he's now saying, 'Look what I can do.' Yet, of course, he did remove her fingerprints. He doesn't want us getting too close, too fast. That makes him all the more dangerous. Then again, it opens the door for a mistake. Or it may mean that he's preparing to leave. To take his act on the road, so to speak."

"Christ!" blurted a state investigator.

"Is there anything, time-wise, that's setting him off?" an agent asked.

"His clock appears to be purely internal," Jarvis said. "We have our *why*, or much of it, and I expect in the next few days I'll be bringing you more whys and wherefores about our Harvester, a quaint name. But I'm perplexed by the *how*. What about this man entraps these disparate women? The hulking monster is a silly image.

"So what key did he use to enter these women's lives? I would suggest we find it. Quickly." He scanned each face at the table. "Don't you agree?"

That night, I curled on the couch beside Jake. I held a glass of cabernet and leaned my head on his shoulder. I'd tucked my body close to his, trying to feel an intimacy that was elusive.

Even if I'd dreamed of being close to Jake, it wasn't going to happen when he had a big show coming up.

The front door buzzed and I jerked upright, which

spilled my wine, making me curse and Jake laugh. Penny yipped.

Jake sprang for the door. I got some wet paper towels and started cleaning up.

"We finished!" Donna and Mary stood in the doorway, bubbling with excitement. "The Web and phone responses!" Donna laid a thick folder on the table.

"Way to go!" I smiled. I'd forgotten about them once Reen had been killed. "Gert didn't give that stuff to the FBI?"

Mary shrugged. "Well, she would've, but we figured you should see it first. I mean, after all, *we* did all the work." She shot a conspiratorial smile Donna's way.

"Any good stuff?" After I read it, I'd hand it over at tomorrow's meeting.

The front door buzzed again.

"I'm up," Jake said, again striding down the hall.

Mary frowned. "We didn't see much."

"Wait, Mare," Donna said. "What about that thing you found on Della Charles?"

"Sure," Mary said. "I noted it with a Post-it."

I fanned the stack. "Excellent."

"Hello Ms. Whyte. Girls." The imposing FBI agent crossed the room in a flash and reached for the folder.

"Pardon?" I said with asperity as I clung to the stack of pages. "Can I help you?"

My bodyguard offered a false smile. "I think that packet belongs to us."

"*Really*?" I stood. "I'm doing a read on Mary's novel." I gestured to her.

He chuckled. "Is that why it says Web responses on the cover?"

I forced myself not to glance down. "I don't care what the cover says, Agent . . . ?"

"Gilpin. A novel. Mind if I check out a couple of pages?"

"What the hell is going on, Tal?" Jake said.

"Nothing important," I said.

"Look, Ms. Whyte," Gilpin said. "We know these girls—"

"Women," Mary repeated.

"*Women* have been collating data for you. We've been eager to review it. So when they showed up with this folder in hand, I . . . You see my position?"

"Not really," I said.

"How will it look if tomorrow you arrive with this in hand? That could be construed as harboring evidence, obstructing justice. You see?"

I saw. "It's pretty ballsy of you to spirit it away before I've reviewed it."

He slid the folder from my slack hands. "We're nothing if not ballsy. Ladies."

"*Women*," Donna and Mary chorused.

Penny's fur bristled as her eyes followed Gilpin to the door.

Chapter Thirty-four

Sunday morning I was relieved to finally get my period. While the cramps did the conga across my belly, a migraine sizzled beneath the surface. So after I took my meds, I called in to tell the group in the conference room I'd be late.

"Heard you mixed it up with Agent Gilpin last night," Lauria said.

"To put it bluntly, he was a pain in the ass."

She laughed. "He's a good watchdog, but his social skills are that of a Rottweiler."

"Hey," I said. "I know some really sweet Rotties."

"Point taken. Were you aware that Agent Maekawa was paralleling your Harvester investigation?"

"Not really." It hurt, but I told her about my last conversation with Reen.

"She was what I call free soloing. From her resulting death, you can see why we disapprove of agents or *anyone* doing their own thing."

I kept my mouth shut.

"Her apartment turned up very little," Lauria said.

"I thought you agreed to take me along when you checked it."

"We had to go in last night," Lauria said.

Like I was in Florida? I leeched the anger from my voice. "Huh. Anyway, I'll be late, but I'll be there."

Urgency boiled inside me. Migraine or no, I had to see Reen's apartment. Now.

Since I was being watched by Gilpin, I couldn't go as me. As I gathered my costume, I appreciated the irony of it all. Didn't the Harvester do the same thing?

Gray wig from Halloween, cane from a knee injury, two layers of clothes, and my ancient sneakers. I pancaked my face, a la Mary, ran some age lines down my cheeks, blended, and voilà—ten years older, easy.

I gave Penny a treat, then snuck out the back door and down the steps. I carried a small bag of bird seed for Reen's birds.

I was about to unlock the tall wooden fence gate, when I remembered Jake had failed to oil its hinges.

I'd vowed to do it, but had forgotten. Hell. Oh, how bad could climbing over it be?

I hadn't figured on my costume's bulkiness. I made it to the top of the fence, tossed the cane and seed over the side, and tried to lurch over the wooden points.

"What the hell are you doing?"

Up three floors, Jake stood naked in the window, hands on hips.

So much for secrecy.

I motioned him to shut up, lost my balance and began sliding back down. My sneakers came to the rescue, and I scrabbled back up the fence and flung myself over.

Clutching the bird seed and cane, I ran in a crouch down Dartmouth Place. At Dartmouth Street, breathless and sweaty, I looked to the right. No Gilpin.

I'd made my escape.

The taxi dumped me several doors down the street from Reen's place. I fished out her key, then stood on the sidewalk, assessing if I'd been followed.

Like I'd know?

I hobbled toward Reen's leaning on the cane, unlocked her apartment door, and went inside.

A shiver of memory. I rested my hand against the wall, head bowed.

Oh, Christ, Reen. I miss you.

Red walls, black lacquer objects d'art, white couches. Austere.

Fingerprint dust over everything. And mud on the sisal floor. No blood, though. Reen wasn't killed here. Drawers and cabinet doors open.

I whispered to Cliffie and Bruno and Bubba, sniffling the whole time, as I dished out extra-large portions of seed. Not that they needed it. From the pile, it looked like Mrs. Maekawa was feeding them.

When I finished changing their water and laying fresh newspapers, I inhaled a stuttering breath, blew my nose, and looked around.

I found nothing of interest in the kitchen or the living room, except mementos that made me want to cry. I reached for the bedroom knob. A creaking, like the springs of a bed inside the room.

Run! my brain screamed.

I pressed my ear to the door, heard nada, then carefully turned the knob and pushed, listening, listening . . .

I peeked through the slit of the door. I couldn't see very well. Reen's dresser. Her closet. The end of the bed. Someone's butt rested on the end of the bed. A guy's.

Dear God. Kranak. What was he doing?

He had his jacket off, left shirtsleeve rolled way up, as he sat at the end of the bed, his back toward me. He raised a vial, then stuck a syringed needle into the vial's rubber end and drained it.

He tapped the full syringe twice.

Before I could speak, he plunged the needle into his upper arm.

I raced to the bed.

Kranak's hand snapped around my throat like a vise.

"Jesus, Rob," I choked out. "What are you doing?"

His hand dropped. He glanced at his arm and flushed. His scar was a white snake down the side of his face. "Nice getup, Tal."

"Are you okay?" I asked.

He finished what he'd started, plunging the liquid into his deltoid. When he pulled the needle from his arm, a crimson bead oozed from the needle's entry point.

"Are you all right?" I repeated.

"A course I'm all right. Lucky I didn't strangle you."

"What are you doing? With this? Here?"

He produced a black nylon bag from amidst the rumpled covers. "Doing? What's it look like, Tal?"

I rocked back on my heels. "Shooting up."

"Hey hey! There ya go. Ms. Samantha Spade scores again. Except you don't shoot heroin into a muscle, like I just did."

"Oh. I guess I knew that."

"Sure ya did." He swiped a hand across his face. "I'm a diabetic."

Talk about the wrong ballpark. "Oh, Rob. I . . ."

"The famous counselor without words. A first."

"I'm so sorry. Does anybody in the department know?"

"No." His grim face said it all.

"I won't say a word. Reen knew, didn't she?"

"She did."

I felt a spurt of jealousy, which was ridiculous.

I turned away from the hard-faced stranger and began going through Reen's bedroom. I searched her dresser drawers, between the folds of lingerie and sweaters, behind her photos and paintings. All while Kranak's eyes tap-danced across my back.

"You won't find anything," he said.

"Maybe." I sifted through her closet, clothes and boxes and shoes. I left her black-lacquered jewelry box for last, and after I opened the lid and eyeballed the neatly arranged earrings and bracelets and necklaces, I again felt the prick of disappointment.

"This sucks." I sat beside Kranak on the bed. He started to get up, but I slung an arm around his shoulder and held tight.

"Fuggetaboutit," I said. "Tell me. Please."

He sagged, turned his head away, and said something I couldn't hear.

"Rob?"

"I should have listened to you about the dickhead dicing up women."

"You did listen."

"Not enough. I got sidetracked by that organ-selling crap. You know the warehouse thing was drugs, Tal? Nothing but drugs. Oh, we thought it was corneas at first. But we were wrong. They were using Coleman coolers, dolling up homeless people as couriers, all the signs. . . . If I hadn't dropped the ball, Reen would—"

"How often have you lectured me on this? It wouldn't have changed a thing."

"Fuck you. Why do you think I haven't been talking to you? I knew you'd give me that touchy-feely shit, and I don't want to hear it."

"Well, fuck you, too. Okay? Now can we get past that?"

"No."

"Did you love her?"

"Love her? Yeah. She was also my crutch when my diabetes turned so bad I had to start shooting the insulin."

I pressed my cheek to Kranak's shoulder, my arm wrapped around his waist. "How long, Rob?"

"Nine months."

"Let me help?"

"Reen got it. You wouldn't." He stroked his scar.

"It's not gonna be the same between us, Tally."

"Of course it will."

"It won't."

I'd felt worse gut punches, though I couldn't remember when. "I'm here for you, Rob, and I'd like to understand. Remember that."

"I'll give ya a ride." He tossed his keys into the air.

I snagged them from midair and spread them on my palm. "Where did you get this charm?"

"Reen." He reached for the keys.

"Wait." The charm was a figure, a jointed one, made of gold. "Did she say where she got it?"

"Nope. Just gave it to me when . . . never mind. Just one night."

The charm was a twin of Della's earring. And the one worn by the VW guy.

"Whoever gave Reen this charm," I said. "He's our killer."

The air was frigid as Kranak drove me back to the town house, and I don't mean the weather. In fact, it was one of those February cheat days, where the New England temps soar as if spring was just around the corner. Trust me, it's a hell of a big corner.

After Kranak dropped me off, I cleaned up and arrived at the Grief Shop around noon. My blue mood worked beautifully with my menstrual cramps. Just beautifully.

I headed upstairs, gloomy with the knowledge of Kranak's diabetes, how much he was hurting about Reen, and that he wouldn't let me inside. I called Veda to say I couldn't come for Sunday dinner, which depressed me more.

In the conference room, I asked Lauria when I'd have access to the information abducted by Gilpin.

She pointed to a collated stack of pages in front of my seat.

"Each person got a set," she said.

"Found anything?" I asked her.

"So far, no. You received a lot of crank calls. And we haven't seen much interesting in the Web or e-mail messages. Maybe you will."

"Maybe," I said, still irritated at my watchdog's highhandedness. "Did Kranak tell you about Reen's charm?"

"Yes," Lauria said. "He and his CSS staff are examining it. We're going after stores that might sell it. A shame it's mass produced."

"What about Trepel and the taxidermy connection?"

"He's legit. And we're tracking down everyone he visited on his sales trip. So far, they look legit, too. Even the infamous Harry Pisarro doesn't seem a part of this."

After Gert filled me in about the morning's doings, I slipped into the empty chair beside Kranak. "Hey, Rob. Feel like going over some stuff with me?"

His eyes slid toward me, and I braced myself for one of his scathing comments.

He turned in his seat and gave me his back.

It appeared I'd lost two friends the day Reen Maekawa had died.

"We're not fucking getting anywhere!" said one of the Boston detectives.

I'd been mind-surfing. Zoning while I read through the Web and phone replies. The morning's blues had deepened. I felt empty and hopeless.

Except . . . "There's something here, in the Web responses."

"What?" barked the same detective. Fifteen pairs of eyes snapped my way.

"I . . . I don't know," I said, feeling stupid.

"I do," Gert said in a small voice. "At least, I think I do."

Now all eyes swiveled to her.

She blew a bubble. An immense one. "I think," she paused, chomp, chomp, peered around the table. "I think the—"

In walked Jarvis.

He held up an enlarged scan of the charm, as well as the polybagged charm itself. He began to speak.

Jarvis speculated that the charm was the Harvester's "tell." Gee, a surprise. He droned on about how the Harvester took things and had to leave this charm behind in order to feel fulfilled. It was a trade. He received a precious and perfect body part and in return left a gold charm representing the person he'd killed.

"It's more than that," I blurted out. Shit.

Jarvis's glasses almost skied off his pudgy nose as he peered down at me, frowning. "Pardon, Ms. Whyte?"

"I didn't mean to be so abrupt," I said. "It's just that he's left so few of these charms. Della. Now Reen. The man I saw in the Volkswagen."

Jarvis nodded. "And?"

"My gut says that your theory, forgive me, is a little off. First of all, he gave Reen the charm. When she was alive. There's something else, but . . . I wish I knew what."

His lips curved into a smile. "I never discount gut feelings. Imperfect though they are, they're usually based on some hidden knowledge that refuses to surface immediately. I'll keep your words in mind."

Jarvis continued to talk about the earring.

Gert leaned close. "Della appeared in some magazine."

"And you got this from?"

"The Web stuff." She turned a stack of pages over. "See?"

A talent agent recognized Della's face from some potential modeling shoots.

"Excellent, G. Della modeled years ago. I guess . . ." I rested my face in my hands. "Wait. It's something that . . . Yes!" I dived into Angela's box, piled stuff on the table, and pulled out a framed magazine page of Angela with some other college girls. Also on the page was a head shot of Angela, with a caption about her amazing eyes. The page had appeared three years earlier in *Glamour*.

I put it aside, shoved the rest out of the way, and pulled over Elizabeth Flynn's box. I lifted out albums until I came to the scrapbooks. There, in the second one. An article with photos about Elizabeth in *Shape* magazine.

"Magazines!" I shouted.

"Are you *done* with your demonstration, Ms. Whyte?" Jarvis said.

"That's how he picks them. I'd bet on it. After they appear in some magazine—national, regional— doesn't matter. He likes what he sees, then finds them."

Agent Lauria dragged my ass, along with Jarvis's and Gert's, down the hall.

Lauria paced the small room. Jarvis and I sat across from each other at a circular table. "You're sounding very sure about this magazine connection."

"I'm not," I said. "Sure, I mean. But it's the first thing that's made any sense."

Jarvis nodded his large head. "Yes. It *feels* right, as Ms. Whyte here would say." He tossed me a smile. "You see, Kathleen, it works. Oh, take a seat, for heavens sake. You're giving me palpitations."

Lauria laughed, then pulled out a chair and straddled it. "Go on, Jarvis."

"He'll come across a particular woman in a magazine who fascinates him because of something remarkable about her. The Pisarro girl's eyes. Or the Blessing girl's hands. Boch's legs, because she was a runner. And now it seems this Della Charles appeared in a magazine. He was drawn to her eyes, too. I'd wager that when we see the article, her eyes will be prominently featured."

"Della modeled years ago," I said. "Until we talk to the guy who sent the e-mail, we won't know if it's old or something new. I was told she wasn't currently modeling."

"By whom?" Lauria asked.

"An old friend of hers."

Lauria arched her eyebrows, but let my evasiveness pass. The less they bothered Mrs. Cheadle, the better.

"Okay," Lauria said. "What about the other women?"

"*Boston Magazine*, the *Boston Phoenix*, the *Globe*, and *Herald* must have run pieces on Patricia Boch, with photos. I bet they ran stuff about Moira Blessing and Inez, too."

Lauria looked from me to Gert to Jarvis. "A good hit." She pushed from the table. "I'll put a bunch of people on it. There are a hell of a lot of magazines and newspapers."

I turned to Jarvis. "He tracks them, doesn't he? He finds out where they live and work and then somehow he insinuates himself into their lives. The research is part of the fun." I quivered, knowing his cruelty. "Be nice if he got lots of subscriptions."

Jarvis laughed.

"Unfortunately, Tally," Lauria said, "we're not dealing with your run-of-the-mill stupid crook who robs a bank wearing a hard hat with his name written on it."

"A girl can dream, can't she?"

Chapter Thirty-five

That night we got out late from the task force. Although I'd missed going to Veda's and Bertha's, I felt hopeful for the first time in days.

When I walked through MGAP's doors the following morning, I slammed into a wall of tension. Donna's back was rigid, and she bustled out of the office carrying a load of files before I opened my mouth. Andy flipped his hands up and shrugged.

I tracked down Donna. "Okay, D, what's up?"

She didn't pause in her filing. "Nothing."

"Right. Spit it out. You always do in the end."

"I'm pissed at Mary. She left me high and dry this morning. You and Gert are working upstairs. And now Mary blew us off. She just left. So it's only Andy and me."

"You couldn't call anybody?"

She thrust out her bottom lip. "I called. And, yes,

someone's on the way in. But it's very uncool what Mary did."

"What happened?"

Donna shrugged. "She took some call from a friend of yours over at the lab in Sudbury. I could tell he didn't want to talk to her, but she wormed the information out of him. I don't know. She slammed down the phone and ran out of here, leaving us shorthanded and . . ." She rested a hand on her hip. "And I guess I'm annoyed and worried about her at the same time. And that's really annoying me."

After I calmed Donna down, I called Billy from my office.

"Doc Strabo was filled with tranqs," he said. "Enough to anesthetize a horse."

"So he was unconscious when he took that fall from the warehouse window?"

"Yup. Unless he was Superman."

Which meant that someone had pushed him.

After MGAP's relief arrived, I raced upstairs.

Gert gave me a one-fingered wave. Kranak was talking with a Boston PD cop. I assumed he knew about Strabo. Lauria looked tense when I walked over.

"Did you hear about John Strabo?" I said.

"Yes," Lauria replied.

"I never could see Strabo selling body parts or drugs. The whole thing smells."

Lauria notched her head and we moved to a corner of the room.

"You see it, don't you?" I continued. "How Strabo's death was a setup to draw attention away from the Harvester. John was a patsy, like Blessing and the Binny kid."

Lauria held up a hand. "Maybe. Yes, he was most

likely a homicide. But Kranak believes the Harvester and your Dr. Strabo were somehow connected."

"The killer's a pro at befriending people." I caught Kranak staring at us. He cut contact. "It's lousy, Strabo getting killed like that."

"Sure is," Lauria tapped keys on her laptop. "I do have some good news. The magazine connection seems to be panning out. Moira Blessing appeared in *Boston Magazine* and the *Phoenix*, among others. The same for Patricia Boch. And one of the other women had modeled on a national level."

"I sure didn't recognize her," I said.

Lauria smiled. "She was a *hand* model. The Harvester took her hands, too, six months before he cut off the Blessing girl's."

"It's like he's shopping!" I said. "He takes a pair of hands and adds it to his hands collection. Ditto for the eyes and the ears and . . . Christ, it's gruesome."

"They're all panning out," Lauria said. "Except for Della Charles."

"I know she modeled years ago."

Lauria shook her head. "The agent who contacted you said late last summer, he sent Ms. Charles on some tryouts for print modeling jobs. She never made it to any of them and he finally cut her loose. If she did appear in some magazine, we don't know which one. We're circulating the sketch of her to agencies around Boston. It's a matter of time."

I sighed. "Time that will give the Harvester a chance at his latest sweetie."

On my way home, I stopped at Mount Auburn to see Mrs. Cheadle. She was asleep, a hint of smile on her lips, her breathing natural. I felt good about her recovery.

I stayed for about forty-five minutes, but she never awakened. Maybe tomorrow.

Did she know anything about Della's modeling? Could that be why the Harvester had sent her the bees?

I stopped home briefly, then took Penny to the park for a run, where I was pestered by some jogger who thought Penny was the cutest thing. He couldn't stop petting her and talking about her three legs and what a beautifully shaped head she had for a German shepherd. Suddenly, that day's FBI shadow materialized. After he shooed off the jogger, he lectured me, hand on shoulder, about the dangers of conversing with strangers in strange places.

I tolerated it—he was only doing his job—but mentally ground my teeth. I loathed being followed by anyone, including my protectors.

I entered my living room to find Jake enthroned in a chair, eyes focused on a guy in a hideous green warm-up sprawled on my couch, an ice pack draped across his face.

Penny trotted over to stranger and began her sniffing routine.

"Christ, Jake." I whispered. "We've got all this weird stuff going on and—"

Jake shut me up with a kiss, then Mr. Lackadaisical started trolling my fridge. He handed me a Diet Coke and popped a Coors for himself. "Mighty annoying, I'll tell ya." He took a swig of beer. "I'm in the john and I hear the front buzzer—"

"Why weren't you at the studio?" I asked.

"Meeting with a client. Upstairs. So I'm in the can,

and it takes me some minutes to get downstairs. When I do, this dude was collapsed on our stoop."

"Did you call EMS? The cops?"

"I'm lifting my cell when he wakes up and says not to call anybody. Then he staggers to his feet, flashes an FBI badge, and orders me to help him inside."

I rolled my eyes. "What if the badge was fake? What if—"

His finger shut me up. I liked the kiss better.

"I half carry the guy inside," he said. "He's a big mother. He makes a call, and I go get an ice pack. 'I'm calling EMS,' I tell him. 'Don't fucking call anybody,' he says."

"You must have been batshit over that one."

He shrugged as he took a sip of beer.

Penny positioned herself by her food bowl, a hopeful look on her doggie face.

"This is a mess," I told Jake as I uncranked the can of dog food. I scooped kibbles into Penny's bowl, added some water, then said "okay."

"Hello."

I twirled. Two-hundred and fifty pounds of FBI agent stood rubbing his head.

"Glad to see you're okay, Ms. Whyte," the agent said. "Might you have some bottled water to drink? And some aspirin?"

I filled the agent's requests after I made him sit back down. He swallowed the aspirin dry and chased it with a guzzle of Poland Spring.

"What happened?" I asked.

"A small accident," the agent said.

"What really happened?"

He sighed. "You're my concern, Ms. Whyte. I'm relieved you're home safe."

I hooked my arm though the agent's. "Not to worry. Your other guy was all over me." I told him about the jogger in the park who'd admired Penny.

He massaged his temple. "Excuse me for a minute, ma'am. I've got to call in." He swiveled, so his back was to me, and whispered on the phone. Unfortunately, his muffled conversation gave me time to think.

When he snapped the phone shut, I cleared my throat. "Now that I think about it, I was told 'an agent' would be watching me. So how come—"

"Special Agent Lauria is on her way over." His voice was flat and hard.

"That wasn't an FBI agent in the park, was it?" I said.

His fog-colored eyes shuttered. "Could I have another bottled water, ma'am?"

"Oh, come on. Cut it out. There was no second FBI agent on me, was there?"

"No, ma'am. There was not."

Later that evening, Jake sketched as I described the guy in the park for Jarvis, Lauria, and the hulking agent.

Pulled-down baseball cap, sunglasses, buck teeth, lisp, jeans, and an Emerson College sweatshirt.

It didn't matter. Not Jake's sketch. Not my memory. Not all of their concern over the fake agent's appearance.

The Harvester had stood beside me, touched me, examined my face. He'd given my shoulder a friendly squeeze just before he'd walked off.

"I wish he'd do *something*." I raked a hand through my hair. "Instead of just—"

"Watch?" Jarvis said. "I suspect, in his mind, you play a special role."

"I can't begin to tell you how thrilled I am about that," I said.

"We'll add another agent," Lauria said. "There'll be two on you at all times."

It wouldn't make a difference. If he wanted me, he'd get me.

Jake and I made love that night. It was a frantic, desperate coupling.

I was spooked. Jake insisted I hide out at his cabin in Vermont.

I searched his face. It might be unconscionably handsome, but I'd found enough craggy lumps and bumps to make it dear. I suddenly realized what a swell support he'd been over the past few weeks. He'd taken great care with me.

Hiding out at his place sounded so appealing. Except . . . "I can't."

"Makes sense." Jake laced his words with sarcasm. "You acting as bait."

"Don't you see." I sighed. "I've been tracking him, learning about him from the day Blessing spouted off at Chesa in my group. Somehow, I've become a part of it all."

"What part, Tally?" Jake's voice was gruff as he cradled me.

I chuckled. "It can't be my face. I'm no beauty."

A growl. "Dammit, woman, you are."

"That's such bullshit. Maybe it's my hair, on a good hair day."

He stroked it, pressed his face to it, and inhaled

deeply. "Don't think that way. The FBI. The cops. They can't protect you. You've *got* to go away."

A fleeting thought, one I captured and turned this way and that. "You know, Jake, maybe you're right."

Tuesday morning, I saw a subtle change in the men and women occupying the conference room. Jackets were off and some of the agents and police officers wore jeans and polo shirts. Even those in suits had undone their ties. Kranak had doffed his, which lay like a parti-colored ribbon on the table.

We were in for the long haul, the euphoria of the magazine connection having dissipated when no new leads surfaced.

March was still roaring like a lion. Sleety snow spit from a pewter sky.

"I hate this weather," Lauria said, as we walked toward the small meeting room.

She laid the folder she carried on the formica table. "What's up?"

"I have an idea about my, um, situation."

She pointed to the manila folder. "This is all about you and your 'situation.' "

The thing was an inch thick. "Is J. Edgar Hoover alive or what?"

"SOP, given your relationship to the killer." She tapped the folder. "I don't like it, Tally. Everything points to him watching you for months. Yet he took out Reen, not you." She rested her cheek on her hand. "McArdle. Trepel. The VW guy. The whole side issue with Roland Blessing. Now this fake agent in the park. There could have been other instances where you encountered him, but didn't know it."

My laugh was hollow. "I'm sure there were. These are just the guys we've recognized. And let me say up front, it gives me the willies. It's even creepier that he could've made a move on me any time, but hasn't."

"I agree. So what's your idea."

"Tit for tat. I'll assume a disguise. I'll dye and straighten my hair. Bangs. Yeah. I look awful in bangs. I'll wear padding. Different lipstick. Red, I think. Definitely glasses. I'll drop off the radar as Tally Whyte, but still be involved. I can change my walk, too." I bent my shoulders and slumped. "I used to do that. Round my shoulders and all, when I was a kid. I was embarrassed by my height."

Lauria's smile was sardonic. "Can you imagine a guy being embarrassed by that? Sometimes I hate being a woman."

"I agree. Once I'm not me anymore, I'll reappear as an FBI agent and go back to work finding the bastard. What do you think?"

She nodded. "It's absurd, yet I can see it. Your vanishing could infuriate him."

I nodded. "Maybe it'll be a trigger. If I'm an object of desire, he'll get frantic, panicked, when he can't find me. I think that's just swell."

She licked her tooth. "Have you thought about if he sees through the disguise?"

"Sure. He'll already be furious with me. So he finds out who I am? He won't bother with the game anymore. He'll just kill me."

"Absolutely not." Veda folded her hands on her desk. "I forbid it."

"You're afraid," I said. "It's gone beyond that, Vede."

"Oh? Has it?" She waved a hand.

"Your bag of tricks is empty. I'm not a teenager anymore."

"You never listened to me then, either." Her shoulders sagged. "I'm too old for this. Too old. Who will be in on your little masquerade?"

"You. Jake. Lauria."

Her hands slid across the desk and she clutched mine. "If I lost you, it would be the end for me. Bertha would feel the same."

"You both survived the camps. You'll survive this. I love you, Vede."

"Remember. I want to see grandchildren."

I told the MGAP staff that I had to attend an essential conference. Gert knew there was no conference. I felt like crap lying to her.

When I left the Grief Shop, I ignored the fact that Gert and Kranak would kill me for not including them in the deception. Heck, they'd be my test subjects. If they didn't recognize me, no one would.

Jake glowered and railed against it. I survived, even after he stomped out shouting, "Who gives a good fuck what I think? I'm just the landlord!"

Lauria arrived and instructed me on a slew of things, from my getaway to enhancing my disguise.

Wednesday morning, a phalanx of FBI agents drove me to the airport and put me on a plane to Florida. I got off at Newark, was met by a petite agent who reminded me of Reen, and was carted off to New York where my transformation took place.

I had a ball. What girl doesn't love a makeover?

A day later, I deplaned in Manchester, New Hampshire, feeling weird. In the ladies room, I primped. My straight black, banged hair came just below my ears, exposing my skinny neck. Yuck. My ruby lips curved into a bow and my eyes hid behind smoky glasses that made them look larger. Unlike the real me, I wore eyeliner and mascara and shadow. My B-cup breasts were flattened to A cups, which felt awful. I hunched, so I looked about five-eight, and took smaller steps than my "Tally" stride.

I'd used a brooch to pin the neck of the disgusting frilly blouse that flourished beneath my black suit jacket. I hated the cut-her-off-at-the-knees straight skirt that topped a pair of awful black pumps with little gold buckles. The whole rig screamed "conservative," making me feel like Ms. Talbots. Blech.

I wheeled my suitcases to the rental car I'd booked as Emma Nash. As I drove toward Boston's Marriott Hotel, where the Washington FBI agents were staying, I fingered the small ruby ring on my pinkie. It was also part of my disguise.

I missed wearing the gold starfish ring that Veda had bought me on our long-ago trip to the Bahamas.

I practiced my Southern drawl. Lauria said the accent would go far in disguising Tally's voice as long as I didn't overdo it. I also pitched it higher than normal.

I tried to blow the negative thoughts from my head as I sped toward town.

Was I crazy? I felt a yawning uncertainty. Already I missed Jake, missed Penny.

I missed Tally, too.

Chapter Thirty-six

Lauria met me in the hotel lobby and showed me my room. After she left, I quickly changed into another alien and determinedly preppie frock, a dressy one I intended to wear to Jake's gala opening that evening.

I hadn't mentioned my outing to Lauria, so she had a fit when she caught me in front of the hotel hailing a cab.

"Already we've got problems," she said in a tone like Veda's. I cringed.

"I won't miss Jake's opening."

"It could be disaster," she said. "For you, I mean."

"Then come with me."

"Why the hell would I go to Jake Beal's gallery opening?"

"Because you love art."

She squeezed her eyes tight. Counting to a hundred?

"You hate dealing with nonprofessionals, don't you?" I said.

"Wait in the lobby. I'll be down in ten."

I moved across the SoWa gallery's parquet-floored, people-stuffed room. The flats I'd bought for my "costume" killed. So did the breast band, aka a vise.

Screw it. I slipped off the shoes and carried them. My feet sighed. So what were a few raised eyebrows? I was some stranger from Washington.

I was feeling pretty good. I'd seen Gert and Veda and Andy and Donna and Mary and a slew of other people I knew. None appeared to recognize me.

"Hurrah," I thought, just as Penny trotted up, a lacy bra held between her teeth.

Oh, Christ. A present for Mom. Adorable.

Of course Jake had brought Penny, just as I did to each of his openings. And of course she'd recognize me.

Lauria was in the toilet, Jake was schmoozing some bejeweled patron, and I was stuck pretending I didn't know my own dog, whose tail thumped against other guests, as she offered me her prize purloined bra.

If I walked away, she'd follow me. If I tried tugging it from her mouth, she'd tug back—a fun game.

I sidled to my left, aiming for the bowl of doggie treats Jake usually put beside the centerpiece of his exhibits. Jake has a great sense of irony.

I made it just as Lauria returned, spied Penny, and paled.

"Leave her alone," I said. "Trust me, it'll only make it worse if you try to lead her away from me. She'll growl and cause a fuss, which will make everyone notice us." I offered Penny the dog cracker.

Penny studied it, sniffed, then reluctantly dropped the bra into my waiting hand, while simultaneously scarfing up the treat.

David Copperfield had to have it easier than this.

"Ms. Nash!"

I quickly stuffed the wispy bra into the shoe I was carrying.

"Ms. Nash," Jake said, grinning. I'd swear he'd seen the whole thing.

Lauria gave me an I-told-you-so face as Jake shook her hand.

"Officer Lauria." Jake beamed.

"She's a special agent," I whispered to Jake.

"Have you seen what all the fuss is about?" he said, gesturing to the exhibit centerpiece hidden by a throng of people.

"I'm afraid not, Mr. Beal," I said.

He hooked an arm through mine, then parted the clump of "oohing" and "aahing" bodies. Lauria trailed after us. I could tell she was pissed.

I didn't care. Jake's sculpture blew all thought from my head.

The bust was twice the size of a human head. Made of steel, redwood, and ebony, it was of a woman. Women, actually. "She" took my breath away.

I played the tips of my fingers across her face. She was cool and smooth. My hand explored her chin and nose and eyes and hair.

She was me, but not me.

The nose and right side of the face were mine, but the left cheek and forehead belonged to Nola, Jake's sister. The chin belonged to Jake's mother.

The ebony hair . . . For a minute I saw her—Reen— in all her beauty. I couldn't lose it. Not here, not now.

"I did Reen's hair for you," he whispered. "A last-minute thing."

I stroked the ebony waterfall. "Thank you for understanding."

"I've been working on her off and on for two years now."

The piece was incandescent. "A keeper," I finally said, trying to keep it light.

"She's yours," he replied.

"But, Jake, I can't. She's a hundred-thousand-dollar sculpt—"

"*Yours.*"

The title, carved in steel and brass, on the base was "Beloved."

Oh, my. I couldn't stop staring at her. She wasn't beautiful. Not classically so. Yet her disparate parts synchronized and drew the watcher in with enormous power.

Shock rippled my body. "Jake, has anyone tried to buy it?"

"Sure. Not for sale, though."

"No one saw it before this evening?"

He puffed out his cheeks. "No."

"Excuse me," I repeated a thousand times as I made my way thought the crowd, desperate for air, for relief.

I looked back once. Jake was staring after me, a quizzical look on his strong face, while he gripped Penny's collar.

If he only knew what I'd seen. But I could never tell him.

Outside the gallery, I slipped into the pumps and stuffed the bra in my purse.

"What's wrong, Ta—Emma?" Lauria asked.

"Back at the hotel. We'll talk back at the hotel."

She grabbed my arm. "Was someone there? I've got people inside. Tell me."

"No. No one was there. But everyone was. Let's go."

I scrubbed my face and donned my pj's, my very own. When I exited the bathroom, Lauria handed me a bourbon. She held one, too.

"What happened back there?" she asked, sipping her drink.

I sat on the bed and folded my legs. "I know what he's doing."

"The Harvester?"

"Yes." I took a slug of bourbon. Maybe it would help me sleep that night, but I doubted it. "He's assembling a woman. He's taking a part from this one and another from that and assembling his perfect woman. His beloved."

Her glass halted midhoist. "Making a woman. You mean *Silence of the Lambs* making?"

Adrenaline juiced me to where I was trembling. "Not exactly. The book's killer wanted to *become* the woman. Our man is creating a collection of perfect parts that in his mind become the whole of his loved one."

She shook her head. "Except he took Angela's eyes, then Della's. That's two sets of eyes. The same for the hands."

My nerves settled to a rolling boil. "True. He keeps the best one for his woman. So if he sees a new part he prefers, such as Della's eyes over Angela's, he goes after it."

"Sure," she said. "I get it. I wonder what makes him choose one woman over another?"

"This is a guy with a borderline personality disorder. A man with a terribly shaky self-image. He over-idealizes people. That's how he chooses his victims.

"He wants to kill himself. Often. So he buries those feelings beneath a mountain of homicides. I'd say all his life he's been a poor little schmuck. Made fun of by the jocks. Ignored by the girls. And yet he's so damned smart. Genuinely so."

"A lot of guys are made fun of. They don't start collecting body parts."

"I don't mean to simplify. It's more complex. *He's* more complex. But he sees himself as a screwup, a loser, because someone he loved saw him that way. I can almost feel it—his longing to get it *right*."

"Right? Gross. Aren't these body parts going to shrivel up?"

"In reality? Sure. But not to him. They no longer have a reality for him. They always keep their beauty. He's collecting the flawless woman. The woman he idolizes. The woman he lost to a killer. I wonder, maybe he knew and loved her killer, too."

That night, the drums wouldn't stop pounding. They were strident and loud, and I finally reached for a shot of bourbon to quiet them.

That smoothed the edges, but I still couldn't sleep. I punched the spongy pillow, wishing I had my down one, and I longed for Jake's reassuring warmth. Penny's too.

The Harvester. A loved one of his—a victim of homicide. Aborted grief. I'd seen the scenario a thousand times. Poor thing.

Christ. All I needed was to start feeling sorry for him.

I must have dozed, because it took a while to surface at the phone's insistent brrring. It was Jake. The show was an huge success. He'd sold almost all the pieces.

We laughed over Penny and the bra thing, speculating on who owned the lingerie and why it was floating around the gallery. I was shocked how much I missed him. Before I blurted it out, he said "Missing you's like a bad bellyache."

Romantic as hell. That was Jake.

We were both horny and thought up dozens of

ways to sneak him into the hotel, most of which were hilarious and none of which were practical.

Then I had a bad thought. I wasn't there. Maybe he'd taken home one of the models that had flocked to his opening. That was his former MO. Still could be.

I said not a word.

While I was "gone," he was camping at my place to take care of Penny and answer the phone. I'd half hoped the Harvester had called, since my phone was tapped. But Jake reported no hang-ups or strange calls. He said I *had* received a call from a nurse. Mrs. Cheadle was talking a bit, were the nurse's words.

"You're not going to visit her, are you Tal?" His voice was brittle with worry.

"Of course not. I'm undercover, right?" I laughed. Jake swore.

He knew I was lying.

Chapter Thirty-seven

Thursday morning, feeling sleep deprived, I followed Lauria up the stairs to the conference room. Whoa. There was Fogarty, schmoozing up some FBI agent, probably mining tidbits for *Street Fighter*.

Lauria introduced me to the group as her assistant, and neither Kranak nor Gert gave "Emma" more than a glance. Around noon, half-a-dozen people broke for lunch, while the workaholics submitted take-out orders.

Kranak sauntered over to ask Lauria a question,

then offered to get lunch for Lauria and myself at the deli around the corner.

I upped the pitch of my normally husky voice. "Thanks. But I'm going out."

Kranak shoved a hand in his pants pocket. "Want to join me? The deli's decent."

Oh, great. Kranak wanted to be friends with "Emma."

"I'm afraid I've a few errands to run." As I breezed out, I overheard Lauria give Kranak an order for a Reuben.

"Ms. Nash," Kranak hollered as I was exiting the front door. "I'll give you a lift."

Oh, *peachy.* "Thanks."

Outside, icy rain blasted from the skies. Even the parking lot seagulls looked disgruntled. Kranak held my elbow as we skittered to his car. I made sure he did the leading, since I wasn't supposed to know what his car looked like.

We belted up and wheeled out of the lot.

"Where to?" he asked.

"Newbury Street." I'd take a taxi to Mount Auburn from there.

"So you live in Washington," Kranak said. "Where?"

"Arlington, actually."

"Huh. You ever been to Boston before?"

"A couple of times, years ago."

"Lousy weather," he barked.

"It sure is."

"So, tell me, what do you do for fun at night?"

He didn't really say that. Not only was it a lousy line, but Reen was dead less than a week. Did he know I was "Emma" and was yanking my chain? With

Kranak, it could be more complicated than that. I felt like a rat for not telling him.

"This okay?" He pulled up in front of the Ritz.

"Thanks again." I reached for the handle.

He laid a hand on my arm. "Um, Emma? I asked you a question."

My lips formed yet another lie. But as I looked into his sad, sweet eyes and that lumpy face I'd known for years, I couldn't.

I stalled. "Why, Officer Kranak?"

He puffed out his cheeks. "If I'm honest? I lost someone recently. You don't look like her, but . . . Well, your hair's the same color. She'd wear that red lipstick, too, sometimes. No ring, either, so . . ." He swiped a hand over his flattop. "I don't know. I just thought it might be a good idea."

Kranak *didn't* know it was me. And he'd hate that I'd been privy to his feelings. "There's someone special in my life, too."

He shrugged, grinned. "So how come I feel relieved?"

"Maybe because you miss her a lot?"

"I do. More than I ever would of thought in a million years."

I felt like a perfect shit.

The key to seeing Mrs. Cheadle was getting past Bones. The FBI agents shouldn't be a problem. I'd just tell them I was Lauria's assistant. I remembered to alter my normal stride, and minced right by the room where Bones usually waited.

Other than an elderly man reading the *Herald*, the room was empty. Where was Bones? Eating? Peeing?

In with his nurse flame? And where were the agents?

I entered the ICU. I wasn't surprised when no one looked up. I walked up to the circular station and cleared my throat.

"Can I help you?" the nurse said.

My mouth flapped, a buzzer buzzed, and she said "excuse me" as medical people raced to one of the rooms. I zoomed to Mrs. Cheadle's.

She lay in the bed, eyes open, staring at the ceiling. Someone had washed and brushed her long white hair, and it shined.

"Mrs. Cheadle?"

Her head slowly turned, but the eyes didn't focus on me. "Yes?"

I pulled up a chair and kissed her cheek. "Hi," I whispered. "It's Tally."

Her eyes moistened, then tears trickled down her cheeks. "Tally?"

My eyes burned, too. Just what I needed. "I'm in disguise and undercover. You can't tell anyone you've seen me."

"Ah." She gave me a conspiratorial smile. "What fun."

"How are you feeling?"

Her lips trembled. "Like I've been kicked by a cow."

"You'll keep feeling better and better. You'll see."

She patted my hand. "Of course I will."

I hugged her, terribly conscious of the tubes snaking into her body. "Is there anything I can get you? Do for you?"

Her voice rasped from disuse. "I'm all set. But how are my kitties doing?"

"They're great. Promise." She smiled while I detailed the doings of each cat.

"That nice Mr. Bones told me you and a group of friends were taking care of them and I wasn't to worry."

"And you shouldn't. They want their mom home, though."

She chuckled. "Their mom wants home, too."

A nurse poked her head into the room. "You are, ma'am?"

"Mrs. Cheadle's second cousin once removed," I said.

"Are you, now?" The nurse smiled. "Enjoy your visit."

"Well aren't you the hoot," Mrs. Cheadle whispered. "Saying you're my cousin."

I cheered that Mrs. Cheadle seemed sharp as ever. Her lids drooped. She might be enjoying this, but my visit was tiring her. "I need to ask you something about Della."

"I've dreamt of Della," she said. "And Chesa. And so much more."

I stroked her hand. "Had Della done some recent modeling? For a magazine? A newspaper, maybe?"

She squeezed her eyes tight, then finally shook her head.

"It's okay. It really is. Thank you for trying."

Her blackberry eyes opened. They were bright and knowing. "Not modeling, dear, but she had her picture taken for some article or other. Della was embarrassed by it all. It had to do with the homeless. My memory . . . It was last summer, I think. I asked for a picture for my albums." She shook her head, her lips compressed. "Never got it."

That letter hadn't been in Mrs. Cheadle's scrap-books when Reen and I had looked. "I'll try to find the magazine. If I do, I'll get you Della's photo. Can you remember the name of the magazine that did the article?" I crossed my fingers.

Mrs. Cheadle pressed a hand to her breast. The room grew quiet, the syncopated sounds of the ma-chines loud and rhythmic. Her lids drifted closed again.

I waited, but she'd fallen asleep. I kissed her cheek, then rose to my feet.

Her eyes snapped open. "Don't leave."

I smiled as I sat down. "I thought you were sleep-ing."

"Easy to do in this place. But, no, I was thinking. The magazine's name was something like *Camera In-side*. Or *In Photo*. Something. I can't quite catch it."

"You've done great. Just great. I'd better go. Oh, but you're doing swell."

A smile crept up her face. "Yes."

"I'll see you tomorrow."

"I hope so, dear Tally."

"Promise."

On my way out I collided with Bones, who stuck a gun in my belly. Cripes.

We sailed out of ICU, down the corridor, and past the waiting room.

"Thank you and good-bye," I said to him, trying to shake off his hand.

"Not so fast." He shoved me into a eight-by-ten room stacked with supplies.

I wanted to strangle the little pit bull. "What *is* your problem, suh?" I said in my best Georgia-peach drawl.

He pushed out his chin. "My problem is who the hell are you, lady?"

I gave him the second cousin spiel.

"You got ID?" he said.

I held up Emma's license. "Ah'm up from Washington, as you can see."

He jabbed a finger. "Well, that's just adorable. Where the hell have you been? Huh? She's only had one other relative visit since she's been here! *One!*"

One other relative? Friends, yes. But . . . "Suh, what other relation's been here to see my auntie?"

His eyes widened. "What's it to you?"

"Ah'm her cousin, *suh*. I have a right to know who's been visiting her. Heah?"

"Right, right, right. I can see you're related. Another cousin. From the darker side of the family. Couple days ago."

I didn't like it. Mrs. Cheadle had no living relatives. Period. "Her name?"

"*He* was from away, too. I forget his name. John. Dan. Real cheerful fella. George! Yeah. That's it. George Davis."

"Did you get an address?"

"No. Why should I?"

"Because, dammit, he's not her cousin. I'm it. Her only relative."

"Bullshit. He knew all about her."

"I don't give a flying fart. He could hurt her. Got it, suh? So don't let him near her again. Don't let anyone in but me and this Tally person." I stomped out and went in search of Mrs. Cheadle's FBI guards.

Guards my ass.

I found them in the cafeteria, eating bagels. I hoped they choked. I introduced myself as Lauria's assistant and asked where the hell they'd been when I'd gone in to see Mrs. Cheadle. I felt a childish burst of satisfaction as they stuttered out their excuses.

I told them about "George Davis," that I believed he was the Harvester, and that if a flea got past them to Mrs. Cheadle, Lauria would hear about it.

I left them with their mouths agape.

Would it take an army to keep Mrs. Cheadle safe?

Chapter Thirty-eight

"I've got a magazine name!" I whispered to Lauria. "Well, a sort-of name."

She hauled her "assistant" to a conference room corner, and I survived her tongue lashing about seeing Mrs. Cheadle, after which I told her about George Davis, Mrs. Cheadle's *other* cousin.

"The Harvester in blackface, no less," she said. "I wish the old woman was less delicate. Maybe in a day or so we can question her."

"I doubt it," was all I said.

She licked her crooked tooth. "The magazine won't be hard to find. As far as breaks go, it's a decent one."

"Mrs. Cheadle thought the photo shoot took place last summer. She said Della wasn't modeling. That article was about the homeless. And that it embarrassed Della."

She grinned. "What do you say we find out exactly what it was?"

We searched the Web for the photography magazine. My gut said this was the key. All we had to do was figure out how to turn it.

"Got it!" barked one of the agents. "*Inside Photographer*. Sound right?"

"Could be," Lauria said. "Where's it located?"

"Maynard, Mass." the agent said.

Lauria scrolled her finger down the wall map of Massachusetts. "Here. About thirty miles west of Boston. See?"

I peered at the map. "Huh. Out in the burbs. Let me be the one to call."

Her eyes surfed my face. "Don't screw up."

Lauria and I hotfooted it to the small office. We donned headsets and plugged them into the phone jacks. I dialed while she sat across from me, jiggling a pencil.

"Magazine Media Resources," answered the chipper-voiced woman.

I started. The name was . . . I couldn't catch the thought. "Hi. My name's Emma Nash. I'm trying to locate an article with a friend of mine in it."

"I'll need to know which of our five publications it appeared in, the date it was published, and the name of the article."

"*Inside Photographer* is the magazine, I think. I don't know when the article was published, but it dealt with the homeless."

"Sorry. Not enough information for me to find it. But let me give you Jenny Case's phone number. She edits the magazine. She'd know."

"You can't just connect me?"

"Our editors telecommute."

I jotted down Case's number. When I reached her, I did my spiel. It was followed by a conspicuous silence.

"Ms. Case?" I said.

"Um, yes. When did you see this article?"

"A friend of mine told me about it, actually. It was published maybe a few months ago. I'm just guessing. That's the problem."

"I see. And as I understand it, you're looking for a photograph in the article?"

The woman's authoritative voice had hardened. Lauria's eyes said I was blowing it. "It was of a friend of mine. Della Charles. She appeared in the article."

"And why do you want this photograph?"

Lauria tapped my hand, then mouthed *tell her the truth*.

I hesitated, then amended Lauria's instructions. "My friend, Della Charles, is dead. I'd like her photograph. A memento, you know?"

The editor's voice softened. "I'm sorry. Forgive my suspicions. We've got a pretty heated war going with a rival photography magazine. Never mind. You see, Ms. Nash, the odd thing is that the homeless spread was originally slated for our October issue, but got bumped back. Not unusual when a piece isn't time sensitive. It hasn't appeared in print yet. It's now slated for *Inside Photographer*'s April issue. That issue's at our pre-press house. The actual magazine won't hit subscribers for another three weeks."

Not published yet. "Just so I'm clear on this, Ms. Case. Only someone within *Inside Photographer* would have seen my friend's picture in the magazine spread?"

"Pretty much. We've got five trade magazines here.

So the staff of any one of those might have seen the article. You say you just want your friend's photograph?"

"It's complicated. Can you tell me a bit about Della's piece?"

Case described it as more photo essay than narrative article. It was titled "You Think You Know the Homeless." She couldn't remember who shot it. I asked Case if I could meet with her and to please not mention our call to anyone.

"There's obviously more going on here than you're telling me," she said.

"Yes. Important things that I can't talk about on the phone. I'd like to meet you today and see the article, if you have a copy of it."

"I do," she said, steel in her voice. "I can meet at two at our offices."

I looked to Lauria, who shook her head and mouthed "not there."

"How about somewhere I can grab a bite?" I said.

Case suggested a coffee shop. "I'll be frank, Ms. Nash. I don't like what you're asking me or the way you're asking it. Please arrive with some identification and a better explanation for all of this cloak-and-dagger stuff or you'll get nothing from me."

When I hung up, Lauria was busily tapping keys on her laptop.

"If I'm reading this right, Kathleen," I said, "the Harvester would *have* to be connected with one of the five magazines at Magazine Media Resources to have seen the article on Della. He could either work there, have something to do with the film lab, or could be a friend of the photographer."

She stared at me, grim-faced. "That's how I read it, too. His first mistake."

A thrill rushed through me. "Yes!"

Minutes later, Lauria softly closed the laptop. "This Jenny Case is clean. She's got a few unpaid Maynard parking tickets. Her credit info, license, social security number look fine. No prints on file. Doesn't rule her involvement out, but it helps."

I waited for the slam about not following orders.

Her grin was lopsided. "You'd never have made it in the FBI, Tally. You don't take direction well enough."

"I just thought mentioning that Della was a homicide would make for trouble."

"And maybe you were right. *In this instance*. You've got to listen to me, kiddo, or you could end up as a body part. First the sculpture show, then the Cheadle thing, now this. Disregard my instructions again and you're persona non grata with the case."

My face got hot and tight. "Don't even think it, Kathleen."

"Sure you're not living the fantasy?" she said.

"*Fantasy*? Day after day I counsel people left with the wreckage of homicide. The dead walk with me. I'm scared. I'm angry. My dad . . . I'm still trying to fix things."

"You can't, Tally," Lauria said.

"But it's me—who I am. With or without your permission, I'll see this through."

She nodded, but her eyes asked: *Will you end up dead, too*?

*   *   *

Maynard wasn't hard to find. We drove out Route 2, then followed Route 62 to the small industrial town that first was a mill town, and then home to Digital Computer. Nowadays, high-tech firms filled the mill.

Maynard's few downtown streets were narrow, and the three central ones were one-way. We parked and easily found the corner coffee shop done up Starbucks-style. I had described "Emma" to Case, and when we walked through the door an attractive brunette waved us over. Her smile was guarded as she pointed to the order counter.

After a short wait, we carried our food and drinks onto the small round table beside Case's coffee.

"So what's the scoop?" Case said without preamble.

Lauria whispered in Case's ear, the woman's eyes widening as Lauria spoke.

"I'd like to see a badge," Case said in an assertive voice.

"Keep it low." Lauria passed Case the leather holder.

The editor carefully examined it, then returned it to Lauria. "Looks real to me, but what do I know?" She barked a warm, loud laugh.

"This is no joke," Lauria said.

Case sobered. "I can see that, even though it sounds like a bunch of pulp fiction. So what do you want from me?"

"A list," I said. "Of people who could've seen that article."

"Can do." Case pulled a legal pad from her bulging canvas bag and scribbled across the yellow page at a furious pace. She handed me the list.

Lauria and I looked it over. "What's this group?" Lauria asked.

"Production people," Case said. "They've already got the article's Quark files and transparencies, so they would've also seen Della Charles's photograph."

"Idaho?" There were two names with Idaho Tech beside them.

"Our lithograph house. They'll have scanned the transparencies, so either one of those two people would have seen the woman's photograph."

"Okay," Lauria said, although she was mentally deleting them, too.

Two dozen names with Maynard next to them remained. "So all these people here in Maynard could have seen that photo spread with Della Charles's picture."

"I don't know if they all did," Case said. "It depends on how the file was passed around and which of the editors did what we call final reads, and which office, production, and graphics people worked on the spread."

"Would you tell us about the Maynard people, Ms. Case?" I asked.

She raised her eyebrows. "Isn't that your job?"

"We can find out the facts," Lauria said. "But we're looking for more than that."

Another bark of laughter from Case. "I was just busting your chops because the two of you make me very nervous."

"Sorry," Lauria said.

"How come I haven't heard anything about it?" Case asked. "The media."

"Ah, the media," Lauria said. "We've managed to keep that pressure cooker momentarily sealed. The killer knows we're onto him. But he doesn't know that we've discovered the *Inside Photographer* connection.

We don't want to give him publicity. And we don't want to scare people."

"Might be a good idea," Case said. "Don't you sometimes intentionally bring in the media?"

Lauria looked like she'd swallowed something distasteful. "Yes, although I don't belong to that camp. Not one of our people would talk about this situation."

Case waved at someone entering the cafe, then shook her head. "My assistant editor. She won't come over."

Lauria's patience was fraying. "Ms. Case. Why are you being so reticent about telling us what we want to know?"

"Because I protect my people."

"Oh, puh-lease," Lauria spit back. "How trite. Ms. Case, I'm a hunter. I like tracking my quarry. I like apprehending him even better. It makes me feel good. So it's simple. We can keep it low key and casual, which is what I thought this meeting was all about. Or you can accompany us into town and we can make it all official. Your choice."

Case stiffened. "That sounds like a threat."

Lauria smiled. "It is."

"Ms. Case," I said, interrupting. "Jenny. Both Agent Lauria and I understand all about loyalty. And we could be off base here. Maybe it wasn't someone involved with *Inside Photographer*. But what if it was? What if he found Della Charles because of that photo spread? Della wasn't the first. Nor was she the last."

"How many others?" Case asked.

As I reeled off the victims by name, Jenny Case paled.

"A lot of women, isn't it?" I said. "Overwhelming."

"Yes, but . . . it's not that. You said Moira Blessing? I read in the *Globe* a few years ago that she'd been raped and murdered. I thought the rapist did it."

"That's what was believed at the time. A smoke screen."

"I'll help," Case said. "Sure, I'll help. Three years ago we did a spread on Moira. She was a delicate, sweet kid. I remember the piece. Vividly. It won a prize. We titled it 'An Artist's Hands.' "

"What if I went inside Magazine Media Resources as a temp?" I said to Lauria as we were getting ready to leave. "I could start tomorrow."

Case nodded. "I don't see why not. We're always buried with work."

"Could you call in the editors for a meeting tomorrow?" Lauria said.

Case tapped a finger on her chin. "No. Several are traveling, which they do quite often. Trade shows, conferences. We hold an edit meeting each Monday. They all come—all of the telecommuting editors and in-house graphic artists. It would look strange if I spun the meeting date on one day's notice. Everyone'll be back for this Monday's weekly meeting."

Lauria peered down the street, as if she was studying the Maynard traffic. She was weighing options. If we waited until Monday, four precious days would pass. Another woman could be taken, killed, mutilated.

"Are any of the men on your list out of town?" Lauria asked.

Case nodded. "Harv Britt and his assistant are at a conference."

"We'll wait for Monday," Lauria said, an edge to her voice.

"I can still start tomorrow," I told Lauria on the drive back to town. "Sure, it's a Friday, but I can get to know people, check out the magazines, get gossip on the staff."

"I'm not sure it's going to be you, Tally."

"I'm the only one who's seen the Harvester up close and personal."

"In disguise, remember. I want to think about it. I'll call."

I flopped onto the hotel bed, emotionally wiped. Lauria said she'd call.

After an hour, the phone remained silent.

I called my apartment hoping to catch Jake. All I got was my machine. I left a message, called his cell, and left a message there, too.

My brain felt stuffed. So did my nose. I was coming down with a cold.

I took a fistful of vitamins and a hot shower, then tucked my lonely self in at the ungodly early hour of eight-thirty.

I dreamed of Reen. It wasn't pretty.

A buzzer jerked me from sleep. I checked my watch. Only eleven. It buzzed again, and I slid from the bed and shrugged into some sweats.

Maybe it was Lauria telling me we were on in Maynard for the following day.

The peephole showed me a waiter hoisting a room service tray while he conversed with that night's FBI guard dog.

The agent started manhandling the waiter, so the tray tilted precariously.

I squinted. The waiter was Jake. No wonder the agent was giving him a hard time. He looked about as much like a waiter as I did a gymnast.

I swung open the door.

"It's cool," I said to the agent. "I know the guy from Washington. He's my boyfriend."

"No visitors," the agent said. "That's what I was told."

"Run it by Special Agent Lauria. Just tell her it's my artist boyfriend."

The agent hung onto Jake, whose self-satisfied face was pissing him off, while he whispered into a cell phone. He clicked off and released Jake with a shove.

"Know this, fella," the agent said to Jake. "I'll be watching the door every second. Anything happens to the lady, you're dead meat. Got any problem with that?"

"Fuck you," Jake said with a smile, and entered the room.

I shut the door and leapt into Jake's arms.

We surfaced, sighing, after a long, wet kiss.

"I don't like this undercover shit, Tal."

I started to giggle. "You should talk."

He peered down at his uniform. "I look pretty fine, eh?"

I hugged his waist. "How's Penny?"

"Madly in love with me."

"Cute. You're such a pain in the ass. But I've missed you."

"Missed you, too. Nobody's around to nag me. Gets lonely."

"You're a riot." I lifted a dome on the tray. Blech. "Half-eaten pork chops?"

"I stole it from some doorway." He took my hands and led me to the bed.

I swooped in for a kiss, but he held my shoulders. "What?"

"The reason I came over," he said. "There's something . . ."

Shit. His face had hardened and his eyes had turned puppy sad. He chewed the end of his mustache.

"Someone's dead, right?" I said. "The Harvester got another woman? Is that it?"

He shook his head. "Your friend, Mrs. Cheadle. She died."

"Bullshit." I pushed him away. "I just saw her yesterday. She's recovering. Oh, Christ. He got to her, didn't he?"

"No one got to her, Tal. I was at your place when the hospital called. The nurse was very kind. She said Mrs. Cheadle slipped away a couple of hours ago."

"It was him. I'm sure it—"

"No. I asked if anyone had been in to see her after her cousin had left yesterday. The nurse said some guy named Bones was either at her bedside or peering in through the window. He never left her after you'd gone. He's the one who alerted them. She stopped breathing. They couldn't revive her. That's it."

I slumped on the bed, swiped at my tears with the back of my hand. "She's not! She can't be. Please. She

said she was feeling better. I saw her. She *was* better.
She was."

Jake held me, but I couldn't stop crying. That bastard had killed her. Maybe not today. But he'd killed
her, all right, by sending her those damned bees.

Oh, God, I didn't want any more of this.

I turned away from Jake, my hands covering my
face. He spooned himself around me, held me, and I
drifted into a sleep filled with shadows and fog.

I awakened in the middle of the night, groggy, remembering I was sad, but unsure why.

Then I saw Mrs. Cheadle's sweet face.

It wasn't fair! I sighed and ran my hand across Jake's
hair, spiked from sleep. He'd been sweet to come over
and tell me in person. Kindness mattered more than
just about anything.

I padded to the bathroom, closed the door, and used
the phone on the wall to call Lauria.

I told her about Mrs. Cheadle. Told her she could
add one more to the Harvester's list of homicides.
Told her she had to place me undercover at the magazine.

"Sorry, Tally. No."

I weighed my options. "I hate saying this, but I either go inside the magazine or I'd go to the media."

"You won't do that," Lauria said.

"Okay, you're right. But I'll rip off this damned wig
and use myself as a lure."

"Blackmail is an ineffective tool."

"I don't give a shit, Kathleen. Not anymore." I
pushed back the tears and swallowed hard. "I'm the
best person to do this."

"I'll arrest you so fast your undies'll turn inside out."

"Big whoop."

"You can't be objective," she said, softening her voice. "You've got too much personally invested in this thing."

"I can deal. Believe me. This is a cakewalk compared to my dad's murder. Your choice. I go in as Emma or I become Tally again and let the Harvester come get me."

"Out of the question." All business.

"Dammit, Kath, you're not offering me any options. Let me go in there."

Silence, then "No." She hung up.

Chapter Thirty-nine

Jake was awake when I returned from the bathroom, and we made love. Afterward, he instantly fell asleep. I tossed and turned, and I finally took one of the books on serial killers into the bathroom and read there, so I wouldn't awaken Jake. And I cried. For Mrs. Cheadle. For Chesa. For Reen and Della and Elizabeth and Moira and Inez and Patricia. And for all the women with promises of tomorrows who would never see them because some crazy man thought he was collecting perfection.

We were close to catching him.

I pictured myself embraced by the Harvester, and I was afraid. I wanted to run off to palm trees and ca-

lypso music and sugar-sand beaches. Kathleen was
right. I shouldn't be doing this stuff.

But if not me, then who? Ego. That was ego speaking. But, dammit, I was different from the cops, the
FBI, Kathleen, or Kranak or any of them. Because I
let the feelings in, just like I taught in my cop class.

Except I hadn't felt him that day in the park when
he'd played an FBI agent.

Oh, screw it.

I brushed my teeth, showered, and applied
"Emma's" makeup. As I settled her wig on my head,
I studied Emma in the mirror. Was this how the Harvester felt each time he donned a new disguise—trans-
formed?

I touched my breasts, pleasantly sore from Jake's
lips and hands, then bound them with the Ace ban-
dage.

As Emma, was I pretty to men? Alluring? Desir-
able?

Even with the bound breasts, I felt sexier as Emma
than as Tally.

Why?

I had to do it, didn't I? I had to go get the Harvester, right? As much as I'd like to hide, I couldn't
abandon the dead.

I left Jake asleep on the bed, a note on my pillow.
I saluted my FBI watchdog as I traipsed downstairs to
the dining room. I ordered French toast, bacon, and
downed coffee while I phoned Jenny Case on the cellular given me by the FBI.

I implied this was an FBI-orchestrated deal. She
agreed to my temping as an office worker at *Magazine
Media Resources*. I'd meet her there at eight-thirty.

I lingered over my meal—even with the drive, I

couldn't leave for another hour. I finally called Kathleen and told her what I'd done.

"Good," she said.

"You're supposed to be livid."

Kathleen laughed. "I can do the shrinky dink thing, too. I reasoned that if I didn't go for it, you would. It would mean you were committed to this thing heart and soul."

"I hate a wiseass."

"Takes one to know one. You *are* the best person for this, much as I hate to admit it. But it could get very ugly."

"I know. And I'm scared."

"You better be. Me, too. We'll watch your back. We've also got people on each of the Magazine Media Resource men on Case's list."

"What about the women?"

"We're watching them, too. But statistically and behaviorally, our killer is a man. Remember, Tal, he's gathering parts for his ideal woman."

"I agree," I said. "Except there's something we're missing here."

"What?"

I sighed. "Again, it's a feeling, rather than a knowing. I'll try and work it through. Like Jarvis says, these feelings spring from our subconscious understanding of things that our conscious mind has yet to acknowledge."

On my way to the car, I literally bumped into Kranak.

He doffed an invisible fedora. "Excuse me. Just the lady I was looking for."

"Sergeant Kranak. I'm afraid I'm on my way out. And in a rush."

I got one of his toothy grins. "No problem. Later?"

He was up to something. Oh, why the hell not? "Tonight? Here at the hotel?"

He made a pistol with his fingers and shot it. "Gotcha."

Magazine Media Resources was nothing like I expected. Instead of expansive offices, hushed cubicles, and plush carpet, there was a small main room, not unlike an optometrist's showroom, with five mismatched metal desks crammed into a too-small space. A couple of fluorescent tubes flickered in the cheap ceiling, a fax machine burped and wheezed, and a photocopier ka-thumped. Phones rang, incessantly. Tchotchkes were everywhere, from Beanie Babies to a postcard of Laura Bush holding a whip.

The atmosphere felt casual, warm, and busy.

Four female faces swiveled my way as I entered behind Jenny Case.

"Hey, Jens," hollered a women who sat in front of a desk mounded with paper.

Jenny introduced me to the four, including the office manager and the production manager, a Botticelli look-alike. My desk was front and center, the better to sign for FedEx and UPS deliveries that I was told streamed into the office.

"We're bare bones here," Case said. "The editors all telecommute. So does the design director, although his assistant is here. Come on, I'll introduce you."

We walked through the cluttered front room and down a narrow, short hall. A ten-by-twelve conference room sat on the left. The door on the right held a cube-sized room where a graphic artist was hunkered over a massive Macintosh monitor.

Mark Ellsworth was twenty-four years old and one of the four male names on my list. He also stood six-foot-three, was pipe-stem thin, and wore the distracted face of an intellectual dreamer. I didn't see how he could be our guy.

Case left me to my duties, reminding me that I'd meet the entire editorial and design staff on Monday, when they'd all attend the edit meeting.

Friday came and went. I spent my day filing, answering phones, signing for packages, and running errands. I took time to review several back issues of *Inside Photographer*. They were filled with ads for professional developing and printing machines, film, digital, and other stuff useful to the photography trade.

Articles offered tips on studio and landscape photography, film and digital, photo supplies and equipment comparisons, and trends in the business. Along with *Inside Photographer*, MMR also published magazines for graphic artists, digital artists, and professional painters. I'd seen their magazine devoted to sculptors at Jake's studio, which focused the niggle of familiarity when I'd first heard the corporate name.

Magazine Media Resources' trade magazines were aimed at professionals, rather than consumers, and were only available by subscription.

As I was signing for yet another delivery, a female editor and her production editor breezed in. "Blues" had arrived. The office manager patiently explained that "blues" or "blue lines" were the dummy magazine, and editors, assistants, and production people looked them over for any mistakes or marks on the pages before the magazine shipped to the printer. Theirs were actually in color, not blue.

According to her, blue lines were a dying commodity in the digital era.

I chatted up the office staff about the names on Jenny Case's list. I learned that all four men were single and between twenty-five and forty years old, which fit Jarvis's profile. I learned little else except they liked staff photographer Harv Britt, although he was exceptionally quiet, and that they didn't much care for Britt's assistant, who, when he wasn't working with Britt, shared the office in back with Ellsworth.

It felt like a futile day, and the mind-numbing filing and phone answering gave me far too much time to think about Mrs. Cheadle. It was my evening to feed and water her beloved cats, and I made a mental note to find homes for them.

Case called me once, on some fabricated pretext, while I was reviewing the magazine library in the cellar. I told her I'd learned little.

I again asked her who had done the homeless spread. She said it was staff photographer Britt. I made sure Lauria knew.

I left for town feeling exhausted and missing MGAP and its people.

After a stop at Mrs. Cheadle's, I arrived back at the hotel. I called Dave Haywood, pretended I was on some faraway isle, and began making arrangements for Mrs. Cheadle's funeral once OCME released her remains. He asked why she was at the Grief Shop and I explained that her death was being treated as a homicide. When we disconnected, I again found myself heartily sick of the repeated lies I told friends and loved ones about who and where I was.

How did undercover cops stand it? How long could I? And then I remembered I'd agreed to meet Kranak that night. A stupid move on my part, if there ever was one.

Kranak knocked on my hotel room door on the dot of seven. He wasn't alone. Gert and Veda marched in behind him.

Gert looked uncomfortable, Veda, resigned, and Kranak positively jolly.

"You know who I am," I said to Kranak.

"I do." The unsaid words were "I'm gonna kill you when we're alone."

Veda sat at the small table beside Kranak, in front of the windows that offered a view of the harbor. Gert took a seat on the floor, rather than beside me on the bed.

I felt like I was on trial.

"Gert figured it out," Veda said. "You'd better tell them all of it."

I told. The faces on Mount Rushmore were more lively.

When I finished, they got up to leave.

"Come on, guys," I said. "Say *something*."

Veda left, head shaking, followed by a stiff-backed, bubble-blowing Gert. Kranak turned in the doorway, his hands curled into white-knuckled fists.

"You couldn't trust me." Sad eyes reflected his profound disappointment.

"Rob, I . . ."

He closed the door softly behind him.

I felt like crap all weekend as we worked gathering

dossiers on the employees of Magazine Media Resources.

We learned that the spread on the homeless with Della had been Britt's idea from the get-go. Not unusual. His assistant, Steve Vellner, was disliked by the office staff. Apparently Vellner got into lots of credit-card scrapes. Jim Spinelli was the design director and a bit of a prima donna. Finally, there was Mark Ellsworth, the graphic artist who worked on all of the magazines, as did Britt and Spinelli.

The FBI had assigned an agent to each employee, male and female alike. But the four men remained our focus, even though Ellsworth seemed too tall for our killer.

I hoped the info on one of the men would wave a red flag, signaling he was IT.

Didn't happen.

I longed for Jake, annoyed by my increasing need for the guy. Lauria strongly suggested Jake not return to the hotel, citing my safety as her reason. I agreed, except it was my emotional safety that worried me when it came to Mr. Beal. When I called him, I nagged, giving him a million instructions for Penny, all of which he already knew.

Kranak was back to avoiding me. And Gert was firmly camped in the Tally-as-pariah group. Made me feel swell. Gert was working in the conference room, as were Mary and Donna, who'd volunteered to help over the weekend.

Did I mention Lauria had grown decidedly cool to me? Not fun.

Even Veda wouldn't talk to me, except for raking me over more burning embers for my undercover work at the magazine.

Saturday night, I holed up in my hotel room and held a self-pity party. It wasn't that much fun.

I felt trapped in my masquerade and disenfranchised from everyone I loved. I called Kranak, then Gert, then Veda. Each time, I met with a machine and hung up. I searched in vain for the long picture.

At the FBI's expense I got drunk on Old Grandad, then maudlin about my dad, and even more so about the mom I'd never known. I crashed around midnight.

Sunday was a repeat of Saturday, minus the bourbon.

I switched to milk to quiet the drums, which of course didn't work, and woke at 3 A.M. I read about serial killers until dawn broke over Boston Harbor.

By Monday morning, the day I was sure I'd meet our killer, I believed that Tally Whyte was a dream. My reality was Emma Nash, and she was in a pissy mood and primed for a fight.

Bodies jammed Media Magazine Resources' conference room—almost two dozen of them. In my best chirpy voice, I took orders for bagels, muffins, tea, and coffee from the clack-clacking editors and design staff that crowded the room.

Upon my return, I made sure I could hand each person his or her order and get a good look at each face.

The babble continued as I passed out food and drinks. I felt like a frigging stewardess.

Steve Vellner weighed about two hundred and fifty pounds. He stared at my nonboobs, yet kept yapping to some female editor when I handed him his muffin.

I pictured McArdle and the thin VW driver. Even

the Harvester wasn't *that* good at disguises. Vellner was out of the running.

I set Jim Spinelli's and Mark Ellsworth's food down. Spinelli, somewhere in his late twenties like Ellsworth, remained on the list. Not too big, not too small. He wore a buzz cut and was clean shaven. His chiseled chin reminded me of "Trepel." My hand shook from the adrenaline rush as I set down his coffee.

He probably thought the new temp was a junkie.

I passed out more food to women editors, then finally squeezed behind the line of folding chairs to Harv Britt.

Dressed all in black, his back was to me. I set down his coffee as he turned to an editor across the table from him.

Holy moly. Britt looked more like McArdle than McArdle had.

When he tugged his ear, just as McArdle had done, I freaked.

I plunked down the tray with the food, mumbled, "Excuse me," and fled.

Back at my desk, I got control of my shakes. Okay, I couldn't tell Britt's height. But his hair was shaggy and he had large, Dopey ears. He didn't wear a beard, which made sense. All the better to paste on different fake ones.

His outfit—black T-shirt beneath a black jacket and black jeans—was as trendy as McArdle's suit was staid. But clothes don't make the man.

Britt looked more fit than McArdle, but "Emma's" slouch was diametrically opposed to my normal posture.

Britt wore thick glasses, and I hadn't caught whether his eyes were pale.

It didn't matter. Britt and McArdle had to be one and the same.

I lifted the phone to alert Kathleen. I hadn't even talked to the guy. I hadn't heard his voice or seen his walk or even his height. I set the receiver down on its cradle.

I didn't want to just guess or go with my gut. I wanted to *know*.

Two nail-chewing hours later, the meeting broke up. Per our agreement, Case made a point of introducing me to the three men I'd yet to formally meet.

Vellner was definitely out. But if I hadn't seen Britt, I would have said that Spinelli was still a candidate.

I put his face, with makeup, on top of McArdle's, Trepel's, the VW driver's, and the ballcapped FBI agent who'd "rescued" me in the park.

They all worked.

In turn, Spinelli examined me as if I were a piece of beef. I guess he liked what he saw, because he started oozing testosterone as he chatted about his exalted position at MMR. He used the pronoun "I" a million times, further attempting to endear himself to me.

I was relieved when Case, much to Spinelli's obvious annoyance, ushered me over to Britt, who was talking to the production manager. Britt stood about five-foot-eight—just the right height—and looked to be in his midthirties.

A tremor again passed through me at his shocking resemblance to McArdle.

We shook hands. Mine, I'm sure, was sweaty. His was firm. He smelled of Bay Rum aftershave, the kind my dad had always worn. A sea of memories washed over me. Always did.

"So you're here temping, Ms. Nash?" Britt's affect was low-key and affable. Here was a guy who people easily liked.

"Call me Emma. Please. Yes. I'm hoping it'll lead to something in publishing."

He tugged his ear, laughed, and rocked back on his heels. "God forbid. They pay nothing. They overwork us. I should've stayed in Maine."

"I'm from Maine, too. A long time ago." I smiled. "But you wouldn't do anything else but take photographs, right?"

He pointed a finger at me. "You've got my number."

He was nothing like Spinelli; no projection of a slimeball on the hunt. Which made me like him better for our killer, not to mention that his eyes *were* pale. "Your work's striking. I've seen it in the magazine."

"Thank you," he said, again tugging his ear. "I think it's okay, too." He tilted his head. "You're a pretty woman, Emma. Mind if I take your glasses off?"

"Not at all."

He gently drew them off, then grinned. "Great bones. I'd like to shoot you."

I laughed, embarrassed. "No way."

He slid my glasses back onto my face. "Think about it."

"I do a little photography. Hacking around. Some handcoloring stuff, too."

He rested a hand on my shoulder. "Bring it in. Show me some."

"Thanks. I will." I tried to get a rise out of him. "I've some stuff published in the *Harvard Post*. Are you familiar with Harvard?"

"Great apple picking." Not a shadow, not a flicker. "Oops. Duty calls."

He wove across the room jammed with clumps of chatting editors and slung an arm around one of the editorial assistants.

How stupid—letting him take off my glasses and stare at my face. And yet I'd agreed—instantly. Been flattered, in fact.

Had I just revealed myself to the Harvester?

Odd. With all of the physical evidence telling me that Britt was our killer, why wasn't I convinced?

Chapter Forty

Lauria and I sat around a small table in my room, feasting on room service.

"It's him, Kath." I dipped a shrimp in cocktail sauce. "So how come I'm having problems with it?"

She tapped her lips with the linen napkin. "Happens. You find the guy, but you can't believe it's *really* the guy. You're excited. But then you start having doubts."

"Maybe." I poked my fork at the quiche Lorraine. "It's too easy."

She shook her head. "Nothing about this case has been easy."

"No. No, you're right." I told her about allowing him to remove my glasses.

"We can't afford those mistakes, Tally," she said. "*You* can't afford them."

"I know. Britt was so nice. It was weird. Here I was

liking the guy, and flattered that he wanted to photograph me, and at the same time thinking he'd killed and mutilated more than a dozen women. Although he looked like McArdle, his persona was so different, I didn't associate him with McArdle. It was bizarre."

"You know, you're right." She waved her steak knife like a sword. "Absolutely right. Get it? How disarmed you are by the guy? It makes perfect sense."

She watched me with those intense eyes of hers, as she slid a piece of steak into her mouth.

"If he'd given me the creeps," I said, "like that Spinelli guy, it would be different. Spinelli couldn't lure me down the hall. Britt? Sure. I can see it." I laughed. "He even wore the same aftershave as my dad. And we're both from Maine."

"Huh?"

"It's not a biggie, Kath. It made me like him more. That's all."

"Well, *I* don't like it." She chewed, slowly. "No. I can't say I do."

"It was nothing. Just some overripe memories."

"Hope so."

"So what's next?"

Midchew, she smiled. "We catch 'em."

When I returned from the bathroom, Lauria had cranked one of the windows wide, lit a butt, and was yapping on the phone.

"Freezing in here," I said. I turned up the heat, sat, and gave my scalp a good scratch. How anyone could wear a wig day in and day out, I'd never understand.

"He's clever, Kath," I said. "Clever and cunning."

"So are we. Unlike that dope out in the hall."

"My watchdog?"

"I dated him once. A lousy lay. And not a lot of spare change upstairs."

I smiled. "I'm glad I met you, Kathleen."

"Me, too."

A knock at the door. Lauria checked her watch. "Too early for the troops. You stay put."

I donned my wig and glasses, while she peered through the peephole.

"Who is it?" I asked, hoping it was Jake. She waved me over.

I pressed an eye to the peephole. Mary stood in the hall looking anxious, her nose peeking over the stack of paperwork she carried. "It's one of my counselors. I'll hit the bathroom. Without the whole costume bit, she might recognize me."

I skedaddled, thinking how much this incognito stuff stank.

"What was that all about?" I asked after Lauria signaled the all-clear.

"Some paperwork on our poster boys over at the magazine. I needed it tonight. Your Gert sent it by."

"I wish Gert had come." I plopped onto the bed. "She sent Mary because she's pissed at me. They all are." I told her about my visit from Gert, Veda, and Kranak.

"Shit. I didn't want Kranak and Gert knowing. The more people, etc."

"I should have told them."

"I hope they don't screw up." She lit another cigarette.

"They won't. I'm pooped, Kath. I'm going to bed."

"Not yet, Tal." She wagged her cigarette. "We've got a powwow about to begin."

*   *   *

Eight FBI agents were jammed in my hotel room, including Jarvis, Kathleen, and an agent orchestrating a conference call on speakerphone.

Too tired to discover why the party was in my room—better view, maybe?—I sat back on the bed and watched the show.

The agents reviewed again and again the dossier they'd collected on Harv Britt.

Britt lived alone on a large estate in Lexington he'd inherited from his parents. His father had been a surgeon. A prestigious and famous one. His mother, a homemaker. They not only left Britt the house. They'd left him rich.

He'd gone to Phillips Exeter Academy, where he'd repeatedly gotten into mischief. After his parents were mugged and murdered, Britt flunked out of Harvard, then disappeared for several years. No credit cards. No driver's license. No nothing.

When he resurfaced, he was into photography and landed several low-paying jobs at a variety of small publications. He then arrived at Media Magazine Resources and worked his way up from assistant to his present, senior staff photographer position.

His love life appeared nonexistent, which fit with my take on the killer. Much volleying took place across the table as to whether he was gay.

Several agents, along with Jarvis, thought so. Lauria didn't. I agreed, but kept my trap shut, hoping the seemingly endless debate would soon wind down.

According to FBI documents, I'd counseled one James Harvey Britowsky nine years earlier. A shock, and Lauria showed me the picture of the then thin, acned twenty-two-year-old, producing a ripple of memory.

I didn't believe much in coincidences.

Britowsky had in the intervening years, legally changed his name. The FBI hypothesized that my first meeting with McArdle/Britt in the funeral home is what set McArdle/Britt to stalking me.

"So was Blessing just Britt's pawn?" I asked, and was ignored.

Everyone agreed that Britt looked good for it, especially given his striking resemblance to McArdle. One of the agents held Jake's sketch of McArdle beside Britt's photo in the magazine. The resemblance was uncanny.

"Let's go get him," Lauria said, her eyes seeking those of her fellow agents.

"I agree."

"Agree."

"Yes!"

"Hold it," came the disembodied bass voice on speakerphone.

"Pardon, sir?" Kathleen said.

"I don't feel we have enough evidence on this Britt to take him."

"But, sir," Lauria said. "We can—"

"No, Special Agent Lauria," the bass voice said. "Trap him instead. Isn't that what Ms. Whyte is there for?"

Eyes pinned me to the headboard. Before I could speak, the bass voice continued.

"If she's compliant, we'll use a standard setup. Will the state and Boston law enforcement be amenable?"

"I expect so," Lauria said. "But—"

"Absolutely," another agent chimed in.

Lauria leaned toward the phone. "I strongly disagree that this is the action we should take, sir."

"Jarvis?" the bass voice said.

Jarvis's eyes drooped, while he ran a finger back and forth across his lips. He sighed, looked at me, then at the speakerphone. "Yes, sir. I'm afraid I agree with you."

"Kathleen?" the voice said from the speakerphone.

Lauria's forehead furrowed. "If Ms. Whyte agrees. Tally?" Her eyes were soft and open as she said my name. She mouthed, "Think about it."

She was right. I should mull it over. But, hell, what was the point?

"Sure. I'm game." I savored the irony of the word. I just hoped I wasn't the sacrificial lamb.

Tuesday morning around ten at Magazine Media Resources, I took a breather. I wore my very own wire taped to my torso. When the fashion mags said accessorize, wires weren't exactly what I'd pictured.

We'd begun casting our flies for the Harvester. The supporting players included dozens of FBI agents, Boston police officers, and state cops. Now was the time to call Harv Britt at his home office.

I told him I'd not only reconsidered having him take my photograph, but had pitched a story to my editor at the *Harvard Post* and wondered if I could interview him. I'd also bring my photography portfolio.

"Super, Emma. We could meet this afternoon after work, here at my studio."

Perfect. His home was where everyone wanted me

to be. Except today was too soon. I followed the script I'd rehearsed with Kathleen.

"I can't today," I said, oozing disappointment. "Would tomorrow work?"

"Hang on."

I hung, zoning while the office hustled and bustled around me.

"Emma?" Britt said. "I have a shoot at a barn in Acton tomorrow. I should be done by four. If you can get off work early, you could meet me there. I'll be all set up and can photograph you there and then."

"Sure," I said. "I'll treat you to dinner and we can do the interview while we eat."

"Um, no, I can't do dinner. But we'll work something out about the article."

"Excellent!" I positively bristled with enthusiasm. "I wanted to tell you—I've got a magazine spread that I appeared in last year. Mind if I bring it?"

"I'd love to see it," he said. "And don't forget your portfolio."

"Not a chance."

We were off and running.

I called Kathleen at lunch, and was disturbed when I couldn't reach her. She was supposed to be available to me 24/7 while I posed as the Harvester's next pigeon.

I called her second-in-command, who was also unavailable.

Gee, I was getting a real feeling of security here.

I could call the "alert" number they'd given me, but hesitated. This wasn't an emergency, just informational.

If I didn't reach her in fifteen minutes, I'd call the alert.

I filed, checked my watch, signed for a UPS delivery, and answered phones.

As I was again checking my watch, my cell phone vibrated.

"Be right back," I said to the office manager. I made my way to the bathroom, shut the door, turned on the faucet, and answered the secure cell phone given to me by Kathleen. "Emma here."

"Get off work now," Kathleen said. "Play ill and meet me at your hotel room."

"Why?"

"Problems. Just do it. Now!"

I varoomed into town and flew into my room. "What happened?"

No one answered. I got one of those crawlie feelings, as if I'd been set up.

I chewed my lip, then pulled out my pepper spray, slipped off my shoes, and padded to the bathroom door. I wrenched it open.

Nada.

I flung back the shower curtain.

Empty.

I crept back into the bedroom, and as silently as possible bent on my knees, and peered under the bed.

Not a soul.

I flopped onto the bed. Unless my hotel room had a hidey-hole, like Mrs. Cheadle's place, I was alone.

Where was my FBI watchdog? Where was Kathleen?

The door crashed open.

Kranak stood in a crouch, both hands gripping his 9mm, which pointed straight at me.

"You that mad at me?" I collapsed back onto the bed in relief.

"I heard noises." Kranak holstered his gun. "How'd you get here so fast?"

"I zoomed." I propped myself up on my elbows. "I got this weird call from Kathleen. She scared me. What's wrong?"

Kranak slumped on the end of the bed. "I was supposed to be here when you arrived."

"So you weren't here. Big deal. What's happened, Rob?"

"It's . . . It's Gert. She's missing."

"*What?*"

"Fa' Christ's sake, get your hearing checked." He wouldn't look at me.

I grabbed his arm. "Explain exactly what you mean by 'missing,' Rob."

"That's where Kathleen and half a those FBI suits are. Looking for her. She disappeared. Car parked on the street in front of her place, no sign of struggle there or inside her apartment. I got my team going over her place with tweezers. But she's gone. Poof. They're not gonna find her."

I sat back, smothered by the weight of his words. "No, they won't find her."

We didn't race around, didn't make calls, didn't even scream "Gert!," when that's what we both wanted to do. We just sat there, numb.

I looked at Kranak, for the first time noticing the sag of his jowls, the whiteness banding his lips. His scar looked like a worm undulating across his worry-lined face.

I was sure I looked worse.

My cell phone vibrated. "Yeah?"

"I'm on my way over," Kathleen said.

Kathleen paced, flipping pages of a steno book as she read. She looked as disheveled as Kranak and I did.

Gert's day sounded normal. "She spent maybe an hour working upstairs with us," Kathleen said. "Your guy Andy said it was a busy day for MGAP."

I wished I'd been there. Maybe . . .

"Don't, Tally," Kathleen said.

"Yes. Sorry."

"A security guard named Charlie waved Gert good-bye at five-thirty. But she failed to show up at some bar known as Trip's at eight."

"Our gang meets there pretty regularly." It felt like decades since I'd shared one of our convivial evenings. "How did you find out she didn't show?"

"That Dixie chick called me on the boat," Kranak said.

Kathleen rolled her eyes. "Which he didn't answer!"

Kranak sneered. "Yeah, I did. Or you wouldn't know squat."

"Two hours later, you mean," Kathleen said.

Kranak notched his head. "Fuck you."

"Stop it!" I lurched off the bed. "How can you have a pissing contest when the Harvester's taken Gert?"

"We can't swear she was taken," Kathleen said.

"Oh, right." Kranak stood. "I'm going to the office, *ladies*. You need me, holler."

Kranak stomped out. He felt squeezed out of the loop, was furious at himself for not calling Dixie back sooner, and felt helpless about Gert's disappearance. I didn't blame him at all. "Go on, Kath." Defeat cuddled me like a soggy cloak.

"This Dixie did say she thought Gert was dating someone new. A possible lead."

I sighed. "Gert's always dating someone new. Any chance she went home to Brooklyn, to see her parents? Some emergency?"

"We checked. Without alarming them, we learned all was well. Gert had called last Sunday, like every week, no new men mentioned, yada, yada."

"Her brother—"

"Is in California and hasn't talked to her in weeks."

"What about Donna or Andy or Mary or the other MGAP people?"

"All appear to be in the clear and know nothing, except for Mary. The girl and the guard, Charlie, were the last to see Gert."

"Gert sent Mary over here with those papers. What did Mary say when you interviewed her?"

Kathleen lit a cigarette. "Not much. One of our guys made a stupid comment about her makeup. Clammed her right up."

"Swell. We're sort of friends. She's worked with us for three years. She has this mentor thing with me going a little bit. What if I talked to her as Tally?"

"Not a chance."

"What about you interviewing her and 'Emma' playing secretary? If I'm there, maybe I could nudge a bit this way or that. Come on, Kath. We're desperate here."

"All right. Fix yourself up, *Emma*, and we'll head over to the conference room."

"No, wait. Let's bring her over here. It's less intimidating."

Kathleen inhaled deeply blowing the smoke out through her nose. "Fine."

Chapter Forty-one

We had to meet with Mary before four, since she had an appointment. Lauria stressed the urgency, and Mary surprised us by asking if we could connect at Trip's.

I followed Lauria into the bar. I felt uncomfortable, haunted. I saw Gert flirting. Gert laughing. Gert drinking those awful sloe gin fizzes.

And Gert telling us about her latest man. It was always a man with Gert. I pressed my thumbs to my burning eyes.

This last one might be the end of her.

We took a corner table by the window. Lauria opened the drapes, and afternoon light filtered through cloudy glass into the nearly empty bar.

Toots, unlit cigarette drooping from full lips, polished the counter. The room smelled sour from bodies and booze. Someone punched on "A Boy Named Sue."

Although I salivated for a bourbon, I ordered a Diet Coke. Farful, Trip's dog, trotted over and flopped his muzzle down on my lap.

"Lose the dog," Lauria said.

"How am I supposed to do that?" I snapped.

Lauria sighed, shook her head, and wagged a fry

Farful's way. My "best friend" abandoned me without a backward glance.

"We're all tired and spooked and upset," Lauria said. "Let's try and relax."

Mary arrived moments later. My heart lurched. She'd smeared an extra ounce of that awful makeup on her face, maybe in protest, and glommed on the eyeliner and mascara. Her armor.

Damn that agent for bruising the kid's self-esteem. Now she had Lauria's grilling to look forward to. If Lauria took off the gloves, I'd end it.

A mini tape recorder whirred, and I flipped open my steno pad for notes. Lauria's voice was soft and welcoming. "As I understand it, Mary, Gert gave you the stack of papers to deliver just before she left work."

"Yes," Mary said, checking her watch.

"Then what did she do?" Lauria asked.

"She, um, said good-bye to Charlie and me, and left."

"Did you see her go to her car?" Lauria said.

"Yes. She forgot to tell me what room you were in, so I ran after her."

"And where was she when she told you the room number?"

"At her car. She told me the room, then she said she'd see me that night at Trip's." Mary's hand stroked Farful's head.

"And was that the last you saw her?" Lauria said.

"Yes. May I leave now?"

"Where are you off to?" Lauria said.

I saw it as a bid to make Mary more comfortable. Instead it made her more nervous. She fiddled with a loose thread on her sweater.

"I guess you'll find out if you want to," Mary said. "Nothing's private anymore."

"Mary, you—"

"It's okay, Emma. It's an AA meeting. In college, I had a problem."

I was surprised, but it made perfect sense.

Lauria patted the girl's hand. "A lot of people have problems. I'm glad that you've done something about it."

"You won't tell, will you?" Mary said.

"No," Lauria replied.

I felt lousy having discovered a secret I was never meant to know.

"Only a couple minutes more." Lauria reviewed her notes on the security guard's interview. "Did Gert mention anyone new in her life? Boyfriend? Friend? Anyone?"

"Not to me," Mary answered.

"The guard said that he caught the taillights of a car leaving just after Ms. Gomez left. Did you see the car, Mary?"

Mary chewed a nail. "I don't know."

I felt Lauria's frustration. And if I felt it, so did Mary. I pitched my voice to Emma's.

"Mary," I said. "Was there an odd-looking car in the lot or a stranger wandering around or anything out of the ordinary?"

"No," she said. "But, well . . ."

"Anything at all, Mary. It doesn't matter how small."

Her head bobbed up. "It was really cold. I was out-side without my coat, so I was freezing and . . . I saw the exhaust steam from another car near where Gert was parked."

"So you saw a parked car running," I said. "No lights?"

"Not that I saw."

"Could you see the car? Did the car follow Gert out?"

More nail chewing. "I didn't see. Not when I was outside. Like I said, I was really cold, so I ran right back in. I didn't pay that much attention. I'm really sorry."

"Nothing to be sorry about, Mary," I said.

Lauria pinched my knee so I'd shut up.

"Try to describe the car," Lauria said.

"I don't know cars very well. All I remember is that it was big and dark. Long. Maybe like an SUV. Sort of like Tally's, but a different color."

"Doesn't Ms. Whyte drive a Jeep?" Lauria said.

"Yes." Mary smiled. "I think so. But . . . I don't know if it was a Jeep, exactly. Can I go now?"

"One sec," Lauria said. "You said the truck was dark. Try and picture the color."

"It was dark out. The lights were on in the lot. All I remember is that maybe it was black. But I don't know. I wish I knew, but I don't."

Lauria patted her hand. "Thanks for the help."

Tears puddled in Mary's eyes. "Gert said she'd see me later. I'm so upset. We were supposed to meet here. Have some fun. Is she going to be all right?"

"We'll find her," Lauria said. "Not to worry."

"So we shouldn't worry, huh?" I said after Mary had left.

Lauria lit a cigarette. "Yeah we should worry. You drive a Jeep, right?"

"A dark green one." The bar was filling up. All I wanted to do was leave.

"SUVs are ubiquitous," Lauria said. "It could've been blue, green, black. And all the guy did was turn on his car. He could've been warming it up. But at least it's something. What does Britt drive?"

"I don't know," I said. "But lay money it's a dark SUV."

We left Trip's, and I talked Kathleen into taking me over to Gert's studio apartment. It was the funkiest, funniest place—all Day-Glo colors and sixties paraphernalia. I missed Gert terribly and heard her voice in my head as I scoured the large room. I felt invasive. I didn't belong there, looking into her most private things.

Like it mattered? The FBI and the CSS people had already been through the place, covering it with black-and-white fingerprint grit, leaving drawers open, and piling sofa and chair cushions in stacks.

As I moved around the room, nothing perked my antenna. Kathleen assured me that all leads were being followed, all phone calls and such investigated, that FBI forensics were the best and on and on and on.

I told her she sounded like a law-enforcement recruiting agent, and I was ready to sign up, by golly, and for some reason she found that funny, and we both laughed, tears streaming down our faces. The relief was intense.

It didn't last, of course, and as we trudged back to our hotel, the euphoria fizzed.

I desperately hoped that tomorrow we'd find Gert and catch Britt in the act of adding me to his collection.

Would Emma appeal to him?

I'd make damned sure she did.

* * *

Hunkered in my bed, I watched TV, pretending to be interested in an underwater exploration of Cleopatra's sunken palace. Now *there* was a woman who attracted men. What would The Harvester have gone for? Her fabled eyes. Sure.

I kept seeing Liz Taylor's.

I was having sick thoughts. All night. Picturing Britt peeling back Reen's face and scooping out Della's eyes and sawing off Inez's feet.

Who was he, really, this person with such desperate cravings?

I didn't drink. Couldn't eat. Wished I still smoked.

When the phone rang, I snatched it up and barked "Yeah?"

"It's Kathleen. We found a charm."

"You mean the jointed-man one?"

"Yeah. In the parking lot of OCME."

Wednesday morning, I dressed in a black turtleneck, a loose one, since I again wore the FBI's recording device. I pulled on a black tube skirt that ended just above my ankles. I wore a circle pin, echoes of the Talbots image I'd semi-abandoned for a sleeker, more alluring style.

I painted my nails and applied my makeup—more than Tally would wear, but still subtle. I slashed my lips with red.

I spritzed on Chanel Number 5. Classic, but still great.

Hell, I was trying to interest the creep, wasn't I?

Lauria called around noon. Britt drove a black Suburban. Bingo.

I returned to my desk, sure that everyone there believed I had a bladder problem.

I was to meet Britt at four. By three-fifteen I was humming.

At three-thirty, Spinelli sauntered from the cave he shared with Ellsworth to inform me that Britt had postponed our meeting until six. The shoot was running late.

"Six?" I said to Spinelli, thinking that at six it was dark. "Um, that might be a problem. Do you have his cell number?"

"Nope." He smirked, then said something to the production manager that annoyed her. She took a swat at him, and he scooted back to his den.

Hard to believe, but no one in the office had Britt's cell phone number.

Swell.

I called Jenny Case and struck out with her, too. Apparently Britt's cellular was personal. He liked keeping it that way.

I didn't like it one bit. Had Britt sensed the trap? That I was Tally? Did he prefer the cover of dark?

Or had Gert replaced Emma in his plans?

Or were we wrong? Was Spinelli the Harvester? Or in league with him? Maybe Spinelli was setting me off, having me stand up Britt so he could arrange something more comfortable for himself?

I didn't like the not knowing.

I made yet another trip to the toilet to inform Kathleen.

"Why don't you just turn on the wire?" Kathleen said.

Duh.

Two more hours of waiting. I was going to go nuts here.

Except for Randie, the production manager, everyone at Media Magazines bailed by four-forty-five. Gee, I had a whole extra hour to ponder unanswerables.

"Hey," she said on her return from locking the back door, "were you planning on hanging around for a while?"

"Yeah. I've got some work to finish up."

"Do you have a key?"

Crap. "No, I don't."

A chagrined smile crept across her face. "Harv's notorious for postponing stuff, including his deadlines." She laughed. "I'm going to happy hour down the street. A bunch of us always go on Thursdays. Why not come along and bag the work?"

Sounded like a plan to me.

"We're going to a place called SinJin's on Main Street," I said to my watchers as I followed Randie's pickup truck. "We're parking out back, behind the CVS, in the lot."

"Gotcha," Lauria said.

"I'll be with a group, so it's hard to talk. But I'll keep you posted."

"Excellent," Lauria replied.

The place belonged to the dark pine, dim-lit, cacophonous school of bars and grills. Maynard memorabilia hung on the walls. I followed Randie past the bar and into the dining area alongside it, where we were hailed by four coworkers. A food table held the typical buffalo wings, fried mozzarella sticks, and other high-calorie-nosh.

As we sat, a waitress in black jeans and a white shirt

materialized, and I was gently teased for my order of Diet Coke.

We huddled almost head to head, those of us who wanted to talk. Spinelli ate, gobbling food as if it were his final supper. Maybe it was intended as mine. I didn't much like the covert looks he kept sneaking my way.

An editor joined us, and some apparently deaf soul cranked up the jukebox. A few desultory glances were cast by table members at other tables, but SinJin's, at least at five, was no meat market.

I went for a potato skin, oddly ravenous. Periodically, I checked my watch. Time moved at the speed of a dozing sloth. I half-listened to the conversation, the excitement about a new magazine launch and how bummed they still were when two old magazines had folded. Interesting, but I was too antsy to give it my full attention.

After forty minutes, I gathered my stuff, unable to stand the waiting any longer, though I still had more than a half hour before I met Britt in Acton. What the hell. I'd drive really, really slow to the barn.

Our production manager hailed someone standing at the entrance to the room. A man. One in a too-large brown coat and brown fishing-style cap pulled low on his head. Spinelli looked his way and groaned. He knew the guy, too.

As the man turned toward the bar, he waved at our group, and one of the faded lights caught his face.

What was Britt doing at the bar?

Chapter Forty-two

More people piled into the restaurant, and the noise ratcheted up another notch.

I grabbed a lipstick from my bag and hotfooted it to the ladies room. Somebody entered right after me. I slipped inside a stall.

"Can you hear me?" I whispered into my earpiece.

"Got you, Tally," came Lauria's reassuring voice in my earpiece.

"Britt's here. I . . ."

A flush of the next toilet muffled her reply.

"What?" I said.

"We're on him," Lauria said. "Ditto for you."

"Stay close." I was juiced on adrenaline.

"We sure will."

After the other woman left, I emerged from the stall. I reapplied my lipstick and rejoined the group. Everything seemed normal. Randie was talking to Spinelli, the others were laughing at a joke, the waitress was replacing dirty glasses with full ones.

Britt waved again, then left the bar.

I waited a couple beats, laid some money on the table, said my good-byes, and walked deliberately and slowly out of SinJin's.

When I hit the street, it was dark, empty.

Britt was headed out back.

It creeped me out, following him like that, but I was desperate to find Gert.

"You there?" I whispered.

"We're here," my watchers said.

Britt had parked a couple cars down from me in the same lot. He bleeped his Suburban open, then hopped in. The taillights winked on.

I unlocked my rental Taurus—damn, why wouldn't it open? There! I slid into the car, started it up, then followed the Suburban.

I caught my breath as I drove. The Suburban's lights snaked over back roads that led from Maynard, through Lincoln, toward Lexington.

"You still there?" I said.

"Sure are," Lauria replied. "Try and relax."

I could do that. Right.

The steering wheel felt cold beneath my hands. I tugged on my gloves, pushed a Stevie Ray Vaughn CD into the player, and tapped a beat on the dash— anything to not picture what Britt might have done to Gert.

We curved through dark back roads overhung with branches of fir and pine. I disliked driving the unfamiliar car. Why had Britt arrived at the bar, rather than met me at the barn? Had Spinelli spun me a yarn, so that in actuality, I'd stood up Britt?

Or, more likely, was Britt playing some game? I knew too well how the Harvester loved games.

I cracked the window and breathed in the snapping cold air. The flick of a memory. Something said in the pub. And . . . ?

A four-way stop peppered with a few shops and a restaurant sat beside a frozen cornfield. The Suburban turned left. My rearview mirror glistened with the lights of two cars, one of which was an SUV. Agents. A clutch of them, ready for the kill.

Cars streamed by me, preventing my turn, but just

as the light flicked orange, I made it. The SUV made it, too. The second car of agents would find us.

The Suburban chugged on at a reasonable 40 mph. More frozen fields, with farm stands flanking the road. Easy to see Britt's truck.

What had been said at SinJin's about a magazine that sparked my noggin?

"Holy shit," I said.

"You okay?" Lauria screeched in my ear.

"Fine. Just fine. Sorry." Was it possible?

The pub group had been talking about two of their magazines that had folded. I remembered that clearly. One I'd never heard of, but the second—*Restoration*—I'd heard the name before.

From Mary.

When she'd come aboard at MGAP, Mary had been assistant editor at a magazine called *Restoration*. In fact, she'd worked the two jobs for more than a year.

I could either sing "It's a Small Word, After All," or . . .

Mary?

Coincidences like that just didn't happen.

I squinted in the darkness. The Suburban remained a couple car lengths ahead. Dense woods crowded the narrow, winding road.

Were we in Lexington yet?

The SUV in my rearview mirror remained glued to my tail.

Mary.

Ridiculous. Absurd. What was I thinking?

Of course Mary wasn't helping the Harvester.

Except that funny little niggle wouldn't go away.

No, Mary wouldn't do that. Help some man create his lost beloved.

I tugged a bottle of Poland Springs from my purse and sipped.

Gert would tell me to turn the cube. *Dammit*! I smashed the bottle against the seat. He had *Gert*, for Christsake.

I was breathing hard. I had to calm down. Think. *Reason*.

Mary must have been at Magazine Media Resources for several years while she worked on *Restoration*, yet when the company name came up in connection with the Harvester, she'd said nothing.

What did I know about Mary? A lot. But did I really? Her mother was a homicide victim. So were Britt's parents. Mary was studying at Harvard for her master's in psychology. Britt had flunked out of Harvard. She loved museums. Britt was an exceptional photographer.

She could be dating Britt. Hungry for affection, would she do almost anything he asked?

Lauria would say I was nuts. Wouldn't she?

The Suburban made a sharp right, past yawning iron gates, down a long drive.

I hung until the truck vanished around a driveway curve, flicked off my lights, then followed.

"You're there, right?" I said.

"We've got you," Lauria said.

My eyes gradually adjusted to the flood of dark. Soon, the starlight and half moon gave off enough light so I could inch forward without headlights. I drove for a few minutes. A curve, past a row of bushes, then I spotted the darker outline of what could be a rambling one-story house.

I jammed on the breaks.

Although he was still quite far away, I could make out Britt walking up the path. He opened the front door and stepped inside.

Gert could be in there right now.

I had trouble seeing Britt as Mary's lover.

I turned off the car. The gates far back up the drive clanged shut.

Hell.

"You're there, right?" I said. "Behind me? You made the gates?"

"Gates?" Lauria hissed. "What gates? And why the hell did you just walk into Roche Bros grocery, of all places? That wasn't the plan."

Roche Bros? But . . .

"What have you been doing?" I whispered. "Where are you?"

"In the damned Roche Bros parking lot, obviously."

"But I'm in the middle of the woods near Lincoln. Roche Bros is in Acton."

"*What*?" Lauria screeched. "Then who the hell have we been following?"

"Good question, Kathleen." I wasn't amused. "Maybe the *wrong* person."

"That's ridi—Hold on."

Christ. What a mess.

A light blinked on inside the house.

"I don't know what's going on," she said. "But we'd better figure this out fast. We did see another green Taurus pull into that lot behind SinJin's. A balding man was at the wheel. We saw *you*, driving in your rental Taurus toward Acton on Route 62 after you signaled us from the pub that you'd spotted Britt."

"Whoever's in that car ain't me, lemme tell ya."

"Where are you? This isn't funny."

"I couldn't agree more. I'm somewhere between Maynard and Lexington. I think it's Lincoln, but it could be Concord. I'm not sure. A side road. Lots of trees. And a gated driveway."

"Get out of there. Simply back up fast and smash through those gates."

I could do that. It made the most sense. But the Harvester wanted me here. Had led me here. Well, dammit, now he had me here. "I can't leave. Gert's inside. Find Mary's house and I think you'll find me."

"Tally! Tally!"

"I'm going to do this, so you can either go with it or keep screeching in my ear."

I slipped out of the car, crouched low, hoping I wouldn't get a gun to the head. I felt like IT in some sicko's game.

I tried to glide toward the woods, except a patch of ice tripped me up, and I slipped and slid down a hilly slope. Not far, thank God.

Still in a crouch, I inched into the woods.

More lights came on in the house.

Now what, Samantha Spade?

God, I missed Kranak.

I leaned against a tree, breathing hard.

What better place to prowl for the emotionally wounded than at MGAP? Sure. The families, all strung out, looking desperately for any comfort they could find.

And Mary liked giving comfort, didn't she?

Oh, I was crazy thinking these things. Could Mary be that monstrous?

"Sure I could." Snick.

"What?" I knew that sound of a trigger being cocked, had *waited* for it, in fact.

"You asked out loud if I could be that monstrous," said the disembodied voice.

I remembered to stay in Emma's persona. "Where are you?"

"Nowhere. Believe me."

"I'm here to get Gert."

She walked toward me, gun aimed at my chest. "You figured it out, huh?"

"Sure." I enjoyed the lie.

"Take off the wire," she said, hand outstretched.

With considerable tugging, I pulled the rig off my body and handed it to her.

"Now that we can talk, come on in and see the place."

"Is Gert alive?"

"Yes."

"Where's Britt?"

She chuckled. "Here, of course." She hooked her arm through mine. "I don't want you to slip."

She pulled me forward.

My fear sharpened. I hummed with the adrenaline rush, heard a branch clack, smelled a hint of smoke, saw a cat cross the grass. Not a soul anywhere in the world, but here.

Mary. Me.

Dark laughter in my ear. A memory. Where? Trepel. Yes.

I realized my mistake.

There was no conspiracy.

The real Britt was never in the bar. No. He was off t some photo shoot, waiting for me.

Britt looked like McArdle *not* because he was play-

ing McArdle. But because Mary modeled *her* McArdle
after Britt, a man who'd known me, who perhaps
talked about MGAP and the work it did, a man who
unknowingly sent Mary to us.

Mary was McArdle. And Trepel. And the VW guy.
And . . .

She'd gone for Blessing right after their confrontation in group. Or maybe even before then. She'd set
him up for Chesa's murder, then cultivated him,
sucked him in, used him, until she arranged for him
to get shot by Kranak.

Except he freaked out when he saw *her* standing in
the doorway, and killed himself. Just like he'd been
waiting for me in the parking lot, but when he'd heard
Mary's voice, he'd disappeared. She was the trigger
the whole time.

Poor Roland Blessing. He'd never stood a chance.

We walked through Mary's unfurnished house. An
odor, fetid and antiseptic and chemical, drifted from
somewhere, getting stronger with each step we took.

My whole being screamed "run!"

She led me down a narrow staircase to a brightly
lit cellar that reminded me of a doctor's suit of offices.

I gagged. Not at the corruption of death, not that,
but the smell of formaldehyde, of death's *preservation*.

She turned to me, smiling.

Mary was dressed as McArdle. Or Britt. Whichever.
Longish hair, big ears, thick glasses, beard.

She thrummed with excitement.

"Where's Gert?" I said.

"I'll be back." She shoved me into a room.

After she'd closed the door, I trolled my purse for
my cell phone and dialed.

All I got was static back.

I groped for the light switch, flicked. The room sprang into view.

"Cripes."

Barbie, everywhere—on the sheets, comforter, wallpaper. And the dresser. Dozens of Barbies peeked from opened dresser drawers, clustered on the miniature chair, and assembled in a corner of the room by the Barbie dollhouse.

And my doll, Gladdy, lay against the pillow, staring back at me.

I grabbed Gladdy, and sat on the bed clutching her so tight I expected her stuffing to erupt. Finding Gladdy in this creepy room sickened me.

I was also rip-shit with anger. I hugged Gladdy for the fiftieth time.

A cold glass of milk and Oreos sat on the nightstand. I took a sip, then split the Oreo in half, licked, then munched. Was she watching, I wondered?

Did Mary know Emma was me? Why else would Gladdy be here? Or maybe she was just one of the Harvester's trophies, and Mary still believed I was Emma.

Did it matter?

The room did a tilt-a-whirl. Oh, crap.

What a fool to drink drugged milk.

Zoom.

A clanking awakened me. My eyes flew open. The room swam. Dizzy. Then it righted itself. I sat up. I thought I'd be sick. I was cradling Gladdy. I moved her away.

I was naked, my wig gone, my breasts unbound, and facing McArdle/Mary.

She'd changed into a trench coat that fell to the floor. God knew why. And a hat, pulled tight on her head. She pulled her chair up to the bed where I sat.

While she watched me watching her, my stomach was doing the samba.

Lauria would find Gert and me. I hoped in time.

She tugged her ear, grinning. Just like McArdle had. And Britt.

"Where are you keeping Gert?" I asked.

"Here."

My stomach flip-flopped. "Bathroom?" I pleaded.

She shook her head.

I raced to the garbage can and retched. When I finished, I staggered back to the bed. Boy, that sucked.

She'd watched, hadn't moved her eyes away once. She handed me some tissues, and I wiped my mouth and watering eyes.

"This stinks," I said.

She shrugged, but she was smiling. She held out a glass of water. "It's fine."

I drank, which helped a little. At that point, I felt so lousy that I didn't care if I passed out again.

She began to peel off "McArdle's" beard, then the eyebrows, then the wig. She pulled the residue of spirit gum or whatever she'd used off her face, then yanked at her large front teeth, and they came free, revealing her smaller ones. She plucked more tissue from the bedside box, worked on the nose, and pulled that off, too.

She couldn't stop grinning. She was loving this revelation.

The body language changed, and she momentarily became the Mary I'd known for years. Then she threw back her shoulders and laughed and slapped her knees

"I'm amazing, aren't I?" she said. Her dancing people earrings glinted in the lamplight. I itched to throttle her.

I tried to make sense of the Harvester being a woman.

Mary unbuttoned her coat and shrugged it off. She wore a long turtleneck and yoga pants reminiscent of an outfit I owned. The top was turquoise, a favorite color of mine. The pants highlighted her thick calves and ankles. Not a flattering style for her.

She flung off the hat, and her hair billowed, as much as thin, silky hair could. She'd curled and bleached it. Frizzed it, actually, so it resembled mine when it wasn't damp from sweat and fear. There was a sensuality to the whole getup that heightened my unease.

If I hadn't had the creeps already, the outfit and hair would have sealed it.

She was me, and she knew "Emma" was me, too. Talk about surreal.

Maybe I could bash her head in with the lamp. "How about some clothes?" I said.

"Soon," she said. "I like you naked."

Christ. I still was having trouble processing that Mary was Britt/McArdle, that she'd killed more than a dozen women, that she'd stolen their body parts. That she was a psychotic killer.

"Where's Gert, Mary?"

"Resting in another room."

"I'd like to see her now."

"No."

Just the sparest of answers. Interesting. "You drugged her, too. Didn't you?"

She lifted one shoulder in a half-shrug.

I slowly sipped more water, buying time, trying to figure things out. "Your mother, how did she die?"

Mary's eyes cut to the floor. "She was murdered. You knew that."

"Where were you?"

"Around."

"Were you just 'around,' Mary? Or were in the room when she died?"

"I know what you're trying to do. Cut it out."

She tugged at my shoulder, and I staggered up. My wobbly legs almost collapsed. I braced myself on the table. She pulled again, and this time I was able to move forward.

She dragged me from the room.

"It's your mom, isn't it? You're trying to reconnect with your mom. How old were you when she died, Mary? Eight? Nine? Ten?"

"Eleven! And shut up. You think you get it. But you don't. You'll have to see."

She pulled me out into the hall, where I cringed at the bright lights. "You're clever, Mary."

"I am."

"And smart."

"That, too."

I could reach out and shove her, except I had no strength. She'd done to me what she must have done to the other women, drugged them to where their legs felt like Gumby and their arms like Flubber. Dammit.

She began dragging me down the hall. I resisted, staggered more than necessary, groped for a wall. "You create amazing men, Mary."

"Thank you. Obviously I based my Mr. McArdle on the real Mr. Britt. The VW guy was some asshole

I went to high school with. Trepel was Harrison Ford in *Presumed Innocent*, with just a touch of Spinelli. Did you get it?"

"No."

She pouted. "I took some theater classes in college. One was a theatrical makeup course, and after class, I got a job as a makeup artist at a repertory company. That's how I got rid of my accent, too."

"Let's get back to your mom. Did your sister die with her?"

Her whole body quivered. "*Ants, ants, ants.*"

"Problems?"

Her head shook. "Nothing. *Nothing!* I won't talk about my sister, either."

Our little Mary wasn't entirely in control. I got an image of Inez, which produced the sweats. Oh, shit. I couldn't think of the women. Not now. Or I'd never make it.

"What about your dad, Mary. Wasn't he a butcher, or something?"

She punched me in the face. I staggered backward, bounced off the wall. A blow to the belly bent me double, and I retched, vomit mingling with the sweat streaming across my face. Christ. Guess I'd hit a pressure point.

I slid to the floor, gasping for breath. "That was fun," I wheezed.

She poked her face inches from mine. I suddenly realized her heavy coat of makeup was gone. Faint, crosshatched scars ran from beneath her eyes to her chin.

What had been done to Mary?

Chapter Forty-three

I used my hands to climb up the wall so I could stand. I teetered over to Mary. That's when I saw the small caliber gun tucked close to her body. I had to think, *think*. That was the only way I'd get Gert and myself out of there.

I couldn't be scared.

I giggled. Nerves. Christ. I was scared shitless.

And Mary was astute enough to know that.

"Having a good time, aren't you?" I said.

"I don't know. I never thought of it that way. But I guess I am."

Think. Think. "Why the gun? You won't shoot me. The others, they didn't have bullet holes in them."

She smiled. "I wouldn't shoot to kill. But I'll wound you if I have to. It'll hurt. And I don't want to hurt you, Tally."

"Just to take a piece of me, right?"

"If there was any other way . . ." She sighed. "I'm working it through."

Time for more proactivity. "Tell me about your dad, Mary."

"Stop it! Or I'll hit you again."

"So? You think he'd be proud of you, once they find you, Mary?"

She laughed. "Of course they won't find me. I'm invisible. I always have been. I'm plain. My personality's plain. No one sees me. No one except . . ."

She sounded terribly sad. I wanted to touch her.

but didn't dare. "Who was the exception, Mary? Your mom?"

Here eyes dilated. "She was wonderful." She tugged at my hand.

I stood my ground. "I want to see Gert."

"Fine," she spat. "You touch her, she dies."

We turned down the brightly lit hall. The floor was tiled in white and so cold it pained my bare feet. We approached a door at the end of the hall that was cracked open. I got a glimpse of an even brighter room filled with shelves and . . .

Mary yanked me hard, so I was facing her.

"Not yet." She opened one of the doors, revealing a huge, walk-in closet. Shelves held manikin heads wearing wigs, a theatrical dressing table crowded with makeup and clumps of hair. A rack of clothes jammed with jeans and dresses and T-shirts and coveralls. From a dresser, she pulled out two sets of green scrubs and masks.

"Put these on."

We donned the scrubs, then she opened a second door. Another bedroom. This one done up in blue roses. More Barbies. Same rug. Same chair facing a bed that held a seemingly sleeping Gert.

She looked terrible. Her hair was a snarling halo, her face a pasty white. Mascara tear tracks scored her cheeks.

Was she breathing?

I exhaled a pent up breath when Gert's chest rose, then fell. Thank God. As we moved into the room, Gert twitched, pushing the white sheet from her body.

Except for the nipples, her full breasts were smeared with an orangy brown something. Betadine, I'd bet. Oh, shit.

I started to shake. Mary expected something of me. What? Dammit! "Why Gert's breasts, Mary?"

Mary snapped on latex gloves and knelt by the bed. She caressed Gert's breasts. "Because they're so beautiful."

She gripped one breast with a latex-covered hand and suckled.

With Mary on her knees by Gert, I could make a dash for it.

Mary, her mouth still embracing Gert's nipple, laughed with her eyes.

I'd never leave Gert, and she knew it.

Mary abruptly stood, tears wetting her eyes. "I'm so happy! Elizabeth's breasts proved too small, but Gert's will be perfect." She sobbed into her hands.

I moved to hold her.

The gun appeared.

I backed off. I was beginning to get the drift of Mary's disturbing desires. "If you take them, they won't be there to suckle. What happened with your mother, Mary?"

"Shut up!" she screamed. The gun snapped up.

I gasped, primed for the pain.

She calmed and her gray eyes grew clear, like when the sediment from a recent storm settles, leaving the river transparent to its very bottom.

"My mother?" she said. "Come and see."

She tugged me as we walked. Her step was springy, her lips tilted up in a small smile. Down the short hall to a brightly lit room, maybe twelve by twelve. I stopped. No way did I want to go into the room.

Mary pushed me inside. A chipmunk and a squirrel

were mounted on the wall beside two bucolic land-scape paintings. Shelves lined the walls, too, and held dozens of lit aquariums filled with turgid fluid that bubbled slowly from the tank's pump. Big aquariums. Small ones. Round ones. Rectangular ones.

I walked toward the tanks.

I shrieked, stuffed a fist against my mouth so I'd stop.

A body part bobbed in each aquarium. I jerked, my eyes panning the room. Arms and feet and ears. And eyes. Many, many eyes. Each tank held a wrinkled or distended specimen.

I'd imagined it, or tried to, but I sure as hell wasn't prepared for the reality.

Mary took my hand. "There's more."

She led me through a door, me, like a rag doll, boneless, mindless, spineless.

What had so diseased her mind? Nature? Nurture? God knew. I certainly didn't.

We entered a room maybe fifteen by twenty.

White-tiled floors, white walls, lab counters, a steel gurney, sinks. I faced a steel table, much like an autopsy table.

This was Mary's operating theater, where she carried out her mutilations. I stumbled when the smell hit me—putrefaction. From where?

Not the trophies, which were spaced at intervals on the walls. There was an elk, as well as a deer, a cougar, a bear, and a lynx. There were mostly heads, but the cougar and lynx were complete animals, posed in predatory positions and expertly mounted.

I couldn't get the dead women from my head, heard their haunting pleas for help over and over and . . .

Gurgles and ka-thunks came from behind a curtain

that closed off the left portion of the room.

"Marvelous, isn't it?" Mary aimed the gun at my belly.

"No, Mary. It's horrible. Did you shoot those?" I pointed to the animals.

"Gosh, no. I would never shoot an animal."

She'd said it with a straight face. I wanted to laugh. Irony ran rampant. "I see."

"My father was a taxidermist. My sister thought it was gross. I found it totally cool. With taxidermy, at least the poor dead creature is preserved."

Which was how she knew Trepel.

What must each woman have felt when she was first brought to this room of horrors? "Those creatures. They're all so hollow and dusty. Emptied of everything. Is that how you feel, Mary?"

She rubbed the back of her gun hand across her forehead. "They're beautiful. My father was a genius. He taught me everything he knew. They retain the spirit of the creature. Don't you see?"

I saw, all right. If I didn't get Gert and myself out of there, we'd end up as a part of Mary's little theater. "Of course they don't retain the creature's spirit."

"Creations do! Fuck you."

"I'm feeling woozy. Mind if I sit?"

"No!" She took my elbow. "This is from the drug. We'll go back to your room."

She wagged the gun toward the hall and my room.

"I'll be fine." I worried I'd never awaken. "I'll just sit for a minute."

I slid onto a tall stool beside one of the lab tables. Now what? I rested my head in my hands, feigning a wooziness I didn't feel. How to get Gert and me out of there?

There were glass beakers. I could smash one on her head. A hose ran from a swan-necked faucet to the drain. I could turn on the hot water and try to scald her. Or I could pretend to pass out, slide to the floor, and when she bent over me, I could overpower her.

Swell ideas. None of which would have much effect against a bullet. She'd drugged the others, including Gert. Why not keep me drugged?

"It's time," she said.

Shit. "Time?"

Her face grew sad. "For Gert. I've got to lock you up again. A shame. I wish you could watch me work."

"And afterward?"

Her thin lips vanished to invisible. "We'll talk some more."

"Will we? Or will it be my turn?"

Her eyes pinballed around the room. "I don't know. I don't know. But it's time. I've got to do Gert *now*! Ants, ants, ants."

Stall, my brain screamed. "But I haven't seen everything. What's behind the curtain?"

"Nothing." She wagged the gun, indicating I should get up.

"Oh, come on." I stayed firmly planted on the stool. "Something special must be hiding behind the curtain."

"Forget it. I have to get started."

I slid off the stool, appearing to acquiesce. Then I sprinted across the room, my back prickly, expecting the thud of a bullet. I reached the curtain and flung it back.

"Dear God!"

* * *

The corpse was hideous. It lay cradled on pads connected to ceiling wires, suspended in an aquariumlike tank, maybe six feet long. The tank gurgled, and bubbles sluggishly surfaced from the viscous liquid that surrounded the corpse.

"Get away from her!" Mary screeched.

The tank's top was open, and I grabbed the edges so as not to fall backward. I wagged my head like a wet dog, willing myself to keep it together.

I'd seen horrors. Sure I had.

But none like this.

"You like her." Mary said. "I'm so glad. I wasn't sure you would."

I felt Mary at the bottom of the steps. I sensed her excitement, her *thrill* at my seeing her creature.

I peered down.

Dear Reen's face looked up at me. I muffled a sob. Tiny stitches surrounded eyes that weren't Reen's but Della Charles's golden, catlike eyes. Except Reen's face was distorted, a Halloween mask, and the Della's eyes drooped inward.

"Did you toss Angela's eyes when you found Della?" I didn't turn to Mary, afraid she'd see my revulsion.

"I liked her eyes better that Angela's. You saw the other room. The spare parts room, I call it. I keep those jars in there just in case there's a problem. Don't you see? I keep changing. Della's eyes better suit Mom."

MOM?

The poor creature had no breasts, although holes marked where a row of tiny stitches had once been. Mary must have recently removed Elizabeth Flynn's breasts in preparation for Gert's.

Whose poor arms had Mary stolen? They were lean and tan and long. Where would we find her remains? Who was she?

At the ends of the tan arms floated the small, pale hands that had once glided over a flute. Moira Blessing's hands. I pressed my own into the glass edge of the tank. She been a child. A child!

The sewn-on legs, heavy boned, sturdy, belonged to Patricia Boch. They were white and freckled. But the feet were a golden shade. Bony, callused. Inez's feet.

What must each woman have felt when she'd seen this horror? "Why did you let Inez live?"

"Jazz was good to me. Inez was a gift."

How pointless it all was. How stupid. "John Strabo?" I asked, unable to shut up. Unable to *think*.

"He was such a loser. That worked out well, for a while, anyway."

He had kids, Goddamnit, who loved him. "Why kill Chesa?"

She giggled. "She got in the way. Asked too many questions. Typical. Her ears were tempting. But they weren't quite good enough for Mom."

I had this terrible urge to strangle her.

Instead I reached out to touch the thing in the tank. To soothe it. To tell it that it would be okay. I heard their voices rise like some mournful Greek chorus. I clenched my hand into a fist.

"Isn't she beautiful?" Mary said.

"Was your mother very beautiful?" I asked in a calm voice I was far from feeling.

"She was perfect."

"Was she? Really?" I tried to find some pity for Mary. What was she but the twisted product of some horrible homicide? I lifted my head. I still had my back to her, couldn't look at her. "So this creature represents your mom. Is that it?"

"You don't understand," she said, her voice a whisper.

I glanced to my right. A smaller tank sat beside the large one. Inside, a little gray-and-white dog hung suspended from similar tethers.

McArdle's dog. What was it's name? The dog had loved her, and of course that was part of the equation.

And if I was going to get Gert and myself out of here, I'd better use the weapons I had at hand.

I turned to her. "I love you, Mary." And it was a lie. Yet I could feel her sad and desperate yearning that had brought her to this monstrous state.

For she was me, and countless other "me's" who ached for that missing someone who we idealized in our minds. Didn't I want my father, almost more desperately than life? Didn't I yearn for him to hold me? To cradle me? Couldn't I still smell his aftershave and hear his voice?

"You can't love me," she said.

"I can. Because I understand. You've created that which reminds you of your idealized mom." I wouldn't turn, not until my plan was finalized.

She moved up a step and gazed rapturously at the cobbled together woman suspended in the tank. "More than that. Don't you see, he hacked her up? Tiny pieces all around me. Tiny. Tiny. For days and days and days. It was impossible to put her back. That's why he chopped her up, because he knew she couldn't be put back."

"Who, Mary? Who killed your mother?"

"I don't know."

"Sure you do."

"I don't!" she screamed.

My plan sharpened, strengthened. All I had to do was . . .

"So now it's up to you," she said. "Once I have your heart."

"My *heart*? You've got to be kidding me."

"You're kind. The kindest person I know. Then Mommy will be complete."

"Complete?"

Her smile was slow and sly and insane. "*Mommy*. I've saved her pieces all these years. I'll transfer them into the new mommy, and she'll come back to me. You see?"

Chapter Forty-four

Whoa. It just kept getting stranger. Mary really thought she could bring her mother back in some sewn-together *thing*. Talk about transference! I'd just tripped into a Mary Shelley novel. I laughed. I couldn't stop.

"Mary Shelley," I said. "Shel. Short for Shelley. The name in Della's letters. The name Blessing repeated to me."

She grinned. "I have a sense of humor. Sometimes. I couldn't resist the irony."

"You'd better get yourself another heart, kiddo. Saint Tally I ain't."

"From the very beginning, your heart's been the one I've wanted for Mommy."

She'd reverted to her hunched posture. Her bleached hair lay limp, her lips wobbled, her eyes pleaded for understanding.

"That's how you got them, even Reen. Pretending to be a sad sack."

She fired the pistol, and pain blazed through me. I bit my lip, dug for control. A rivulet of blood trickled down my left arm.

"Mary, I—"

"Beg. Go on." Her eyes filled with cruelty and self-satisfaction. "All of those beautiful women—they all begged." She giggled.

"Reen didn't."

"But she freaked out, like the rest of them, when she saw my beautiful Mom."

Another layer, a well-hidden one. I'd been feeling pity. No doubt Reen had, too. "Having fun, are we?" My torn flesh hurt like the dickens.

She chuckled. "A little. Maybe."

"Had me feeling sorry for you."

" '*I love you, Mary,*' " she parodied in my voice. "You don't love me."

"Not as you are now. But there's sweetness in you, too. I've seen it."

She smiled. "I wished my beautiful Mommy had scared you. That's when they knew what was going to happen was real. I liked that."

Nervous sweat greased my armpits. Oh, it was real, for sure. "This is all about your not finishing with Mommy. How didn't you finish, Mary?"

"None of your business."

"Did she die before you got to say good-bye? Or was she mad at you, and then she died, and you never had the chance to say sorry? Was that it?"

"Come away now." A click.

She'd recocked the gun. My injured arm twitched. "What was unfinished, Mary? What part of your grief didn't happen? Did you hate Mommy as much as you loved her?"

"Move! Now!"

I dived my arms into the tank and wrapped them around the body.

Mary screamed. "Get away! You'll infect her!"

I jerked the corpse up, too hard, the momentum carrying me backward.

I teetered, the weight heavier than I'd imagined, tried to regain my balance.

Over I went, horrified that the body might land on me.

Thump! Right on my shoulder, clinging to the cobbled-together corpse. One of its legs partially ripped off. Dear God.

A shriek.

I clung to the corpse, thinking frantically about the size of guns and bullets, and if one could tear through the corpse into me.

Screw it. I shoved the pickled flesh at Mary, detaching part of an arm in the process.

I ran. What would stop her? What? What?

Over my shoulder I saw her frantically trying to lift her mother's precious cocoon. She raised it by its armpits, then began tugging it toward the tank.

The other leg ripped. She screamed, but her hand still clutched the gun.

I grabbed the wheeled gurney and ran at full tilt toward the tank.

I smashed the gurney into the side. Not a crack in the tank. Nothing.

"Stop!" Mary screamed.

I bobbed and wove backward, then forward again. Smash! Vibration running up my arms, legs, but I hung on. Into the tank again. The boom of the gun. Bobbing, weaving, backward, then forward, hoping to hell I wouldn't catch Mary's bullet.

I slammed into the tank again.

Hands pulling at me, nails digging in. A sear of pain from my grazed arm. I flew backward, let momentum take me, put force into it, and rammed her.

Over she went, sliding on the viscous slime right into the corpse.

I scrambled to my feet, out of strength, out of breath.

But I'd cracked the tank. Yes!

It spidered with cracks.

A boom. Heat from the bullet whizzing by my cheek. Shit.

I backpedaled, dived for the lab counter. Protection.

Another boom, my shoulder on fire. I barked in pain, rolled.

Mary screamed again, shrieking screams that didn't stop.

The tank's thick liquid oozed across the floor.

I crawled on my belly.

Mary sobbed, cradling the creature as she swiveled the gun toward my head. "You fucking bitch! You ruined her house. You bitch! You bitch!"

I pushed forward, rolled, slithered behind the counter, leaned back, panting. I rested my head in my shaking hands. Everything hurt. Where the hell was she? How many bullets did she have? What was she doing?

Moans. Coming from Mary.

I peeked around the edge of the counter.

She was cradling her creation, rocking it, roles reversed—a mother and child—her head buried in the thing's breastless torso. Surrounded by gelatinous liquid and shards of glass from the shattered tank.

I was numb. Not much pain. My shoulder and side coated with blood. How much could I lose?

Oh, hell.

I swiveled on my bum, opened the lab counter door on my right. Heavy metal stuff. Too heavy for me to throw.

The second door revealed neatly stacked plastic containers.

The third door . . . Empty. *Empty*, dammit!

I peered around the corner.

Mary hugged the body, her right arm outstretched toward the lab counter, her gun arm steady. Her face—a mask of fury, eyes bugging, teeth bared.

"Come out, you shit!" she said.

"Not in this life."

"You'd better believe it." She hiccoughed a sob. "I'm gonna fucking mount you like a fucking buck."

Glass beakers on the counter. Perfect as missiles. If I could just reach them.

I snuck my fingers to the slate counter and, thighs protesting, side whining with pain, pulled myself up.

A sleepy naked Gert appeared in the doorway.

"Whazzhappening?" she mumbled, scratching her head.

Mary smiled, slow and mean. Her right arm swiveled toward Gert.

"Gert down!" I screamed, lobbing a beaker. I grabbed another, hurled it, too.

Mary swiveled the gun to me.

"Wha' the fuch'?" Gert wandered in Mary's direction.

The gun swiveled again toward Gert.

I threw two more beakers, then launched myself at Mary, shouting a bansheed "eeekkkk," arms flying.

"Noooo!" screamed Mary.

I thudded onto her and the corpse, setting off the gun.

Panting again, harder, prickles of pain everywhere. I looked down.

Mary appeared unwounded and unconscious. I kicked the gun away from her outstretched hand, and it skittered across the floor.

The corpse's detached left arm lay beside me. I tasted bile.

Mary could be faking it. I slammed an uppercut to her jaw. It better have done the trick.

I crawled my eyes sideways.

Gert lay on the floor, arms spread eagled, legs splayed.

Oh, Christ. Had the bullet . . . ? "Gertie? You okay?"

Her head bobbed up. "Tally? I don't feel so good."

"Are you hit?"

She sat up. "With what?"

Cripes. "Gert, you've got to get up and find something to tie Mary's hands."

She scratched her head again. "Yeah?" She pushed herself to her feet, then thumped back down again.

Swell. I stood and pain ricocheted around my body. I minced over the broken glass, found some duct tape in a drawer, and bound Mary's hands and ankles.

I left her lying there with the creature she'd stitched together while I checked Gert. Although hungover from the drugs, she seemed physically okay.

I found a phone in the lab and called in the troops.

It was over.

I folded my arms on my knees and sobbed.

A week later I snuck through the gate in my backyard wearing Emma Nash's wig and makeup and clutching a small, heavy bag. With my injured arm and side complaining, I gently closed the gate. Dartmouth Place was empty. I'd managed to give the ferocious media the slip. Yes!

From the time I'd left the hospital four days earlier, I'd been assaulted by questions and strobes and microphones. So had Gert and the people at Media Magazine Resources and anyone else associated with Mary Armstrong.

Even worse, somebody had leaked word of Mary's stitched-together woman. At least no shutterbug had managed to take a picture of the poor creature.

I walked down Dartmouth Place, looked first, then hooked a left onto Dartmouth Street. I slipped into the idling navy sedan driven by Lauria.

Things were a bit hinkey between Lauria and me. She blamed herself that they'd fallen for Mary's ruse. Mary had hired a decoy to wear an Emma wig and drive an identical rental Taurus from Amory's to the Ames parking lot in Acton. The incident stuck in Lauria's craw.

Lauria brushed a speck of nothing off her collar.

"Kath, come on."

"Don't. I'll get over it. Just don't."

I sighed. "Are you ready to tell me what you learned about Mary Armstrong?"

Lauria sighed. "It's some story. Our little Mary grew up in a small, West Virginia town with an older sister, a homemaker mother, and a father who was a banker with a taxidermy hobby. The parents were big muckety-mucks . . . until the father killed the mother. Apparently mom was a harpy who demanded perfection from her youngest daughter, Mary, and the father killed her when she went after Mary one too many times. He strangled her, then chopped her into little pieces. Mary was eleven at the time and—I'm sure this is no surprise to you—idealized the mother who constantly berated her.

"There's a recipe for psychosis," I said.

"It gets worse." Lauria turned off Dartmouth Street. "Mary, eleven and plain, was home. The older sister, fourteen and gorgeous, was at boarding school. The sister's out of it, right, but Mary sees the whole thing come down. After the father does the mother, he shoots himself. And Mary? She stays in the house for three days, along with her chopped-up mom and dead dad, until her seventh-grade teacher comes over to see why the kid hasn't been in school for a few days.

"As McArdle," I said. "She talked about her mother's unmarked grave. It was a fantasy—perhaps meant to erase some of the guilt she felt over her mother's death. How she must have hated her mother and loved her at the same time. Certainly she had unfinished business with her." Just like I had with my dad. I shivered.

"Our little Mary had to have been odd from the start. Listen to this: four years later, Mary's only living relative, her sister, drowns while swimming in a local quarry. Some who watched said Mary dove in and tried to rescue her. Others said less pleasant things. A cursory autopsy was performed by the local coroner, and the case was never seen as suspicious. We're exhuming the sister."

"My guess is that Mary drugged the girl first," I said.

Lauria continued, explaining that with the sister's death, all the family's substantial assets had gone to Mary. She'd left town on her sixteenth birthday and didn't resurface for two years, when she entered Syracuse University as a theater major. She dropped out her sophomore year and again disappeared. She reappeared six years ago, purchased the estate in Lincoln, and was hired by Media Magazine Resources. Much of Mary's life, like Mary herself, remained cloaked in shadow.

"How's she doing in Bridgewater?"

"She won't say a word, not to us, nor to anyone, including Jarvis, who hasn't gotten 'boo' out of her. The same for Bridgewater's psychiatrists. She's been scratching her face."

"Shall I give it a shot, try and talk to her?"

"Don't, Tally. We found seven more women at Mary's house of horrors. Three remain mysteries, although I believe we'll eventually identify them. Some of the body parts she had in those jars we'll never identify."

I felt cold. "Mind if I crank up the heat?"

"Feel free," Lauria said.

"Look, Kath," I said. "I'm not angry at you. Can we get over this?"

"Maybe. Give me another week. I *worked* with this monster during the task force. I should have spotted her!"

"And I shouldn't have? She was at MGAP for three years."

"Let's drop it. When are you going back to work?" I folded my arms.

"Oh, ho. Touch a nerve, did I?"

A lot of them. Looking in the mirror in the morning was almost impossible. How had I missed so many signs with Mary?

"The girl you worked with was just one disguise of our killer. You know that."

"I do. And, yes, I am going back to work. But... I'm chilly. Can't we have more damned heat?"

Lauria turned the blower higher.

"Why did you insist on picking me up?"

We climbed a ramp and hopped onto 128. "One, because I knew you'd drive yourself. Your wounds might be superficial, but you're still healing and shouldn't drive. Two, because any of your people, including Veda or Kranak, would have been spotted chauffeuring you."

"Three?"

"There is no three."

"Did Jake get Penny?" I asked.

"Yes. He'll meet us there."

I looked behind me, suddenly paranoid.

"No media," Lauria said. "They didn't follow us."

"What about the others?" I asked.

"They're clear on the setup."

"I hope you're right."

I pulled off Emma Nash's wig and began my transformation back to Tally.

*   *   *

We sped up Route 95 on a late March day that blazed with a bright sun and an intense blue sky. But winter's chill remained, and got chillier still as we drove though New Hampshire, then into Maine. Just above Portland, we turned onto Route 1.

I must have dozed, clutching my precious package, because when I awakened, I saw the glistening harbor and quaint shops of Camden.

Lauria drove through town, then turned down toward the harbor, where a tall windjammer rocked amid lesser boats and ships.

The harbor lot was partially filled and more cars were pulling in. As I opened the car door, I spotted Kranak, Gert, Donna, and Veda, all bundled in sweaters and down coats. Penny bounded toward me, followed by Jake. And there was Chief Flynn walking up the dock. When we reached him, he enveloped me in one of his swift hugs, then said, "This way."

He'd been the one to suggest, then arrange for the windjammer, which normally didn't return to its Camden berth until later in the year.

Nearly one hundred somber-faced people streamed down the dock and onto the tall ship. When I stepped on board, I spied Dave Haywood. He stood in front of a mahogany coffer the size of a cedar chest that was secured to a stand on the ship's bow. I'd asked him to perform the ceremony.

I saw the Pisarros come aboard. They didn't meet my eyes. Behind them was Danny Brown, minus Inez, and Tom Fogarty and Dixie. They walked over and I made introductions, and we produced small talk. There were others, many others, whom I didn't know. When everyone had assembled, the crew released the lines and we chugged from the harbor as the immense sails were unfurled.

An hour later, having sailed behind an island that protected us from the wind, we held the ceremony. First a minister spoke, then a rabbi, then a priest. I saw Mrs. Maekawa mouthing a prayer.

When all the prayers were done and with tears running down our faces, we queued up. A piper in a down vest and kilt blew the first notes of "Amazing Grace." Haywood opened the casket's lid, and we each took a scoop of dust and bone, freed it to the sea, and said a final farewell.

In the casket lay the mingled cremated remains of Mary's victims. For some, that meant their loved one's torso or hand or eyes. Here, too, were the remains of Mary's cobbled-together woman. And as I took my scoop and released the powdery essence, I said my farewells to Reen and Della and Patricia and Moira and Elizabeth and others. I apologized to Inez, who remained unaware, and to the unidentified woman whose arms had become a part of the creature, and to all the women whose identities remained mysteries. I said good-bye again to Chesa, for she was so much a part of this, too. And to Arlo, and finally, to Roland Blessing. As I walked away, I tried to believe that they were in a better place.

I headed for the stern. Kranak met me there, as did Jake and Lauria, Veda and Gert, and the rest of our circle. I removed the urn I carried from its wrapping and we said words to Mrs. Cheadle, and we gave her to the wind and sea, too.

When I turned away, I found Kranak beside me. He hooked an arm though mine and walked me over to the starboard rail. He leaned on it with his fore-arms, hands threaded together.

"You've forgiven me," I said.

"You ever pull somethin' like that Emma shit again, I'll bop you one."

"Point taken." I kissed his cheek and started to turn back to the others.

He wrapped his hand around my forearm. "Wait."

"What's wrong?" I said.

He shook his head. "I'm bugged."

"By?"

"She set me on Blessing, Tal. Bugs me, is all."

"You mean that night at class?" I said, knowing that "she" was Mary.

"Remember I said I forgot my notebook? It wasn't mine. *She's* the one who sent me back to your class-room. *She* forgot her notebook, not me."

So it wasn't chance, but Mary. "She must have seen him."

"And got worried," Kranak said. "Maybe she thought he'd hurt you. So she left her notebook. And sent me back to get it. She was protecting you."

"No," I said. "I think she believed Blessing would tell all. His face when he looked at you—abject terror. But it wasn't you he was looking at, it was Mary."

I'd told only Jarvis that Mary had coveted my heart. I hadn't wanted to repeat it. Yet I felt compelled to tell Kranak.

"So she was following you, too," he said. "For how long, I wonder. She set Blessing to stalking you."

I nodded. "She pulled all the strings. Easy for her to get inside my house. She just made copies of my keys, which I leave in my desk at work. I remember the day she 'happened' upon Jake and me at the museum. The way she fed on grief. What better place than the Grief Shop?"

I thought of how I missed my dad. How I pictured him every day. How I yearned for his love. How I couldn't let him go. Yet something inside me had changed when I'd seen Mary revealed and I'd held that poor cobbled-together corpse. A window had opened, and with it a sharp breeze that embraced the spirit of my dad.

It wasn't a resolution. I had yet to say a final farewell to Dad. Like it should be that easy? No way.

But beginnings are good, and this was one.

What would I have become if my father, like Mary's mother, had expected perfection in both form and intellect? What would I have become after he'd been murdered, if I hadn't met Veda? Hadn't received her and Bertha's love and praise and nurturing? What would I be now?

I licked my lips and tasted the sea's salty spume mix with my tears. I saw two girls playing HORSE at a playground hoop. I was still here, when Chesa had been robbed of her life. It wasn't fair at all.

Jake walked over. Penny nuzzled my hand with her cold, wet nose and Jake wrapped an arm around my waist. I slipped one of my dad's meerschaum pipes into Jake's suit pocket. Jake didn't say a word—I knew he wouldn't—and we turned to watch as mourners sprinkled handfuls of flowers across the surface of the sea.

THE
CRIMINALIST
WILLIAM RELLING JR.

Detective Rachel Siegel is a twelve-year veteran of the San Patricio Sheriff's Department. But she's never seen anything like the handiwork of the Pied Piper, the vicious serial killer who's been terrifying that part of California for months. Because she's the best at what she does, it's now her job to catch this maniac—but she has very personal reasons, too, for wanting him stopped

Kenneth Bennett works for the Department of Neuropsychiatry at St. Louis's Washington University. There's something special about the Pied Piper case that draws Bennett almost against his will to the west coast. He has no choice but to help Siegel in her frantic search—even if it gets both of them killed in the process.

ATTENTION
BOOK LOVERS!

Can't get enough
of your favorite HORROR?

Call **1-800-481-9191** to:

— order books —
— receive a **FREE** catalog —
— join our book clubs to **SAVE 20%!** —

Open Mon.-Fri. 10 AM-9 PM ^{EST}

Visit
www.dorchesterpub.com
for special offers and inside
information on the authors you love.